W9-DEE-342

Magic and Misery

Magic and Misery

PETER MARINO

Holiday House / New York

Copyright © 2009 by Peter Marino
All Rights Reserved
Printed in the United States of America
www.holidayhouse.com
First Edition
1   3   5   7   9   10   8   6   4   2

Library of Congress Cataloging-in-Publication Data
Marino, Peter, 1960–
Magic and misery / by Peter Marino.—1st ed.
p. cm.
Summary: TJ, a sturdy teenaged girl with little self-confidence,
becomes best friends with a new, gay student in her high school, and
when he is bullied and she tries to convince him to tell the authorities,
he refuses.
ISBN 978-0-8234-2133-6 (hardcover)
[1. Homosexuality—Fiction.   2. Best friends—Fiction.
3. Friendship—Fiction.   4. Bullying—Fiction.   5. Dating (social
customs)—Fiction.   6. High schools—Fiction.   7. Schools—Fiction.
8. Self-confidence—Fiction.]   I. Title.
PZ7.M338782Mag 2009
[Fic]—dc22
2998024600

UWEC McIntyre Library
DISCARDED
JUL 2 9 2009
Eau Claire, WI

Fic
M3897m
2009

14965869

To Lisa "Scorcher" Luderman,
with great affection

INSTRUCTIONAL MEDIA CENTER   DISCARDED
William D. McIntyre Library
University of Wisconsin
Eau Claire, Wisconsin

acknowledgments

A sincere thank-you to the people who read and critiqued *Magic and Misery* in its various stages: Julie Amper, Aaron Broadwell, Mary Cash, Tom Ecobelli, Regina Griffin, Courtney Reid, Bill Reiss, and Nancy Seid.

chapter one

I assumed I was in love with Pan from the start, but looking back, I think it was more like fago. Fago is an emotion Mrs. Burrell, our English teacher, told us about. She knew everything—she made so many asides that I forgot most of the trivia, but not that piece.

"Fago is from a tribe in the Pacific Islands," she had said. "It's hard to explain, but it means something like feeling both affection and worry for someone at the same time. You might feel fago for a friend who is in a dangerous profession, a firefighter, an astronaut."

It intrigued me to learn there was an emotion I'd never heard of. Later, when Pan was gone, I realized that was definitely what I had felt for him most often. The first time I saw him—not interacting with anyone, his handsomeness so out of place in our classroom—I felt very attracted, but also a sense of worry. Because as radiant and confident as he came across, it couldn't have been easy transferring into a new school in November. And there was just the slightest something about his face, a pinpoint betrayal of sadness or vulnerability or longing, I'm not sure.

He was probably the most beautiful person I'd ever seen, and while that may not be saying a lot in Mungers Mills, in any location it would be true. I watched him, and sometimes he would catch me and give me a quick smile. He stayed completely to himself those first weeks. There were rumors about him, all dumb, and I think people eventually forgot about this new, tall boy who didn't say much. He sat in the cafeteria alone, at a small square table right in my line of sight from where I sat with Amanda. I kept wanting to invite him over, and if I'd had more confidence I would have, but he was too good-looking. And he appeared content to be by himself.

I knew what it was like to be the new kid. At the end of the first day of ninth grade, over two years ago, the bunch of us Holy Spirit Redeemer girls—me, Amanda, Mary, Emma, Sandy—had all huddled at the high school's front entrance for comfort and to compare stories about this new world of public school. It was so big to us then—more than one hallway—and there were strange faces and the constant reality that everyone who had gone to the public middle school together was summing us up. Now that I was a junior, it was hard to remember that I had once considered this place huge.

Our principal, Dr. Jackson, had the annoying habit of revealing birthdays at the end of morning announcements. People cringed when homeroom rang out with the birthday song, and on November 28 it was my turn. But I had a cringe buddy because it turned out that Pan's was the same day.

"I should go say something to him," I said to Amanda during lunch, sneaking another glance. He looked the same as always, not uncomfortable in solitude. But knowing it was his birthday made his solitude unbearable for me—and gave me an excuse to approach him.

"Do it," Amanda said. "He's really cute. Better than cute. Try to find out if he has a girlfriend."

"That would be the last thing I'd ever do," I said.

"TJ," she said, "get over yourself. The only one who thinks you're not pretty is you. So get over there and meet that hot guy."

"I'm just going to say hi, to be friendly," I said, standing. "No one should eat alone on his birthday."

"Maybe he can be more than a friend," she said too loud. I waved her off.

I might as well have been about to ask him to marry me the way I was trembling as I approached.

"Happy birthday," I said. "I guess."

He hadn't looked up at me until I started to speak, and I was sure this was going to be even more humiliating than I had planned. He smiled, and it seemed genuine.

"Sit," he said, pointing to the chair across from him. "We need to celebrate."

"Why don't you come sit with us?" I asked. "My friend Amanda's over there waiting." He smiled again, then picked up his stuff and followed me. I had never felt so self-conscious in the cafeteria before, and never so elated.

"Any free seats?" he asked when he got to our table. He had this rich, smooth tone that made him sound like James Bond. Amanda looked up as if she were staring into the sun. She pointed to one of the two empty chairs.

"Thanks." He took the one next to me. "If you sit alone for more than two weeks, they assume you're going to shoot up the school."

"You're not, are you?" Amanda asked, smile blazing.

"Nope, I'm totally ammo-free. I don't even carry a comb."

I tried not to stare at him, and at the same time tried not to avoid eye contact. Those eyes demanded contact. They were a piercing green. I was not going to survive this meal.

Trying to pull myself together, I commented on the fact that we'd all brought our lunches.

"My mother is completely organic," he said, "as well as a teensy bit insane. She packs mine for me."

"I make my own," said Amanda. "Always have. Just a habit by now."

"Yeah," I said. "My mom's sandwiches are better than school food."

"Anything is," Pan said.

"Yeah." I didn't mention that the reason I brought it was I didn't have the money to buy, and there was no way I was applying for free or reduced lunch. Maybe I should have said so because the conversation dried up. If Pan was disturbed by the ensuing silence, he didn't look it, just kept eating. When I didn't think I could stand it another second, he said, "Happy birthday to us." He opened the lid of a square plastic food saver, revealing a huge wedge of unfrosted chocolate cake, which he took a plastic knife to. His willowy, strong fingers worked like a surgeon's. He placed one piece next to my sandwich and one next to Amanda's, no discussion. I'm glad too because I would have felt obliged to decline if he'd asked first, and it was incredible.

"My mother made this. All natural ingredients. Whatever that means."

This was maybe what chocolate originally tasted like when people believed it needed only a little sugar rather than a crate. It was ripe and fresh and full, and I immediately wanted what was left of theirs, maybe the whole cake if I could find out where this guy lived.

"Good, right?" he asked.

"Yes, um . . ." I said.

"Excellent," said Amanda.

"And not one insect was harmed in the production of this wheat."

The cake must have contained some kind of relaxing agent because I immediately felt like we were all friends now. This most gorgeous boy had not rejected me—he was feeding me.

"We're both late babies," I said.

"Yeah," said Amanda. "You guys should be seniors."

"My parents held me back because they thought I wasn't ready for school," he said. "Which is amazing, since they can't wait to get rid of me now."

"My mom thought I wasn't social enough to start school," I said, "so she kept me home. Back then she liked the company. But with my baby brother, she wants him to start kindergarten as soon as he can walk."

I collected crumbs with my thumb and tried not to look too hoggish getting them into my mouth.

"This is so good," I said.

"It could bring you to tears," said Amanda.

"There's plenty more where that came from," Pan said. "But you'll have to come to my house for it."

Somehow I knew that he was not inviting either of us as a date, that this was as innocent as Amanda inviting me to her house. Still, it was thrilling.

"Happy seventeenth." He held up his juice bottle. Amanda and I held up our milk cartons and we toasted.

"I guess we're the class elders," he said to me, smiling, and showing that peephole of longing.

Pan sat with us at lunch from then on, which was a daily thrill. It wasn't just the rippling, very blond hair he adamantly denied lightening when Amanda asked. He had the body too. It wasn't the pumped-up, dieted-down-to-no-fat look or the steroid deformation. Pan was a tennis player—or had been at his last school—and he had a natural, lithe shape. And don't make me think about those legs. Our gym classes were coed, and the first time I saw him in shorts, I felt like I was high on nighttime cough syrup. That's it, I thought. I'll pass out into his arms. When I wake up, we will be in love forever.

I didn't faint on him, although I imagined every strategy and gimmick possible for making bodily contact, to make it clear that I was available for deep friendship leading to intense romance. I don't know what gave me the spirit to flirt with him, since it had never worked with any other boys. I hoped that if he had no interest in me—like all the rest—he would wait a while, not rush reality.

I started to entertain—a little too intensely—a fantasy life with Pan. I had it all planned out, which is a little sad in retrospect. First of all, he would realize his attraction to stout, sturdy girls and not be able to stay away from me. Next would be our higher education. I couldn't get into Harvard like he could, since, as it turned out, he was also genetically smart, and was taking the only two honors courses our school had to offer. Hard classes like chemistry and math were like swinging a tennis racket for him. I would have to forge my college plans around his because we couldn't have a commuter relationship. I wouldn't want him falling in love with some other strapping Italian babe with an inordinate amount of arm hair. I could get into someplace a little less competitive than the Ivy Leagues, maybe a state school nearby. Finances would be tough, but I was used to having no money. We'd make the sacrifices for four years, and then Pan would go to medical school or law school while I worked at my new career. It would all pay off, with both of us making so much money that eventually I could work part-time while we raised our beautiful children. We wouldn't consider signing a prenuptial agreement, since in this fantasy we would stay together forever and always be in love despite being married before we were old enough to drink.

It was in Science and Society with Mrs. Mercado that Pan burst this fantasy dead. She was telling us something about domestic abuse statistics and made some related reference to "the gay and lesbian community." Mrs. Mercado was not the kind of teacher kids fooled around with, but there was no missing the whispered comments from Patrick Torno and Boz Samson when she said this. I looked over at my new friend, embarrassed that he had to see what kind of idiots we harbored here, and saw that he stiffened, lowered his eyelids a little. Then he said what I'm sure no person at Mungers Mills High School ever had.

The stillness in the room was like waiting for a piece of an iceberg to collapse. Amy Conrad, another girl I'd known from Holy Spirit Redeemer, folded her hands and looked more sour than usual.

Finally Mrs. Mercado smiled and said to Pan, "I think that's the bravest thing I've ever heard. If you're being serious."

"I am," he said. "If one-tenth of the world is gay, I'm the fraction in this class."

chapter two

The disappointment had such a stranglehold on me that I couldn't look at him the rest of the class. I avoided him after the bell and left the building when school let out without making eye contact with anyone. Maybe I had known in some recess of my brain, and that's why I'd had the nerve to talk to him at all. Maybe that's why I had been bold enough to fantasize about him.

Pan called me that night. If he had called me the night before, I would have been orbiting the earth on a rocket of joy. But now I was numb.

"Hi," he said. "You looked upset, and I . . ."

"Why did you have to tell me?" I blurted.

"I'm sorry."

"It's just that . . ."

"Forget I said anything," he said. "It's not true. I was memorizing lines for a play."

"No, no, no, I don't mean that."

"Then why are you so mad?"

"I'm not mad," I said, which was true, being more like devastated. And in that state I was having trouble controlling my mouth. "I wanted to think you weren't gay so I could dream about us getting married someday."

There was nothing on the other end, which was to be expected after such a ridiculous outburst. I would never be able to go to school again after saying that. But then he said, "We could get married, if you want. We've got a week off at Christmas."

I laughed, almost hysterically, and tears came pouring out.

When I had calmed down a little, he said, "We might as well. It's not like many guys are knocking on my door in this town."

I wiped my eyes, blew my nose. "That's what every girl wants to hear. 'I'll marry you if a better guy doesn't come along.'"

"That's not what I meant."

"Why couldn't you at least have held off until we graduated? Let a girl have some hope."

"I could go through reparative therapy."

"What's that?"

"They show you pictures of bodybuilders and then zap your 'nads till you're not aroused."

"But how could you be aroused by anything ever again after that? Least of all me?"

"I won't know until I try. Okay, here, I've got some wires. I'll hook them up now, and . . ." He did something in the background, then let out a howl.

I didn't want to laugh again but couldn't help it. "Are you straight yet?" I asked.

"My hair is."

"I knew it wouldn't work. Nothing works for me."

"I'm sorry. Again."

"Why couldn't you just pretend, you know, like other boys do when the rumors start?"

"That was inconsiderate of me," he said. "But there are some things you have to share with your only friend. Your dreams, your goals. Especially your goal of meeting the right boy someday."

"My entire love life is set in fantasy. Now I have to face reality again. I've had enough reality in my life."

"I'm sorry. I'm a dud."

"No, I'm the dud," I said. "That's been proven."

"You're not a dud, TJ."

"A girl who's seventeen and never even had a date?"

"There's nothing wrong with you. You're just leading an alternative lifestyle."

"If you're going to be so handsome, you need to expect a few plain girls to go crazy for you."

"I don't see plain. I see an Italian princess."

"That's not a compliment where I come from."

"Do you want to fight about who's the bigger loser?" he asked.

"It'll give me some time to get over my disappointment," I said, though even as the words came out I was getting tired of pitying myself. I cleared my throat. "Anyway, I thought it was brave, telling the whole class that way."

"Really?"

"Really."

"Because it got so quiet that I might as well have told them I was Osama bin Laden's water boy."

"Yeah, you even shut up Boz Samson for a few seconds."

"He's a piece of work. And what's with his friend, slouched in his seat like he has no spine. Is that some kind of yoga position?"

"That's Patrick Torno. He scares me a little. But I don't want to talk about them. I'm still mourning my lost prom date. I had such a great night planned for us, too. Dinner, then the dance, then . . ."

"Then great sex?"

"Well, in my case, first sex. I wouldn't care if it was great."

"What's the problem? I can still be your date.

There's not like a homo screening at the door, right? I can't imagine Mungers Mills has that kind of technology. Will I have to wear a tux?"

"I can wear the tux if you want." I sighed. It would save me from doing a waxing that day.

"You wear a nice dress and I'll wear a nice tux, and we'll be the prettiest people there."

"Well . . ."

"Is it a deal, TJ? We are officially prom dates?"

"Do you swear it wasn't the thought of dating me that scared you out of the closet?"

"I'm serious," he said.

"In that case," I said, "I have a few conditions."

"Let me guess: You want to go in a limousine, not a dump truck like everyone else. Easy enough."

"No, but you are not allowed to be the best dancer in the place. I know that's a stereotype and all, but just in case."

"That will be hard. I used to be in a boy band."

"Second, you may have to ugly yourself up for the evening."

"That'll be even harder."

"Work on it. I want you to tone down your radiance."

"Radiance?"

"I don't want people so blinded that they don't see me at all."

"I won't take a shower or brush my hair. Not for days."

"That ought to do it," I said. "Well, this has been one unusual conversation. But I should get going on my homework."

"Okay," he said. "Now don't conveniently forget about our prom date. The only deal breaker will be if you find a real guy between now and then. Which is easily possible because you are pretty."

"Oh sure. Good night."

"Sleep tight. Loves ya."

"Loves ya?"

"Yeah, you know, when you're too shy to conjugate the verb correctly? Loves ya."

"I see. Loves you," I said. "That doesn't exactly roll off my tongue."

"It will."

In reality, people would snicker at us for our arrangement, but too bad for them. My date might not want to kiss me passionately, but I would have the best-looking one.

Amanda called me right after to discuss Pan's announcement in class, but I had no interest. I did manage to tell her about the prom.

"This could be viewed as progress," I said. "It's only December and I actually have a date for a dance five months away."

chapter three

Ironically, it may have been Pan's revealing why he was yet another boy who would not be my boyfriend that slid him toward the best-friend slot. Or maybe it was his story about his real father. Or the story about his mother pulling him out of Buckingham Heights because she couldn't stand suburbia anymore, which was not their first move. Or that we both loved to walk, at a time in our lives when everyone else was driving like they had invented it. Or our mutual love of big, splashy movies, which he could take me to in Holland Park, where they had an actual multiplex. Or the fact that from then on he called me every night to catch up on whatever he might have missed since the final bell. If I'd had a cell phone, he would have called me during class or when I was on the toilet.

Maybe it was because I had stopped hanging around in groups after ninth grade. My old group, the Holy Spirit Redeemer transplants, had long since assimilated, and no one thought of us as new anymore. We were still friends, and I still felt the old bond with them. But somehow, between then and now, the schedule of my life had gotten complicated, leaving me with no energy to go out at night. Because of homework, babysitting my brother Paolo, and my job at the pharmacy, I usually saw my friends only in school. Otherwise, it was the phone, and I spoke mostly to Amanda.

Amanda was short and kind of round. She smiled all the time, her big cheeks swelling up, but not so much that they detracted from the animation in her eyes. She was the easiest friend a person could ask for, but she—like everyone else—was more into socializing than I was. She was always bubbling about an upcoming dance or the bonfire before a big football game on a Friday night. But Friday mornings I would wake up and think about the full day of school, then about doing an hour or so with Paolo and some housework, then going to work until nine. Imagining going out after all that and getting home late, only to have to get up early to work again, made me want to crawl back into bed. So I had given up on Friday nights. Eventually, Saturday nights got away from me as well.

Amanda and I always had lunch together, and now

that Pan had come out, she was back to talking about the topic she liked best—boys. She focused on males elsewhere—TV, Internet, movies, the mall in Holland Park—because there was only so much you could say about the boys here. When we had first started at MMHS, it had been the land of tall boys, so far out of reach we could only dream about them. But now that we were older and our eyes were more open, we could see that so many of them were fuzzy and zitty and, worst, not always looking clean. The boys in Mungers Mills wore baseball caps as if they'd been born with them. Probably they wore them to bed. I'd seen them worn in church, even in the line for Communion.

Amanda had the same issue with romance that I did: always longing. But she was willing to take risks, while I was waiting for someone to discover me. Because of her drive, she did have dates here and there, and even had a boyfriend for a few weeks. But each time the guy hinted he was looking for someone else, someone better, I'm sure he was thinking, a girl who wasn't short and round and giggly.

It was becoming clear that Pan neither liked nor disliked Amanda. He was polite and attentive to her, but I could see that even though he liked boys too, he didn't find her constant stream interesting. Maybe what finally clinched our best-friendship was that Amanda's lunch mod got changed when she made All County Chorus and had to take a lesson in the middle of the day.

Pan's and my nonromance progressed so fast that before long I was someone he could say pretty much anything to, someone he could arm-wrestle with, the brother he'd never had. He even called me Bro for a while. And I did feel different with Pan than I had with my other friends. I once heard that if you hung around with smart people, you got smarter. The same must be true about other traits because in trying to keep up with Pan, I was more glib and more sarcastic. Usually I tended to be polite and deferential, but with him the naughty girl came out to play. I enjoyed her, I'll admit.

For instance, you might be thinking that he was named Pan because he looked like some Greek god with a flute, minus the goat hooves. But his real name was James, and Pan was short for Pansy because after Pan made his little revelation, Boz Samson and Patrick Torno started calling him Pansy. Pan's reaction to it surprised me.

"That's it?" he asked, almost bewildered. "With all the gay slurs available, they come up with 'pansy'?"

To show them just how dull they were, we co-opted Pansy and changed him from James to Pan.

"I like it," he said. "Kind of subversive."

The story of my own name was not rooted in protest. It started with my older brother. My father regretted not having named Teo after himself right up to the day I was born four years later. Since I turned out to be a girl and Teo had gotten used to his name by then, my parents had settled on Antonia, the Italian female form of Anthony, my father's name. They gave me Mom's name for the middle, JoAnne. Antonia JoAnne Fazzino didn't have a flow to it. And Antonia had the flavor of someone delicate and ethereal, while I was dense and kind of furry. Also, neither of my parents had the patience for a lot of syllables, so I became Toni, for a while. But Tony was my father's nickname, so I became TJ. When I explained all this to Pan, he started calling me Tojo, until we found out it was the name of a Japanese prime minister who was hanged for war crimes. He then changed it to Joto, which I also came to regret when we learned that it was Spanish for "faggot." Pan was amused, and said it was solidarity for me to be an honorary joto.

Incidentally, when Mom and Dad became parents one more time, sixteen years after I was born, they must have been too worn out to remember that Dad had wanted a male namesake, and they called my baby brother Paolo.

chapter four

I was a stock person and cashier at Polaski's Pharmacy on Broad Street, which used to be the main shopping area in town. There was never enough time between when school got out and when I needed to be at work, but Pan insisted that I meet his family; so on the Friday he took me to his house after school, I was more anxious than usual.

Pan didn't have a job. His problems were not financial. He lived with his mother and his stepfather, and his dying grandmother.

"I have to warn you about Gram. She's been dying for thirty-one years. I believe her bouts of meanness are preserving her, like brine. One day she'll like you and the next she won't remember that she did."

"Which day is today?" I asked.

"Not sure. It depends on which way her blood is flowing."

He was wrong. Her mood shifted much faster than every twenty-four hours. When we walked in the front door of their gigantic house, she smiled like she was recognizing an old friend. I felt sure she was just a sweet old lady, a typical grandmother sitting in a broiling living room. She was dressed in a white blouse with a high neck and long sleeves, and black pants. She held a cane, which was pointed at the floor even though she was sitting.

"Gram, this is TJ."

"TJ?" she asked, still smiling.

"Yes, nice to meet you, Mrs. Lockwood."

"TJ?" she asked again.

"Yes. How are you?"

"What kind of name is that for a girl?"

"Sorry?"

"TJ sounds like something you call a boy."

"Gram," Pan said.

"It's a polite question."

"If it were a polite question, you wouldn't be asking it."

"Why didn't they name her something that sounds like a girl?"

"It's a nickname. A girl's nickname. Now be nice."

She looked at me, her eyes trying to bore into my head. "Are you one of those she-males?"

"What?" I asked, taking a step back.

"Gram, that's enough."

"I want James to go out with a real girl."

"Okay, Grandmother. You've terrorized enough children for one day. We have to go."

Pan took me by the arm and led me toward a lustrous oak staircase. I couldn't help glancing at the old woman, as if she would take back her question if I looked troubled enough. But she wasn't aware of us anymore. She seemed to be staring at something that I couldn't see, dust motes or invisible aliens.

Pan's bedroom was like the rest of the house, high ceilings and natural wood moldings. There were no posters on his walls—paintings and drawings and photographs, but no posters. I would have taken more interest in the bookshelves and the dressing room and the private bathroom, but I was too rattled to be curious.

"Sorry about her," Pan said. "She started dying when my mother was in college. She keeps taking a turn for the worse. But it's a maze."

"What's actually wrong with her?" I asked. "Medically."

"No one knows. They diagnosed a bunch of things

over the years, every disease you can think of, but she keeps scaring away the microbes."

"What's this about me being half boy? Have I finally morphed completely into my father? His side of the family looks like lawn gnomes."

"You are not a lawn gnome, Joto."

"And you didn't tell her about my shaving ritual, did you? I've never told one of my girlfriends about that, not since fifth grade when I had to start. You're the only one I would trust with that information."

"She and I don't have the kind of relationship where we chat about you shaving your arms. Don't listen to her. You're beautiful."

"Then what did she mean?"

"She's daft, as my stepdad calls her. Ever since I told her I was gay, she's been trying to find the right girl to cure me."

"And I don't qualify."

"She wants a fake girl. Makeup, big hair. She'd fix me up with a drag queen before she let a real woman near me."

"That doesn't help."

"Forget her. She's been bitter lately. She's always been loopy, but now she's adding dimensions."

"This does wonders for my self-image, Pan. I really love that your grandmother thinks I'm not feminine enough for her gay grandson."

"Don't even think about it. She can sense heat, you know, like a missile? The more hurt you act, the better her aim."

"God," I said, thinking I might cry.

"Oh no," he said, and came close, lifting my chin. "Don't let her do this to you. If you cry, I'll kiss the tears right off you."

"But . . . your grandmother thinks I'm a hermaphrodite."

"She thought I was here to read the gas meter the other day," he said, putting his hand on my face. "She's only got half a mind, and today's half is focused on the she-male thing. She must have seen something on TV. You could go down there and flash your noony-cooch for her and she still wouldn't get it."

"That would be a picture for your parents," I said, recovering a little. "Me flashing your invalid grandmother."

"Are you kidding? They'd be thrilled she finally made a friend. Anyway, she's already forgotten she insulted you. She's already forgotten she ever met you."

"I can't deal with this."

"I think you're beauteous and I'm all that matters," he said. "So, this is my room, but let's get something to eat before you go to work. I believe the fridge is full."

"I'm not going back down there," I said. "You've got a window. I'll land in the snow."

"She's harmless. Look at my stepdad. She hasn't killed him yet, after all these years. And she's tried. Then again, he has the patience of a dead person."

"I'm not hungry."

"Yes you are. Let's eat. You're not on a diet, are you?"

"She-males are only half-concerned with their weight."

"Very good. Very very good. Now come with me."

He took my hand and we went down the stairs. We had to go right past her. Mrs. Lockwood turned to us. I braced myself for another jagged observation.

"Is this your girlfriend?" she asked.

"We've been down that bumpy road already, Gram."

Suddenly she grabbed my arm and peered so intently that I thought she might hypnotize me.

"I don't care," she said, holding tight for such a frail woman, "I don't care if Jesus Christ himself comes down from heaven and says it's okay to be a homosexual. It will never be okay."

"I, uh, thought you were atheists," I said, looking for a door. "Um, I mean, I thought you didn't, like, go to church. And stuff."

"Don't be fresh with me, missy pants."

"Stop it," Pan said.

"In my day, if the nelly didn't stay at the organ

bench away from the congregation, he got run out on a rail. Now they want to be at the front of the church in a wedding gown!"

I frowned. Pan would probably look better in a wedding dress than I would.

"Let go." He pried her hand off my arm.

"I think if he found the right girl."

"Go toward the light, Gram. Faster."

"You look like a nice girl."

By now I didn't know who she was talking to. She looked so earnest that it was harder for me to hold a grudge for her believing I bore two sets of genitals.

"Don't turn that TV on in here," she called as we walked toward the kitchen. "I can't stand the noise."

"You really are a good friend," Pan said, kissing my cheek.

"You're not kidding. Someday you'll appreciate me."

"Someday?" he asked with a smile so delicate I wanted to kiss him for real. But the afternoon had been confusing enough.

In the kitchen—which was so magnificent it could have been the set for a cooking show—we found his mother. In other circumstances I might first have noticed her lustrous hair and gorgeous skin. But what I noticed was that she was holding a washrag and sniffing at cereal boxes. Pan's family had money, but so far they were definitely odd.

"What are you doing, Mother?" Pan asked.

"What does it look like I'm doing?"

"It looks like you're smelling the cereal."

"Exactly."

"Somewhere an airport dog is unemployed. This is my new friend TJ."

She turned and smiled. She was very beautiful, with high cheek bones and Pan's green eyes. But there was something aggressive about her look.

"Ah dah," she said. I looked confused.

"Ah-duh," said Pan. "Other people pronounce it 'Ada,' but she has an aversion to long vowels. Second question, Mother. Why are you sniffing the cereal boxes?"

"For pesto."

"Pesto."

"Yes, James. Now get over here and help me smell these packages."

"Other kids get grounded."

"I had a jar of pesto in this." She held out a plastic grocery bag.

"Exhibit A," Pan said to me.

"And it was leaking, and I'm afraid everything is going to smell like garlic for months"—she lowered her eyelids, raised an eyebrow—"if I put them in the cabinet without wiping them off first."

"Why are you whispering, Mother? Hidden microphones again? Anyway, a sniff search is good enough."

"No, you're wrong. They need to be washed."

"What's the point of having a dishwasher if a person has to scrub every box of cereal by hand?"

"Here," she said, holding out a box with a sober design. She pulled it back, took a whiff, then wiped it. "It's been contaminated."

Pan looked at me. "There's really no defining my family, is there?"

I smiled. Ada was so confidently strange.

"All clean." She smelled the suspect package one final time before putting it into one of the long, windowed cabinets. She turned and saw that we were watching her. "Someday you'll look back fondly on these moments," she said.

"We're going to eat something, Mother. But it's been really, really fun."

"Can't you wait until I get the fruits and vegetables washed? Soap is the key. Make them clean as a whistle."

"And we can blow bubbles too."

"They were out of organic produce. Ever heard of pesticides?"

"The Pesticides," he said. "Sounds Greek. Are they the ones who owned the house last?"

"A pesticide," Ada said. "That which is used to kill insects. Simply rinsing with water will not do."

"Whatever. We have to get a snack. And you better go yell at Gram. She called TJ a she-male."

I swatted at him lightly. It was even worse in the repeating.

"I'm sorry, TJ," she said. "That really is obnoxious, but she tends to repeat things she's heard. My mother's illness makes her rather confused. And unpleasant."

"That's okay," I squeaked.

"No, it's not. I apologize for her now and for any future remarks. And there will be those."

"Gram's going to chase away my only friend here if you don't shut her up."

"It's better here than Buckingham Heights, that hell of subdivisions and strip malls," she said. "Can I tell you something?"

"Can we stop you?"

"If I'd had to hear one more time about Clarence's violin lessons in New York City with a very well-known instructor, I was going to break the damn thing over his head. The people of Buckingham Heights claim to be so multicultural . . ."

"Well you found the right place, Mother, because no one can accuse Mungers Mills of being multicultural. Unless you count that Taco ¡Hola! on the outskirts of town."

Ada looked just at me. "And they shove their new babies in your face. 'Lookee what we adopted!'"

"Mother."

She looked annoyed, before the tiniest amusement peeked from her eyes.

"Have I gone on too long? Again?"

Pan took her arm and led her toward the dining room entrance. "Rhetorical questions. Go speak to Gram."

"I'll go talk to her. Fat lot of good it will do. Nice to meet you, TJ."

"Bye," I said. She left.

Pan motioned for me to sit at the table. Then he took a glass baking dish from the refrigerator, along with some cans. "Homemade chicken potpie. Soda?"

"Any diet?"

"No dieting. I will wrestle any can of diet soda out of your hands, missy pants. Even with this limp wrist."

"That wrist is too thin."

He held his right hand out in front of him. "The butter knife can also cut. There's no diet. All of them natural soda too. Though we have yet to define 'natural.'"

He poured himself a glass of cola, then scooped us big plates of pie, nuked them for a minute or so, and placed one in front of me, along with a fork and a cloth napkin. "*Mangia, signorina.*"

"I don't think you can use *mangia* with this kind of food."

Actually, it was better than what I usually got at

home. His mother cooked basic food but with expensive ingredients. I didn't want to admit I could taste the difference, but it was true. Better ingredients, better food. Poverty was so unfair.

The back door opened and a man walked in who I assumed was Pan's stepfather, Kevin.

"Hey, youngsters," he said with the smile of a kid holding a giant candy bar.

"Kev, this is my friend TJ."

I stood up, and Kevin hugged me. "TJ, I'm so glad to meet you. We've heard nothing but good things."

"Thanks, Mr. Ashford," I said into his shoulder. When he let me go, he hugged Pan, who allowed it from his sitting position.

"You call me Kevin," he said. He was so boyish-looking that the informality felt right. His thick dirty blond hair was combed tightly to one side like his mother had prepared him for a school photo. He wore goofy round glasses on his pointy nose. He was what I would call nonthreatening, unaware handsome. I would have allowed myself to think he was even a little sexy if he weren't Pan's stepdad. Only in a few poses could you see that he was a grown-up, some crow's-feet, a bit tired when he wasn't smiling.

"Set up any interesting networks today?" Pan asked.

"Oh, I don't know how interesting it was," Kevin said. "You two having a snack?"

"TJ has to go to work, so I'm feeding her."

"That's a good boy. She works too hard. You work too hard, TJ, from what I hear. Eat up. No skipping meals."

Kevin, I was to learn, loved to give advice, but it was never the finger-wagging-in-your-face that made you stop listening immediately. He also loved telling stories.

He put his hand on my shoulder. "Look at that boy," he said as if he and I were watching Pan from a distance. "Six feet tall. You know, TJ, James was not the kind of kid to climb on my lap, even when he was a lot smaller. And whenever he was taken away from his mother for any reason—any reason!—there was a hurricane of a tantrum."

"I could throw one now," Pan said.

"Aw, it wouldn't be the same," Kevin said. "A baby's tantrum is forgivable. Cute even. A teenager's? Not cute."

"Mother and Gram have already sunk their fangs into TJ."

"Sorry. We are the fun family, after all."

"There's more food," Pan said. "Want some?"

"No. I don't want to spoil my supper. Can't eat like the old days."

"You might as well. We're having cereal for dinner. Freshly scrubbed."

"I won't ask," Kevin said. "You kids have a good time. I mean it."

"I will," I said as he was leaving.

Then he turned and said to Pan, "Oh, and if you need me tomorrow, I am happy to go."

When he was gone, we chewed a few blissful moments. It was American food, as my mom would once have called it. She used to ignore any food without a red sauce whose name didn't end in a vowel. That was before Paolo. Since then, she rarely cooked the good stuff. Now all we had was cheap American food.

The flavors were making me love everything in the world. "Kevin's really nice, isn't he?" I said.

"Yeah, I guess. People always assume he's my real father anyway."

"I would have if I hadn't known. The hair."

"His is getting gray. Although sometimes people mistake him for my older brother."

"I can see it."

"Which irritates my mother greatly."

"Your parents know you're, you know . . . ?"

"Oh yeah. Long time ago."

"How did they take it?"

"I'm sure they always knew. When I was a kid, I made my mother sew pajamas for my GI Joe."

"That might have given you away."

"Kevin had no problem with it. He said something

like, 'You're still number one with us, buddy.' You know, the kind of thing he would say."

"Oh my God, that's so sweet, Pan. Let's face it, the typical boy in this town won't even show his dad his report card."

"My mother was more concerned with how I was going to be treated at school, whichever one I was going to at the time."

"Did you? Have trouble?"

"There has been this and that. I think it's easier than being the fat kid. I think people can pretend that what they can't see doesn't exist."

"That's what I tried to do."

"Will you ever forgive me?"

"If the food continues to stay this quality."

"Kevin was good about it, but he doesn't know when to stop. He always wants to help, so he started on this gay slang thing, 'Let's go, girlfriend,' and crap that I would never say. I tried to give him the hint by laughing really loud and obnoxious, but he didn't take it. Finally I had to punish him."

"Oh, don't say it. He's so good." At that moment I decided I would find out when Kevin's birthday was to make sure Pan didn't neglect it. I would do the same thing when Father's Day came around.

"It had to be done. This one time he said my mother wanted him to take me to a place called Ginger

Snap's for a haircut. Then he just had to say it was going to be our ladies' day at the beauty parlor."

"He was trying."

"Too hard. So I told him Ginger should shave his ass while he was there."

"That's awful."

"He thought so too. He got this deep rose color in his face and spoke in an almost whisper, something like, 'You know I don't like it when you talk to me like that.' "

"Good. You deserved it."

"I was kind of scared of him then, but I did manage to explain that I was in fact still a boy and so was he."

"Was that the end of the slang?"

"Should have been. Every once in a while he forgets."

"Sounds innocent enough to me, Pan. Makes me like him even more."

"Yeah, he can come across like a dorky older brother, but he's a pretty good father all told. He went to all the tennis matches and school plays and orchestra concerts. Which is way more than I can say for my biological father."

Out of curiosity, Pan had contacted this father, whose name was Robertson, a year before, and the guy had responded. After some hesitation and delays on both ends, they arranged a meeting at a diner in New

Rochelle, where Robertson lived. It didn't seem to me like the best setting for that kind of reunion.

Pan started to withdraw as he ate.

"Are you nervous about seeing him?" I asked.

"I shouldn't be. I don't expect a lot from him. I just want to see for myself. He's the one who disappeared."

"That must be strange, meeting him for the first time since . . ."

"I want you to come with me."

"That would be weird, right?"

"You should come. For moral support."

"What would I do while you're talking to him?"

"You could go to the Galleria. You can shop while you're waiting for me."

"And you know how I love to shop. Maybe the spring fashions will be in."

"Please? I'll buy you lunch. Give you the money for it anyway."

"I'd better not, Pan. It's my one Saturday off a month. I promised my mom I'd watch Paolo a few hours during the day."

"Pretty please? With chocolate pound cake on top?"

"Your mother made chocolate pound cake?" It was what he had served me on our mutual birthday.

"And I know where it is."

"You know, Pan, any other boy would get a girl drunk so he could get her in bed."

"What's this getting at?"

"That you, on the other hand, try to ply me with cake so I'll go on a road trip with you to see your father."

"And?"

"And? And when is someone going to get me drunk and try to take advantage of me? When is it my turn to mean no when I say no?"

"I could do that if you want. Take advantage of you."

"You're a pansy."

"No one is totally, one hundred percent anything, Joto."

"I can't go. My mom needs me."

"Don't make me beg."

"I can't go in with you, right? You have to face him yourself. So what's the point?"

"You're my best friend. I want to talk to you as soon as it's over."

"You can call me as soon as it's over."

I finished my chicken potpie, fighting the impulse to lick the plate.

"Cut me some cake."

"No cake unless you agree."

"I'll look for it myself if you don't bring it to me."

He got up and went to the counter and lifted the top of a cake saver. He cut me a moderate piece, put some vanilla ice cream on it, and placed it in front of me. Then he cut himself a giant one.

"Eat much?" I asked.

"I don't gain weight, ever."

"Don't ever say that to a girl," I said, then plowed in.

"So, is the answer still no?"

The cake was so good and Pan was so handsome, probably he could have gotten me to dance for his grandmother.

"Really, I would do it for you. But my mom looks forward to this one Saturday a month like it's parole. My baby brother has problems with his ears. Lots of screaming. It might be dangerous if she saw you taking me away after I'd stranded her."

"I could send her some cake."

"Nice try. But you stay home with a shrieking child all week long, then have your Saturday bowling taken away. No, cake would not do it for you."

"I guess it's Kevin, then," he said, "though it will be strange talking to him about it. He'll only go so my mother won't have to. She tried to hide her bitterness, but it was like stuffing a hot air balloon into a lunch bag."

I was about to ask him why anyone had to go with

him, why he couldn't just drive there by himself, but at that moment it struck me as cruel.

As it turned out, Robertson wasn't there when Pan and Kevin arrived, and he never showed up. After it was established by cell phone that Robertson had forgotten and wanted to reschedule, they headed back home. Pan told me the basics on the phone and more of the details on Monday in school.

"Eh, who needs him?" he said with just the curl of a smile. We walked into the building without saying anything more. I couldn't imagine anyone not wanting to know his own son. I wanted to know Pan, even if he would never be mine in the way I had dreamed of. Good friend, not girlfriend. I could play it.

chapter five

Mungers Mills High School, according to Pan, was the opposite of Buckingham Heights, his last school, where the smartest kids ruled. The cool kids at MMHS were not rich or particularly academic, and the smart kids suffocated under the social heap. I think there was some rule on the books about not allowing them on any athletic team, because when the honor roll was published in the paper, I never saw the name of any star player except Caspar Phillips.

I would not have been in the ruling class at Buckingham Heights. My grades were good, though I could have put in more effort, especially with the hard sciences, where I would get mostly Bs and an occasional A. I hadn't ever qualified for advanced math, and I probably wouldn't pursue any college credit courses when I was a senior. I found high school classes pretty straightforward: Here was a task that wasn't simple, but you did it and you got rewarded. I couldn't understand why other kids got terrible grades. It was like owning a car and letting it die for lack of an oil change.

The one exception was Science and Society, which might have been the most interesting class I'd ever taken. Mrs. Mercado tried to "foster intelligent debate," as she put it. We saw pretty graphic videos and listened to guest speakers and watched demonstrations, and once a boy named James told us he was gay. I especially liked The Circle, where we were allowed to voice our opinions on "world health issues." I wasn't good at public speaking, so I didn't say much in The Circle, and Mrs. Mercado was a little sarcastic, which made me more nervous. But she did make me think, and I was caught up in every topic. The problem with a democratic process was everyone had a right to express an opinion, including those who should have been self-conscious, like Boz Samson. Amanda always referred to him as Samsonite because, as she'd said, "He has a lot in common with a suitcase, an impervious shell outside, dirty underwear inside. The only major difference between Samsonite and luggage is he can make noise on his own without being dropped first." And hating Samsonite was as useless as hating a suitcase, which couldn't help what it was.

I wanted The Circle to be something to show off to

Pan, for him to see a strength in our school and our teachers so he wouldn't think we were a bunch of hill-billies. But Samsonite always contributed in the only way he knew how. He would say something ridiculous and then smile like he had just scored a touchdown, looking around the room for acknowledgment. Today he was on to some nonsense about socialized health care—not that he used the exact term—which was way off the subject.

Pan interrupted him. "People would live longer if they could all get to doctors."

"Like you'd know." Samsonite smiled big, looked around.

"It's logical."

"It's logical," Samsonite mocked, then added under his breath, "Pansy."

That's when Mrs. Mercado said, "Boz, remember the most basic rule of The Circle? I'll refresh your memory: We respect other people's opinions."

"I was just saying . . ."

"If that's too much for you, then say nothing."

All expression left his face.

"Oh, and as for name-calling? Zero tolerance—that's a school rule, not just mine. I'd hate to interrupt class to escort you to the office. Perhaps you already know the way." Mrs. Mercado brought the topic back, which had been quarantining.

There were some intelligent remarks—from Amanda, Pan, Sandy Willis—while Samsonite took a brief rest. But he wasn't done with us yet.

"You know that dentist?" he asked, peering around The Circle.

Mrs. Mercado sighed. "Which one? There are several in the area."

He dipped his head as he looked around, as if each person were in on the plot. "No, no, like in Chicago or someplace. He's the one who gave those people hepatitis. Put them under gas and got hepatitis into their mouths. That guy ought to be shot." His smile reappeared.

"Shooting someone? That makes it sound like it's a simple problem. It's not a simple problem." Caspar Phillips said this in a voice that was so bass it could have been electronically altered. "If diseases were simple, we would have wiped them all out a long time ago. Look at tuberculosis."

Caspar was a curious person. He had started in our school as a sophomore. He was a big, hulking guy, a talented football player, but there was an old man inside him. The rhythm of his speech was one thing. When you first heard him, you were sure he was doing an impression. Then when you realized he wasn't, you wouldn't be listening to what he was saying, because how he talked was so interesting. When you got beyond that peculiar voice, you saw that he was very thoughtful in his opinions.

"Yes," Mrs. Mercado said, "and how do we approach wiping them out? For example, Typhoid Mary. The issue of putting people in quarantine. That's where we left off."

"My dad told me there had been talk," Caspar said, his face almost immobile, "of concentration camps for certain infections. Putting everyone with contagious diseases on an island somewhere so they wouldn't spread. That sounds like a pretty dangerous precedent."

"Precedent?" asked Samsonite.

Caspar turned to Samsonite. "Setting the standard."

"Precedent," Samsonite repeated.

Mrs. Mercado rubbed her eyes. "Oh, for heaven's sake, Boz. Let's get back to the quarantine islands."

"It's where they couldn't spread their disease." This was from Patrick Torno, Samsonite's best friend, who rarely talked. But his silence was menacing. When he did say something, it was always like a threat. He slouched in his desk, legs extended, cap pulled down over the tops of his eyelids. Since Pan's revelation, Torno's occasional looks at him were unblinking disgust.

Caspar continued. "If you start quarantining, you might be locking up people who don't have any disease at all. How do you know where to stop?"

"She said before," Torno said, indicating Mrs. Mercado with a lift of his head, "that an epidemic can spread anywhere."

"Even here?" Samsonite asked with childlike wonder. Everyone laughed.

Almost everyone. Caspar never laughed at anything. "Putting people away . . . I don't know," he said. "I don't think we want to be like that." He cleared his throat. He was definitely interesting and smart, even if listening to him was a commitment.

"Yeah, whatever," said Torno.

"We heard at church that sometimes God in the Bible, like, sent a plague," said Samsonite, teeth flashing. "Because people were so evil."

Pan asked, "What church?"

The bell rang before Samsonite could invent one.

As we stepped into the hall Patrick Torno gave Pan an efficient cuff upside the head. It was incongruous because Pan was tall, and tall people generally didn't get slapped by shorter people.

"Don't get too close to the school pansy," Samsonite said, and screeched. "You might catch it."

"Yeah, you might catch pansy," Pan said. "Do you even know how to spell that?"

"F-a-g," Torno said, before turning a corner.

I pulled Pan the other way.

"You should report them to Mrs. Guten. You shouldn't have to put up with their crap."

"Don't let it bother you," Pan said. "Our friend Boz has found religion, I see. Although I'm wondering how he can fit church into his busy schedule of football, weight lifting, and devolving."

From behind us we heard Caspar's slow voice: "Some people use religion to keep from thinking."

We both spun around.

"Sorry," he said. "I overheard you." Then he kept going, as if he hadn't been speaking to us.

We looked at each other, thrown off.

"Is he like the school visionary or something?" Pan asked.

"I don't know," I said. But I was curious about him.

chapter six

It was time for Pan to meet my family. At least to meet
Mom and Paolo. I had avoided bringing him over as
long as I could, hesitating and fumbling when he
insisted. I told him the truth, sort of, that I liked being
away from my house and all the responsibilities I had
there. I told him it was a pleasant escape for me in his
big, fancy old place. He had a TV in his room, so we
could watch terrible shows and make fun of them. And
his house was in a nice part of town. Kids on my street
called it the rich neighborhood because that's where the
doctors and lawyers had always lived. Still, he wanted
me to take him to my side of the tracks, and eventually
got suspicious of my stalling.

"Why are you keeping me away?" he asked. "Is it
the G thing? I understand if it is."

"No, not at all," I said. "I never even thought of that. In fact, I told my mom, and she was fine with it, like I knew she would be." I didn't tell him of Dad's silent reaction.

"So?"

So the whole truth was I was embarrassed to have Pan at my never-quite-clean house, with the constant howl of a baby brother. I didn't want him to see the neighborhood I lived in. And worst, I was ashamed of the way Mom looked these days. She had given up on her appearance since Paolo was born. Everything she wore made her look older than she was, cheap polyester pants and T-shirts with loud designs. She still had beautiful hair, thick and black, but it had streaks of gray that she could easily have colored. Instead, she covered her hair entirely to keep from having to fuss with it, but not with a cotton bandana or a headband, or even a wig. As if to make it clear she was in retreat, she cut the legs off old panty hose and wore the waist part on her head like a nylon skullcap. The stretch pants and the T-shirts and the gray hair I could overlook, but not the pantyhose hairnet.

I could not bring myself to tell him any of these things, so one day after school as we walked toward my place instead of his I said, "My house doesn't smell good. I might as well warn you."

"Don't worry."

"It's not offensively bad, like farts or cat pee. It's just kind of stale. Old, musty house odor. No amount of cleaning will scare it out."

"My grandmother keeps our house at ninety all year long. How good can it smell?"

"Look, Pan, my dad's auto shop failed, and he's still paying off the business loan. Now he repairs cars for someone else. And my mom is unemployed. We don't live in a castle."

"You're being melodramatic."

"You'll see."

My heart went cold when Mom met us in the living room wearing that beige sausage skin on her head.

"This is my friend Pan."

"Pan?" she asked. "I thought you said it was James."

"Long story," I said.

"Nice to meet you. I'm JoAnne." They shook hands.

"You must be TJ's sister," Pan said. "Is your mom home?"

Mom's smile started in her eyes, and she did look younger than she had in years. "Just for that," she said, "I'm fixing you a snack. Sit. Relax." She scuttled out of the room with a new energy.

Before long we smelled garlic sautéing.

"Come on in here," she called. On the table were

two bowls of pasta. "Just a little spaghetti to take the edge off."

"This is incredible," Pan said, twirling a huge circle onto his fork and sticking it in his mouth. "You just whipped this up? Will you be my mother too?"

Mom's eyes were dancing. And I realized that she had at some point removed the panty-hose hairnet and tied up her hair.

"It's just garlic and oil," she said. "Nothing to it."

She didn't eat with us, but she was full of questions.

"So, Mr. Pan, are you starting to look for colleges? Do you know what you want to be when you grow up?"

"Well, my stepfather does computers and my mother was a psychologist, so neither of those."

"What do you mean she was?" I asked, though I was more interested in Mom's return to cooking.

"She doesn't practice anymore. Maybe I'll be a doctor. Lawyer. A few years ago I thought about professional tennis, but now we're here, so that's not going to happen. TJ says she's going with me, wherever I go."

"Not likely," I said. "The community college looks good enough."

"With her grades she could probably get a scholarship," Mom said, "unlike her mother and father, who were not so swift in their day. All my kids are going to get four-year degrees, if I have to do their work for them."

"Two years at Mohegan ought to give me some

career inspiration," I said. "It would be nice to get a job around here, close to my family. Teaching maybe."

"Teaching must be the last industry left in Mungers Mills," Pan said, then worked another spool of spaghetti into his mouth.

"Teachers get maternity leave, and I could spend the summers with my kids. That's what I want—a real job, a decent husband, some kids."

"A few years ago I would have nixed Mohegan for TJ," Mom said. "Her brother Teo is at the University at Holland Park, in the business school. No small accomplishment. But with Paolo in the picture, I could use a couple more years of help. Then she will be transferring, no question. Her father and I got married a few weeks out of high school. Oh, I'm boring you kids."

"Not at all," said Pan, "although I was thinking about bringing you home to be our chef. Keep going."

"Well," she continued, "Tony and I thought, no more classes, no more 'in' groups. We thought we were tasting freedom. Who'd have known it would leave such an aftertaste?"

"What do you mean, Mom?" Pan asked. I looked at him. His eyes were set on her, very interested. And he didn't call his own mother "Mom."

"Oh," she nearly sang, "instead of taking the advice of our elders, we took jobs and made money and had babies. Now, I don't regret my children, but after fifteen years of sitting in an office, I decided I wanted more from life than working for a doctor. I wanted that piece of paper. Then I got pregnant again. It was during my first semester at Mohegan."

"No cause for celebration, huh?" he said.

"Well. Little Paolo has . . . his ears have been a problem, and they make him, let's say, cranky." Mom and I exchanged a look, "cranky" being way generous.

"I tried to take a course or two but couldn't keep up," she continued. "TJ helped me through it all. She practically adopted her little brother, but I had to give up. College became a disappointment instead of a dream. That's why I tell my kids, 'Go to school. Get an education first. You can always have a family—'"

At that moment Paolo wailed from his crib, loud and angry.

"If you really feel the need to—" She started to get up.

"Mom, no," I said, "I'll get him." We were done eating anyway. Pan got up too.

"When we come back down," he said, "I want to hear about you managing the doctor's office. My mother used to have her own practice, and she said the office manager was the most important person there."

"Oh!" Mom said. I couldn't remember the last time I'd seen her delighted.

Waking up was just one of the many things that

Paolo resented. His wake-up crying sounded more like despair than a cranky baby. Usually, when he saw me, he started to cry harder, as if to convince me he hadn't been faking. He did turn up the volume, for a second, but then he saw Pan and he was startled silent. Pan picked him up before I could warn him, but instead of Paolo shouting an objection, he took an interest in this new being, especially the wavy blond hair.

I wanted to take a picture. Paolo never liked strangers, and he never got quiet so fast for any of us. When Pan nuzzled and tickled him, then played peeka-boo, Paolo giggled. It was like magic.

"I should call my mom up here," I said. "Too bad we don't have a video camera."

"What are you talking about?" Pan asked. "He's a cute little kid." He held Paolo up and made him laugh again. I looked at the baby with wonderment. Laughing. Life was full of possibilities.

Pan carried Paolo downstairs.

"When he stopped crying so soon, I thought I'd better call an ambulance," Mom said, amazed. "Look at that. Paolo's first friend."

"Does this mean my brother's gay too?" I asked.

Mom grunted. "No one will ever use that word to describe this child."

* * *

As we walked to the pharmacy I told Pan about Paolo, about his ears and his noise. He was otherwise a normal baby, just not a happy one. No one had ever said he was cute or anything close to the compliments most babies got. People made comments like, "He's big, isn't he?" Once when I had him out in the stroller, a woman had peaked in and disappointment quivered over her face.

"Now that's a baby."

I nodded and pushed him on our way. I knew what she meant, and I could have told her she wasn't all that pretty herself, but each insult and every burden in Paolo's life made me want to shield him.

After Mrs. Burrell explained fago to us, I was pretty sure I felt it for my baby brother. I loved Paolo—of course I did—but I was also a little bit afraid for him, afraid he would start to sense Mom and Dad's disinterest, afraid he would have no friends, no girlfriend ever, afraid that he would be that one kid in school no one wanted to be. For now, I tamped these fears down by taking care of him the best I could.

Pan was listening the whole time, I felt sure, but when he finally spoke, he said, "I like the smell of your house. Garlic and basil. It makes me feel comfy."

chapter seven

I suppose it had something to do with my mediocre ambition, but I was actually fond of my job. Maybe I should have had some fago for Polaski's Pharmacy, because it was one of the few long-standing businesses left on the main strip of downtown Mungers Mills, and it tried to survive against the two chain drugstores on the outside of town.

"These old buildings could be a movie set for a period piece," Pan remarked once. Sometimes I imagined them in their prime, imposing brick and steel, fancy concrete moldings, cornerstones with dates like 1875. I tried to picture a time when downtown was proud and necessary, the sidewalks and streets bustling with people and trolleys. Now it was begging. Our store was hardly a gem, old and forlorn underneath abandoned offices upstairs. The Historic Preservation Board kept the buildings from being torn down, but that meant they stayed up and empty.

Pan's parents made a special point of coming down to support an independent business, and therefore my continued employment. The store owner stopped in once in a while to whine about sales. We were always barely holding on. Most of our customers were elderly, or very poor, or living in the residences for the developmentally disabled nearby, and they came in only for little things. We had a credit card reader at the register, but we almost never used it because our customers seldom had anything but small amounts of cash.

I'd worked there since I'd turned sixteen, actually a little before, although now I worked more hours. My parents hadn't forced me to find a job, and I knew Mom would rather have me help with Paolo. But if I didn't work, I would have to ask them for spending money. I hated to do that because of our endless financial straits.

I got such a silly glow of contentment from working on a Friday night. Pan would usually spend half a shift with me, talking, helping out, walking casually to the door when the owner came in. There were insurance concerns, and since he was not an employee, he was not supposed to be there lifting boxes. It wasn't an exciting life trying to keep my nonboyfriend's presence from being too obvious while we stacked deodorant and body wash. Other kids my age were having parties somewhere. Yet I often felt completely fine in our decaying part of town with my predictable job. Since Mom was making me go to college, a career at the pharmacy was not an option. She had warned me that someday the coziness and predictability of the job would not be a consolation when I looked back at my wasted youth. But I didn't feel any dissatisfaction yet.

The job was not all that difficult. Sometimes I could do some reading while I waited for customers to straggle in. My only concern, besides whether the pharmacy would survive another year, was the assistant manager, Tammie Speers. Tammie had to be reckoned with when our shifts collided, especially if I had homework to do, because she had this work ethic that any sitting around—on my part, not hers—was a waste of company money.

Another irritating thing about Tammie was how she flirted with Pan. I understood the reason—I'd done it too—but she was worse. It had crossed my mind to clarify for her why this was pointless, but I'm sure Tammie would just pretend she already knew and then lecture me about acceptance. At least when he was around she was on her best behavior, like she was with the pharmacist or the owner, and not bossing me. Pan was his most complimentary with her, and she loved it.

Tammie was twenty-eight, and it was no secret she really wanted a husband. When she had as much as a date, the words *my boyfriend* found their way into every other sentence. When that relationship crashed, the references disappeared. Until the next guy. One boyfriend in the series had even risen to fiancé status before she stopped mentioning him altogether and stopped flashing the ring.

My mom used Tammie in her lesson plan for my life many times. "She's a perfect example of what happens when you don't go to college and make something of yourself. More perfect than me. At least I don't have to make up for my shortcomings by giving everyone around me grief. But it's all she's got. Her life is inside those store walls."

I knew I was never going to like Tammie, though I tried to have some sympathy. She didn't make it easy. Besides always looking to keep me busy, she wasn't the most competent employee either, or even that hard a worker, since she didn't have patience for the kind of menial tasks she assigned to me. She did a lot of flitting around, sounding important. When she talked to a customer, she got very loud and formal.

"Now here is your receipt, which I can hand to you or put in your bag, whatever you wish. Please keep the receipt in case you need to make a return, and please have a very good evening."

Despite the formality, she was not good with customers. When there was something I couldn't figure out on the register or a customer who complained and wouldn't go away, Tammie would buzz around for a few seconds, call out some pointless comments, then disappear. I'd wind up handling the problem myself, at which point she would be back, asking how it had worked out, then evaluating my performance. She never said good job, only a short list of what I could have done. She would sprinkle in phrases like "When I was a cashier . . ." or "As assistant manager, I know that. . . ." When I'd first gotten the job, I would get defensive and say I'd done the best I could. She'd give me her placating you-are-still-in-high-school smile and tell me it was all a learning experience. When I eventually figured her out, I stopped defending myself. Her life made me uneasy. I knew what it was like to want a boyfriend and not have one. And I wondered, if I didn't go to college, would I be the same way someday, annoying a younger employee because I could? That was as good a reason to get an education as any.

One night Pan was studying for a test in his advanced math class and couldn't come down to play at the pharmacy until later. A sleigh-riding scene blinked in our window, forcing cheeriness onto Broad Street. I was doing some reading. Tammie and I were alone in the store most of the evening. A sweet, older customer named Larry walked in shortly before closing time. He was looking for a birthday card for the woman who cooked at his residence, and much to his misfortune Tammie was hovering near the rack. "Hi, Larry," she shouted, even though he was not hearing impaired. "You have to hurry because we're going to close soon. Hurry."

He looked worried. I would have gladly stayed open a little longer to let him finish because he was painstaking and serious about his meager purchases.

"Do you want a funny card?" Tammie shouted. "Do you want one like this, that's funny?" Then she practically screamed, "Funny? That means ha-ha, it makes you laugh."

Larry did not laugh.

"Do you want one like this, that's got a picture on the front? Picture? Or do you like these cartoon ones, Larry? You have to hurry, Larry, we're closing. We open at nine and we close at nine. You know that by now." She continued plucking more cards for him, getting in his face like a lip-reader while he got more and more frustrated and began counting the change from his pocket. I was in agony myself.

"The rules apply to everyone," she sang.

"I've got it, Tammie," I said.

"What?"

"I've got it. It's okay."

"If customers stay late, we have to stay late," she said. "I have to stay late."

"I know. I'll take this customer, and I'll cash out really fast after."

Then Pan walked in.

"Tammie, hi," he said. "Wow, have you lost weight or what? I mean, you were never heavy, but now you're downright lean."

"Finally someone noticed!" Tammie said, forgetting Larry and switching to flirt mode. I stole the chance to let Larry choose a card and pay for it with change that he counted out again and again. By the time Tammie returned to earth, Larry was on his way out the door with a slim white bag. Tammie called a good-bye to him and waved energetically, then said, "And remember, we close at nine, sir."

I cashed out and did my other end-of-shift routines. When Pan and I were about to leave Tammie said, "James, TJ seems so uptight lately. Maybe you can bring a smile to her face. You both have a great night. Bye bye, kids."

I could barely make conversation as we walked home.

"She is so miserable sometimes," I said. "You got the tail end of the Larry drama."

"The way she kept shouting his name when I first

walked in, I thought someone named Larry was in a coma."

"Poor guy. I had to put some money in for him. I couldn't let him keep counting his coins, so I just took what he had and told him it was perfect. Not exactly honest."

"At least you got him out of there before she lectured him about carrying enough money."

"Yeah. She once told me they'll never learn, *those* people, if you do things for them. The whole point is to get them to be independent."

"Like her."

"She just doesn't get it. She thinks she taught him a lesson, but what she really taught him was to be afraid of coming into our store."

"Forget it. Soon enough she'll mess with the wrong person, and she'll be history."

Something about that depressed me—Tammie losing such a humble job.

"She's not qualified for much else," I said.

"She does have managerial experience," he said.

"Assistant," I said. "Assistant managerial."

chapter eight

In early February, Pan and I had to take Paolo to an interview at a day care center. Mom was meeting with a counselor at Mohegan yet again, this time to investigate the nontraditional student route, and she would need two days a week off to take a couple classes and do the homework. I had offered her some of the money I'd earned at the pharmacy to help out.

"The dream may not be completely dead," she said. As it turned out, the day care required an interview, and the only time the woman could do it was at the same time as Mom's college appointment.

Since I'd never gone to day care as a child, I was surprised that Paolo, at age one, had to audition for a spot. I was not optimistic.

Mom leaned into Pan's mother's car. She blew a kiss to us.

"Make sure you two do all the talking," she said. Desperation weakened her voice. "Keep him quiet. Let them think he's the most silent baby on the planet."

"We'll try, Mom," Pan said.

"Try hard. James, you may have to come with me every time I drop him off."

"Okay. We'll open the door, hand him off, and run like we're on fire."

"Fine. Afterward I'll cook something nice for you."

Paolo, who had been unhappy about having to wear his snowsuit, was even more displeased at the idea of Pan sitting in the front seat. Since a car is only so big and can hold in quite a bit of sound, Pan had to sit in the back next to him, bent sideways so Paolo could pull his hair. I had to drive his mother's car, which made me more anxious.

A few minutes' drive from the center of town where I lived and we were practically in the country. The homes were farther apart here, huge yards and long driveways, no sidewalks, lots of evergreens and bushes. These days the better-off people were moving here, out of the city, even out of the nice neighborhood Pan lived in. The day care had green shutters and trim. A painted sign on the lawn said GREEN GOOSE DAY SCHOOL.

Mrs. Purcell introduced herself and led us into her office. We could hear children playing in another part of the house. She was a short little penguin of a woman. I quickly took Paolo's snowsuit off so he wouldn't get hot and start yelling about it. Then Pan took him. Mrs. Purcell was pleasant enough. That is until she got right into Paolo's face. "What a little chunk he is!"

Paolo let out a scream. Pan laughed as if this were entertaining.

"That's Godzilla playing a kazoo," he said.

"He likes you," I said to Mrs. Purcell. Pan turned Paolo toward him and Paolo stopped to grab some hair.

Pan stayed busy trying to keep Paolo from destroying my mom's future while Mrs. Purcell asked me a lot of what I thought were very personal questions about my family—how many of us and how old, what jobs we had, and if anyone had ever been convicted of a crime. Finally, after she'd asked for way too much information, she closed her notebook and looked over at Pan and Paolo.

"He's good with kids," she said. "He'll make a good father someday." My heart beat a couple aches, not that Pan might never be a father, but that he would not be fathering my children.

"Yeah," I said, "Paolo adores him."

"Your boyfriend, I assume."

I knew any hint of truth might destroy our chances

of getting Paolo in. You could never tell with old people which side of this fence they were on.

"Yeah, my boyfriend." I looked at him. She had really given me a compliment.

"Are we ready to go, babe?" Pan said in his James Bond-iest voice.

For a second I drank in the rapture of that. "Sure, uh, honey."

"Let me hold that chunk of a baby," Mrs. Purcell said, standing up and holding out her hands.

Pan looked unsure. But I was struck motionless.

"Here we go, baby boy," Pan said, handing Paolo to Mrs. Purcell, but backing him away so that Paolo was still facing him, thinking it was a game. Paolo, with a drooly grin, gurgled a laugh as Mrs. Purcell put her hands around him. Pan kept mugging as he let go, and Paolo was unaware that he'd been passed off. Then Mrs. Purcell sneezed, and Paolo whipped his head around and saw that he was being held captive. There was a second of silence—Pan and I had stopped breathing—as Paolo took in the full horror of the situation. Mrs. Purcell turned him, put her head against his, and cooed.

At that moment Paolo emitted one of his famous guttural explosions. We were used to them, but Mrs. Purcell looked startled.

"That's okay, sweet cheeks," she said, nuzzling his

face and stomach. Paolo stopped for a second, terror and indignation sharing his pudgy little face. His next wail was louder, if that was possible.

"Now now," she said, sounding a bit annoyed. "Would you like to try the indoor swing? It's too cold to go outside this time of year. We'd have to get you all bundled up."

Paolo stopped again, as if not believing her impertinence. Then he erupted, like a maniacal sound-effects machine. Pan tried to be nonchalant as he lifted our little ball of fury from Mrs. Purcell and turned him. Once Paolo saw Pan, he stopped immediately.

"That's interesting," Mrs. Purcell said, more scornful than interested. "I usually have a way with fussy children. Let's try again." Before I could object, she took Paolo. Pan looked like she had pulled off his arm. Paolo had had quite enough of this woman, and when he was facing her again, he vomited thoroughly. She yelped and practically tossed him to me.

"He's had a little tummy ache," I said. "Really, I'm so sorry. His teeth give him a lot of trouble too."

She picked up a diaper and began wiping the mess off herself.

Paolo had by now forgotten the nightmare of Mrs. Purcell and was laughing at Pan, who had taken him from me and was putting the snowsuit back on him. We were all tainted by his barf, though she had gotten the worst of it.

"I'll need to call your mother. We need to discuss his separation anxiety. And I hope he doesn't have the flu."

"No," I said. "I don't think so."

"I can't believe you'd bring a child with the flu to someone's home."

I couldn't think of anything but apologies. I considered throwing myself at the woman's little penguin feet, begging her not to reject him, promising we would find a store that sold baby muzzles. "I'm so sorry," I began, but Pan interrupted.

"He doesn't have the flu," he said, looking Mrs. Purcell in the eye. "He's just anxious."

Mrs. Purcell seemed to have caught something in his tone.

"Thanks for stopping by," she said, and moved toward the door. Pan carried my oblivious brother.

"Bye, Mrs. Purcell," I said. I could hear the pleading in my voice when I added, "I think he'll like it here. It's perfect for a kid. Lots of space outdoors. In the spring."

"We'll see."

"You run a day care," Pan said. "You ought to be able to deal with a kid crying."

"Have a nice day," she said, guiding us out.

"You flaming amateur," Pan said just before the door shut hard behind us.

We were solemn in the car after. Finally Pan said, "I'll be glad to babysit twice a week. Especially since I insulted the old hag and nailed the coffin shut. I'll even skip school if Mom Fazzino needs me."

"Thanks, but I'm afraid Paolo's going to the orphanage when she hears about this."

We pulled up in front of my house.

"Good," he said. "Mom's not home yet. I'm not sure I could stand the look on her face."

chapter nine

Mrs. Burrell, in English, was our most intense teacher. Every movement was charged, like she was dancing on electricity. She reminded me of a Chihuahua, a smart, interested, determined Chihuahua. There wasn't a single worksheet that she wasn't excited and exacting about. Now she was having us take a real life experience and make things up so it sounded more like a story. We spent a lot of time reading famous short stories and figuring out what elements made them work. We used real people's journals and diaries to get ideas.

"Uh, how long is this supposed to be?" Samsonite asked.

"The story can be as long or as short as you want, but it has to have a complete story arc," Mrs. Burrell responded. Unlike Mrs. Mercado, she wasn't too concerned with a free flow of conversation with people like him. So when he attempted to ask another question, she reviewed what a story arc was in details that I'm sure he ignored.

"I'm going to photocopy each piece for workshopping, as it's called. You're going to give your opinions on the story to the person who wrote it, both out loud and on paper. You are going to get graded not only on your story—please listen to this carefully—but also on how well you participate in each workshop. Of course, your responses have to follow specific guidelines. You can't just say whatever comes to mind."

Samsonite raised his hand. Instead of answering, Mrs. Burrell passed out a sheet and spent a lot of time going over the guidelines with us. This was as hard as a science lab, and I wasn't going to be able to get by with regular effort this time. When I tried to write a draft, my creative process dripped dust. I didn't think my story was especially good, though I had Pan and Mom read it before I handed it in, and they liked it much better than I did. The workshop schedule listed me near the beginning, and I was brittle tense that day. I was tempted to skip school and claim I had a dentist's appointment, but Mrs. Burrell would reschedule me, so that was pointless. Pan said he would defend me, and I also figured out a good strategy for being in the spotlight, which was taking notes as people criticized my story. I knew they would be giving me written notes too, but I wanted something to do while I was being grilled alive, rather than fighting to look calm.

But the other kids thought it was okay too—there was no brutality. They weren't exactly enthralled by my story about a college kid who makes his bunk bed collapse on his roommate. I had gotten the idea from my older brother, Teo, who, as a freshman at UHP, had been in a dorm room with two other guys who hated each other. I might have thrown in a little of "The Tell-Tale Heart" or "The Lottery." Most of the comments were about the incompleteness of the story, and how the bed collapsing needed to be more important than just something that happened. That made sense and gave me some new ideas.

Pan did defend me, and without sounding defensive. "I like that evil-in-the-hearts-of-men concept," he said in his smooth tone. "We get to see into the head of someone whose anger has taken over. It shows the irrationality from the inside."

"Yes," said Mrs. Burrell, "and she also has a nice way with figures of speech."

That was kind, but mostly I was glad it was over. Once the focus had passed from me, workshopping was kind of fun. I enjoyed it more with each class. Using a new set of words to respond to the stories made me feel more like an adult than a high school kid. And Mrs. Burrell was taking us very seriously, like she cared what we thought. I didn't say anything out loud, but I enjoyed writing the critiques and listening to the discussions.

I knew Pan's would be excellent, since everything he did was. But when he gave me a draft, I had to read it a second time to understand why I didn't like it.

"This is a slam on Samsonite and Patrick Torno," I said. "That's all it is."

"Yeah?"

"I know what she's going to say. She's going to say it's not a real story because it's not truthful."

"It is truthful. They're like twins who develop their own language. A really primitive one."

"You have Samsonite falling in love with the school groundskeeper?"

"It could happen."

"Who bears a striking resemblance to Patrick Torno?"

"So?"

"So the ending is a joke. I can't believe you have them sailing off into the horizon on a riding mower."

"I thought you'd think it was funny, Joto."

"It's hilarious, it really is. Let's keep it for a joke between us. But don't go public with it."

"Well . . ."

"Besides, I'm afraid of Patrick Torno. You can't tell what he's thinking."

"Probably not much."

"So why give him the honor of a starring role in your story?"

"If you insist, I'll write something new."

He did, and this time it was elegant. He wrote about a boy who meets his real father and manages to help the guy stop drinking. It made me choke up a little, and the class gave him good reviews, with some raves. Torno and Samsonite didn't say a word between them but did offer a few snickers and sneers.

Eventually we did Samsonite's project. There were no limits on subject matter, which turned out to be a problem. I don't know why Mrs. Burrell didn't make him rewrite it before she made copies, because parts of it were incomprehensible from all the mistakes. But we knew it was directed at Pan. A man pretended to be gay so he could have an affair with his secretary, who wore a fat suit to look unattractive. Every time the boss had to say a word with an *s* in it, Samsonite replaced it with *th* to show lisping. The boss constantly made references to anal and oral sex. At the end the boss revealed himself as a normal guy after all, and he ran away with his girl-friend, who tore off her fat suit revealing a beautiful body.

We got the copies on Thursday and were supposed to have read it and written notes for Friday's class. I despised it, I told Pan that night at the pharmacy.

"Why waste your energy on a fool?" he asked. "If she gives him even a D on it, we'll know she's the one wearing the fat suit."

My stomach turned a notch. If people liked anything about it, were amused by or praised any part of it, I would have to admit that we Mungers Millsians were hopeless.

The next day in class Pan sat frozen like the Sphinx. The kids who did speak up—I didn't—were usually careful with Mrs. Burrell's guidelines. Not this time. Most of the comments were so critical that within a few minutes Samsonite's satisfied grin began to tremble.

"I didn't believe any of it. It was like you made us read seven pages to get to a punch line," Amanda said, breaking the ice for a flow of criticism. "You're not taking your story seriously. Who are these people?"

"It's a long joke," said Sandy Willis. "Not a very good one either. I was waiting for something to make sense. It never did."

Caspar Phillips was the one person in the class I expected some diplomacy from. His comments were gentler than the rest, but not that gentle. "I couldn't figure out the point of the story. Why does the guy pretend to be gay in order to have an affair with his secretary? If she had a husband, then maybe I could see it, but that still doesn't exactly work."

"Yeah," Amanda said. "Did the boss just start acting like a flamethrower when they began the affair? Wouldn't the other people in the office be suspicious?"

"And no one in the office minded him talking about getting it up the butt constantly?" Sandy Willis asked. The class laughed at that, most of the class anyway.

"Didn't anyone notice that the secretary suddenly got fat?" Amy Conrad asked in her pinched voice.

"I felt like I was wasting my time reading it," said Sandy. "I could see if you were pointing the finger at someone who made fun of those people, you know, the fat people, for example. But otherwise it was like a joke on a bathroom wall."

Amanda brought it home: "I had to look it up, but the word is spelled *f-a-g-g-o-t*, not *f-a-g-e-t*."

"Maybe it's French," said Caspar, making everyone laugh again, though by his look he hadn't intended to.

Samsonite might have been shrinking.

There was only one positive remark, and it wasn't from the teacher. Probably even Mrs. Burrell couldn't think of a kind thing to say. Instead, it came from Patrick Torno. "I thought the surprise ending was pretty cool. I wasn't expecting it."

"But the ending didn't make any sense," Pan said.

"Yes it did," Torno said, like he was drawing a gun.

"I made it to the end," said Caspar Phillips, a tape

playing too slow, "because I wanted to see if there was a payoff. But I drew the conclusion that this was making fun of writing a story, not writing a story."

Mrs. Burrell usually interrupted people who veered away from the guidelines, which everyone had, but she had stayed quiet through Samsonite's trial. Finally she broke in.

"Maybe we need to review notes about plotlines and character development," she said, and then took examples from Samsonite's story as models of what not to do. There was no mistaking how sharp she was being, but she did try to offer suggestions for him to rewrite by including an occasional, "What you could do, Boz, is . . ."

I wondered if she had meant to let Samsonite hang himself by allowing him to use this scrap for the project. As cruel a joke as he had played, the whole episode had been a disaster for him, sitting there while people shredded his work.

But someone had to pay. After school Pan was packing up at his locker and I was waiting for him. While he was bent over getting books Samsonite and Patrick Torno appeared, and Samsonite slammed him from behind. Pan's head practically got caught inside. Torno gave one more shove before I fully grasped the situation and shrieked something at them.

Samsonite was down the hall already, but Torno was not in a rush. I turned back to Pan, afraid of what I might see. He had straightened himself, blood on his lip, a whitish scrape down his face.

"Are you okay?"

He blotted the blood from his lip with the back of his hand and examined it.

"I'm going to tell Mrs. Guten right now," I said, louder than I needed to be for someone next to me. "This is a bunch of crap." I had never been in a room alone with our vice principal, and I was a little afraid of her, but I was moving on furious energy now.

"No. What's she going to do? Suspend them because their brains don't have any folds?"

"It's harassment. It's illegal. You can get thrown out of school for smoking a cigarette. They've got to care a little bit about people getting their heads smashed in."

"Is it smashed in? If they destroyed my face, they're dead."

"I'm going. She's hearing it from me."

Pan licked at his lip.

"Salt. Maybe a little Coke too."

"Does it hurt?"

"Only in my heart."

"Pan, let's go to the nurse, and then I'm going to see Guten and tell her what's going on before they do something really obnoxious."

It was only minutes later that Pan and I were walking to his house.

"Why am I letting you get away with this?" I asked.

"What?"

"They beat you up and I'm the one fighting with you to turn them in."

"That's one of your many qualities. Always looking out for your man."

"You won't let me look out for my man."

"Think about it. If we tell, they'll say I hit on one of them or something. Perfect justification for kicking the gay boy's ass. The rich gay boy."

"But what if you do nothing? Just let this go on forever?"

"They don't have that kind of perseverance. And wasn't it worth a little head bashing to watch Samsonite swinging in the wind today?"

"No. Nothing's worth it."

"Did you see his face? He had this big look, like he was a stand-up comedian who just knew he was gonna kill. And then one person starts on him, then the next, and before you know it, he looks like they just published his report card in the paper. Everyone hated it. And I didn't pay a single one of them."

"Well, I'm glad Mungers Mills proved its integrity today. But I am going to report this if you don't."

"Don't push me into a corner, Joto. I've already been in a locker."

We walked along awhile. His indifference confounded me, but there was no penetrating it.

"You're not going to cooperate with me, are you? I really think you need to tell someone—Kevin at least—about those two."

"I'll be all right. Just always promise to be my friend. That's all."

"Come on."

"Promise?"

We walked. I didn't answer.

"Joto? Are you still there?"

"Yeah."

"Is that a yeah you're still there or a yeah you'll be my friend forever?"

"Yeah to both. I'm sulking."

"One of the many reasons I loves ya so much. Now promise."

"Okay, I promise," I said, looking at him. "If someone better doesn't come along."

But he didn't smile. He just gave me this small lift of his eyes, where I could see something that made me feel what I would later realize was fago.

chapter ten

Before the bell, Mrs. Burrell had passed out Caspar's story for us to review over the weekend. He was intelligent, and it was only my prejudice that his playing football didn't fit with that, probably because his teammates Samsonite and Patrick Torno were such bad examples. Caspar was also on my mind because that morning Dr. Jackson had announced his birthday, and during lunch Samsonite and his table of friends had made a huge deal of it, singing and shouting. Caspar had looked miserable through every second.

At work that night I read the story, and I was really gripped by it. I wanted to read it again. Then I heard Tammie broadcasting at an unnecessary decibel.

"Maria, you have to go to the bathroom before you

leave your house. You can't come in here every time and use ours."

Maria was maybe fifty. From enough of a distance, you might think she was somebody's grandmother. Up close you could see her exaggerated features. She always came in to buy gum. For this I was grateful, as it meant something was being bought. But the price of gum didn't include bathroom privileges, not with Tammie.

The argument went on a few minutes, back and forth, Tammie's piercing volume resonating through the store, dwarfing Maria's muffled responses. I considered closing up my drawer and going back to plead Maria's case, but before I could decide, she shuffled out the front without buying so much as a gumball.

Tammie came to the register.

"Those residents!" she said. "I'm going to call her house and tell the folks on duty that they have to make sure the clients use the potty before they go out."

I said nothing. She waited, then turned and marched back to whatever she had pretended to be doing before Maria came in. I went back to Caspar's story.

It was about a high school senior whose only wish for a graduation present was that his older brothers show up at the commencement. They were his father's kids from a previous marriage, and they were absent from his life for long periods. They only swung into town when they were on the run from their mother. They would stay for a while, until arguments with the father and his wife turned into free-for-alls. There were Person in Need of Supervision petitions and juvenile detentions, and one time a knife fight. The narrator had me holding my breath by the end. He grew up in a big, luxurious house, always waiting for these brothers who didn't remember him until they needed a place to stay.

I made some notes on the pages to remind myself of what to put in my written critique, especially that the story was honest. Then Pan came in.

He leaned over the counter and kissed me. "How's business tonight?"

"Dry as a desert." Then I whispered, "Tammie scared off our only potential buyer."

"She's got a shrewd head for business. She ought to sell typewriters."

"She makes me crazy sometimes."

"Let's pretend she's already gone home," he said. "What have you been up to, beautiful?"

"Reading Caspar Phillips's story. It was excellent."

"Hmm."

"I'm not kidding."

"Doesn't he play football?"

"You bigot. Although I thought the same thing."

"And?"

"You've heard him in class. He's smart. A little slow on the draw, but smart."

"What was so great about it?"

I explained it to him.

"We'll see. I'll read it before I go to bed."

"James, hi." It was Tammie.

"Hey," Pan said. "How are things? Great hair, by the way. Wow."

Tammie smiled like she had been elected May Queen.

"Thanks. TJ, don't get so dreamy-eyed looking at James that you miss customers coming into the store."

"It's hard for me to concentrate," he said, "with all these pretty women around." Tammie's flirtatious giggle made me turn and grab the bottle of cleaner to wipe down my counter.

"'All these pretty women around,'" I mocked when we got outside. "Are you queer or not?"

"I like to make people happy. Look how she lights up. Besides, she's less likely to kick me out of the store when I need to hang with my real best girl. Let's forget about her. She's over for the night."

He was right. I started to feel cozy again.

"I think you're going to be surprised by Caspar's story," I said.

"Maybe."

"It's the best one I've read so far."

"What?"

"Besides yours."

"Quick yet clumsy recovery. Are you sure it was his you read? He talks like his vocal cords are in reverse."

"I know, but if you listen to what he says, he's got a brain."

"Listening to him takes a lot of patience."

I felt defensive and wasn't sure why. "It's a good story, Pan."

"I said I'm going to read it later," he said. "But I don't want to give him the benefit of the doubt. And I don't want you to either. He's probably like the rest of his buddies. And we know what they think of me."

That next Monday in class I made a positive remark about Caspar's piece, even though I hated talking in big groups. I had reread it and still liked it, seen things I hadn't the first time. Pan looked at me once with a wry smile, but he didn't comment at all. Meanwhile, Samsonite, in retaliation for Caspar's treachery the previous class, said, "Dude, there's a lot of run-on sentences."

I looked at Pan, waiting for a smirk, but he didn't seem to be paying attention.

"Where?" Mrs. Burrell jerked her head like she had picked up a scent. "I didn't notice."

Samonsite read a sentence from the piece aloud.

"That's not a run-on, Boz," Mrs. Burrell said. "That's a long sentence. There's a difference."

Then she wrote the whole thing on the board and showed us the grammar.

Trying to save face two classes in a row, Samsonite said, "It's too long. It's hard to pay attention."

"That may be, for you," she said. "But it's not a run-on."

That worked. He sat back in his seat.

After class Pan said he was going to the bathroom and would meet me at the front entrance. I must have packed up too slowly because I was one of the last people in the room. The other person was Caspar.

"I loved your story," I said. "It was really emotional." I wished I hadn't opened my mouth. That had not sounded intelligent.

"Thanks," he said, and looked down at his pack.

Maybe I'd insulted him. I started to leave, embarrassed to have been so gushy and gotten such a laconic response.

"It took me a long time."

I looked back at him unsure of who he was talking to, since there was no one else in the room.

"I felt like it was agonizing work," he said. "I must have rewritten it ten times, and then I still wasn't sure. Maybe that's it. You're never sure."

He was looking at me now, pulling at his pack. He

had very nice eyes. A light shade of brown. I hadn't noticed them before, probably because his hair tended to hang in front of them.

"Yeah, uh, I know what you mean," I said. "I thought it would be simple at first. But when I got started, I didn't want to do it at all."

Again he didn't respond. Again I turned to go. Then when too many silent seconds had passed, he said, "Yes, that's exactly it. Once I was in, I didn't like the feeling one bit."

Every word was deliberate, as if he were translating from another language. I began to say something, but he wasn't done.

"But at the same time, I felt like it was a baby. You can't leave a baby alone. You have to take care of it."

That was a strange comparison, but I was intrigued. I didn't know if he wanted to talk more or if I should really go this time.

"See ya," I said, which sounded absurdly out of place.

All I heard, or thought I heard, was him saying something like "Huh."

When I met up with Pan for our walk home, he said, "What are you up to?"

"What do you mean?"

"I don't like the look on your face."

I shook my head. There was no look on my face, I was sure.

I don't know why, but a feeling of resignation came over me as we walked.

"Pan, maybe I should investigate lesbianism," I said. "Life would be easier, at least my love life."

"Not following your logic, Joto. But don't worry. You'll find someone. Just not a Mungers Millsian. I mean, what kind of pickings are there here?"

"None, I guess."

"Maybe less than that. You must never, ever date anyone from this town. Except me. That's final."

"But Pan, even if I couldn't stand him very long, at least I could say I'd had a date."

"I think it's better to always be picky. Maybe a guy from out of town would be worth the effort."

"What town? Look at the names of the towns around here."

"That's true," he said. "Netherford. Who came up with Netherford?"

"Or Triangle Center?" I said. "What about Root? Do you think I can find a quality boyfriend in a town called Root?"

"I would guess not."

"So it's hopeless."

"It's not easy for either of us, Joto. What do you think it's like for me living in a place like Mungers Mills? What exactly is a munger anyway?"

"I don't know. Probably we learned it in fifth grade social studies."

"It doesn't bother me that much, being single," he said. "I've got you, and I've got Mom Fazzino to cook for me. What else could a boy ask for?"

"But you do find people. You told me about that guy you met online. And your parents took you to Cape Cod where you had the romance of your life with some Portuguese kid."

"He never answered my e-mails, if that helps any."

"But he had sex with you for two weeks. Do you realize that's fourteen more times than I've had sex?"

"We did it more than once some days, so it's closer to thirty."

"I hate you. When we went on vacation a few summers ago, before Paolo was born, I didn't have meaningless sex. I got sun poisoning. And sand fleas."

"You got souvenirs anyway."

"Do you see how unfair life is? You are gorgeous and blond and thin, which makes it easy for you to find someone. And you get to go on vacations."

"Speaking of the Cape, we're making plans to go for Memorial Day."

"I thought you were going to Florida."

"That's spring break. Those tickets are already bought. But we all want you to come with us to Chatham at the end of May. The pharmacy can spare you."

"I'll think about it. But what'll I do while you're playing all weekend with another kid in the changing hut?"

"I exaggerated. I only saw that Portuguese guy a few days. He was terrified of his parents finding out. Or any of his friends seeing us together."

We had reached his house by now.

"So think about it, really. You've got two months to get ready. Mother and Kevin have said a hundred times they'd like me to invite a friend so I'll be less sullen."

"I'll think about it," I said, though I had already decided that if there was any way I could afford it, I would go.

chapter eleven

Imagine being on your own little float making your way along the water, and you look up to see that an ocean liner is coming your way. At first you think that it must see you, that it will at any second make a slow and steady turn. But it keeps getting closer. And you keep waiting for it to veer off, at least enough to miss you. Seconds before it's about to plow through the middle of you, it stops. You wait because you cannot ignore an ocean liner. That's what it was like that next Wednesday, April Fools' Day, during lunch when Caspar Phillips came toward our table with his tray and a look in his eyes like he didn't know who was navigating.

"Do you mind if I sit here?" he asked with that hard-to-believe voice. "Just for today?" From this angle his face was as innocent as a little boy's, despite the boulder of a body beneath.

"Uh, no," I said, "go ahead." He proceeded to situate himself. Pan looked incredulous.

"I really appreciated the comments you made about my story the other day," he said. It wasn't exactly clear who he was talking to since he was looking between me and Pan, but I was the only one who had remarked on it.

"Yeah," I said, "it was really good." I pretended to keep eating.

Caspar turned his head slightly to Pan. "Some of the comments were okay, but I feel like TJ's really helped."

"Thanks," I said. Pan would mock me later for blushing, but I couldn't help it. "You're a good writer."

"I don't know about that," he said, and kind of smiled. "To tell you the truth, that's the first story I've ever written."

"Me too."

"The first thing I've ever written that I cared so much about. Most of the time I do the assignment and turn it in and worry about my grade. But this time all I cared about was whether I was going to like it or not. Like I was painting a picture to put up in my house and I had to do the best I could."

Then he saw Pan looking at his watch and trying to

stifle a yawn. Caspar stiffened, and his face got even more expressionless. "I'm sorry. Were you having a private conversation? You didn't seem to be talking much, so I thought . . . My mistake."

"It's okay," I said. "We weren't talking about anything important."

"No," said Pan, "nothing."

"Oh, okay," said Caspar. "So it's nice to find out how other people approached the assignment."

"I approached it from behind," Pan said.

"What?"

"Nothing."

"James," he said, "I think you are an excellent writer. Way beyond the rest of the class."

I think Pan actually blushed this time, then bit on his straw.

"I'm not as good as you," Caspar said, "but I wonder if I have an aptitude for English that I didn't know about."

"You've definitely got talent," I said.

"I've always been good at science."

"And football," Pan added.

"Yeah, but the subject of schoolwork never comes up there," Caspar said, and I giggled. "I would like to say football is my favorite subject of all, if only it were a subject. But then too many people would get credit who didn't deserve it."

I couldn't help giving Pan a sardonic smile. Caspar continued as if there weren't something else going on. "Math comes to me with little effort. But I might go into political science. I guess my politics have always tended to lean toward the liberal side."

I'd never thought about which way my politics leaned.

"I really like science too," he continued, "but I've never felt excited like I did in English these last few weeks. *Excited* is not the right word. Because like I told you before, I was in the middle of my story and I just wanted to get out. I didn't enjoy it. It was like being haunted. Possessed, maybe. I've never felt that kind of emotion about a math problem."

"I've been haunted by math problems," I said.

"There's some kind of trap to making up a world you've based on real life," he said. "It makes you feel like you're inside of it instead of doing the work."

I didn't know what that meant, but I thought I could listen to him all day. He didn't say things for filler. He examined every word.

Pan got up. "I'll see you tonight," he said to me. "I've got my physical, like I told you, so I'm getting out early."

"Bye," I said. He left me and Caspar sitting looking at each other. Rather, I looked at him and he looked somewhat to the left of me. The noise from the cafeteria was conspicuously loud compared with our table.

Finally, finally, Caspar formulated a new sentence. "Your friend doesn't like me, I guess."

This was probably true, but Caspar sounded so vulnerable that I had to make up an excuse.

"He's very shy," I said.

"But he talks in class."

"Yeah, but you know, the guys give him a hard time. Really just a few of them. Most people leave him alone."

He sat with that. I was learning that when Caspar went silent, he was thinking, not bored.

"I suppose if I were in his position, I would feel the same way. Anyway, I hope I didn't spoil your lunch."

"No, not at all," I said, though it was plain I'd not eaten anything since he'd dropped anchor.

"Okay, then, would you like to go out with me sometime?"

I might have been less startled if he'd asked for my bra.

"What?"

"I'm sorry."

"No, it's okay . . ."

"Have I offended you in some way? That's not what I had in mind at all."

"No, no, it's that . . . nothing. You took me by surprise is all."

He grinned. He was very handsome when he

smiled. "Will that help my cause? The element of surprise?"

"I guess."

"I don't mean to put you on the spot. Do you work on the weekends?"

"At Polaski's. Downtown. Weeknights too."

"I can give you my e-mail address if you want, and you can take some time to think about it."

My impulse wanted to say yes. Saying no was like turning down a lottery win. I was about to respond when a tiny mosquito of paranoia bit me. There was no evidence for it, but since he did sit with that table of jerks, possibly he had been put up to this: I hung around with Pan. I wasn't one of the babes. And it was April Fools' Day. No one had ever asked me out before. I thought of my thick hair pulled back in an unimaginative braid. Then I could almost see the reflection of my dad staring back at me from the tabletop.

"So," he continued, "do you have a phone to put it in? Or a notebook or something to write it down on?"

His insistence made me want to squash the pesky mosquito.

"That's okay," I said, surprised that my voice still worked. "I don't have a cell phone. Or a computer at home. Uh, I have to see my guidance counselor." I got up and grabbed my lunch bag.

Caspar leaned back a little, looking straight ahead, his face a snowman's melting into confusion.

"Uh, bye," I said.

"Yes." His voice rumbled in his chest. "Good-bye."

I took a quick look at the jock table. Not one of them was paying attention to us.

"Thanks," I said, no idea why.

He turned his head to me and those beautiful eyes were cloudy with hurt, but I couldn't go back now.

"For what?" he asked.

"Nothing. I mean, see ya."

"Sure."

I was in the hall so fast that I had no time to figure out where I was really going.

That night I couldn't concentrate on work. A couple of people from the residences came in, and I was patient, if not particularly friendly. Tammie snapped at a woman named Edith, who lingered over the body washes too long.

"She's okay, Tammie," I said. "I'll take care of things." I didn't know if it was the injustice or my irritability making me say it. Either way, Tammie gave me her frigid smile and disappeared. I felt completely dismal when Pan came loping in.

"Kiss me, Kate," he said, leaning over the counter. For some reason I didn't want this kind of playing tonight, but I kissed him anyway. "So, did you have a proper din-din, or do I have to go down to Samantha's Fried Chicken and get you a bucket of the bad HDLs? I just got an all-okay from the doctor, so I can eat whatever I want until next year."

"I had something at home . . ."

The front door opened and Caspar Phillips came in. Bewildered, I thought that possibly Caspar was related to Tammie somehow, though she had never mentioned any relatives. Before I could unjumble my thoughts, he came straight to me.

"I'm very sorry for being so abrupt today," he said. "In the cafeteria."

"That's okay."

"You see, I tend to work out a situation in my head for a long time before I say something. So I forget that when I'm ready to say it, the other person isn't necessarily ready to hear it."

Pan coughed. Caspar slowly turned to him.

Caspar was an inch taller and I don't know how many inches beefier.

"I'm sorry, again," Caspar said. "Was I interrupting another conversation? I didn't mean to."

"No," I said. "You don't have to apologize."

"As a matter of fact, I do. That was really inappropriate. I asked my dad about it, and he said that my intention was good but the execution was off."

"What are you talking about?" Pan asked.

"You don't ask a girl out in the middle of talking about something else," Caspar said. "You've got to lead up to it."

Pan drew back.

"It's okay," I whispered. It wasn't—nothing was. I had to get them out of here. I could pull the fire alarm or hit the panic button under the counter. Tammie's impeccable timing made it even worse.

"Isn't this nice, TJ. You're surrounded by admirers tonight. Not just one this time, but two." She followed with an exaggerated sigh. "A girl should be so lucky. But boys—and I hate to sound like the pushy grown-up—if you're not here to purchase a product, you'll have to be going. No loitering. You can read the sign." She looked around for a sign to that effect, and not finding one, turned back. "Those are the rules."

Pan didn't even try to flatter her, just left. Caspar stared at nothing for a few seconds, and then looked back at me. "I've made a big mess. Now I've gotten you in trouble at work, too. That's not what I intended." Big as he was, he left without a sound.

Tammie raised her eyebrows at me almost imperceptibly, then turned and went back to the office.

chapter twelve

When I got home, it was nine thirty. Pan had a cell phone, so late-night calls to him didn't wake up his whole house, especially his porcupine of a grandmother. But I didn't have the nerve to call him. I don't know why I hadn't told him about Caspar asking me out—I just hadn't wanted to. And I had said no to Caspar—sort of—by running away like an electrified hen. But the agitation persisted, and at ten, a much less acceptable hour, I dialed Pan's cell.

He answered with, "You have exactly thirty seconds to explain."

"People with manners say hello," I said.

"Not in the age of caller ID. No more stalling. I'm plugging in the cattle prod I'm going to use on you. Or him."

"That's what Father Francis always said at Holy Spirit Redeemer."

"You actually had a priest in Catholic school? I thought they were extinct."

"He almost was. He was ancient. And he was always threatening us with a cattle prod."

"Speaking of cattle, explain all this about Caspar asking you out."

"Which one is the cow?" I asked, annoyed. "Both of us?"

"I would smite anyone who compared you thus."

"Speak English."

"You speak English, Joto. You're stalling."

"He asked me out. Is it so unbelievable that someone might do that?"

"No, not a bit. Any one of those endomorphs would be lucky to have you for a girlfriend."

"So what are you so mad about?"

He laughed. "Mad? Is someone feeling just a wee bit paranoid? Do you need some of my mother's medications?"

"You said he was a cow."

"Boys can't be cows."

"Come on."

"Okay, I apologize. I don't have anything bad to say about Caspar. Nothing particularly good either. Now wait—don't get dizzy again. I just mean I don't know him. That's all. But let's examine the real issues. There are two. One is that he had the audacity to move in on my girl."

"So you are angry."

"Two is that you hid it from me for hours and hours."

"I was going to tell you, I swear."

"So out with it. What did he say? Word for word. I want exact syllables."

"It's not that dramatic."

"The prod, Missy Pants of the Parochial School."

"He's kind of blundering, Caspar is," I said.

"Kind of. He never gets a joke either. You could tell him your brother was a marmoset and he would consider it."

"We talked a little about homophobia, that is, after you disappeared."

"Homo—What do they even think that means in this town? Haunted houses?"

"Honest. He was talking about how hard it must be in our school for you."

Pan was quiet for a moment. "That works in his favor. But he may just have been trying to get into your pantaloons."

"In the cafeteria?"

"You know how boys are."

"Can I finish?"

"Go."

"So we're talking about that, and then, like he pulled it out of the sky, he asks me if I want to go on a date."

"With him?"

"No, Pan, with a marmoset. Of course with him."

"And you said no?"

"I said I had to go see my guidance counselor."

"Hmm . . . innovative."

"For a second, a billionth of a second, I thought that he was doing this for the sake of his friends. The guys he sits with. You know, like on TV when the ugly girl gets asked out by the football captain, and she falls for it, and everyone laughs?"

"That's as much as I needed to hear, Joto. My grandmother must have a grenade in her Hope Chest."

"No. That wasn't it at all. I was completely wrong. Maybe because I've watched too much bad TV. Or because no one's ever asked me out before. He's too nice . . . honest or something."

"Or maybe subconsciously you knew he wasn't your type."

"I don't know what my type is, so neither does my subconscious. No, I was wrong. He was asking me for real. I looked over at that table of clowns and they didn't even realize he was gone. Don't you think they'd be sneaking looks and doing all that obnoxious stuff guys do when they're watching a good show?"

"So?"

"So I'm an idiot. I shouldn't have been so abrupt with him. And then tonight when he came in, I didn't make things any better standing there like a coatrack."

"What were you supposed to do? Tammie Eye Shadow was throwing us all out."

"I could have spoken up. That's two times in one day he's been snubbed. He doesn't deserve that. I think he's an okay guy."

"Wait. Let me rewind one itsy-bitsy second. Am I hearing that you don't care that I got thrown out, only that Caspar did?"

"I didn't say that."

"Yes you did, and I intend to let my feelings be hurt, but not until after we discuss issue number three."

"You said there were only two issues."

"That's why I'm in advanced math. Number three is you really want to go out with him. Now that you know he wasn't fooling, you are actually considering it."

"Oh, all right. So what if I do want to go out with him? He's got beautiful eyes."

"So does a gray wolf. I can fix you up with one."

"There are other things. He's kind of sweet, and a girl needs a little romance once in a while."

"I love you for your spirit. I appreciate you the way no straight guy can."

"Come on, what's the big deal? So he asked me out, and if I weren't such a mushroom, I might have said okay. You meet guys and have your little fun."

"That's different. That's just boys in a hostile land desperate for affection."

"That could be the title of your next story."

"You wouldn't like it as much as you did Caspar's story, now would you? That's issue number four, the way you raved about it in class."

"Oh my God, you really are jealous. And if you're going to be this crazy over my one venture into dating— and a date that never happened—then you need to fake being straight."

"Maybe I will. And what's this crap about comparing yourself to ugly girls on TV who get set up by the popular guys? Haven't I taught you anything? You're beautiful."

"Inside."

"No, outside. That's why he asked you out. Not because he's capable of seeing some inner beauty. Boys his age aren't."

"You're a boy his age."

"Quiet. And I'm not saying you aren't innerly beautiful too. I can see it."

"So if that's true and he's only after my body, shouldn't I decide if he's worth it?"

I waited. I could hear him breathing, fiddling with something on the other end.

Finally he laughed, like he had been kidding the whole time. "If you want to go out with him, then you should. He's not a total idiot like his friends. Not even close."

"Really?"

"Don't press me, Joto. I don't give much, or often."

"Okay."

"You have my blessing."

"You sound like somebody's father."

"I feel like somebody's ex-husband."

"It's too late anyway. I blew it."

"He'll be back. He's as slow as a caterpillar, but he's persistent. Just remember you are my prom date. I've already bought the trick boutonniere."

"I can't believe you're insecure about that too."

"So are you going to call him?"

"I don't know. We'll see. Tomorrow maybe. I'm going to try to sleep."

"Loves ya."

"Loves ya."

I hung up.

*   *   *

Lying there, I plotted how to tell Caspar that I would like to go out with him after all. But when I had the script worked through, I wondered, What if he doesn't want to go out with me anymore? What could be more humiliating? Then I had to rewrite the whole thing and focus on apologizing for being so abrupt. And apologize for Tammie. Then if he wanted to repeat his request, I would seize it like a life preserver.

Once I got settled on that course, I remembered how slow Caspar was. What if I apologized, but he didn't understand that he was supposed to repeat his request? An apology wouldn't be enough. I would have to word things so that he grasped my intentions toward his original intentions. But what if my hints were too subtle and I ran out of material before he got it? That required a whole new script, more rehearsal.

I was putting myself out on a frayed tightrope. I had hinted to other boys in the past that I was available for dating. I might as well have been trying to sell them housekeeping magazines. The last time had been at the beginning of ninth grade, when my wishful imagination had led me to believe Ted Karsinski wanted me for his fall dance date. Only in retrospect could I see what a fool I must have sounded like: asking him if he liked to dance, what his schedule was, what price the tickets were, making a big deal about how the tickets should be free, since it was a school activity and we were paying for it with our tax dollars. Really cringe material. Ted must have understood the hint too well because he avoided me hard after that. This was one of several small incidents that made me believe I was not date worthy, at least not at this school. So though I was anxious to get the invitation from Caspar again, I was just as concerned about avoiding another rejection. That one potential date had turned into a tightrope act was ridiculous, but I couldn't get myself off it. When I was so tired I couldn't go at it anymore, I fell asleep for what was left of the night.

By morning I was in such a daze I had to keep reminding myself that it was in fact a school day, and I had in fact done my homework. Nerves and fatigue were making me dizzy. I couldn't have been shakier if I'd been about to give a speech to a huge audience. I'm sure I looked like a wreck. I might not survive this near-dating thing.

Pan was no help. He pestered me in every class we had together, and even threatened to ask Caspar himself.

"Maybe he'll change his mind and go out with me," he said. "I've never been out with a certifiable jock."

"You wouldn't dare," I said, then was overcome by a deep yawn.

At lunch Caspar did not come over to our table,

and I tried hard not to look in his direction. In English his face hung like he had been drugged. When Mrs. Burrell called on him, he said, like a proper old man, "I apologize. I seem to be lost in thought today." Something about the way he said it made the class laugh.

Pan waited for me to pack up after, but I sent him off. Since Caspar was lagging behind as usual, this was my chance. If another day went by I would lose my nerve, and I might worry myself into never sleeping again.

"Caspar," I said, thankful that Mrs. Burrell had left the room. At first he didn't move at all. This worst scenario—that he wouldn't even speak to me—seized my throat. I had no plan for his indifference, but I forced myself forward.

"Caspar?"

He turned his head toward me. "Oh, hello, TJ. I hope I didn't get you into too much trouble last night. I wasn't aware I was loitering."

"No," I said. "That's my manager. Assistant. She likes the sound of her own voice. You—you two—didn't do anything wrong. You can come." The weight of my ineptitude made my knees buckle. "To the store."

"Thanks." It sounded final.

I could barely remember my lines, but I had to get through this. "So I'm the one who needs to apologize."

"Apologize? For what?" He looked at the floor as if the patterns puzzled him.

"For yesterday. In the cafeteria?"

His expression didn't change.

"When you, you know, sat with us? Me and Pan. James?"

He looked up at me, his face relaxed back to the drugged look, and he stared just long enough for me to fear he might drool.

"Yesterday, during lunch," I said. "We were talking, first, about the stories we wrote?"

"I know. I was very crass."

"No, not at all. I was the crass one. I shouldn't have been so rude like that. It's just that I was surprised, is all."

"Oh, I see."

Then the words sneaked out: "I would love to go out with you."

A mistake, I was sure. I should have stuck with the script, feeble as it was.

But his brown eyes looked recharged. A slight smile lifted his big face.

"You would?"

"Yes, sure. Anytime. I mean, not right this minute since we're in school and all."

"My schedule only includes spring track these days. When would be a good time for you?"

I couldn't think of anything, not one single thing, never mind when I was free. Then my identity came back to me. "Saturday nights are good for me. I don't work," I said. Usually I spent them with Pan, and though he had given me his consent, saying that made me feel like I was plotting an affair.

"Why don't we exchange e-mail addresses and . . ."

"Uh, I don't have a computer at home."

"Oh, that's right."

"Easier to call. I mean, only way is to call. My house. No cell either."

"Sure. That's even better."

I ripped a piece of paper from my notebook and scribbled my number. "Don't worry if some crazy people answer," I said. "Eventually it will filter down to me."

"Thank you," he said. "I'm really looking forward to talking to you." He got up, lighter and even springy now. "Can I walk you to your locker?"

I prayed that Pan was not lurking.

"Yeah, sure."

He stood up. He was easily a foot taller than me. Wider by a person. He had on a light cologne. As we walked through the hall I thought how it would be nice to put my arm around him, but it remained a thought. From a distance behind I heard Pan sneeze an amplified sneeze, but I couldn't turn around. When we got to my locker, I looked up at Caspar.

"Thanks," I said.

"May I call you tonight?"

"That would be great."

Before I could see that ocean liner coming at me again, he leaned down and kissed me, lightly, on the cheek. Then he smiled like he had no confidence at all, turned, and walked off.

My body was vibrating.

I tried three times to get my locker combination right. Then Pan was there, pushing me out of the way.

"Here, I'll do it." He opened it, and I grabbed for things without any purpose. I shut the door, tried to be casual.

"You look like you just saw a fairly large ghost," he said.

I mustered a laugh. Pan put his arms around me and kissed me on the lips. Twice.

chapter thirteen

I had to work that night, and my family had strict instructions about contacting me when the call came. "If a boy calls, just give him my number at work," I warned them. "It will not be James. James knows where to find me at all times, so he won't call here when I'm at work."

"He won't call to talk to me?" Mom asked. "I thought we had kind of a bond." Dad grimaced.

"Do not attempt conversation with this male caller. Do not let him hear Paolo screaming in the background."

"I'm going to want to talk to him a little," Mom said. "Show him we're friendly."

"No," I said. Then seeing her flinch, I added, "Please."

"A father should have a talk with the boy who wants to date his little girl," said Dad.

"His little girl will not appreciate that."

They exchanged a she's-at-a-difficult-age look.

"Just give him my work number. It's next to both phones, so you won't have to go looking for it."

"What's he like?" Mom asked.

"Questions later. Does everyone know what to do?"

"I guess so," she said.

"Do not engage with him. Just give him my number."

"We've got it."

"Dad? No meddling?"

"What does that mean?"

"You know what I mean. Don't disappoint me."

"Yeah, all right."

"TJ, why are you so nervous?" Mom asked.

"This may be my only call from an interested guy ever," I said.

"Nonsense," Mom said.

"Your mother's right," Dad said. "Look at that skin. You've got rich lady's skin."

I felt my eyes tear up. My wonderful, dopey parents loved me like I was something special. I cleared my throat so they wouldn't be able to hear what I was choking back. "I'm going to work."

They didn't disappoint me, because Caspar never called. Every time the phone rang at work, I jumped for it. Once when I was checking out some customers, it rang and I almost turned away from them to grab it. But it was not Caspar. Pan called twice. Usually I loved to hear from him, but tonight I had trouble paying attention.

"Are you trying to get rid of me, young lady?" he asked during the first call.

"No."

"I suspect I am being rushed."

"Okay, yes. I can't help it. I'll call you just as soon as I hear from him."

"You'd better."

"I will."

"We'll squeal like impish schoolchildren."

"Good-bye."

"And Joto?"

"What?"

"When you two get married, I will not refer to him as my brother-in-law."

I hung up.

He called back again an hour later, but when there was no news, he didn't try to keep me. He sounded worried himself.

The whole shift went by and the call never came. There must have been some screwup at my house. When I got home at nine thirty, everyone was in bed. That was okay because I didn't want to find out that there had been no screwup. Mom looked into my room when I had just turned off the light.

"How was work?" she whispered. We always whispered when Paolo was asleep, the silence so fragile.

"Not bad. We had a little business tonight."

"Your friend didn't call. Your father and I kept off the phone all evening."

"Thanks, Mom."

"Maybe we should get you a cell phone. All the kids have them these days."

"That's okay. He's kind of an airhead. He probably forgot. I'll talk to him in school tomorrow." I attempted to yawn indifference, but I could feel that tears would get away if I did.

"That's it, I'm sure. Boys your age are scatterbrained. Good night."

"Night."

Nothing could comfort me in that dark hour, though I tried to reason away the dread of school the next day. I was pretty sure that on Fridays Caspar was only in one class with me—English—and I could avoid him for forty-five minutes. Then the weekend would come and go, giving me time to build up resistance.

What a relief Friday morning not to see Caspar anywhere in passing, and then in English to find he was absent. By Monday I would be strong again, and I could even smile and say hello to him without too much faking.

Pan was another story. I wouldn't be able to fake anything with him. During my restless night I hadn't had the energy to think about how he was going to take it. All the way to school he had chided me for not calling him before I went to bed. Then he said, "I believe Mister Caspar needs to be punished somehow. How does a bullring sound? We get him drunk, pierce his nose, and he goes through life getting yanked by magnets and harassed at airport security."

"Between best friends," I said, "I have a request. This situation is not to go any further than you and me. Got it?"

"Of course. Who am I going to tell?"

"I'm just saying, if you start something with him, he's going to know it got to me. It's going to look like I put you up to it."

"Up to what?"

"To whatever. I like my humiliations private. Please don't say anything to him at all."

"Tell me this: How are we to get him to learn if we don't point out his bad behavior?"

"What bad behavior? He probably forgot. You know how he is."

"He stood up my best girl, that's what I know."

"Don't make it worse."

"I'm not making it worse. I'm making it right."

"Please."

"All right, then, silence to Caspar. But I'm not sure he'll know the difference. He could be a sheepdog with that hair in his eyes. He doesn't seem to know where he is most of the time."

"Enough about him."

I wanted to call in sick to work that night. I never took time off, because it was hard for Tammie or the owner to get someone else on short notice. But I didn't want to be there. I wanted to stay home, sulk, get my strength back. What a waste to have worried myself into convulsions, making sure I phrased my apology just right so Caspar would ask me out again. And I was annoyed with him in advance for any apology he might make. Even if for some reason he had not gotten through to my house, he could have picked up a telephone book and looked up the pharmacy number.

Still, a persistent blip of hope kept squiggling through my mind. Why had he made the special effort to come to where I worked? Then the hope would be stomped by confusion: Why, so quickly, had he forgotten me? I knew guys could lose interest in girls as soon as they'd gotten what they wanted. Had Caspar skipped that step and gone straight to the dumping?

I went to work anyway. It added to my anxiety that Tammie was on because she was sure to explain in detail her boyfriend plans for the weekend. When I got there, though, there was something comforting about being back to normal after the emotional storms of the past two days. Maybe this was my future: working on a Friday night, looking forward to seeing Pan, hearing about his adventures when he had them.

Just when sorting greeting cards made me stop thinking for a few minutes, Caspar walked in. Actually, I didn't know how long he was behind me before he said something.

"TJ, I've had a rough couple of days."

I spun around. "Hi," I yelped. I was not ready for this. I hadn't planned to be strong until Monday.

Caspar kept his voice low. He remembered that much at least. "My dad had a heart attack Thursday," he said. "I found out when I got home from school. A myocardial infarction."

"Sounds bad," I said, though it really sounded kind of dirty.

"Yes, it was. He had to go in for emergency angioplasty."

"Oh, okay. What's that?"

"It's really an interesting procedure."

"It is?"

"They use an instrument that's kind of like a balloon to unclog the artery. Then the blood can pump like it's supposed to."

"Oh, that. Yeah."

"It's actually fascinating," he said, as if it were not his own father getting the balloon.

"Is he all right?"

"Things look okay right now. He's in Holland Park at the medical center. It was pretty successful, the procedure, and the cardiologist believes there wasn't a lot of damage."

I didn't wish his father bad health, but this was an incredibly good excuse for not calling me.

"I don't know if you remember," he said, "but I told you I was going to call Thursday night."

"Um, yeah, I think you did."

"Oh. Maybe I hadn't said Thursday night. It's quite a blur to me now after all that's happened."

"I can imagine."

"I was worried you would think I was rude or unreliable or something like that."

"No, no," I said. "Of course not."

"It was hard for me to leave my mom through all of this."

"That's where you needed to be. Don't worry about me," I said, then added stupidly, "I got over it."

"I was very worried. Even with my dad sick, I kept thinking how I didn't want to ruin my chance to go out with you."

Now I could forgive him anything.

"I tried calling your house today when my aunt brought me home, but there was no answering machine."

"What?"

"It rang and rang and no one answered, and nothing picked up."

Paolo. Probably he had turned the machine off between squalls. Once he had pulled the tape out and eaten it. At least we were forced to update to digital.

"Sorry," I said. "My house is a little disorganized."

"Are you still interested in going out?"

"Yes," I said too vigorously. "I mean, sure. When your father gets better, and all."

"I was thinking about tomorrow night, like we talked about in school. Or at least I think we talked about Saturday night. I sound disoriented." He sighed. "Because I am."

"You've got good reason to be," I said, wanting to put both my arms around him.

"Would you like to see a movie? I know the theater here is not great. I have better movies at home. But it's something to do, and we don't have to worry about transportation. My truck is in the shop. It's not in great shape even when it is running."

"Are you sure? With your dad in the hospital so far away?"

"My mom thinks I should go out and have some fun after all this. Try, anyway. I really would like to see you."

"Then let's do it."

We stood and looked at each other, then away. We looked at the ceiling, the aisles of products, the floor. One of us was going to have to make a suggestion.

"Let's look at the listings and see what's playing," I said, walking to the register and grabbing the last copy of the local paper from the rack in front of the counter. I tried to be cool, turning the pages deliberately. I wasn't really concentrating on the task, but thinking about Caspar inches from me.

"I think the table of contents is on the first page," he said. There was no sarcasm in his tone.

"That's right," I said as if I'd just remembered. I found the movie schedule. A comedy started at 6:40 at The Moving Picture. We agreed to meet at 6:15 to be sure to get seats. That would give me exactly one and a quarter hours to get home, clean up and change, and get back. I would have to get a ride. Pan might drive me, but that could be awkward. Dad or Mom could give me a ride, but they would ask questions. I could walk, if I ran. I'd figure something out.

"You'd better show up," I said, and smiled.

"You bet I will," he said, and bent and kissed my cheek again. It was just a peck, but I almost hoped Tammie saw us.

chapter fourteen

Having had it withheld from me for so long, I expected dating to be magical, mysterious, or at least different from going out with a friend. But maybe a first date is like the first Halloween you realize you're too old to trick-or-treat, but you go anyway. There's a needle of reality pricking the excitement.

To start, Mom gave me a warning: "People get their expectations up. Don't make a big deal if it's not the best night of your life. Just enjoy yourself. You're young. You've got many, many years of dating ahead of you."

As if that wasn't curse enough, she added, "Most first dates don't result in any long-term relationship."

I nodded, without saying that Dad had been her first date.

She dropped me off, but I didn't let her stay to meet

Caspar, because she was wearing her recycled head cap. Caspar came out of the theater, having bought our tickets. We didn't have much to say, so we went in. I hadn't been to The Moving Picture in such a long time that I'd forgotten how old and run-down it was. Nobody escaped from Mungers Mills alive without knowing it was an old vaudeville theater, whatever that meant, but it had something to do with live shows. Mom had told me that when she was young, a man playing an organ would rise out of the floor in front of the screen. When she was a little girl, she had been terrified, but as teenagers, she and her friends had thought it was hilarious.

Caspar and I watched the trailers without a word between us. Then the movie began. Throughout the show I was expecting something to be happening in the audience as well as on the screen, something between us. I would have settled for some conversation. I would lean over to remark about this or that on-screen, and he would nod, very minutely. That's all. After three tries I quit, but I looked at him a few times to see that his lips were parted as he watched the screen with strict concentration. He surely had forgotten he had company. I felt homesick for Pan, who was on a date of his own. He and I whispered our own narrations during bad movies—much like we did when we watched TV in his room—until our disparaging comments provoked people around us. We mixed candy and popcorn for the effect of salty and sweet. He would put his lean arm around me, and I'd snuggle against him.

Caspar, by comparison, was like one of those Easter Island monuments. His mammoth shoulders and torso, which I had found quite attractive earlier in the evening, spilled over into my space. If he was going to touch me, it should at least be inappropriate. But he was so still that at one point I was sure he had stopped breathing. I'd have a story for my grandchildren about how I hadn't realized my first date was dead until the lights came up.

The movie was all right, when I paid attention, but mostly I sat and analyzed what was not happening, how our evening wasn't even approaching magical. I was supposed to be sexually charged, and instead I was fantasizing about organic mac and cheese with naturally cured ham chunks at Pan's house. When the credits started, I jumped up, conceding failure. My life wasn't bad the way it was: I had an okay job and a roof over my head, and a handsome best friend with lots of money who adored me. Who needed this?

Caspar sat and watched every name roll up, to the last gaffer and best boy. I had to sit back down. Finally the lights went up.

"I didn't think that plot was very credible," he said, turning as much as he could in the restrictive area.

He was alive, and he did remember me.

"I don't know," I said, trying to recall.

"Remember what Mrs. Burrell said in class? If you set up a certain logic, you have to stick with the logic throughout your story."

"Yeah."

"Yes, they have broken a cardinal rule here. They wanted something to happen, so they forced it to happen, even if it didn't make sense."

He was starting to interest me, like he did in class. It could be that Caspar operated in different gears. When he was in, say, first gear, he was nearly catatonic. Then he upshifted, and slowly you realized he was not only animate but intelligent. He never got into overdrive though. Maybe on the football field. But I had not yet seen him excited or agitated or quick.

"What did you think of it?" he asked.

"I agree," I said.

"You don't have to. People have many different interpretations. That's just how I see it."

"I wasn't paying as much attention. To the logic, that is. It was a typical love story."

"Yes, that's it. The usual Hollywood stuff. Suspension of disbelief. You can let something slide if the story is entertaining."

"I might not be smart enough to know better," I said.

He put his nearest hand on mine, and held it there.

It wasn't like when Pan held my hand . . . Well, the first few times I'd nearly passed out, but the electricity had shut off when I knew it was only brotherly affection. This was real, and it had been worth waiting for in silence. Caspar managed to maneuver himself so that he could kiss me, a gentle kiss on my lips.

I didn't know what to do next, so I sat there like a display. When he didn't try to kiss me more, I stood up again. Caspar remained seated. I was conscious about lagging behind in an empty theater with the lights on. People would be coming in for the next show soon. Caspar looked up at me—there was not much difference in our heights with him sitting down—and he had such pretty eyes to peer into. He also looked so innocent. He put his hands on my hips and sat me on his knee, and kissed my lips once again. It wasn't a comfortable position by any means, an armrest pushing deep into my butt and me twisting to match my lips to his, but I was getting delirious.

"Time to go, lovebirds," someone called, someone who sounded a lot like Pan, who was supposed to be in Holland Park with an Internet date. This pulled me back through the levels of my delirium. I looked behind us, but no one was there. It had to have been Pan. He didn't have a stereotypical voice, the dripping affectation Samsonite used to imitate him. It was deep and sometimes musical, often mildly amused.

"I guess we should go," Caspar said. We made our way out of the theater, his hand in mine. When we got outside, he put his arm around me. I enjoyed this, though I was also afraid the phantom Pan might be planning more commentary from the shadows. We walked, neither of us said saying anything about which direction we ought to be going.

"I had a great time tonight," Caspar said.

"Me too."

He stopped and went in for another kiss. This time he moved his tongue in, and his mouth was minty. I tried to go with it, but I felt rigid. I wasn't sure how this was done, so I opened my mouth a little. Caspar knew what he was doing, or was good at pretending. It was the strangest sensation, but one that made me curious for more. Soon my head was in chaos and everything below my waist ached. I tried not to pant. Years of deprivation made me want to make up for lost time, get too into it and open my mouth too wide, but I let him lead. Caspar was patient, gentle, and constant, and I pushed back my impulses.

"A so-so movie. But a wonderful girl," he said when we finally broke.

I didn't care that the movie had left me completely now, although he would doubtless bring it up again for discussion. I might have to sneak back and see it on my own to be prepared.

"I should walk you home, TJ."

"Sure. It's pretty far. About a mile or so."

"That's fine with me."

"And we're heading the wrong way."

I turned us around.

When Caspar and I got to my house, my parents were waiting.

Mom bubbled down the porch steps. Her appearance hadn't changed since she'd dropped me off. "You must be Caspar. I'm TJ's mom. And this is Mr. Fazzino." Dad stood on the porch like a column.

"Very pleased to meet you," Caspar said, reaching out and shaking her hand. He looked at Dad, whose head might have moved.

"So, did you kids have a good time tonight?" Mom asked.

I gave her a hug. When my mouth was close to her ear, I whispered, "Go inside. Now."

She pulled away from me. "It's been nice to meet you, Caspar. I hope you're taking good care of our girl."

"Mom," I said with a smile she needed to fear.

"Good night, you two." She turned and went back up the porch steps. Dad kind of nodded, looking like a mime with arthritis, and went in behind her. The door shut, and the porch light, which had not been on when we'd arrived, lit up.

"Mother," I called, loud enough to be heard

through the door she was spying behind. The light went off. I was unsettled now. Our front porch looked like a poverty cliché, especially with that socket and bulb hanging from wires. And my parents were acting like fools.

"Sorry about them," I said.

"What was your mother wearing on her head?"

"Some kind of head thing," I said, nonchalant.

"It looked like a do-rag," he said. "But not exactly."

I couldn't explain her. "She wears that under her wig."

He looked confused.

"Not really."

"They seem nice, at least your mom. Your dad looked like he was suspicious."

"He doesn't much like boys my age. He's always been really cold to Pan—I mean James. I thought it was because he's gay. But maybe he just doesn't approve of anyone."

"I would really like to see you again. I can't make firm plans right now, though I don't want you to think I'm being rude. My dad is still in the hospital, and I have to wait and see how we're going to schedule things."

"Sure," I said. "Don't worry about me. I'm pretty much always here." That sounded pathetic. "Or at work." That wasn't much better.

But Caspar kissed me, the serious kind, and I loved reaching my arms around his wide, muscular body.

The porch light went on again. I would be wrapping my hands around someone's neck soon. To spite them, I pulled him out of the range of light and resumed the kissing. The light went off and on again. I couldn't tell whether my heart was racing because of Caspar or because I was going to be an orphan soon. I pulled back. I didn't want to stop, but I had to before my parents got the floodlights out.

"How are you going to get home?" I asked. "You're like miles from here."

He pulled out his cell phone and pressed some numbers. He spoke cryptically—quicker than usual— then folded it and put it back in his pocket.

"My aunt can pick me up. She was already out and she's going to swing by."

I could have gone in and made Dad offer a ride. That would have served him right. But I didn't trust what he would say on the way. And also I felt weird about Dad and me and Caspar riding together after my first real kissing.

A car pulled up.

"Good night, TJ," he said, giving me one last earnest kiss despite an audience of three now.

"Bye," I said as he got in the car. I went into the house, snapping off the porch light as I closed the door.

Mom wanted details, but she wasn't getting them.

"You could have woken Paolo," I said, "with your trotting in and out of the house. And what's with the lights?"

She drew back. Then I felt bad. Her life was so flat, and all she wanted was some girl talk.

"Mom," I said, "I think he's really nice. He's got the sweetest eyes."

"Why don't you invite him in next time?" she asked.

"Okay, maybe. Good night," I said, and went to my room.

Lying on my bed, I let the irritation pass. There was Caspar to dream about. Maybe a first date—a good one—truly is like the first Halloween you realize you're too old to be asking for candy. After the initial disappointment, you find there are other treats to be had.

chapter fifteen

Pan called first thing Sunday morning. I confronted him about the lovebirds remark in the theater, though he swore it had not been him. I wasn't convinced, but I let him off. I never had the energy to spar with him for long.

When he demanded information about my date I felt shy, like there was a confidence between me and Caspar that I shouldn't share. Pan interpreted my condensed version as a lack of interest. That worked, for the time being.

"Sounds like it was boring."

"He's nice. Not exactly traditional. As far as conversation, that is. But really nice in his own way."

"Now you're getting defensive. I didn't say he was boring. I said it was boring."

"I have a few questions for you about your little date, Pan."

"Not so fast. Are you going out with him again?"

I didn't answer.

"I repeat: Are you going out with Casparino again?"

"Not sure."

"You don't sound thrilled."

"It's not that. He can't make plans with his father being in the hospital and all. He said he'll call me when he can."

"That old excuse. 'My father's heart stopped.' I've used it."

"Your father's heart did stop," I said. "In a manner of speaking."

"So in a way I'm being truthful."

"Are you saying Caspar's trying to ditch me?"

"He better not. Mom Fazzino and I will march right over to his house with the cattle prod."

"That's really sweet. Now, how did your date go? You'll notice I'm not interrogating you about your boyfriend last night."

"He's not going to be my boyfriend," he said. "That much of the future I can predict."

"Why? What happened?"

"Nothing much. Nothing good, anyway."

"Was he cute?"

"Yeah, kind of."

"So what's the problem?"

"How shallow do you think I am? He only has to be cute?"

"Tell me."

"He was old."

"How?"

"Online he was twenty. In person he wasn't. He said people tell him he looks twenty even though he's thirty-one."

"Oh my God, that's disgusting."

"He even had a few gray hairs. And some missing ones."

"He knew you were only seventeen and he still went out with you? Isn't that illegal?"

"I don't know. But I wasn't exactly honest either."

"What did you tell him?"

"Twenty-one. He was supposed to think I was his elder."

"You shouldn't have."

"It's different than telling people you're younger than you are."

"I'm not following your reasoning here, Pan. Why not just be honest?"

"Because saying 'seventeen' is like a death knell to online dating. Why should I be honest when no one else is?"

"You might meet another boy your own age and actually have fun."

"Someone my own age with a mortgage is what I met."

"I'm afraid you're going to get hurt. Some predator is going to lure you into his den."

"I don't meet them just for sex. It's dating, just like you normal kids do."

"I know . . ."

"And I can't go making a date with someone in the hall at school, like you normal kids. If it weren't for online socializing, there would be no socializing."

"I know. But I worry."

"I won't go home with anyone craggy. I swear."

"What did you wind up doing when you found out he was ancient?"

"Went to a movie. When we sat down, he asked me how old I was. I told him eighteen at first, forgetting what I had told him online. When I saw how uncomfortable it made him—and because he had lied really bad himself—I played bashful and told him I was really only seventeen. The younger I got, the more he squirmed like he needed Preparation H. So I just couldn't help but say I was really only sixteen. Or just about to be."

"You are cruel. And did he believe you?"

"That's when he got up and left."

"He left?"

"He didn't give me a chance to get any younger. He was frozen for a second, then stood up and said he needed to use the bathroom, and tried to get by me. That's when I whispered that my father was a state trooper."

"He must have had a panic attack."

"He didn't even react, just stepped past me, headed for the bathroom, and never came back. I ruined his evening. He wasted mine. Although I noticed you two were having a good time. Eventually."

"You lying sack of . . . You spied on me, Detective Pansy."

"At your service."

"I can't believe you."

"What else was I supposed to do? My date left me in the middle of the movie. I had to entertain myself. And I wanted to make sure Caspar didn't go too far."

"Pan, if your jealousy didn't amuse me so much, I would end the friendship right this instant."

"I just wanted to make sure my best girl was okay. I was looking out for you. And weren't you two into each other when the lights went up."

"I continue to hate you."

"Is he a better kisser than me?"

"How would I know?"

"I'll show you kissing if that's what you want. Don't underestimate me, Joto. I'm already plotting to get you away from Caspar Phillips and make you mine, all mine."

"How much did you see?"

"Why? Did you go all the way, right there in the theater?"

"You're acting an awful lot like my parents. They were waiting for me when I got home. I was ready to kill them too."

"They are good people. Taking care of what's theirs. Maybe if you tell your father I chaperoned you, he'll like me a little. Or dislike me less."

He sounded very lonely saying that. My indignation melted.

"If it helps any, Dad wasn't exactly a great host with Caspar either. He didn't say a word. He just stood there on the porch."

"Maybe he thinks Caspar's a homo too."

"It's not because you're a homo. He doesn't warm up to people all that fast."

"Like an ice age."

"I've got to get ready for work."

"I'll be by to torment you and make your day pass faster," he said. "Especially now that I'm in competition for your affections."

"I will never forgive you, Pan, ever."

"What about now?"

"No."

"Now?"

"Maybe."

"Good enough. Loves ya."

"Loves ya, and good-bye."

chapter sixteen

Caspar had invited me over for pizza and a movie Saturday, the night before his father was coming home from the hospital. He didn't know what things would be like at home after that.

When Mom found out about this second date, she casually brought up the safe-sex rules she had taught me many times before, about how my body worked and how a boy's worked and what could happen if they worked too well together.

"Mom, come on. It's just pizza," I said, wanting the lesson over.

But she would not be stopped. She went beyond the basics of being responsible, warning me that the first sex probably wouldn't be that great, that we would be awkward with each other. I might not like some things—positions, sensations, odors.

"Here, I want you to have these," she said, handing me a box of condoms as if passing down her grandmother's wedding ring. "Very important. These will prevent disease and pregnancy."

From his bedroom Paolo let out a squall.

She bit her lip. "When used correctly."

I was sorry I had her worried. She would be destroyed if I got pregnant and had to save up my meager pharmacy earnings for my wedding reception at the Knights of Columbus hall. She did not want me living her life with all its missed fortunes. I wouldn't. But she was going to have to give me some privacy. I didn't want to spoil any potential magic by letting her turn it into a textbook chapter or cautionary tale.

I didn't tell Pan about this second date, not immediately, and I felt guilty about it. As he and I made our long trek to his house from school midweek, he asked, "So, what do you want to do this weekend? It's supposed to be spring, although it's taking a long time to get here. You guys are behind in everything."

I told him I was taking Mom to a movie Saturday night, which was not a well-planned alibi.

"That's great," he said. "I want to come."

Mom would have liked that, had she been going. Then when I told him it was girls' night only, he wanted to know who was babysitting for Paolo, and I could barely look him in the eye.

"I hadn't thought of that," I said. "My dad, I guess."

"Really? Doesn't he work all the time?"

"Yeah. Usually."

"Are you sure you don't want me to babysit? You know I'd do anything for Mama-Mia Fazzino."

"On a Saturday night? You must want to find another date to make up for the bad one."

"With who? I'd rather do your mother a favor. It's better than spending my time with some granddaddy who tells me online how young he's not."

"It's okay, thanks. Dad will be home. He never goes out."

"I'll misses ya," he said, putting his hand on my shoulder and pulling me close. He smelled good in the brisk air.

Before we walked another three yards, there was a knot of guilt in my throat.

"The truth is I have another date."

I felt his arm go limp around me.

"Caspar," I said after a long silence.

"You're a terrible liar, Joto. You sounded false."

"I don't know why I made that up about Mom. I feel like I'm cheating on you. Dumb, huh?"

"Trying to spare my feelings."

"I'm sorry. It was stupid."

"He'll have to take you somewhere else," he said. "I'm not sure I can handle another two hours in The Moving Picture."

"What? Am I still under surveillance?"

"Yes, so please consider my convenience when you make plans with him, will you? It's not easy being a private eye."

"We're going to his house."

"Oh." More silence, then, "That's not convenient at all."

"I'm sorry, Pan. I really am."

"Are you going to make a man out of him?"

"It's only our second date. He's the first boy I ever kissed. I'm not real forward in these matters, as you know."

"Out with it. Are you going to do push-ups?"

"I don't know."

"You are. You sound fake again."

"I said I don't know. Why rush it? If he's going to dump me after, I might as well hold out for a few more dates."

"No more of that. I won't listen to you trash the girl I love."

"But . . ."

"No, enough. If he dumps you, he's a fool. End of conversation."

It couldn't be the end of this conversation, because I needed his advice, and bad. Mom had taught me the basics, but she hadn't addressed the paranoia I was starting to feel about my body. When we got to Pan's house, I had a list of questions in my head. His grandmother was sitting in the living room. I said hi as we sprinted past.

Ada was not around, but Kevin came in the back door while Pan served me an omelet casserole made with free-range eggs.

"TJ!" he said, like I'd been gone for a year. I got up, and he hugged me. "What's new in your life, youngster?"

"TJ's got a boyfriend," Pan said blandly.

"That's great, honey," Kevin said. "They've taught you about the chirpies in school, right?"

"Kev, please. Can we talk about the weather?"

"Chirpies?" I asked.

"Syphilis, gonorrhea, HIV," said Pan. "In my house the clinical term is *chirpies*."

"Well, that's just what I call them," Kevin said. "They're so ugly. We've got condoms, TJ. We keep them in the downstairs hall closet. I'll show you where they are, and you take them if you need them."

"Uh, okay," I said.

"No questions asked. James knows." He winked at me.

"Bye, Kev," Pan said, and Kevin moved toward the doorway.

"See you, urchins. Have a nice snack."

I was touched by Kevin's concern, if not by his discretion.

"Is every adult on the planet interested in my potential sex life?" I asked.

"Be patient with them," Pan said. "It gives them something to reminisce about."

When we got to his bedroom, I said, "Listen, Pan, I do need some advice. It's true that it could happen any time for Antonia JoAnne Fazzino. I'd been sure until recently that I would be the only virgin in the retirement community. I know the rules and stuff, and I'm going to do close shaves on my arms and legs. But how do I know when . . . you know, if he wants to? If we both want to . . . ?"

"I wish I could tell you," he said. "Sometimes you'll be making out furiously and you're sure it's going all the way. And it turns out the other person just wants to make out furiously."

"That doesn't help."

"It's a case-by-case thing, Joto. All I can say is do what feels right. And don't be afraid to run if you change your mind."

"Maybe being dateless was easier."

"Easier but less fun. Don't worry. I'll be by your side through the whole ordeal."

"That's kind of kinky."

"Funny."

"Pan, the thing is—and I know this should not have astounded me—I realized I would have to be naked in front of him. Like, naked."

"That's pretty much a requirement. Although I did see a movie once where they did it through a sheet. You could bring one along, kind of like a security blanket."

"But I've never . . . only in front of the girls in gym, and only when they force us to shower, which they usually don't. I'm not used to that kind of exposure."

"Everyone is that way. It's not just you."

"Everyone? You? You have a beautiful body."

"I know."

"Then why would you be self-conscious?"

"You never know, Joto, if the other person is going to like what they see. Doesn't matter what the general consensus is. If the guy isn't into you, he's not into you."

"Thanks a lot."

"No, you're getting it all wrong. I'm saying everyone has the same fear. There's some mystery about what the other person looks like under their undies, until the moment of revelation. So I'm a little nervous too that the guy is not going to like how much body hair I have, or . . ."

"Stop right there."

"But you shave your legs, right? It's not like he's going to find a black Lab on your lap. Just relax."

"I'm never going to get this right. What if I smell? Mom said the smells might be peculiar, but what about my smells? They're not strange to me, but what if small, lithe girls smell different? What if he's been with other girls before and my fragrance isn't as good?"

"What if he smells?"

"He always smells good. Cologne."

"You can only use cologne in so many places."

"I'm worried about me, not him."

"You'll be fine. Listen, no one knows exactly what they're doing the first time. And the second time wasn't much better, as I recall. It takes a while to get used to each other. But worrying about it is going to make you hate it. You don't want to be like the girl in the movies who cries afterward. Look, Joto, if this were anybody else, I could see why you might be torturing yourself. But it's Caspar. He's not your run-of-the-Mungers-Mill jerk. He's not going to talk about you afterward. Just be yourself. And if by chance he doesn't like this or that, he can either get used to it or get lost. Remember, he's worried about the way he looks too. And smells."

He took my hand and led me to the downstairs hall

closet, dug through a wall of long coats to the back, and pulled out a strip of condoms. "There are enough here for a water-balloon convention."

"Put them back," I said, looking behind me. "Your grandmother will see them."

"She thinks they're coasters. Now listen. Keep his thing covered up no matter what. You heard what Kevin said: No chirpies. And no babies either. I'll babysit for your sonic brother, but that's it."

"Come on, I'm not going to get pregnant. We might not even . . ."

"Here," he said, putting them in my hand. "Take a six pack."

I took them. "I'll cherish them always," I said.

"Yeah, don't cherish them. Throw them away after."

I put my arm around him. "Loves ya a hundred times," I said.

"Loves you even more than that. Use the rubbers."

chapter seventeen

Saturday night Dad gave me a ride to Caspar's in our truck. He was striped with grease.

"Are his parents home?" he asked.

"His mother and his aunt are," I said, though I wasn't sure of that.

"Did you leave us a number?"

"Yes. Don't worry."

"It's one thing to be hanging around with gay boys. It's another to be going to a guy's house on your own."

"So now you trust James? Before you didn't want him alone with Paolo."

"I wasn't worried. Just concerned."

"What's the difference?"

"A father wants to protect his kids."

"From what, Dad? It would mean a lot to him if

you even cracked a smile. He thinks you hate him. He's my best friend."

"I'll try. It just seems like a waste, you know, a nice-looking boy being like that."

"The nicest-looking boys *are* like that."

"Be careful tonight, honey. I don't want anyone hurting my baby girl."

"Believe me, I'm loving the fact that you're worried about me going out with a boy because I'm really going out with a boy. Worry more often, will you? Maybe it will get me more dates."

"Has your mother had that little discussion with you about things?"

"Sex?"

"Don't even say it until you're married."

"Uh-huh. She told me how well you two did with that."

He may have blushed under his film.

Caspar lived in the newer part of town, where the cursed Green Goose Day School was located. This was money in a different way from Pan's neighborhood, where rich people had built homes a hundred years ago. Here the houses were big but not remarkable, with enormous yards, swimming pools, campers, and swing sets.

"Here. This is it," I said.

Dad stopped the truck, then looked at me. He tried to put a hand on my face, but I drew back.

"Transmission fluid will clash with my makeup."

He grinned, a little. "You really are beautiful, you know that? I know you don't think you are."

I blew him a kiss and jumped out. I was ashamed of being ashamed that Caspar would see the truck or catch a glimpse of Dad all greasy.

He waited while I stood at Caspar's front door. I gestured for him to move on. When he didn't, I started toward the truck to give him an order and finally he drove off. Caspar came to the door wearing a lavender sweater and a pair of black jeans. A second of dizziness hit me.

He showed me inside, then down to his basement, which was more luxurious than any room in my neighborhood.

"This is kind of my home inside my home," he said. I turned to look at him, and he put his arms around me, bent a little, and kissed my lips. He took my hand and led me to a huge leather couch. We sat down and began some more intensive kissing. I managed to pull away for a second to catch my breath, check my pulse.

"If my dad could see us, he'd have a heart attack," I said. Then I remembered that his father had just had a heart attack. What an idiot. I tried to clear up the mess. "He was worried about chaperones."

"You're safe with me," Caspar said. "I would never do anything to hurt you."

His eyes were an intense brown, and he looked at me like I was a rare, brilliant diamond. "You are so pretty," he said softly. He almost seemed confused, his mouth open and his eyes transfixed.

He didn't suggest anything else, verbally or otherwise, and went up to get the pizza his mother had ordered for us.

"No beer?" I asked, joking, as he came back down.

"Oh. I don't drink beer. I don't like it. My dad and mom let me have wine once in a while. I could find some of that if you wanted."

"No, no, I didn't really mean it. You know, pizza and beer. Just sort of go together."

"Oh."

"But I didn't really want it. Wine either. Pizza is fine." I stammered on: "Not that I'm going to drink the pizza. I'll just chew it."

He opened a mini-refrigerator in the basement's kitchenette. "We have all kinds of soft drinks. Mainly diet soda. My mom."

"That's exactly what I want," I said. "Cola."

There wasn't much to say as we ate, but every movement either of us made was charged.

After we were done, he said, "There's something I

want to show you." He opened up the louvered doors of his entertainment center and revealed not just a space-age TV with a bunch of other machines under it but a library of videotapes and DVDs.

"My dad loves movies," he said. "We have everything listed either by the director or by the genre. We also have on-demand movies we can order if there's nothing we like here."

For a few moments I forgot the charge in the room as my eyes skipped through lists and lists of movies I had never heard of, actors whose names were new to me.

"It's just that here in town we can't get the kind of stuff my dad and I enjoy. Like the movie we saw last week. He wouldn't pay a dime for that."

"We should have come here instead," I said. That sounded suggestive. Was I going to say anything right this evening? I took out random DVDs and read their descriptions. "A lot of these sound really interesting."

"This is great," he said, picking one up. "But it's in Spanish. Can you stand it?"

"Yeah," I said. "Let's see if my high school education has paid off."

"I mean, it has subtitles, but some people don't like to read them."

I looked up at him and felt pleasantly light-headed again. He looked younger from this angle but so fine that I wanted to put my head on his chest and just hold it against him. As usual, I didn't go with the impulse.

The movie was interesting in a way movies seldom were for me. It was the kind I really had to pay attention to, the kind with no explosions. I forgot within minutes that I was reading subtitles. Caspar sat close and soon had his arm around me. I sat stiff for a moment, then I relaxed and leaned back on him. He was a muscley, tightly-stuffed chair.

During the closing credits he kissed me.

I can always remember the rest as him seducing me because I never would have had the confidence to push so far. But it was a wrestling match that I had every intention of losing. At first the panic came back like an annoying cough and I wanted to pull away and just go home. But Caspar was in no rush, and as he persisted every touch of my hand on any part of his skin, especially his face, was like vibrating fire. Eventually I let go of all the things that were wrong with me, and I could easily have forgotten how to breathe. This must have been the unspoken part of the First Time rule. While Mom was right that not everything was easy, and Pan was right that we definitely needed practice, I couldn't get enough of the kissing, or that focused, obsessed look on Caspar's face.

Though I could see why people would get so carried away they would forget condoms, I did have the presence of mind to pull out the ones Pan had given me. Caspar grinned because he had some too.

"We'd have to do it twenty times to need that many," he said.

"We've got till midnight," I said.

Contrary to another of Mom's warnings, Caspar didn't lose consciousness afterward or try to get me to leave. I was the one who wanted to go because I really wanted to take a shower.

He drove me in an old red pickup truck that looked out of place among all the pricey toys in his yard. It was in even worse shape than Dad's, which was something of a consolation even if it was his family's junky set of wheels. He looked regretful. If this was where he told me it was nice knowing me or that he just wanted to be friends, I could deal with it. It had been an incredible evening and I could live on it for a while.

Instead, he said, "When can I see you again? I'd like to. Or are you going to be busy?"

"I'm free whenever," I said. "I do have a job, but I don't work all the time."

"You might want to think about being my girl-friend," he said in his sluggish, old man's voice.

"I will. I like the idea."

"Not as much as I do."

"Next Saturday?"

"I'll see you Saturday. Besides in school, I mean."

He pulled up in front of my house, which belonged to another lifetime. He leaned over for a last kiss. Neither of us said anything. I hopped out. I knew I wouldn't be able to sleep now that my new life had begun, and that was okay. Just before I made contact with the first step, the porch lights went on. I loved Mom and Dad, no matter how ridiculous they were. I shook my head and went in.

chapter eighteen

I didn't understand why I felt so odd the next morning. I looked around and my room was the same place I had grown up in, the walls needing spackle and paint, my posters curling and lopsided. Yet I might as well have woken up in France. And when Pan called me to demand a transcript of my previous evening, I felt like I had amnesia. His voice was familiar and strange at the same time. As he talked, I started coming back to myself.

"Joto, you cannot put me off. I knows ya and I loves ya too well. Spill it, baby, spill it."

It was no use lying to him, so he was the third person to know about my adventure. But I didn't feel excited about revealing the details, no giggling or breathlessness. It came across flat, like I was explaining a homework assignment. I even perceived that I was boring him, so I turned the subject away from me.

"The first kid I had sex with?" he asked.

I had always tried not to sound thoroughly fascinated when Pan told me of his exploits, although my demand for details gave me away.

"The first time?" he repeated. "I don't know if I can remember that far back."

"Try."

"I remember Justin Holub giving me a piggyback ride when I was in first grade. That was my first of many schools. He must have been in sixth grade, and he looked like a giant to me. I liked it more than he knew. Then he put me on his shoulders."

"What was the first sex you had that the other person was aware of?"

"Let me think," he said. "Sixth grade."

"You waited that long?"

"That was the year we spent in Vermont. My parents wanted to start camping, but Kevin didn't think he could sleep in a tent. They bought a pop-up trailer and set it up in the driveway. I was friends with Karl Kline, who was a year older than me and this brawny, kind of fat kid. We were best friends that year. I always helped him with his spelling homework. Remember those little workbooks?"

"Get on with it."

"I got to invite him for a sleepover. My parents were very accommodating."

"So what happened with Karl Kline?"

"I don't remember how we got there, but we were wrestling one minute, and then the next minute we were playing an entirely different game. I was the husband and he was the wife. We rolled around in one of the bunks and kissed each other like it was a game. Wrestling and rolling, and kissing, and me saying things like, 'Where's my supper?' You know, boy stuff."

"I am completely grossed out," I said. "Keep going."

"We fell asleep, and the next morning the game was over and we were back to being friends."

"Did you ever play house with your wife again?" I asked. "Did you both join the wrestling team or something?"

"Stop panting, Joto. Last night is over. No, nothing else happened. I wanted a rematch, of course. But he didn't, and I don't remember any big scene or tears or fights. Just didn't do it. We moved away, as usual. Never saw him again. Why are you so interested in my love life this morning?"

"I was just wondering because, you know, of my inexperience."

"You're not inexperienced anymore."

"Anyway, I have to go. I have to work all day."

"Wait, Joto, what are you doing next Saturday after work? There's a movie I want to see in Holland Park."

I had made that date with Caspar.

"That's such a long drive," I said.

This evasion was met by a cold silence.

"Hello? Pan?"

"I'm here."

"I thought you hung up."

"I should. What do you mean it's such a long drive? When have you ever cared about how long the drive is?"

"It's just . . ."

"I'll drive. I'll pay for the gas, the movie tickets, the candy, and some ruby red shoes if you want."

"It's just . . . one night I'd like to stay home and rest."

"Then come to my house instead. You can relax without your brother crying for the moon."

"Uh . . ."

"Liar. You're meeting Caspar."

"Okay, I am."

"Why not just tell me when you're ditching me? Don't you think it makes it worse to invent these stories?"

"I'm not ditching you. Don't be dramatic."

"Do me a favor and remember what I said about trying to spare my feelings, okay? I can tell from the first artificial syllable."

"You're right. I'll stop. It's stupid. It's like I'm worried you and Caspar will have to share me from now on."

There was a pause.

"How am I going to survive in this town without you?" he asked. "Half these people would burn a cross on my lawn if they could figure out which side of the match to strike."

"I'm not going anywhere."

"You've got a boyfriend now. That's the way it works. A girl gets a boyfriend and she drops her best friend."

"I'm not like that," I said, then stopped. I had been like that in the past, able to concentrate on only one person at a time. "Besides, I don't know how serious . . ."

"He wants to see you again, and after a night of passion. That's serious. That's practically being engaged in Mungers Mills."

"Pan, it's my first wade into this pool. Let me enjoy it. You get lots of attention from boys. Why not let me have some?"

"I don't have boyfriends," he said, "I have dates. Once they find out I live here, they run like there's a gas emergency."

"Untrue. Lots of boys would be very happy to be your special friend. I think you're the picky one. I think you're the one who's not ready to settle for one person."

"We're discussing your character flaws, not mine.

And I never let my love life get in the way of our romance."

"But you might. If you started to date one of those guys for real, you might need to juggle your schedule to keep me in it."

"I'd be truthful if I did."

"I get the point. I'm sorry, again."

"Tell me how much you loves me and say good-bye."

"One hundred billion."

"That's all?"

"Good-bye."

chapter nineteen

Caspar's father had not come home from the hospital as planned. The balloon procedure had not been a success after all, and he had to have open-heart surgery. So Caspar and I had the house to ourselves for a few weeks. The second time we were together, I had felt more shy than the first, like I'd used up my charms and he was not going to like me anymore. But he did like me still, peering at me all the while as if I were a psychedelic rainbow.

I would eventually have to bring him around to my house again. But how could I let him see what I lived in, and in the daylight? And what would Mom think of him if they talked for more than the few seconds they had the night of our first date? I predicted she and Caspar would not click. Pan was all personality and charm, and she perked right up when he visited. She could easily become his new best friend. She had even slapped Dad down a few times over him.

"What the hell are you talking about?" she'd said one day when Dad made a crack about me walking to work with Tinkerbell. "I'd rather she spend her time with a nice boy who has manners than the rest of these kids. What's so normal about them, Tony?" That stopped him. But it wasn't going to help with Caspar that Mom was so fond of Pan.

Actually, if not for our meetings at his house, I would barely have seen Caspar at all.

At school, walking through the halls was as important as the classes we were heading to. It was a few minutes of moving and looking around and freedom to talk. Caspar and I might as well have been in different schools for all that we interacted in that building. The only time we talked was a few seconds in classes here and there. It was strange passing in the hallways and smiling at each other as if we were acquaintances. And even stranger that we didn't discuss this weird, naturally occurring arrangement.

The segregated seating at lunchtime also remained. Pan and I would eat together, and Caspar was back at his table. I would sneak a look at him when I thought Pan wouldn't catch me, and see Caspar looking so dismal in all that clamor. Once in a while he would see me watching him and a shy expression would appear on his otherwise lonesome face. I was not going over to that table no matter what, and there was probably some kind of shield Pan was giving off that kept Caspar away from us.

School was out for spring break. Pan was in Key West with his parents. I enjoyed my own small vacation in the suburbs with Caspar, looking out the huge picture window in his room at his endless backyard with its variety of outdoor things—plots for gardens, a seat swing, huge weeping willows. A small artificial pond and an inground swimming pool, even in the bleakness of early spring, were more appealing than anything in my depository of a backyard. None of us had raked this year, and no one had ever landscaped. But, I thought, so what? It was a postage-stamp-sized lot and there was no point dressing it up. Backyards in the heart of the city were meant to be humble. Still, I was envious that these looked so manicured even after winter and embarrassed that Caspar had seen where I lived.

He and I lay together in his queen-size bed, another luxury I had not known to long for. Conversation didn't make me as anxious now that I was more used to his patterns, which included long pauses. I now found his old-mannish style adorable. I might have been in love with him already, although I didn't know what that was supposed to be exactly.

I asked him how big the yard was. He considered the question as if it was very important.

"Big enough for a long forward pass," he said, and kissed me. I couldn't believe this same guy was one of the stars of the football team, my lovable hulk with his brooding thoughts. I was being foolish to worry so far in advance, but already I dreaded this coming summer and football practice starting. It began the last week in July, he had told me. Though he'd given me no reason to, I worried about him getting caught up with that crowd, leaving me behind. He would be a senior after all, and for some of his teammates, that was as high as the elevator went. And what were they saying to him about dating me? I felt very insubstantial against them. As for my penetrating that world by, for example, making the cheerleading squad, well that was as likely as winning a swimsuit competition. Besides, the concept revolted me.

"What's so great about football?" I asked, implying criticism without intending to. "I mean, what do you like so much about it?" That wasn't much better.

"I love football. I don't know why," he said, slow and thoughtful. "I can start with what I don't like and get that out of the way."

"Okay."

"I don't like it when I'm tackled and a mob suffocates me. And I don't like the name-calling. Guys from the other team calling us bitches when we're in formation."

"Really?"

"But even our own guys do that to each other during practices. Everyone's a bitch. They say they're trying to toughen us up, but I think they like it."

This was going to take a long time. All questions—even ones I considered simple—engulfed him. I snuggled into his side, hoping I wouldn't fall asleep. I really did want to listen, but the warmth, the coziness, the rumbling of his voice in his chest, all made me drowsy. I felt like a baby, satisfied and content, growing sleepy in someone's arms.

"I don't have much patience for guys who don't pay attention and screw things up for us. Our team does okay, but considering we're not in the Suburban League, which is much bigger and more competitive, we should be doing great. We should be at the top."

"Oh yeah?"

"Coach Pisetti trusts me, probably because I'm one of the few people on the team to do what I'm told. I don't blank every time and run with the ball no matter what. Some of these guys think it's a race. They just want the ball so they can score. I don't understand what's so hard about doing what we agreed to do when it's time to do it. If it weren't for the size of some of our guys, or their speed, our team would be in chaos."

"Maria Baldini did that in *Once Upon a Mattress* in seventh grade," I said. "I helped make the sets. On opening night she started playing to the audience, making faces and making up lines and calling out to her friends. People were laughing, but she made a big mess. I thought the director was going to faint."

"Yes, that's it," he said. "You rehearse something and then someone tries to steal the show." He breathed in deep, his huge chest expanding. "Maybe things will be different this fall. Every year a team has a different makeup. But we're losing some talent, some seniors. And some of this year's juniors aren't necessarily team players."

"Let me guess," I said.

"Yes, Mr. Samson is the most unsportsmanlike player on the team. He's always lecturing us like he's Mr. Pisetti's assistant, then breaking all his own rules. And the way he treats his teammates. Do you know Fred Conrad?"

Fred Conrad was Amy Conrad's older brother, a year ahead of us. He was a big, strong guy, very athletic, but also an outsider. And homely, no other way to put it.

"He really tried. He wasn't great, but he tried. He was an okay player, just not fast. And Boz always called him Roadrunner because Fred was notoriously slow on laps and lagged behind everyone else. I don't see what difference that makes, but sometimes he was so slow that Mr. Pisetti would make us run another lap because he had taken so long. It was a team joke, but it shouldn't have been. We should have been encouraging him for trying. I wonder why he even stuck with it, then."

"Maybe he was like you—he loved the game."

"When you think about it," he said, as if he hadn't heard me, "it's pretty arrogant to make fun of someone else, like you're going to the pros yourself."

"So what do you like about it?" I asked, afraid I might lose my battle with sleep.

"The order. Everything makes sense—if you follow directions, if you play as a team and not as an individual. And the greatest thing in the world is your players being exactly where they're supposed to be during a play. Order and patterns, I guess."

His breathing got a little deeper, and I thought he might fall asleep himself. But he wasn't done with my question.

"I don't know if I have a choice in playing. Even when our team spirit is lacking and I'm feeling despair, I just want to keep playing. Sometimes it'll work despite us. You know, there's something magical about it, at the end of the season when it gets dark early but practice is still three to six, daylight or not. Running laps in the snow. My hands cracking and bleeding from the cold.

Practice gets over in the pitch blackness, and by the time Mr. Pisetti blows the whistle, we're almost icicles."

"You like that?"

"Well, it feels good in a way, like suffering for a cause. Discipline making me stronger and able to handle things. Also there's a long, hot shower to come. We tear into the building and rip off our uniforms and pads, and I can't get in that shower fast enough."

"I don't much care for taking showers after gym," I said. "The girls are too noisy. Sometimes it's like hyenas getting their first bath."

"It's the same with the guys, but I try to ignore them. Someone hit me right here with a bar of soap once," he said, motioning under the sheet. As familiar as I was getting with his body, I looked quick and then away.

"That must have hurt."

"But when I can get a minute's peace, I love the hot water searing my frozen skin. I let it burn me up. Nothing feels so good."

"Nothing?" I asked.

He looked at me, unsure.

"I mean," I said, "considering you've spent the last hour with me."

"Oh, oh," he said, "now I understand." He turned on his side, looked at me with those eyes. "I meant, nothing feels so good when you're that cold and dirty. I wouldn't even think of putting my arms around you then."

His literalness made me smile. "You know how to make a girl feel special," I said.

"I understand now. No, you see, the two have nothing in common . . ."

I put my finger up to his lips.

"Cas, you are so sweet. I mean it." Then, following a pulse of insecurity, I said, "I don't know how I'm going to keep those girls off you next football season." This was a risk, since it assumed we would still be together that far in the future.

"What girls?"

"All those football groupies. Those cheerleaders."

"I wish they would ride on a different bus for away games," he said. "It's crazy. I don't know how you're supposed to play after you've used up all your energy during the trip."

I did not want to know what kind of energy was used up on the bus. Even though they were only day trips, his away games would be taking him from me next fall. Already I was a possessive girlfriend.

Caspar wasn't done intoning.

"I don't really approve of the things they do, the cheerleaders," he said, lying on his back and looking at the ceiling. "They bake stuff—brownies, cookies—and leave them in guys' lockers. Also candy. Inspirational notes. Clean out their lockers for them. Decorate them."

"Did anyone ever bake you brownies and leave them in your locker?" I asked, feeling slightly cold.

"A few times it's happened."

I couldn't stop myself. "Who?"

"The last thing I remember is a paper plate with fudge brownies, with those candy decorations on top. From Sandy Willis."

I wondered if he could feel my heartbeat change. Sandy had been a Holy Spirit girl like me, chubby back then. Now she was beautiful and willowy. She had done nothing to harm me, but I wanted her parents to get jobs far away.

"It seems to me that stuff has nothing to do with the sport. It distracts the players from the real purpose of the game. And you don't see guys cheering girls on their teams, right? Or any other teams having cheerleaders and groupies."

He was right. But still I wanted to decorate his locker for him, fill it with brownies, show the world who my man was. Unless Pan was watching.

"I'm glad you feel that way," I said despite myself.

"That's one of the things I like about you. You're a very independent girl, aren't you?" He pretended to wrestle, which ended with me pinned underneath him. This was as playful as he'd ever been.

But Caspar was not Pan, so when I said, "If you don't let me go, I'm calling the police," he rolled off and sat up.

"Oh my gosh, I'm sorry. Did I hurt you?"

"Cas," I said, fully awake now and pulling him back, "I was kidding. Kidding."

"I don't always understand your sense of humor," he said. I felt a little impatient, thinking how I didn't know him very well and wanted to know everything.

"I know. I'm sorry. I like to joke around. When I feel really comfortable with someone."

"I see. Well, that's good, then. I like that. As long as you're not going to call the police." He kind of grinned.

"Promise."

After a while I said, "Can I ask you something else, Cas?"

"Sure," he said.

"Was your story for school about your own family? You told me you had two older brothers, but that's all I know. I just wondered."

He didn't say anything. His big chest moved up and down, reliable, impressive. Maybe I had tweaked a nerve and we were in for our first unpleasant scene. If so, I would apologize and drop it.

Caspar, however, was contemplating, not angry. Finally he said, "They were much, much worse than that in real life. They . . . I don't know what to say about them. I haven't heard from them since I was eleven. I don't know who they're currently talking to. Not my dad. I'll bet not their mother either. I'm not even sure my parents know where they are or what they're doing."

He breathed a little faster.

"Mom and Dad had gone out for the evening. This was in our old house. Donald and Joe came over because their stepfather had kicked them out again. They must have been seniors by then. They were a lot older. I can't remember much, but my parents came home and found the babysitter screaming and dragging me out of the house. They were trying to kill each other with knives. Or at least knives were part of the fight. I guess they couldn't get along with anybody, not even each other. Twins."

"I didn't know they were twins."

"Yes."

"Oh."

"That resulted in police intervention, and court, and detention, and all that stuff. I would have to assume it wasn't the first time either. I think my mom banned them from our house after that. It makes sense, but then they were gone for good. They might be in jail for all I know."

His house was so neat and quiet, I couldn't picture him ever having lived in such a violent circus.

"But the strangest thing is, TJ, I miss them. They're in their twenties now, and I barely know them."

I ran my hand up and down his arm. Everything he told me about himself made me surer I wanted to be his girlfriend for keeps. "I'm sorry," I said. "Has anyone told them about your father's, you know, problems?"

He turned. "I don't know. I haven't asked. They're my brothers, but somehow I don't feel it's my place to ask. Isn't that strange?"

"No, not really."

"But you, you are the best thing in my life. You're so normal. Your family is so normal, from what I can tell."

He didn't know my parents very well and he hadn't heard Paolo, so I'm not sure how he was defining normal. But I didn't argue. In the quiet that followed, I realized that a major evolution had taken place so fast in my life. I had wanted a boyfriend since I could remember. Now I actually had one, without much effort and only minimal praying. The girl who was convinced she didn't know how to find a guy had found a great one. I felt serene, peaceful, as if the air around us insisted on it. I had to be at work in an hour, but I let myself fall asleep in that tranquillity.

chapter twenty

There was something I noticed once I was dating Caspar: Pan barely mentioned him. He didn't change the subject when I brought him up, or get angry or anything like that. He just didn't engage.

Other things I didn't notice right away. Pan called me less often. He used to call me three or four times a day, which I had taken for granted. Now it was once a day, usually at night. He also had stopped assuming I had free time. First it was weekends, but then it was weekdays too. He still came to the pharmacy, but less often, and it took me a few weeks to realize that I hadn't been to his house or he to mine in a while. Maybe it was something of a relief that he didn't insist on so much of my time. I didn't argue with this convenience. In school we still ate lunch at our table—just the two of us—and spent almost all our rare minutes of free time together. I didn't feel any strain.

While my relationship with Caspar was going along nicely, as if we had been together for years instead of weeks, things were not going so well for him at home. His father's condition was not improving. He had survived the surgery, but he was staying in the hospital a lot longer than heart patients normally did. Caspar would go visit, but he was alone much of the time at his house. I did meet his aunt and his mother once, in passing. They were polite but in a rush. His mother was thin and wiry with short, efficient black hair, nothing like Caspar. She was clipped and businesslike with me, but complimentary.

"Caspar says such nice things about you," she said with a firm handshake. "I'm pleased he has a good friend."

Finally his father came home. But not only didn't I meet him, I didn't see his mother or aunt again. Caspar said it was fine that we hung at his house, as long as we stayed in the basement, which had its own outside entrance. The cellar was practically an apartment by itself. It had a half bathroom, a bar, and the kitchenette. And the movies were making me feel right at home too. Caspar would spend quite a bit of time explaining two or three that he had set aside as possibilities for the evening. I figured out that it was better to be decisive, tell him which one sounded best even if I didn't have a solid opinion, or else the selection process would go on past my curfew. I had never heard of any of the movies, and only once in a while did I think I recognized a director's name. I was surprised at how much I liked these obscure stories.

Without discussing it, we had been having our private time first, because if we got started during the film, we wouldn't see the end of it. The giant leather couch, which we covered with a sheet, wasn't as comfortable as his bed, but it worked. I couldn't let myself think about how the happiest time of my life was happening two floors below where Caspar's father was fighting for his. Caspar didn't tell me a lot about what was going on above, only that the surgery had not been a cure.

By early May the strange, fragile cafeteria arrangement started swaying. One day Pan caught me making eye contact across the room. I don't remember now what he and I were talking about, but he seemed to go into a trance. He barely talked the rest of lunch. It wasn't like he was mad, more like he had been hypnotized.

"Don't be like that," I said, trying to be funny. "You are so possessive." But I could hear the falseness in my tone, and he would not banter.

The next day Pan was late for lunch. He had an extra advanced math class twice a week, so we didn't walk to the cafeteria together those days. I sat at our table and waited, eating listlessly, growing more uncomfortable.

"It's stupid for us not to sit at the same table," Caspar said, appearing in front of me with his tray.

I looked up as if he were a stranger. "I guess . . ."

He sat down right next to me and settled himself. Pan always sat across from me. This might have been more intimate than being in bed together, especially when he kissed me on the lips in front of all those people. I was taut though, and could barely respond.

"I know James is shy," Caspar said. "But I really would like to get to know him. He's your best friend."

I stopped my robotic eating and put my hand on his. I was tempted to warn him about what the other guys would say about his being friends with Pan, but since Caspar contemplated his every action, I resisted.

"That's really nice of you, Cas."

"We haven't talked about this, but I've been assuming you'll want to go to the prom with me. I shouldn't assume. But now I'm asking. Unless you have other plans."

I tried to remember how serious Pan and I had been about the prom. I wanted to go with Caspar, a genuine date that wasn't a protest or a consolation.

I laughed like I had just heard something silly.

"I would love to," I said. "But I'm not much for that kind of thing."

"Oh," he said, looking stung and putting his sandwich to his mouth. "Oh." He took a halfhearted bite. "I don't know where James is today," I said.

"He's sitting over there," Caspar said. "I just noticed him come in."

I turned around. Pan sat at a table by himself, his tall body arched over his food. He didn't look sad or lonely, more bored and indifferent, like a businessman out for dinner alone. He looked over and I saw nothing but effort in his smile. In just those few seconds I had tipped the two men in my life overboard. The bell rang, and they were both gone.

"TJ, I'm so glad to see you," Kevin said, giving me a long hug. I had not called in advance, just stopped in. Seeing Pan alone at lunch had practically driven me here. "We've missed you so much. I hear your boyfriend is very nice. Honey, I think that's great."

"Yeah," I said.

"James is a little blue that you're not coming around so much. I offered to be his new best friend, but somehow he didn't think much of the offer." He laughed. "What he needs is a little someone for himself. He just can't seem to settle on any boy for too long. Of course, with the way we move around like gypsies . . . So tell me about your guy."

"Uh, he . . ." I couldn't remember Caspar at that moment. I didn't know what he looked like or where he lived or any traits that made him human. He was only a shape in my mind.

"He plays football," said Kevin. "That much I know."

"Fullback," I said, remembering something. "He's a big guy, but fast."

"Might as well be a goalie for all I know about sports," said Kevin. "Good for you, though. Young love. Nothing like it."

"Yeah," Pan said, walking in.

"Well, I'll leave you kids alone. Nice to see you again, honey."

"Nice to see you too, Kevin," I said. I didn't sound like it was.

The atmosphere was heavy when we got to Pan's room, though nothing he said or did should have made me feel that way. We watched a talk show on the small TV on his dresser. But we didn't add any comments of our own.

"Want something to eat?" he asked after a long half hour went by. Usually he didn't ask, just took me down and fed me.

"Oh, I'd like to. But I'd better go home and relieve my mom for a while before I go to work."

"How is my boy Paolo?"

"Uh, the same. You know, he has his good days and his bad days." I was about to say, "He misses you," but that was a kind of admission, and the room felt too small for it.

I could not break this awkwardness. "Call me tonight at the store," I said. "Or come by. Definitely come by."

"Okay. Let me walk you out. I'm not going to make you go by Gram without a bodyguard."

It didn't help that he was with me, because the old woman demanded to know why I was late delivering the paper. "You're getting a little sloppy with your work there, mister," she said.

"See ya," I said, and Pan closed the door. I tried to convince myself it was his grandmother being there that kept us from kissing good-bye.

Caspar called me that night at work. I tried to make conversation.

"Is there something the matter?" he finally asked. "Have I said something to upset you? Was it the prom thing?"

He was so good that I almost laughed. It was the first unwound moment I'd had that day.

"No, no," I said. "It's not you at all. I . . . I'm upset about a friend."

"Your friend James?"

I didn't answer at first, and I was sure he could tell that meant yes. "Yeah, a small misunderstanding."

"Is that why he was sitting alone?"

"Something like that."

"He seems hard to predict."

"He's going through a hard time right now."

"I'm very sorry to hear that. I hope it's not more of people knocking him around."

"Not lately, no."

"Well, I really think he should talk to the vice principal. If he doesn't get anywhere with her, maybe he should think about a lawyer."

Evidently I could fall and fall in love with Caspar and never hit bottom. I wanted to see him tonight, but I couldn't. I had to call Pan and get out of the freezer.

"I'll miss you," Caspar said. "Call me tomorrow. And if you think it's appropriate, tell James I hope he's doing okay."

"I will."

"Good night, TJ. I love you."

To think I would have considered a little fooling around with Ted Karsinski in ninth grade if he would have taken me to a dance. I was glad circumstances had made me wait two and a half years for a special guy. But for now, I had to get back another special guy.

I called Pan from the card aisle where I was sorting. I had smuggled the front-counter phone when Caspar had called, and hoped it remained unnoticed for a few more minutes. "Pan," I said when he answered.

"Hi."

"I'm at work. I had to talk to you. Look, Pan, I'm not very good at this kind of thing, but you're my best friend and I want you to stay my best friend, and I don't want us to be this way. It's my fault, I know."

I waited.

"I'm sorry I've been spending so much time with Caspar."

"You think he's prettier?"

"No one is prettier."

"I know that, foolish girl."

"Why didn't you sit with me today?"

"You mean with us."

"Okay, but I was waiting for you specifically. I was sitting there by myself and feeling self-conscious. I didn't know if you were coming."

"It's okay. I don't mind. He is your boyfriend, after all."

"He is, but he only needs one chair. I can't believe you were sitting by yourself."

"I didn't want to intrude. I figured you wanted some time together."

"You weren't, you know, jealous or mad?"

"No. Would you be jealous if I had a boyfriend?"

"Sure I would," I said. "But I wouldn't tell you. My diary, maybe."

"If that's how it works, then why don't you get me a diary? A big one."

"Caspar came over to my table—our table—without asking."

"He doesn't have to ask, Joto. It makes sense he wouldn't want you to sit by yourself."

"But you didn't have to sit alone."

"That's the only other person I know at school. Me."

"Caspar thinks you don't like him. I mean, it's okay if you don't, but . . ."

"He does? I never said a word."

"That might be why."

"He's kind of an okay guy. Not so bad."

"Not so bad."

"I'm not talking about in bed."

"Neither am I."

"I knew it," he said. "He's terrible in bed."

"I hate you."

"Does that mean everything's back to normal, Joto, that you hate me again?"

"I think it does. I felt so stiff at your house this afternoon. I don't ever want it to be like that again."

"Okay. I want you to come over more often."

"I will. And please sit with me. Caspar wanted to get to know you. He said so."

"Maybe I'll let him sit with us from now on," he said. "Let me bring this to the Tribal Council. How many chairs did you say he requires?"

"Just one. One strong, reinforced one."

"Well enough about him. Any other gossip tonight?"

"There's one more thing. He asked me to the prom."

"What?"

"And I said no."

"You did? Don't you usually flit off to your guidance counselor in such situations?"

"Not this time. I told him no."

"Did you tell him you already had a date?"

"Not exactly."

"What did you tell him?"

"I just . . . said it wasn't my thing."

"So what's he going to think when you show up with me?"

"I hadn't thought about it. Maybe we shouldn't go either. Neither of us really wants to."

"I do want to. To show you off."

A few seconds went by. He sighed, then said, "You should go with Caspar."

"No, I said no, and that's it. I'm not even going to think about it. His father is still sick and not getting any better, from what I can tell. I don't want to jerk him around. He looked like a scolded puppy today when I turned him down."

"Well, all right. I guess I forgives ya for all your faults. All your grievous faults."

"TJ, customers!" Tammie shouted from across the store.

"Got to go. Loves ya."

"Is Tammie in spasm?"

"Full."

"Tell her no one names their kids Tammie anymore."

I hung up, breathing in relief, and ran back to the register to help one of our sweet and special customers who would have a handful of change to pay for a bottle of lotion.

chapter twenty-one

My mom had told me, in one of her less frazzled moments, that sometimes everything just seems to be working. "There have been a few of them, these times," she said, "since I started realizing they existed."

"That's nice to hear, Mom," I said. This was the kind of talk I liked from her—optimism, not remorse about her life, not sex advice.

"Just before I got saddled with your brother was one of them."

Well, maybe she wasn't so optimistic. But then she saved it: "You and Teo were pretty much independent and I was going back to school to do something with my life. Your father's business was humping along at the time. All of a sudden I realized things were aligned, all working the way I wanted them to."

"Then Paolo . . .," I started.

"The whole thing with Paolo . . . well, I don't feel like that destroys my theory. Things were working out, and I don't believe they were destined to get gnarled up." She sucked her teeth. "But having everything parallel is temporary. So you need to enjoy the moments when things are running side by side, instead of into each other. They don't have to intertwine. Just be grateful."

I was going through such a period. If I ignored all the things that were unchangeably wrong—money problems, Caspar's dad's health—things were gliding in unison as if that were the natural way. I had Pan, I had Caspar, my grades were good, and my job was safe for the time being. The owner had told Tammie that two new residences might be opening downtown, and like the others, they would have their prescription accounts with us.

Lunchtime was still awkward. Caspar was now part of our table, and the conversation was almost non-existent. At first our discomfort was like a fourth person sitting with us. But Caspar's presence made me feel secure. No one had ever bothered Pan in the broadness of the cafeteria lights, and having a giant football player on our team gave me a reassurance that now no one would. Maybe the unspoken protection would apply everyplace else. Maybe school was safer for a kid with a friend no one was going to shove into a locker. I decided to lean back into Mom's theory of parallelism.

But that didn't mean no one was watching.

Pan's locker was across the hall from Caspar's, down a few yards. What was becoming routine was that at the end of the day, Pan would wait by his locker for me to say good-bye to Caspar before he went to track practice. Pan stood with his back straight against the row, backpack in front of him. I ignored him because if I didn't, he would point to his wrist to indicate it was time to get walking.

After school one day Caspar and I were talking a little when I heard Samsonite say, exaggerating every word, "Hey, pansy, how's your pussy? Full of dick?" I turned fast, expecting Pan to be slapped or pushed or something, but Samsonite did his rooster walk toward us. Then he stopped at Caspar's locker.

"Yo, it's the Cas-man. Where you been?" He was loud and effusive like they hadn't seen each other in years. "Why don't you eat with us no more, Cas-man?"

"I don't know," Caspar said, starting to pack his bag.

Samsonite bounced on his feet. "Why'd you ditch us? I see you sittin' there with your two sisters."

I don't know what Caspar reminded me of then—a robot maybe. He stood straight and turned, and his hands jetted out faster than I'd ever seen him do anything. He grabbed Samsonite by the shirt and pushed him against the lockers, holding him there.

"Don't say anything about my girlfriend," he said, then lifted Samsonite just high enough so their eyes were even.

"Okay, okay," Samsonite said, trying to laugh. "It's cool. We're cool. I mean it."

Caspar slammed him once against the locker, then dropped him. He went back to packing, as if he'd already forgotten he'd been enraged. Samsonite kept forcing his dry, unanimated laugh. He even turned to me and said, "You know I'm just fooling around. You're cool and all." Then he said, "Caspar Phillips, man. You going to practice?"

"Yes." When Caspar didn't look back at him, Samsonite turned, his head nodding as if things were going as planned, and started walking away.

"See ya," he called. "See ya at practice, okay?"

Caspar shut his locker hard. He looked at me, put his arms around my waist, and kissed me good-bye.

He didn't mention the incident, so I didn't.

"He was pretty good," Pan said on our way home. "Impassive can be scary."

"Yeah," I said.

"I'm glad he's on my side. Sort of."

There was more to say, but neither of us did.

A couple days after that scene, Pan said something that actually made Caspar laugh. Caspar's laughing was something you noticed, since the information had to travel many serious miles to get to his funny bone.

We were at a lull in conversation, which was not unusual, when we heard Samsonite's very loud response to something at his table, followed by raucous laughter. Pan shook his head.

"Too much sugar," I said.

"Makes sense," said Pan. "That breast milk he drinks has more sugar than Dr. Pepper."

Caspar stopped eating, as if to examine the hypothesis. Then his face went from its usual tight concentration to a bursting laugh. It was deep enough to be an entire baritone section.

Pan looked at him with a pleased curiosity.

At the end of his laugh, Caspar nodded to Pan, who, I believe, actually blushed before he looked away.

I took a bite of the eggplant parm sandwich my mom had made, the slices all parallel. It was, like this moment, delicious.

chapter twenty-two

I didn't have the money to go to Cape Cod for Memorial
Day weekend, because I didn't have the money to go
anywhere, not even Triangle or Root. Also, if I wasn't
around, who would help Mom with Paolo? What about
the pharmacy? How could I be sure there would be a job
waiting for me when I got back? I didn't get paid when I
was not there. Tammie disapproved of sick or vacation
days, unless she was taking them. No doubt I would
hear about the sacrifices she'd had to make because of
my absence.

Pan didn't give in to these concerns.

"All you need is some spending money," he said.
"And if you don't have that, I have it for you. I let you
out of the prom thing, but I have my limits."

I told Mom and Dad I would have my own room on

the Cape, which might have been true for all I knew at the time. I didn't bother to update them when the final arrangements were made and I was going to be staying in the same suite with Pan. Dad couldn't possibly be worried that Pan posed a danger, since that would undermine his prejudices. And Mom trusted Pan like he was her own son. Also, they'd both made cryptic remarks about Caspar never coming to our house. They had only met him that once for a few seconds, then seen him with his tongue in my mouth moments later. And they probably suspected that he was my first love, so to speak. So surely they were glad I was getting away from him and all those temptations that they didn't know for sure I had given in to.

Caspar didn't exactly twitch with excitement when I told him I was going away with Pan's family for the long weekend, but he studied it, sat with it for a while, then told me he was glad I was able to go and that I should have fun.

Pan's parents were happy he had someone to keep him company. Maybe they thought I would prevent him from hooking up with strange boys. I enjoyed the thought of spending time with Kevin, but I was a little concerned about Ada. However, I forgot all about being nervous when we got to Chatham and I sunk down into luxury.

The Cranberry Inn was a huge Victorian house

with turrets and massive windows that sat right on the beach. It was a new building, and Pan's mother informed me that this architecture was not historically correct for beachfront property. I didn't care. While Caspar's and Pan's houses were very nice in different ways, this place was amazing. A porch ran all the way along the back, facing the ocean. The main room of our suite had a long cream couch across from a landscape plasma TV, a couple of leather armchairs, a coffee table, and a small desk. Our bedrooms were small, not a lot bigger than the double beds that filled them. I could get spoiled by such extravagance, and for the first time I regretted being poor, truly regretted it, rather than just being burdened by it.

I couldn't bring myself to think about what this must have cost or that I was spending Pan's parents' money, even though they were insisting on it.

"We have to rent a room for James anyway," Kevin had said. "You're not costing us a dime."

The view from our suite wore down the guilt. Outside the sliding glass doors was the ocean. I was torn between staying inside to soak in the luxury and getting out in that sand and those waves. I could watch the sea sending waves in and pulling them back and never lose interest. Sitting near the water, close enough for my feet to get tickled by the frigid surf without a full assault, I could picture living somewhere else besides Mungers

Mills, being perfectly content with a career watching waves crest.

On our first day at the beach, Pan and I were like ten-year-olds. Kevin had put together a picnic basket of drinks and packaged snacks for us. We dared to play in the waves until we lost feeling in our limbs. The sand was warm though, and afterward I fell asleep on that grainy mattress.

Pan wanted authentic beach junk food, so we waited in a long line at a white, open-air shack. When we got our mammoth soft pretzels, some guy who was about eighty asked Pan if he wanted some decent food. His sentences kept ending with things like "a young fella like you."

"You shouldn't eat junk food, a young fella like you."

Then as if there were no police in all of Massachusetts, he told Pan to reach into his pocket and fish out some money. "My hands are full," he said. They were, since he was carrying a cardboard tray of sodas, but it was a pretty lame excuse.

"Mine too," Pan said, waving with his free hand as we walked off.

"Oh, gross," I said. "Can you believe that?"

"Right in public this old fart is trying to pick me up. He's probably got a wife, too."

"Should we tell your mother?"

"Sure. You know how level she is."

"She ought to know."

"She chips a nail and she's planning a class-action suit. Besides, he didn't follow me or try to kidnap me or anything. Maybe he thought I was older."

"You're still a hundred years younger than him."

"Kind of flattering, don't you think?"

"Please be careful. Please don't go off with any old men. They'll get you in an isolated spot and we'll never see you again."

"Until my milk carton comes out."

"Don't even joke about it."

"I'll be fine, especially if you're there to protect me."

"I will be. But you might have to wear a less revealing bathing suit."

Pan and I were on our own mostly. The only thing his parents insisted on was dinner together, and they took us to restaurants where the prices made me blanch. I had cashed and kept all of my last paycheck instead of giving some to Mom. She had insisted. She even tried to slip me some more money, but I wouldn't take it. I had a plan that when the bill came at the end of each meal, I would pull out some cash to pay my own share. When the money ran out—which would be very very soon at these rates—I would just skip eating. I might have to turn to the sea for nourishment. But Pan's parents didn't hear me when I offered. I ordered the cheapest things at first, sometimes an appetizer instead of an entree, though nothing was cheap. As early as Friday night Pan caught on and changed my order. When I asked for a hamburger, he said, "You love shrimp. We're at the seashore. Those things grow on park benches here."

"I'm in the mood for a burger," I said, not even convincing myself. "The sea air makes me hungry."

"You're having the shrimp. You're not in Mungersburger anymore."

So I had the shrimp, another exhilaration. My parents were not even eating together, never mind having shrimp in a pricey restaurant. Paolo would be shrieking intermittently, Dad would be working late, Mom would catch something between chasing the baby and trying to shut him up. Later they would watch TV in our living room with the aging wallpaper. I was sitting here eating like royalty before going back to my suite. I reasoned that this was the kind of life Mom wanted for me. Someday I'd find a way to bring her here to live this life for at least a weekend.

None of the indulgence was wasted, because I ate everything put in front of me. Pan wanted dessert, but I refused because the desserts were like nine and ten dollars each. They would have to force-feed me before I let them pay that. So of course Pan ordered one for each of us. Mine was a chocolate tart with raspberries, which were never in season in Mungers Mills. Kevin paid what must have been a mammoth bill without even blinking.

On Saturday night when we were done eating, Kevin asked us, "So what are you two beach bums going to do this evening? Any plans with the local kids?"

"We're gonna hang out at the surf shop with Dale and Missy," Pan said. "They're swell."

Kevin smiled, tilted his head a little. "Our James," he said. "Light of my life."

"Answer the question, James," Ada said. "Or I'll send you home to Grandma."

"Nothing much," I said. "We're going to walk through town."

"Be careful," Kevin said. "And if you go to the beach again tomorrow, those July fish can take you by surprise. Remember how you used to call them 'July fish,' James? I kept telling him jellyfish come in August!"

"No, Kev, because it didn't happen."

"Did so."

"Did not. You made it up. All your stories are manufactured."

Kevin looked at me. "He used to be such a sweet little boy, TJ."

"So now I'm sour?"

"Heavens no," Kevin said, and winked at me. "Of

course, there was the time when I tried to walk him to school and we passed this nice old woman . . ."

"Kevin," Pan warned.

"Enough male bonding," Ada said. "Let's go. I want to hit that hot tub before too many people get the same idea and fill it with fungi."

The streets in town were lined with pedestrians, T-shirt stores, and taffy shops. Pan wasn't exactly parting the waters as he walked through the crowds, but I started taking note after the fifth or sixth inappropriate double take. I thought it might have been about me being with such a hot boy until I realized that most of the gawkers were male and no one was looking at me at all. Men of all ages checked out my golden-headed friend. Young guys with dress shorts and perfect hair were very observant. Other men, some with what appeared to be their wives and children, stared too long as they walked by. Even old bald or gray geezers took a long look. Maybe some girls looked too, but I was fascinated by the consistent attention he got from other men. And for some reason it made me lonesome for Caspar.

"I need to get a T-shirt for Paolo," I said, turning into a shop. "And I want to buy you one for the best Memorial Day weekend I've ever had." I also wanted one for Caspar, but didn't say so.

"Hi," Pan said to a kid folding a pile of loose tees whose name tag said CHRIS. He looked to be our age, maybe a little older, with white, white skin behind a beard shadow. The sleeves on his shirt could barely restrain his toned arms.

"How may I help you?" he asked Pan with an energy salespeople had for customers they wanted to kiss.

"Need a shirt for my friend's baby brother," Pan said, nodding my way. Chris, with his thin, trimmed black hair, smiled at me a second, then was back to business.

"Where are the toddlers' . . . ?" I asked, but they had both already forgotten about me. I was embarrassed, though I realized this was how the pickup thing was done. I could never do it myself, not with a complete stranger, but it was interesting. I wandered away, leaving Pan to his hyperattentive salesboy. It felt a little awkward spending money on souvenirs when Pan's parents were giving me a free vacation, but it was my first experience at buying something for a boyfriend. Caspar would only wear T-shirts if they didn't have huge logos or graphics on them. CHATHAM, CAPE COD was all right in small letters. I found one, a deep blue with gold lettering. Then I found another, black lettering on white with a minute seashell design near the words. I found an all-black one for Pan that I was sure would set off his blond hair, and a toddler-size one for Paolo that would look the way everything looked on him.

It shouldn't have mattered, but it turned out that Chris was the only cashier. Somewhat flushed now, he bounced over, smiling so wide he looked crazed. Stretched any farther, his face would crack. Pan came too, but like a schoolmaster approaching with a cane. He took one of the giant shirts from me.

"A tent for Paolo."

"Pan . . ."

"Pan?" Chris asked.

"Short for Pansy," Pan said, and turned back to me. Chris looked startled.

"Two tents for Paolo."

"They're for Caspar," I said, though I could have claimed they were nightgowns for my mom. "Which you know."

"Casper?" Chris asked, recovered. Then like he was already part of the family, he added, "Casper the Friendly Ghost?"

"My boyfriend," I said.

"So you two aren't together?" Chris still had that loony smile.

"Now you're annoying me," Pan said to him. Then he turned back to me. "Pay for them. Let's get going."

Chris's smile snapped shut and his face went red. He bagged my four shirts as if he didn't know what he was doing. Pan was already outside on the walk. Chris handed me the bag and tried to look in control.

"Your friend," he said, almost inaudibly, "likes to play games."

"He's got a lot on his mind."

"Have a really great night," he said even though his was obviously ruined.

Outside, Pan walked a little too fast for me. I could feel the thrill of the seashore slipping down a sewer grate.

"What's wrong?" I called, trying to keep up and talk at the same time.

"Nothing. Let's go back to the room."

"Okay, but why are you so mad? Is it because your parents are paying . . . ? I can pay them back. I just wanted souvenirs."

He stopped, turned to me. "Why do you have to rub it in my face?"

Every nerve in my body was jammed in my throat. I had always felt comfortable enough with him to say almost anything, but he had never sounded so mean before.

"Rub what in your face?"

"You said you were getting one for Paolo."

"I did."

"Where is it?"

"It's in the bag with the rest of them."

"They're for what's-his-name."

"Two of them are. One's for you. What's the crime? Like I said, if it's the money—"

"I don't care about money. Let's go."

We made our way, not talking, through the crowded streets. We walked toward the end of the commercial section. By then my bewilderment was turning to anger. I knew I had to say something before we were back at the inn.

It came out sharper than I expected.

"Pan, what is your problem? All of a sudden I'm evil because I buy something for my boyfriend? While you're cruising another guy?"

"I wasn't cruising . . ."

"Oh, please. You weren't exchanging recipes. I may be a small-town girl but I'm not a complete idiot."

Finally he slowed down. "He was cute, wasn't he, my cashier boy?"

"No diversions. You were hitting on each other, and then you remembered I was there, and you threw your fit. And those are the facts."

"It wasn't a fit. Just a tiny outburst."

"You hurt that guy's feelings."

"Really?"

"Yeah, really. Didn't you see how his face fell when you stopped paying attention to him and started on me?"

"Well, no, I was distracted."

"I think you should go back and apologize. He liked you, and you were mean to him so you could be mean to me."

"Was I mean?"

"Oh my God, are you absent today? So I bought Caspar a present."

"Two."

"Two. I'm here with you, aren't I? Why can't we have a good time?"

"Maybe you want to go home."

"I'm not saying anything until you grow up."

He stopped walking, turned, and put his hands on my shoulders.

"Joto, I loves ya awful. Maybe I'm worried."

"No need to be. I'm still your best friend."

"I don't want to share. Not this weekend. This is my time with you, not his."

My nerves unwound a bit.

"I'm a smart girl," I said. "Like I told you before, I can have two people in my life." I understood clearly at that moment how hard this actually was, but I was determined more than ever to make it true.

"I don't want to lose you," he said. It wasn't simpering or pathetic, just plain, as if a little boy had said it.

"You won't, dummy."

"Promise?"

"Promise."

"Okay, but you promised to go to the prom with me, and you broke that one."

"I'm not going at all. You and Caspar can go together. I told him no, and that was the end of it."

"Couldn't you get really tiny so I could carry you around in my pocket forever?"

"Go patch things up with Chris."

"Chris. Okay."

"And while you're doing that, I am going to use that pay phone over there to call Caspar, without acting like a secret agent or something."

"No," he said. "Use this." He handed me his cell phone.

I took a breath, smiled. "Thank you."

"But kiss me first." He pulled me close and I could smell the sea air again.

chapter twenty-three

Caspar's father was like a character in a play who's talked about but never appears on stage. So when Mom called me at the inn Sunday night to tell me he had died, it wasn't quite real. In our phone conversation the night before, Caspar hadn't mentioned his father—he rarely did—so I assumed things hadn't gotten worse. But Mom said that according to the Sunday paper, Mr. Phillips had been "stricken at home" Saturday night and died at the hospital.

Pan lent me his cell again, and I called Caspar. But I only got his voice mail.

I couldn't concentrate on anything else. Pan sensed my disorientation, and he held my hand on the drive home from the Cape the next day in the agonizing holiday traffic. He was a crutch for me during my weird mourning, letting me talk or be quiet when I felt like it.

"You realize," he said when we finally got close to home late that night, "that you have to go to the prom with him."

"I don't even want to think about it."

"You don't have to think about it now. But you will have to go."

"He's not going to want to do anything," I said. "He's going to need some time."

"I just want you to know it's okay with me," Pan said, patting my hand. Then he picked it up and kissed it.

I phoned again when I was in my room that night, and still got Caspar's voice mail. Then I tried his home number, even though his family would surely be deluged with calls. Someone with a husky voice told me brusquely that she would pass my message on to him. I didn't call again. When I told Pan how awful it was going to be waiting to hear from Caspar, he said, "Well, you'll be able to talk to him during the viewing. For a few minutes anyway."

"I guess. I don't like that sort of thing, though."

"Neither do I, but you don't have a choice. He's going to want you there."

"I know. But I don't like dead bodies. Especially when I never met the person alive."

"Yeah, it's a strange way to make an acquaintance. But I'll go with you. I'll stand between you and the deceased."

"Can't we go to the funeral instead? The thing is closed then, right?"

"The paper didn't list any funeral, just that one viewing, so there's no predicting."

"You're so good to me, Pan. You take me to Cape Cod. You take me to funerals. I haven't actually been to one since my Great-aunt Carmeta."

"What about poor Great-aunt Carmeta?"

"They made her look like—I don't know what. They had her hair all done big and poofy, and red like you've never seen. And a full-length, scary evening gown that was also red. And tons of makeup. It was like one of those glamour photos."

"Caspar's father will not look like a hundred-year-old chorus girl, I promise."

"But he's at Bianchini Funeral Home. Ever been there?"

"Never had the pleasure."

"It's downtown, a block from the store, and it's old, and everyone seems to use it, even though it has a spooky setup. You sort of view the body through a window into this kind of cavelike room set off from the rest of the parlor."

"Sounds like a fun house. But at least the body can't grab you if it's behind a window."

"Yeah, but there's the creepy music and the perfumey air. I hate it."

"Everybody does. But we'll get through it."

"We will. You're a good friend."

"The best," he said.

Mom had been invited to an open house for nontraditional students at the community college. She was determined to get to school this coming fall. That would have been great news except it meant Paolo was going with us to the funeral home. Dad was not able to leave work early. There were no babysitters to call on short notice, especially with Paolo's reputation.

I didn't have a dress to wear. It had been so long since I'd worn anything but jeans that I wasn't ready for formal events like this. I tried on an old pair of black wool pants that had been hanging in my closet for years, but they looked awful on me. None of my blouses hung right. There was also an old pair of cords that were worse than jeans. I couldn't borrow Mom's clothes because we had different bodies. I settled for a black button-down blouse and the least-worn jeans I had.

This was going to be awful. And it had started to sprinkle.

Pan looked like a movie star in his black suit and tie. He needed to sit with Paolo in the backseat, so I drove his mother's car. I had to park far away because the lot was full and there were lines of cars on the streets.

As long as Paolo had Pan's hair to pull, he could be taken from the car seat without making a sound. Pan grimaced but didn't stop him. We were walking past the pharmacy when Paolo realized it was raining and began whining. I tried to hold an umbrella over the two of them, getting wet myself.

"I'll take the baby and stay in the vestibule, and you go in and scope things out," Pan said. "He's going to be glad to see you." Paolo pulled his hair. "Go on, before I'm bald."

It was pouring now, and my brother was as angry as the sky. We had to get inside.

"No," Paolo said like a baby drill sergeant as we walked in. "No no no."

A streak of lightning followed by a thunderclap made us trot faster. Paolo went silent so fast that I thought he had been struck. Then he let me know he was as hearty as ever by starting to shout "no" an octave higher. He wriggled fiercely in Pan's arms. The magic was gone, Paolo now indifferent to his best friend, throwing his head back and gargling.

"Maybe we should take him to the hospital," Pan said.

"No, he's okay . . . his color is good . . . we've been through this. Take him to . . . why don't you take him to . . . ?" The attention in the vestibule had all turned to us. "I don't know what to do."

A somber, official-looking man came tapping down the stairs toward us.

"I can take you—," he began, and Paolo shrieked a solid "no" at him. The man leaned toward my left ear. "I can take you to the residential part of the house. We really need to consider the family."

"Give me that," Pan said, taking the umbrella from me. He looked at the man, who must have been the director. "If we get hit by lightning, buddy, we'll be in the right place." Then he opened the umbrella and said, "Oh no, bad luck," and forced it out the door the man earnestly held open. "Joto," he called, "go on. I'll wait for you." The man pulled the door tight. Thunder smacked like a plane exploding over the building.

I forced my way up the stairs and into the main room. I was drenched, and my hair must have looked like it had been vacuumed. People would think there were two corpses in the room. I couldn't remember when I had felt so socially inept. The storm kept coming, juggling rain and lightning and thunder. The place was crowded, and everyone was taller than me. I couldn't even tell which direction I was going as I pushed through. It wasn't until I saw the big glass window that I got my bearings. I saw Caspar standing next to his mother. When I was in front of him, I realized they were receiving a long line of people—including Samsonite and Patrick Torno and other football buddies—which I had managed to butt to the front of. I heard, "Wait your turn," which could have been from any of them.

"TJ . . ."

"Casket . . . Caspar, I have to go. Paolo—my baby brother—is with me. James has him. I had to bring him. You probably heard him. Everybody probably heard him."

"That's okay," he said, "I want my mom to say hello to you."

Just then another thundercloud exploded overhead. I jerked my head the wrong way and saw the cave was lit to display an open coffin with someone in it. I sang backward through my nose and teetered. But it wasn't horror I was feeling. The man I had never met was an old version of Caspar, and a mash of emotions—fago maybe—made me lose control altogether.

"Oh, Cas," I said, sobbing into his chest as he held me, "I'm so sorry." I wanted to explain the many things I was sorry for—including not being there for him sooner, bringing my brother, my Halloween witch hair—but I couldn't say another word. Caspar held me until I managed to stop heaving, as if we were alone in that awful place.

I never did say anything to his mother who was very busy with the receiving line. After Caspar and I had said our good-byes, I turned and squeezed my way through the clusters of people. I don't know how many of them I bounced against or pushed past, but at one point I was face-to-face with Patrick Torno, who without his baseball cap looked like the face of evil.

I tried to find Pan and the baby. I looked for the nearest way out rather than the way I had come in, so I was staring at a hearse as I bounded out a side door. The front passenger door of the hearse opened, and I screamed as Pan got out with Paolo, as if they had returned from the dead.

"I had to . . ." was what I caught from Pan as I grabbed the umbrella and shouted, "Run for the store. It's closer than the car."

Inside the pharmacy, the two of us laughed like insane people. This led to me weeping, Paolo's cries echoing mine.

"I'll never be invited to another death after this," I said.

"Oh, there'll be other opportunities."

Tammie found her way to us. I had never been so glad to see her.

chapter twenty-four

I didn't call Caspar the rest of that week he was absent
from school. I just waited, unsure what he would think
of me. Who would want to keep seeing a girl who
dragged her screaming baby brother to his father's
wake, a girl in blue jeans who took a look at the body
and burst into tears like it was someone she knew?

The next Saturday night was the second without
him, and I seemed to have returned to my previous
social life. If it weren't for Pan stopping by to make sure
I was still sane, the work hours would have been endless. But just before closing, Caspar called me. He
sounded the same as he always did, even and steadily
paced. He said it was nice of me to have come to the
viewing. Before I could object and explain what a true
mess I had been, he asked, "Can you come over?"

When I called home to tell Mom I was going straight to Caspar's, she said she would drive me in the truck. She brought a dish of baked ziti she had made to express her sympathy. I did not want to offer this ziti, but I couldn't tell her no. When Caspar opened the cellar entrance and saw me posing with my casserole, he actually laughed, a deep laugh like early thunder. Unsure, he waved to Mom, then guided me inside. He took the stupid dish and put it in the kitchenette's mini-refrigerator, then put his arms around me.

"I'm so sorry, Cas," I said. "For everything."

He was not in the mood for words. I hesitated, thinking that we were being sacrilegious, like doing it in church. But it was his church, and he was the lead mourner. As usual, there were no sounds from upstairs.

"I'm so happy to have you," he said after.

"I wanted to explain about your dad's wake."

"Explain? It was really kind of you to be there for me."

"I didn't know what to do. It was raining and Paolo was even louder than usual, so I had to leave."

"No, it's okay. I didn't want to put you through any more of that."

"I made such a fool of myself, crying and all. Your mother must think I'm an idiot."

"Nonsense. She didn't even see you."

"Good."

"I kept thinking I wanted to keep you separate from all of it. You're the future."

There was no point apologizing further. This was about his loss, not my lack of social graces.

We lay together, silent for a long while.

"My brothers showed up," he finally said, turning on his side. "They came to the funeral, which was private, but not the viewing."

"Was that hard?"

"They looked really uncomfortable, as if they didn't know how to behave or who to talk to. They stuck to themselves mostly. They made each other laugh."

"Laugh?"

"Not hilarious laugher, but nervous. They barely spoke to anyone else."

"I guess that means they're speaking to each other anyway."

"They said hello to me. More like 'hey' or something like that. I'm taller than both of them. They took off after, and that's probably the last time I'll ever see them."

"Oh, Cas."

"I don't believe they said anything to my mother. I haven't asked her. There's too much going on for her right now."

"How's she doing?"

"She's amazing. She keeps busy all day and all night with what needs to be done."

"I guess that helps."

"She's always been that way. She knows how to take care of things. Even terrible things. Now you have to take care of me."

"I will."

"I thought about you a lot. After this, I kept thinking, when this is all over, I will have TJ back in my arms."

I was ready to fill his locker with candy hearts, decorated brownies.

"How is James? I can't tell you how much it meant to me that he was there. If only for a minute."

"Yeah, he's a real friend," I said, thinking of him and Paolo in the hearse.

"I have to admit, I never really know how to approach him. Sometimes he seems to like me, and other times I feel like he's not listening."

"We talked through a bunch of things on the Cape, and he's cool. He's working on his jealousy."

"What is he jealous about?"

"You know, you and me," I said, wishing I had not brought it up.

"But he's not interested in you. That way."

"And don't I know it."

"What?"

"Nothing. He's not jealous because he wants to be my boyfriend. It's because we're best friends."

"Now you've got me confused."

"It's not jealousy really. He was feeling left out because of the time you and I were spending together. Just a little. Now he's over it."

"You did go on vacation with him, after all."

"Yeah, and I told him I had room in my life for both of you."

"There's no reason you shouldn't."

"See why I love you? You understand everything."

"I would like to understand him better."

"I think he assumes all the boys in Mungers Mills hate him."

"But he doesn't let anyone get to know him. A lot of people in school would like him if they had the opportunity, I'm sure."

"I agree. But I can't force him. I would like you to get to know each other. He's not so bad."

"I don't think he's bad at all," Caspar said with a slight annoyance. "I think he's very smart. James is well-spoken in classes. That's mainly when I hear him talk, even though I'm sitting right there at lunch."

"He needs a little time," I said. "Just some time. Don't worry about it. He's going to his prom in Buckingham Heights, and I'm going to mine with you."

"But you said—"

"No argument," I said. "I want you to relax."

He lay on his back.

"I'll do exactly as you say," he said. "I don't want to listen to my own head for a while."

chapter twenty-five

When my junior year had started, the prom was a concept that had nothing to do with me. Now I was kind of enjoying the complications leading up to it. I'd had two boys ask me. The second of the two wanted me to go as a real date, and the first now wanted me to go with the second to console him. Unpredictability could be pleasant.

This upcoming event had an unforeseen effect in that Mom, Pan, and I became a team for a short while as we shopped for a dress. There was a Day-Mart on the outskirts of town and there was also a Dress Shack. But Pan said no.

"We are not shopping for anything in Mungers Mills," he said, "except tattoos."

Mom jumped at the chance to go to one of the quality malls. This normally would have required a variety of babysitters: Usually when she wanted to go out and I couldn't stay with Paolo, she would lull him to sleep before the victim arrived, and when she returned the babysitter would look like she hadn't slept in five days, take her money, and never return calls. But this time we had a repeat performer, who only made one comment about his being "a little fussy."

Mom was more of a kid than either of us. Pan bought her smoothies, gelato, bags of mixed candy. Shopping with the girls might seem like a stereotypical role for him, but he didn't mince or giggle or make flamboyant remarks. He was all business, as if we were buying a car and had to be wary of the salesmen. Not just any guy could offer a masculine perspective while having the patience to shop for clothes with two women. He and Mom were determined to find the dress that would make me look magnificent.

But there was no team on earth that could pull that off. The fun we had softened the repeated blows of seeing myself in a mirror wearing something I shouldn't. I did not have an evening gown body. Nothing flowed or draped on me. Material clung like gauze bandaging, emphasizing every unflattering lump and swerve. Plus size shops were of no help either, since I wasn't plus size. I was odd-sized, for which there were no special stores.

Pan was honest about each try. So was Mom. I appreciated their candor, but not the reality driving it.

"That makes you look seventy," Mom said about one dress. "Bad cut. No one would look good in that."

"Court jester," Pan said about another, and then later, "Medieval serving wench."

Every dress was a mistake or a costume, including one in which I appeared to be a ten-year-old too fat for her mother's clothes.

When we decided that white would complement my rich skin tone, I tried on a gown that was so staticky, my hair was pointing at the ceiling by the time I was in. Pan flinched when I came out of the dressing room, and I forced him to tell me exactly why it was wrong.

"A ghost levitating down Cemetery Road," he said.

That spectral sight led to a huddle where we settled on one in black, always a slenderizing and understated color for any occasion.

"Put it back on the rack," Mom said as she looked at me, "for the next Sicilian mourner."

This pursuit was doomed.

"We'll have it made," Mom said.

"Yeah," said Pan. "Why should we rely on the fashion gulags?"

"No, it's hopeless," I said.

"My friend Lynn knows someone in town who does customwear," she said. "We'll get an estimate."

"Thanks, Mom, but I'm not paying to have a dress made for a stupid dance."

"Don't worry about it, honey," Mom said. "I'll pay. I want you to have a special night."

"Mom's right," Pan said. "You want to look your best. You'll be the prettiest girl there."

"We barely have the cash to pay the babysitter when we get home," I said. "No, let's just go." Failure pressed on my trachea. "There's no point."

"We'll at least check her out, the dressmaker," Mom said. "That's final."

The retail gods must have heard her because we did find a dress that evening. It was at the fiftieth women's clothing store in the mall, which I would have ignored if Mom hadn't walked in. Pan found a dark blue dress with small, inconspicuous white designs. I had no faith when he insisted I try it on.

"It'll look better on you, Pan," I said. "Go ahead, I'll wait."

"Get in there this instant, young lady," he said, taking my arm and walking me and my latest adversary toward the dressing room.

Once I got it on, I was quite surprised to find myself wearing a dress instead of a fitted sheet. I tore out of the dressing room, in case it was an illusion.

"That's it!" Mom said, and turned me around. "Oh, TJ, you can wear it more than once, too. It's formal, but not bridesmaid formal."

"I believe we have a winner," Pan said.

After sufficient ogling, Mom and Pan sent me back to the dressing room to take it off. I noticed the price tag dangling and grabbed it. Ninety-nine dollars. Not a lot for a dress in real life, but way beyond me. I sat down on the bench and kicked at some pins on the floor. I felt weak and tired and thought about curling up for a nap before going out to take back the good news.

Mom was on to me right away. "What's wrong?"

I tried sounding casual. "It's too expensive. Really, it's okay."

She grabbed the price tag. Her face fell, but then she forced a smile and said, "That, my dear, is a bargain."

"Mom, no, I can't afford it."

"We're buying it," she said. "I have a charge card. That's what they're for. You never have to pay for anything."

"Maaaa . . . I don't want you to."

"No argument," she said. "We've been looking for days, and this is perfect on you. The story's told."

She was already on her way to the register. Pan and I followed. I did not want that dress. I thought of my dad at work, oily and exhausted, dodging irritable customers. Even if Mom insisted on buying it, I could not wear it in good conscience.

The woman at the register scanned it. I couldn't look at the little screen.

"Forty-two thirty-seven," she said. Now I did look, and those were the numbers.

"Oh," Mom said, trying not to sound too surprised.

"Sixty percent off," the cashier said. "It's a good deal."

"At that price she'll take two," said Pan. The woman looked up, vaguely interested, but I shook my head.

In the car we had that light spirit you get from a feel-good movie. For once, I'd gotten away with something, two things, really. Despite the conspiracy of the fashion industry, I had found a nice dress to wear. And even though it was made of something besides synthetics, it had cost less than fifty bucks.

"Don't tell anyone we got it on sale," I warned Pan as he drove us home. "I want the girls at school to think I spent a thousand."

"You keep forgetting I have no one to tell, Joto."

"I can't believe it was so cheap," I said.

"Inexpensive," Mom said from the backseat. "Cheap sounds like it's cheap. It's quality."

"I would have bought you that dress myself for a hundred bucks," Pan said. "You looked amazing. That boy better appreciate you."

"He better not break up with me until this dress has been officially worn," I said.

"That's right," Mom said. "No breaking up until

after the prom. We didn't go to all this trouble for nothing."

I leaned over and kissed Pan's cheek. He kissed me back.

"You kids confuse me," Mom said.

"What do you mean, Mama F?" Pan asked.

"In my day the girl just married the guy and ignored he was gay."

"Really?" I asked. "What was the point?"

She sighed. "At least she got a good-looking husband for a while."

chapter twenty-six

Pan had a prom date, back in Buckingham Heights, with an old friend.

"Nothing romantic," he told me. "But he doesn't want to go alone, and he doesn't want to go with a girl."

Most of the girls at my school were approaching the prom with a ferocious intensity. I'd seldom had any interest in extracurricular activities, especially social ones. Wanting a boyfriend had not meant wanting to parade around a gymnasium, hiding under the bleachers, crying with my girlfriends. If things had been different, I would have worked at the pharmacy on prom night, possibly a little agitated about what the event—like Valentine's Day—represented and how it was being withheld from me.

So I don't know why I expected the prom to be

more than it was, but I did not love or hate it. I should have been grateful that instead of being at work alone, I was actually part of the festivities. Instead I was bored. I wished that Pan had crashed the party with his date. We could have had some defiant fun—me dancing with him, him dancing with another guy—although I don't know how Caspar would have gone for it.

Caspar picked me up in his father's Lincoln Town Car. I was not wearing my only dress in the red pickup. He took me to Flora's on the Lake which was outside of town and had a pretty view of the water. I ate with precision because I didn't want to spill anything on my dress, so I suppose it was just as well that the portions were the size of hors d'oeuvres.

I had been worried about Caspar seeing the inside of my house, and had spent too much of the day scrubbing the living room. You can't really scrub a room like that without it crumbling, but I tried to make it presentable. I took the whole place apart. I considered throwing away the cardboard Christmas fireplace we kept up all year, but it wasn't mine to toss. I powdered the carpet and sprayed the upholstery. When I got it reassembled, it was clear that what the living room really needed was all its contents thrown out, including the walls and floorboards. But that kind of overhaul was not going to happen by six-thirty.

Caspar didn't act like he noticed that my house and

neighborhood were a few bars down from his on the economic graph. The shifting of his emotions was very hard to detect, but he was definitely nervous. He told me later that he had been uneasy about seeing my parents again. Mom was fine, though. She had gotten the new babysitter to take Paolo for the evening. And she wore nothing on her head. She brushed away tears as she shot photo after photo. Maybe it was that deal of a dress that was moving her. Dad was his usual self, looking like he'd come to arrest somebody. I might have detected a crack in his countenance a couple times when Caspar and I stood by the fake fireplace for a few shots. At least he was all cleaned up. Working on the house, I'd obsessed about whether he would take a shower when he got home. He was sparkling when Caspar arrived, and I gave him and Mom unrestrained hugs before we left.

I should have felt like Cinderella arriving at the Courtesy Inn with her tall, athletic prince. But things got off to a bad start and only worked their way up to mediocre. When Caspar and I walked into the lobby, my friend Amanda was taking tickets at the door. She didn't have a date, which bothered me since she was cute and lively and ought to have had one. I hadn't said much to her about my going with Caspar, partly because it was so last-minute and partly because I didn't want her to feel bad. She wanted to be part of the event, so she sat there taking people's tickets and greeting them as if she were happy to. Sitting next to her was sullen Amy Conrad who, not-so-surprisingly, wasn't coupled either. Amy's usual facial expression was sour. But when she saw Caspar do this old-fashioned thing of putting out his arm for me to take, her tiny body shuddered with laughter and she turned her head, as if we wouldn't be able to see her. My heart pumped lightning, and I wanted to turn and go home. Instead, I put my arm through Caspar's, and we headed into the banquet room. I don't know if Caspar saw her laughing, but I wasn't going to mention it.

From that point on, the only connection I had with Cinderella was the feeling of being exposed. We were on display because everyone was. People alternately showed off and analyzed each other's showing off. There was no banquet in the banquet room, just an apricot punch. I didn't think apricots and punch had any association before this, and now I knew why. The planners must not have understood that they had practically invited someone to spike it. I didn't find out if it ever was, because one sip was enough to make me misplace my cup. Caspar and I danced to a few slow songs, and I danced with a couple of my old Holy Spirit girlfriends to faster numbers, and the whole time I kept wondering when the magic would begin. When he wasn't dancing with me, Caspar sat like an immense wallflower. I thought of asking him to ask Amanda for a dance, but somehow I knew they would be awkward together, especially since she was even shorter than me. There was a prolonged court ceremony to endure. Finally I conceded that the fireworks were not going to happen and went over to him and asked if he was ready to go. He smiled for the first time since we'd arrived.

Having had enough of other people, we skipped the after-parties Caspar had been invited to. Since we were both starving, we shared a footlong submarine sandwich on the way back to his place. I wore two paper napkins on my chest to protect my dress. Later, after some very pleasant gymnastics in his basement, he drove me home. The car idled in front of my house while we sat talking.

"Did you have a nice evening?" he asked, looking mournful.

"With you I did," I said.

"Me too."

"I guess I could have lived without seeing Michelle Cooper burst into tears when she was crowned queen."

"I agree," he said. "It was very boring. Not you, of course."

"That's good."

"No, I mean that prom court stuff. It took so long. All that forced anticipation."

"Yeah," I said, "and then Patrick Torno was called as a knight of the court."

"At least he wasn't elected king. Not that it matters." He kissed me. "I love you."

"Why do you look so sad, Cas?" I asked. "I'm afraid to leave you like this."

"I was thinking about my dad. It comes up at the strangest times."

"Then I guess I'll have to stay right here with you."

"No, I'm okay. You made the night worthwhile."

"You too."

"You're my queen."

"Don't say that in front of James, please."

Caspar looked dumbfounded.

"Just a joke," I said. "Are you sure you're okay? Do you want to come in again? It's no problem. I just have to warn you about fifteen different things if you do."

"No, I'd better get home."

I got out. My dress was a little rumpled now. "Drive that big car safely."

"Oh, don't worry," he said. "My dad used to say it has enough air bags to levitate."

One relief was that my parents were both asleep instead of waiting up with their fingers poised on the light switch.

Despite the blah dance, I felt strangely contented, like things had been accomplished. I had done the prom bit and could dismiss its promise. Hopefully Pan's evening had been better, and I was happy that he hadn't sat home alone. I loved my dress. It was too good for this occasion, but there would be others. I looked forward to my normal life of jeans and the pickup. Not adventurous, but comforting, and for the time being, parallel.

Pan called me Sunday morning, in time to get me up for work. Instead of us gushing over our big evenings out, he explained his own lackluster experience, showing up at the Buckingham Heights prom with his friend, both in tuxes. If he had hoped for some controversy, he hadn't gotten it dancing with another boy there.

"Maybe proms are supposed to be illusion-busting," he said.

"Maybe," I said.

"You can't predict magic, can you? Misery either, now that I think of it. They just happen."

chapter twenty-seven

There was less than a month left of school. One day while we were eating, Caspar asked what I wanted to do Saturday night. This was a lapse in etiquette because he and I and Pan never discussed our plans in front of the person who was not included.

"I don't know," I said. "Watch a movie."

"Is there anything new at the theater? We could drive somewhere."

"Not sure. I'll have to look."

"Let's go to my house. I have movies."

I really didn't want him pursuing this in front of Pan. But then he said, "I mean the three of us. James, my dad's collection is huge. There's got to be something we can all agree on."

"Oh, uh, it's like . . ."

Caspar looked very concerned. "Do you have something else to do? I mean, I understand if you have a date or something."

I took a bite of my sandwich, but I tasted nothing.

"No, I wish I did, but I don't. Not that . . ." He paused, looked at me, then back at Caspar.

"Not that I wish I had a date because I don't want to come to your house."

"No, I didn't think that. Let's do it, then."

Caspar bent to take a spoonful of his soup. I didn't look at Pan, but I felt a little expansion inside, as if euphoria was stretching.

I told myself I would let Saturday night happen and not worry. After all, Pan had said there was no use in making predictions. He came to my house, where Caspar was going to pick us up. We were sitting in my living room, Mom's delighted attention on Pan who was swinging Paolo. Dad came home from work looking tired and grim. His mood was not improved by seeing Pan tossing his son around and Paolo loving it. He didn't say anything, but Pan stopped, and Paolo let us all know it. Paolo didn't run to Dad to greet him; he insisted that Pan continue the acrobatics. But Pan tried to move away. It didn't work. Paolo clung to him.

"That's enough, Pow," said Dad, but Paolo didn't care. He howled at Pan. "Pow!" Dad yelled.

Just then we heard a car horn. Pan and I were leaving no matter who was honking.

Mom pulled Paolo off Pan so we could get away. "Thanks, Tony," she said. "Just when I had a few minutes of quiet. Go take a shower."

Pan was fidgety in the truck, not composed and distant the way he usually was around Caspar. He sat next to the door, the three of us squashed in together.

When we got to Caspar's, Pan and I sat in the basement while Caspar went upstairs. I thought Pan was trembling a little.

"This is a huge place," he said, a slight quaver in his voice.

Caspar brought down sandwiches, chips, soda, and brownies his mother had set aside for us. At first it was very quiet while we ate. I thought about suggesting we start the movie, then decided not to meddle. Pan finally said to me, "This is almost as good as your mother's."

"Is her mom a good cook?" Caspar asked.

"She's excellent. Mine's pretty good too. She cooks with the finest, most wholesome ingredients money can buy. But TJ's mother can make something delicious out of what's in the lawn-mower bag."

Caspar had his mouth full, so he added a muffled, "My mom cooks by dialing the phone."

For some reason this struck Pan as hilarious. His

laughter made food burst out of his mouth, which made Caspar laugh.

After coughing out the scraps he had choked on, Pan said, "Do you still want me to stay? I mean, after I almost yakked on you guys?"

"There was no vomit that I could see," Caspar said like a reassuring doctor. "You can stay."

Pan relaxed a little after that, but he wasn't entirely unwound. We selected a movie. It helped that we chose a bad one.

Caspar tried to adjust the settings on the TV and DVD player because the characters looked alternately blanched and in silhouette. Finally he figured it was a problem with the filming, not his equipment.

"My dad liked independent films. Sometimes they are real low budget. Maybe too low. Should we try something else?"

"We can make fun of it," Pan said. "We might not be able to do that with a better movie."

So we watched, and laughed where we weren't supposed to. The movie was so bad that it wasn't long before Pan and Caspar were narrating it. Once when a man lit a cigarette, the entire screen went white.

"That would make a good antismoking campaign," Caspar said.

"Yeah," said Pan. "If you think smoking ruins your lungs, just wait till you see what it does to your career."

In another scene, a woman way older than a teenager went to answer a phone. As she lifted the receiver she was lit from behind, giving her an evil glow. "Hello? Is it true?" she asked into the blanched phone. "Have I made the cheerleading squad?"

"Yes," Pan said. "You'll be cheering for Satan."

"She'll be the oldest cheerleader in Hell," said Caspar.

I didn't try to narrate, because I didn't want to ruin their rhythm. Instead, I enjoyed maybe the best fun I'd had in high school. I thought of how, for all my classmates' talk of other substances, I was completely high on sugar and foolishness.

Caspar offered to drive us home after we had laughed ourselves into pain and eaten way too much. I knew he probably wanted some alone time with me, but I didn't think the evening could get any more perfect than it had been. So Pan and I did what we always did and walked, laughing even more on the way.

chapter twenty-eight

I wanted to be left alone at work the next day, to dream my parallel dreams. But it was a particularly busy day, for Polaski's Pharmacy. Midafternoon, when there was finally a lull and I was thinking about calling Caspar just to say hello, I had quite a surprise. Patrick Torno walked in with two people who must have been his grandparents. Or great-grandparents. Maybe greater. The three of them didn't really walk in. It was a production for him to get them in the door with all their calling and banging. The grandfather walked with a cane that had four feet. Torno appeared not to see me as he and his huddle made their way.

I felt like a detective, observing him without being observed. I wondered who had exchanged souls with him that he was so patient helping these old people around the store. He sounded like an old man himself, repeating several times the names of each item they handled and how much it cost, explaining what it was for. Once in a while he would scold one of them for talking too loud, or both of them for lapsing into conversation instead of paying attention to the shopping, or for a near-miss with a shelf of colognes.

Pan's timing was either terrible or razor-sharp because he came in while the trio was negotiating a second aisle.

"Well, I have another date with my father," he said. "I'm going to beg you to come with me . . ."

I put my index finger to my lips.

"Is Tammie—"

I grabbed him so I could get close to his ear. "Patrick Torno is here. With his grandparents, I think. They're both a hundred."

His smile favored the devil.

There was a small outburst, then the three of them bumbled their way to the front again. Torno must have wished he could fly when he saw Pan. Then the old woman called to me, "We need a urinal. My husband can't get out of bed fifteen times a night."

"Aisle four," I said. "Three-quarters of the way down on the left. With the home health equipment."

Pan turned and fixed a look at Torno. "Aisle four, sir," he said.

Torno, very harsh now, said to the old ones, "Stay here. I'll get it," and jogged off.

He came back with the urinal box, holding it at his side to camouflage it. The old man took the box, examined it, then dropped it. Pan picked it up and handed it back.

"You just hold on to the handle here?" the man asked, pointing to the picture on the box.

"You put it next to the bed and use it during the night," the woman said.

She took the box and opened the top, fumbling a little. Finding the urinal inside encased by thin plastic, she tried to grab the handle. She dropped it, and then the box too, and Pan again bent to pick them up. Torno looked toward the floor. Pan unwrapped the urinal and held it out by the handle to the man. The wife took it again and said, "See? Like this. You hold this part and you pee into the tube or whatever you call it."

"Then what do you do with it?" asked the man.

"Well you don't hand it to me," she said. "You put it down and go back to sleep."

"But it'll spill all over. How do you keep it from spilling? That's just what we need."

"No, look," said Pan as if he'd done this before. "There's a cap, and you close it when you're finished. Peeing."

"Oh, I see," said the man, and took the urinal from

his wife. "So you hold the handle like so, and do your business in the column here, and then snap the lid back on like a can of dog food."

"Just like it," said Pan. "But don't put it in the refrigerator after." The old people laughed, unlike their grandson.

"Let's go. They've got other things to do," said the man.

"Go get us a second one," the woman said. "He loses everything." Both of them laughed again.

Pan took the urinal from the man and put it back in the box, then brought it over to the counter. The man turned to Torno and said, "Would you like one too, Paddy?"

The woman's laugh sounded like a wolf baying. "Oh, for heaven's sake," she said. "He's too young. He doesn't need one."

"Used to wet the bed, though," said the man.

"Now you stop that," the woman said. "All babies do that. He was just a baby."

"I'm just saying. He'll be an old man too, someday. Awful to get old. Like being a baby again."

"But not as adorable," said the woman.

"I'll get it for you," Pan said, and hurried down the aisle.

Gravity was having a marked effect on Torno's face. Any second now it would sag to his toes. I wished the store had a surveillance camera so Pan and I could play the scene over and over. It was wicked, but I rationalized that if we never told anyone, we should at least be able to savor this memory. Pan wasn't going to report him and Samsonite in school, so we needed some retribution, if only in secret.

"Will that be it?" I asked, reaching to scan the boxes when Pan returned with the second one.

Torno's voice came through a pool of phlegm. "We have to get the prescriptions."

"Oh, okay," I said.

"What?" asked the woman.

Torno didn't clear his throat. He sounded like he was waking up from anesthesia. "The medicine. We have to go to the back and get the medicine."

"That's what we came here for," said the man. "The pee bottle was your idea, Rose."

"And I'm glad," she said.

"You can pay for these," I said, "along with your prescriptions, in the back."

Pan took the boxes and said softly, "Want me to carry them for you?"

Torno grabbed them from him.

"Have a good day," Pan said.

"Every day above ground is a good day," the man said.

"Oh, let's go," said the woman.

Then the grandparents forgot about us and were bumping their noisy way toward the back of the store. Torno followed them out of view.

Pan looked like he had just seen paradise.

"What an afternoon it's been," he said.

"Go home. I'll call you tonight."

"But there's no back exit. They have to go by us again. Unless Paddy intends to haul them through the bathroom window."

"That's exactly why you have to leave. He's had enough humiliation for one day."

"What?"

"Go on. Git."

"I can't believe you're ruining this for me. It's like being sent to bed when your favorite show is on."

"It's been a lot of fun, I agree. But enough is enough. Go, Pan."

"You're really kicking me out? I haven't even told you about the thing with my father."

There was another disturbance from the old people in the back of the store, then muffled talking.

"I want to hear it," I said. "Every detail. I'll call you."

He snorted as he left. Then, outside, he pressed his nose against the window and batted his eyes. I turned away.

When Torno and his entourage made their way to

the front again, he didn't look at me, and I said nothing to him. I had felt sorry for him about the urinal scene, and he'd been amazingly understanding and patient with his grandparents. I had done right by not letting Pan stay and gloat, but Patrick Torno wasn't getting anything else from me.

chapter twenty-nine

I'd told Pan to pick me up the next morning at the corner of my street. Mom had not been as difficult about giving up her Saturday morning bowling as I'd expected, especially since I put it in terms of Pan needing my support.

"I guess if he needs you," she said. "I could try taking Paolo with me to the lanes. If he acts up, maybe it'll work in my favor, throw other people's games off." I could see she was not going to attempt it.

"Pan promises to babysit next Saturday morning without fail," I said. This was true, although Dad would not approve.

"It seems like a year away," she said. "Go. Be supportive. Tell him I hope it goes well."

When he pulled up, Kevin was driving. He rolled

down his window and called, "I'm just coming along for extra moral support."

When we got to the diner parking lot, we knew who Robertson was right away. His hair was a little darker, but he was definitely Pan's father, standing by the railing of the diner entrance smoking a cigarette.

Before Kevin parked the car, Pan turned around to me.

"You're coming in."

"No."

"I mean it. I can't do this alone."

When the car stopped, we all got out, and Pan held on to me as we walked toward Robertson. There were awkward introductions.

"I'll be back in an hour," Kevin said. "Have a good lunch."

Pan only let me go long enough to lunge at Kevin and give him a long hug. Kevin whispered something, then gave him a be-strong look. I turned to follow Kevin back to the car. But Pan pulled me into the diner.

When we sat down, Robertson took out another cigarette and lit it.

"I have one of these until I get caught," he said. "So, what do you kids think of this Congress we have?"

Thinking I was supposed to answer, I said, "Um, I—"

"You know what Will Rogers said about

Congress? It opens with a prayer and closes with an investigation."

A waitress came over to our table. "You sneaky snake. You put that out or I'll put you right over my knee."

"Doesn't sound like much of an incentive," Robertson said, stubbing out his cancer stick. "What are we having, kids?"

I ordered a salad that came in a dish the size of a sleigh. Pan ordered a sandwich. Robertson had a giant burger platter. Though he did all the talking, which gave us plenty of time to eat, Pan and I both picked.

It turned out to be a near-endless monologue, Robertson punctuating his sentences with one of our names: "James, that's the way this country is run now, James" "TJ, you've got two kinds of people running the government." He could have been talking to anyone. ("Zelda, the lobbyists practically own Washington, Zelda.")

I nodded and smiled intermittently. He didn't mention that I hadn't been expected. He also didn't seem aware that this was the first time he'd seen his son since he was a toddler. He transitioned from one current event to another. He would be quiet just long enough to insert a mouthful of food, then be back to it. He would sound like he was asking a question, then answer it himself.

"James, your mother? How is she? She was quite a

firebrand liberal when she was a girl. Very active. I wonder if she still is. As we get older we lose our idealism, that's for sure."

Despite all his talking, his plate was glimmering when he was done. Though I hadn't thought it was possible, he found a way to be even more obnoxious. When the check came, he examined it carefully, then told us what we owed. I hadn't expected him to pay for my lunch, but this was his son.

Pan put down a twenty. "For both of us," he said, his voice lifeless.

"Hold—wait—wait there. That's too much," Robertson said, looking at the check again.

"Keep it."

"Maybe you're right," Robertson said. "A little extra tip. She was a good girl, eh?"

When we got up to leave, he shook our hands like we had concluded a merger.

"James, I'm pleased to see you've turned into a fine young man. Your mother has done an excellent job with you, James, as I knew she would. Your stepdad too. And your girl is a peach."

Peaches were round and covered with fuzz. I hated this man.

He did not suggest that he and Pan meet again or stay in touch. The business lunch was over, and Robertson heard a cigarette calling. Pan didn't get a chance to ask him any questions, didn't tell him I was not his girl and why.

Kevin was waiting, always reliable, and his reward was Pan being in the worst mood ever. He alternated between sullen silence and snapping at one or the other of us—for something we said, for the radio being too loud, or for the car hitting too many potholes.

"Well at least tell me what happened," Kevin said, "that you're so angry."

"Nothing happened," Pan said. "Nothing."

"For heaven's sake, TJ, what in the world did that man say?"

"He didn't really say anything," I said. "He just talked about the government, things like that the whole time."

"And he made us pay," Pan said. "Don't you think that if you were meeting your son for the first time in fourteen years, you would pay for his lunch? And maybe even his friend's, who came all this way with him?"

"I suppose I would."

"Jesus, Kevin, can you step on it? We're never going to get home. TJ has plans tonight."

I was practically choking on my own agitation by the time we got near our exit. After he'd slapped me down for the fifth time and Kevin for the millionth, I said, "You only have to look like him, James. You don't have to be a jerk like him."

Kevin caught my eye in the rearview mirror.

"Stop the car," Pan said.

"James," Kevin said.

"Stop the goddamn car."

"No, I will not."

"Kevin, I swear I'll jump out."

Kevin pulled over to the side of the highway and said, "James, you may not get out of this car. If I have to put you in the trunk . . ." But Pan was out. Instead of running down the shoulder aimless and desperate as he had good reason to do, he opened the back door and got in. He sidled up next to me and put his head on my shoulder, resting it there until we got home.

chapter thirty

Pan was as subdued as I'd ever known him to be when we talked Sunday, and his heavy mood had not changed by the next day at school. Samsonite didn't help matters any during Science and Society.

"Why don't they just face reality?" he asked. "Who wants to crap all the time? And who wants to kiss a girl who's puking up her lunch every day?"

We were in The Circle, this time discussing eating disorders. The subtopic of purgatives had gotten him excited. There was no groaning when he spoke. It was June after all, and he had us trained to wait it out.

But Caspar took everybody seriously. He shifted himself in his small seat, wrinkled his brow, and said, "I think the reality is they can't control it."

"Sure they can," said Samsonite. "No one's making them puke."

"I saw a documentary on the Nutrition Channel about it," said Caspar. "They think there's some kind of abnormality in the way certain chemicals affect the brain."

"It's abnormal all right," said Samsonite. "It's sick."

Mrs. Mercado said, "It's too easy to dismiss someone as 'sick.'"

"Do you mean sick like the flu?" asked Caspar. "Literally sick?" I looked over at Pan, but he was idly erasing something on his desktop, then rolling the crumbs.

"Sick like crazy people," Samsonite said.

"That's not very useful," said Mrs. Mercado.

"Maybe," Caspar said, like something was unfolding in his mind, "maybe crazy people can't control themselves. So we can't expect them to make good decisions."

"There's no way I would go out with a girl like that," Samsonite said.

"Maybe they can't control what comes out of their mouths," Pan said, "like you."

"Or what goes into yours," Patrick Torno said, foreboding as a blackening sky.

"Stop it," Mrs. Mercado said, though it was not clear to whom.

"Speaking of crapping all the time," Pan said, "how are those urinals working out?"

"James," she said.

"I'm just asking. Paddy came into Polaski's last week and bought two urinals. It was two for the price of one, right Paddy? Don't you just love a good sale?"

Torno looked like Hell's race car was speeding out of his eyes.

"James," Mrs. Mercado said with a conspiratorial grin.

"Come on, Paddy. How come you and your boyfriend here aren't more sympathetic to barfing girls? Someone who needs a urinal for each hand ought to be."

"James," Mrs. Mercado repeated, a little stern now.

"How does that work, Paddy? All that cheap beer guzzling got you so you can't find the bathroom? Why not just piss on the walls and blame it on Grandpa Noodles?"

Mrs. Mercado cleared her throat and sat up a little straighter. "Okay, James. Let's keep it relevant."

"You're worried about relevance?" Pan said to her. "He—the two of them—sit here and say the stupidest things anyone could think of. Although in this school, that's kind of a race."

She stared at Pan, stung.

"If you were worried about relevance," he continued, looking down at his desktop and blowing away the crumbs, "you should have shut them up a long time ago."

"What?" she whispered, like someone had just broken up with her.

"I haven't gotten anything out of this class. But what should I have expected?"

"Everyone," she said, unsteady, "is entitled to their opinion."

"And my opinion," Pan said, "is that some people aren't. Making us watch them foam at the mouth is not some kind of learning experience, I hate to tell you."

"Pan," I whispered.

"This school is . . . The Honor Society is a joke. Why don't you just pass out a bunch of newspaper clippings, like what's-his-name in Social Studies?"

Mrs. Mercado's face betrayed disbelief and fear. Normally someone would be thrown out for such temerity, but Pan was a straight-A student, top of the class.

"We'll have to agree to disagree," she said, not quite finding her voice.

Pan looked up at the ceiling, then stretched his neck back and forth.

The rest of the period crept by like a dysfunctional family holiday. No one spoke. Everyone avoided glances. Mrs. Mercado tried to continue, but her words were wobbly. It was a circle of muteness. The only thing I imagined I could hear was Torno's percolating blood. He stared at Pan as if programmed to kill. Pan put his head down on the desk, using his arms for a cushion.

The bell rang, like it was granting clemency.

"Congratulations," Pan said to Torno as we were leaving the room. "You made it through without an accident."

I got ready to put myself between them, call for Caspar if I had to. But Torno didn't say or do anything, which scared me more.

chapter thirty-one

Why didn't I make the connection that evening when I saw Samsonite and Torno pass by the store windows just a minute or so after Pan had left? Instead I only thought it odd, and had a fleeting hope that they wouldn't run into each other. I went back to work organizing the paperback book and magazine section. People stood around reading them, but they seldom bought one.

It wasn't long after when Pan staggered in, dirty, sticky, his hair wild. For once he was just repellant. And panic clutched me.

"Pan, what?"

"I need something to clean up with."

"What happened?" As I got close to him, ammonia blasted at me. "What is it?"

"Nothing. Just . . ." His voice was higher, none of his usual self-possession. There were bruises too, scuff marks, a trickle of blood from his nose drying a dirty brown. Then I made the connection.

"Tell me, right now," I said, though I could guess the basics. I could have pulled my own hair for being so dim.

"Nothing, I just need some paper towels or something."

"Tell me," I said with a ferocity I didn't know was in me. "What the hell is going on?"

"It was our friends Samsonite and Paddy. They tried to . . ." The last word slipped into falsetto. He stood almost not breathing, mouthing words. He cleared his throat and tried again.

"They poured piss on me."

I felt like I'd been tazered as I ran through the store. I managed to find a package of body wipes, big disposable ones for people who couldn't take a bath. I sped back to him. He was trembling now, a slight pulsation.

I opened the package and yanked out a few wet cloths. I started with his hair and face. He grabbed one and did his arms. The fumes defied us. Really, he smelled like an alley wall. It was on his clothes, in his hair, and, as it turned out, in his mouth.

"I'm calling the police," I said, going for the phone.

Nothing was going to stop me this time. But Pan was practically on top of me as he grabbed it.

"No."

I wasn't listening to no. I tried to grab it back.

"I don't care what you say, I'm calling the cops," I said. "If you won't let me do it here, I'll call from home. I'm doing it. Someone has got to stop those little freaks."

He held the phone high over me, which wasn't hard considering our heights.

"Please, Joto, I just need to get changed and go home. Can we go to your house? If my mother sees me like this she'll go volcanic."

"I can't take this anymore. I can't watch you get pissed on—for real—and then pretend nothing's happened. I can't." I gasped a few giant breaths. He put his hand on my shoulder. "It's too much," I said.

"Please don't, baby. Don't hyperventilate. I'm okay, I really am. I just need a friend right now."

"No!" I turned away from him and pressed myself against the counter.

Detective Tammie entered the scene.

"James, what's the matter with her? What happened to you? What's that smell?"

But I had no allegiance except to him. I stood straight, breathed in deep.

"Tammie, I have to go. He's been attacked and I'm taking him to the police station."

"But that'll leave us short-staffed."

"You know how to manage a register," I said, which stopped her next objection.

"Come on," I said, taking Pan's tacky arm. "We're going."

If Tammie protested more, I didn't hear her and didn't care. Her limp soul was her problem.

The police station was only a few blocks from the pharmacy. I didn't worry about Samsonite and Patrick Torno lurking between every building. I would protect us, even if I had to scream "Rape!" along the way and punch below the belt.

Pan had slowed down. Already I knew a different fight had begun.

"Joto, I can't go in there. What do you think the cops are going to say? In Mungers Mills? A teenage fag covered in piss?"

"They'll have to make a report. They'll have to find them."

"No, they won't."

"Samsonite will confess as soon as they confront him. Do you really think he can keep his mouth shut, of all people?"

"He's probably related to half the force. Torno's related to the other half. That's the whole department."

"I'll make them do a test or something to see whose urine it is. They won't get away with this."

"There is no test. They'll say I'm some kind of pervert, that I'm into getting peed on. Then my mother will find out about this and she'll murder someone. It'll be more of a mess than it already is. Let's just go to your house."

"Not this time. No. This time we're doing the right thing, not the convenient thing."

He stopped. When he spoke, I was sure he was going to cry. "Please, Joto, don't make me go to the cops like this. Not like this."

"We have to."

"Take me to your house and let me get cleaned up first."

"They'll need evidence. If you get cleaned up . . ."

"Please," he said, and choked. His weeping was soft and musical, like a grieving skylark. I should have held him then, piss and all, but I was horrified by the sight of his defeat.

When he stopped crying, we began walking again, away from the station. After a couple of blocks, he let the story unfold. His voice grew stronger. Samsonite and Torno had pulled him into the void between a sub shop and a vacant bank. Samsonite splashed him with a bottle full of pee while Torno tried to hold him down. Some had gotten in his mouth in the process. Pan was strong, but not strong enough for the weapons of speed and surprise.

"The good thing is," said Pan, more like his old self, "Paddy got a taste of the uric acid too. He punched me, then tried to hold me on the ground, but he was shouting that it was getting all over him."

I could almost not stand this salvaging of a scrap of pride.

"They really should have planned it better." When I didn't answer, he said, "You're the best friend a person could ask for. Don't make me kiss you like this."

But nothing was funny tonight. When we got to my house, I insisted he come in for a shower. He wouldn't budge farther than the porch.

"Don't let them know I'm here," he whispered. "Your father especially."

"I can handle him," I said.

"No, it'll make him hate me more. Being beaten up and all. He'll think I'm a coward."

"Why am I arguing with you, Pan? A crime has been committed and we're worrying about my father?"

He convinced me to throw his putrid clothes in the washer for a quick rinse so he could wear them home. I grabbed my slicker off the rack next to the side door and gave it to Pan. Then I took the hideous bundle into the cellar, hating Samsonite and Torno. If Torno ever walked into Polaski's again, even with the elderly in tow, I would call the cops and say they were shoplifting.

I tried to find something for Pan to wear. No one in my house was thin and tall, so there wasn't a lot to choose from. In the dryer I found a pair of Mom's sweat pants and one of Dad's undershirts. Both hung on Pan like he was a clothesline, and the legs of the pants rode up almost to his knees. I also brought back wet washcloths, which he used on his face, hair, and arms. Then he dried himself with a big towel I'd given him.

I told him we were still going to the police, but I knew it wasn't going to happen. If I had been thinking more clearly, I would have gotten Mom to back me up. Instead we waited on the porch after I put his clothes in the dryer.

By then, sitting calmly on the dilapidated steps in his absurd outfit, he was already looking down on the incident.

"You realize, of course," he said, "that if we go to the cops, they've won, the boys. What a score for them to have the police grill me for information and turn it around so they look like the victims. It happens all the time."

I had lost again. He was back in control.

"You're doing the wrong thing," I said. "The clothes are evidence. If I had seen it happen, you wouldn't have been able to stop me."

"We can't say anything about this. Not to Caspar even. We can't let them think they won something."

I wanted to tell Caspar in the worst way, but it was a violent impulse. I wanted him to grab Samsonite and Torno by their necks and pound their heads together like a pair of cartoon cymbals.

"No one?"

"I'll make sure they don't do it again," Pan said.

"How?"

"Don't worry. I'm not completely helpless, you know."

"You have a gun or something?"

"Guns are for amateurs."

"I don't know if I can handle another attack," I said. "This is the last time I listen to you, I swear. You're going to get yourself killed."

He leaned against me. He smelled better now, his hair a mess of wet tangles from the washcloths. "Only the good die young," he said. "I've got centuries."

chapter thirty-two

It was a perfect morning, the sun burning off the cool of the previous night. Everything—the houses, the trees, anything against the sky—appeared illuminated. Normally I would think it was all beautiful, but I hated going to school knowing I would have to see Samsonite and Patrick Torno. And keep my mouth shut.

My life, for a few weeks, had been the way I wanted it—a best friend to walk me home and a boyfriend to kiss me good-bye before I went. Companionship, real romance, as perfect as a girl from Mungers Mills could expect. But today the light was relentless, and I felt that having those two scumbags hanging over our heads was a bill due for my short period of parallelism.

Evidently I was bearing the trepidation for both me

and Pan, since he was in a light mood. I knew if I even mentioned last night, he would ignore me, so I didn't.

"Are you playing today?" I asked when I saw the end of his tennis racket sticking out of his bag.

"I'm taking a lesson after school."

"I wish I had learned how to play. If the courts here had been kept up, you could have coached me and I would have gradually gotten less bad."

"I believe in your potential."

Pan wasn't being cautious or wary, looking around to see where Samsonite and Torno were perched. Knowing Caspar would be in school chipped away a little of my unease, but still I wanted to skip out before the day was through. I'd never done that, but I couldn't stand the thought of seeing them. I realized with despair that now Pan couldn't report them until they did something else, and the school year was ending. In Science and Society Torno turned his evil head our way a couple times, but not Samsonite, who for once said nothing. Pan asked some questions, which Mrs. Mercado answered in a curt tone.

After the final bell Pan reminded me of his tennis lesson and told me I should go on home, that he was staying to work with our gym teacher.

"Oh," I said. "I thought you said you were taking a lesson after school, not at school. Are you telling the truth, or is there another girl in your life now?"

"Believe it or not, I'm going to practice my swing with Mr. Hicks," he said.

"What?"

"Yeah, spring was so wet that I've missed a lot of practice time. I need to get back into condition. I don't want to lose everything because I moved here."

"Mr. Hicks? What does he know about tennis?"

"He's a gym teacher, or as close as you get to one in Mungers Mills. He used to give lessons. Anyway, gotta go."

I was afraid to leave him alone. "Can I come with you? Just for a few minutes?"

"And watch? We don't do that, you and I, worship at the gates of jockdom."

"I know. That's why I'm willing to watch you."

"Very clever. Go home. You'll be bored."

I followed him out the side loading area where kids waited for the buses.

"Where are you going?" I asked. "The gym office is down the next hall."

"I'm going this way. I'll call you tonight, several times."

I thought I understood: Pan was disguising his fear. He didn't have a lesson at all, and going out a more obscure exit might keep him from getting beaten up again. But being where no one could see Torno and Samsonite jump him was a risk too. I wanted to assure him it was okay to be afraid, but I knew better than to bring the subject up.

There was a picnic table where two wings of the building made a corner, probably a hideout for the bus drivers to smoke between runs. Pan walked over and sat on the top.

"What are we doing here?" I asked.

"I'm going to wait here for him. He said he'd be free at four."

"Mr. Hicks?"

"Yeah. Go ahead home. I intend to bother you all night at chez pharmacie."

I felt a twinge of discomfort at the back of my neck.

"Pan, I'm confused. Are you meeting a guy here? I can handle it. As long as he's not thirty, or something awful like that."

"No. Go on. Go. I am one hundred percent groovy."

"Okay. Call me."

I turned to go back in the door near the loading area.

"Hey, Samsonite, Paddy," I heard Pan call as if he were a coach, "get your candy asses over here." Only then did I realize what he'd been planning, and turned back. I had to get him out of there.

Samsonite looked, then looked away. But like an animal lured by food, Torno stormed over. Samsonite followed, slower.

Pan understood the element of surprise too because before they got close to us, he turned his back on them. Then he was facing them, bringing the tennis racket down on Torno's head. With coordinated precision he did the same to Samsonite. As they shouted their disbelief, I tried to grab the racket from behind, but Pan connected with their bodies as if I were not there. They didn't charge him as he laid on more blows. Samsonite had drawn back, covering his face. Standing like a crumpled sapling, Torno looked up at Pan, dazed. But Pan was not retreating. He brought the racket down again and again—on heads, on butts, on backs, on arms. Sounding like he was calling to it, Torno cried, "My face. My face."

A bus driver charged toward us. I shouted for Pan to stop as he continued swinging, now at the air around him. I forced myself toward him, ducking and dodging, and grabbed the racket. A tirade came blowing out of the bus driver's mouth.

I held the racket as high as I could. "Go away!" I said. He drew back, but I was the terrified one. I didn't know this girl using my body.

"Give me that stick!" he shouted.

"Get back," I said. "They're the ones who started this." I pointed to Samsonite and Torno, now both on the ground. Torno was crawling as if searching for a contact lens.

"You give me that thing," the bus driver yelled, "or I'll shove it so far through your ear it'll come out the other side." He spat every word. He lunged for me, but I stepped back. "Gimme that stick or I'm gonna drive this bus right over you two, do you understand me? Give me it. Give it to me."

"It's just a tennis racket," I said, hoarse and desperate. "Leave us alone. Please, just leave us alone."

He was out of words now, so he howled. A crowd was starting to gather.

The last thing I saw before he fell was his giant red face coming toward me. Then he was on his knees and falling sideways. It appeared that between the two of us, Pan and I had killed three people in less than forty-five seconds.

I took Pan by the arm and pulled him away. I was stronger than I knew, because he was like pulling a broom. As we were running I could hear, but not see, Mrs. Guten on the scene yelling, "We have an emergency situation here. I need you to get on your buses, now. Move it out. On your buses. They need to be out of the way. Get going. That's it. Move it. Move!"

I must have made quite the picture, the short warrior goddess with her spear in one hand and a boy in the other. Once we were far enough from the school, hidden in a patch of woods near an abandoned gas station, Pan dislodged himself. I sat on the ground, sucking air. He stood breathing deep but not spent.

"You okay?"

"Better than ever," I managed to gasp out.

"Guten's got some pipes on her, doesn't she?" Pan said.

"I can still hear her." I tried to catch my breath.

"You didn't have to do that," he said. "I could have taken care of myself."

"That's what I was afraid of."

"I told you to go home, Joto."

"Why did you do that? Why did you hit them? You don't want to spend senior year in a boys' detention home, do you?"

"It has possibilities."

"Shut up. Do you know what they would do with a kid who looks like you? I'm not kidding."

"I'm sorry."

I looked up at him. The sun throbbed without mercy through the trees. He sat down beside me, put his hand on my forehead.

"I'm not kidding either, Joto. I am so, so sorry."

chapter thirty-three

I expected the cops to pick us up on our way to Pan's. When they didn't, I waited for them to come get us at his house. I almost called in to work thinking I would be in jail before I got anywhere near the pharmacy. Pan was not concerned as he drove me home.

"You didn't do anything wrong, Joto. Stop worrying. You won't be spending your summer in Cell Block H."

"You've got to tell them about Samsonite and Torno," I said. "You don't have a choice."

"Listen, if anything happens and in any way, shape, or form you are implicated in this, I will make my case against them. I'll spill every detail. I promise. But if not . . ."

"No, don't ask me to keep my mouth shut now."

"If not, if it's just me in trouble, which it will be,

then please, don't say a word. I don't want to be the cause célèbre of Mungers Mills. I don't want the one reporter at the newspaper doing a feature on the high school's pathetic gay boy."

No matter how many times we had this argument, he was still wrong, completely. But too much had happened and I had no energy.

There were no cops. There were, however, many phone calls, and the next morning Dad, Mom, and I were in Dr. Jackson's office. Mom's face was as stony as Dad's usually was, and I couldn't even look at him. Mrs. Guten was careful with them, but still her one tone was shrill.

When Dr. Jackson motioned for them to sit in a pair of chairs in front of his desk, Mom defiantly pulled up a third.

"TJ, sit here," she said, and I obeyed. I sat between her and Dad, and hung my head. I wanted to arrange my hair over my face, look out through the strands.

Dr. Jackson spoke in a low and dry tone about school policy, with Mrs. Guten nodding her head. Mom and Dad said nothing.

"TJ," Mrs. Guten said in the most soothing voice she could manage, "we're concerned about you. We want you to take care of yourself, be careful whom you hang around with. This was a very dangerous situation, a student who goes crazy like that." She looked at Mom and Dad and added, "Things are not the same as when we went to school."

"That boy has never given us one moment's trouble," Mom said.

"JoAnne," Dad said, putting a hand on her arm.

"He may need anger management—," Mrs. Guten started.

Mom yanked her arm away from Dad. "My daughter," she said, soft but steady, "does not need advice."

"For her own protection. James said there was no provocation."

"We all know the real story here," Mom said. "I can't afford lawyers, but that doesn't mean I don't understand things."

"Mrs. Fazzino—"

"Is TJ in trouble?" Dad asked. "Yes or no? Suspension?"

"No, but she didn't give the racket to Mr. Snibley when he asked for it."

"Mr. Snibley was threatening her," Mom said. "He made some vile remarks to her, which I will repeat to the police myself if I have to."

"Is she suspended?" Dad asked. "My wife and I would like to know."

"No," said Mrs. Guten. "We just want to know if she has anything to say about why James might have behaved the way he did toward these two boys. James's parents claim there must have been bullying because of James's, uh, lifestyle. But James won't tell us. If we don't have a complaint, we have nothing to investigate."

Dad looked at me. His eyes were searching, sad. "TJ, do you have anything to say?"

"Honey?" Mom said, touching my hand.

I didn't feel anything at that moment, not guilt or fear or remorse, not a thing. So I didn't understand why I was trembling.

"No," I said.

"Then we are finished here," Mom said, and we got up to leave. Dad followed and shut the door behind us. Mom put her arm around me as we walked to the parking lot.

"Snibley," she murmured.

"TJ, that boy could have gotten you in a lot of trouble," Dad said.

"Drop it, Tony," Mom said. "I swear to God."

That night I found out from Pan that his experience in the office had made mine look like a birthday party. Ada, Pan's mother, had smiled all the way through it, but in a deranged way. Kevin had told them that the school had not protected their son, and Pan was being punished for standing up for himself.

"We have a zero tolerance policy here, Mr. Ashford,"

Dr. Jackson had said. "We can't allow James to return to school when he's proven to be a danger to other students."

"You don't think James has been in danger? You know the score."

Mrs. Guten had said that they wanted to investigate any claims and that Torno and Samsonite would be punished if it was proven that they had tormented Pan. But Pan had never complained about them, not all year, and he was still saying nothing.

"So it's James's fault," Kevin had said. "If he had just told on his classmates, this never would have happened. Of course he doesn't want to say anything. You know how these things work. Don't be naive. How can you expect a teenage boy to do your jobs for you?"

Dr. Jackson had replied that considering the circumstances, Pan was lucky the parents of the boys had chosen not to get the police involved.

"Why didn't you, then?" Ada asked. "You missed an opportunity."

"We don't call the police," Mrs. Guten said. "The parents have to initiate that."

"Thanks for the primer," Ada said. "I'll remember that the next time someone attacks my son."

"Of course they didn't want to press charges," Kevin said. "Would you want everyone in Mungers Mills to know a boy like James had beaten you up?"

Mrs. Guten repeated that they would investigate Pan's having been bullied, but since he was putting forth no defense, they had no choice but to act on what had been witnessed. He had beaten two kids with a tennis racket in plain sight of a bus driver, who had fainted and had to be brought to the emergency room.

Pan told me this is where it got really nasty. Ada turned to Mrs. Guten and said, "This must be very difficult for you. A single, middle-aged woman. When did you add the *Mrs.* to your name?"

Pan said that judging by her reaction, Mrs. Guten had not seen that coming. But despite the booby trap, she and Dr. Jackson were intractable. Pan was suspended for five days. When Ada and Kevin objected, Pan finally broke in, "I'll take the suspension. I just want to get out of this place. I hate it here."

"You can request a superintendent's hearing," Dr. Jackson said.

"No," Pan said. "I don't want to see any more of you. Just get me out of here."

"We have decided to assign James a home tutor," Mrs. Guten said.

"Yes," said Dr. Jackson. "We're not required by law to do so, since James is seventeen, but in this case we're making an exception."

This patronizing was all Ada needed to fully melt down. She actually got up and started for them. Pan said

Mrs. Guten and Dr. Jackson had their heads back like they were watching a hatchet murder. He was terrified himself.

"Kevin held her back," Pan said, "but he didn't apologize for her. He said manners were for charm schools, and that they were total incompetents and cowards. Then we left."

"It sounds horrible."

"Just another outing with the family. It only could have been better if my real father had shown up to lecture them about political action committees."

"I know I'll never get an answer I can understand, but why didn't you back your parents? Why didn't you say something or let me say something? All those times?"

"I don't know exactly why," he said. "I guess I'm like you in a way. I like to keep my humiliations to myself. But it's all over. We're moving."

chapter thirty-four

As much as I may have cherished things staying safe
and static—or sailing side by side—life was doing neither. My best friend was moving. The pharmacy was
closing.

Tammie told me my first night back after the incident, and she insinuated that my behavior had something to do with it. But eventually she let on that the
funding for the new residences had not come through,
that instead the agency was moving all its people outside of town into fewer, bigger places. Then she grabbed
me and hugged me and said, "TJ, I know you'll find
another job. It won't be so easy for me."

"You'll find another one, Tammie. You will. This
was just a stop along the way."

"No, no, I worked my way up to manager here."

I didn't correct her.

She started to cry into my blouse. "That's not going to happen easy for me again."

I let her weep. I would have thought Tammie's crying would sound like a cat's, but she was almost noiseless.

The pharmacy closing was the prelude for the first real grief of my life, Pan's leaving. I couldn't handle even the thought. Maybe his parents would change their minds and stay. But they all wanted to go now. Pan could take his finals, and then it was just a matter of time. Kevin, who had been putting feelers out for a while anyway, had found a techie job in Brookline, outside of Boston. Their house hadn't sold, but that wasn't stopping them. Pan needed to start fresh again, with a new school record.

"I guess he shouldn't have hit them," Caspar said on the last day of school as we rode in his truck. There was no walking home with Pan anymore.

"That's what I thought at first. That's what I said to him. But didn't they deserve it?"

"They deserved something. But he did the wrong thing. He got himself in trouble instead of them."

"But what else could he do? Really, if he had gone to Guten before, would it have done any good?"

"She could have gotten them suspended. Or something."

"But she would have had to follow him around. She can't keep track of everything that goes on in that school."

"I still think he should have done something else. I really wish he had."

I thought about this. He was right, and yet Pan was right too.

"Cas," I said, "remember how you put Samsonite up against your locker?"

"Yes."

"Well, I know Pan shouldn't have done what he did, but what's the difference?"

Caspar kept driving. His mouth hung open, the look he got when transported by thought. His other functions seemed to have stopped. It was as close to criticizing him as I'd ever come. He was silent so long that I was sure he was angry and not going to talk to me.

"I think you're right," he said at last. "I hadn't thought of that."

"But, I mean, I think what you did was okay. I kind of enjoyed seeing Samsonite scared for once."

"The difference between what James did and what I did is that no one saw me. No one who could get me in trouble for it."

I put my hand on the back of his neck, giving him a light massage.

"I could ask myself the same question," he said.

"What should I have done instead when he made me mad? Go running to Mrs. Guten? I would have felt like a fool."

"Yeah."

"I'm very sorry to see James go. It happened so quick." He thought for a while. "Like my dad. Anything can change in a second."

"I know. I hate it."

"I'm sorry for your sake, TJ. And mine too. He was a friend. I don't actually have a lot of friends, you may have noticed." We sat with that a moment. Then he said, "I wonder if anybody really does."

I could feel loss squeezed in the cab with us, like a hitchhiking ghost. I ran my fingers through Caspar's hair. I was not letting him get away, ever.

"It's not fair," he said. "James shouldn't leave. He shouldn't have to."

The words out loud made Pan's moving away irrevocable.

"No," I whispered. "He shouldn't."

The move came fast. There was little time to prepare myself. Pan came to the pharmacy and helped me and Tammie with our final inventory a few times, but I didn't feel the smallest crumb of contentment anymore. Caspar invited us for a pool party of three, which should have been fun. We were listless, though, none of us enjoying the water. Then Caspar suggested what we should have done in the first place.

"Let's have movie night one last time," he said. "Even if it is afternoon."

"We have thousands of titles to choose from," said Pan. And so we went into the cellar on a beautiful summer day.

Pan and I took some long walks, but my heart was always in my throat, and all I could think of was how there wasn't enough time. Also, I was wary of anyone who came near us, who drove by too slowly, even cops, anyone who might be looking for Pan.

At the end of July, he stopped by my house in his mother's car. It was late in the morning, and they were leaving that day. I'd kept hoping for more time, another day or two, but this was it.

Mom had planned to go shopping, but she stayed to say good-bye. Paolo was entranced watching TV, for once not interested in Pan. Dad was at work.

Pan revealed a wrapped gift and placed it in front of Mom.

"Open it," he said.

The wrapping paper was heavy, with ornate, textured designs.

"You shouldn't," Mom said, her eyes ablaze as she undid each fold as if it were a bird's curled wing. Just as delicately, she pried off the tape.

"Can't a boy give his second mom a present once in a while? Now hurry. I can't stand surprises."

"No, I want to use the paper again," she said. "Several times." Then she sucked in a long breath. "James, no. I can't."

"You just did," he said with the corner of a smile.

The sleek brushed-steel laptop computer looked out of context on our enamel table.

"It's too much, no," Mom said. "Take it out of the house this minute. Before I run away with it."

"Nope, it's staying," said Pan. "And it's used, so don't panic. Kevin gets new geek toys every six months. He never misses an opportunity to buy himself a new computer."

"He does know you're giving this away," I said. "Doesn't he?"

"No, I just took it off his desk. Along with his passport and some large bills."

Mom was too enchanted to hear.

"There may still be some porn on the C drive, Mom. I can show you how to erase it. If you want."

Mom nodded, then lifted the top and touched the power button as if it would open the gates to the mansion.

"Oh, it is beautiful," she said. "In my office we used to have a monitor the size of a microwave oven. This is . . . this is . . ."

"A laptop," Pan said. "But it'll defrost things too."

"Pan, that's really generous," I said. "Where's my present?"

"She's in the car," he said. "You and Gram will be very happy together."

"James, I can't." Mom ran her fingers along the smooth steel.

"It's staying. If you don't accept it, my mother will toss it anyway. This move has pretty much put her over the edge."

"In that case," Mom said, and moved slightly to shield it.

"Your mother buys only organic food and throws computers in the trash?" I asked.

"Don't make me explain her. Anyway, it's yours from me, with full approval from my parents. I think Kevin wanted to come himself and give it to you. He was even more excited than I was."

"I'm going to get familiar with this thing. I'm getting ready for my next try at school. One course at a time. Maybe two. The advisor suggested I do a class online. But how was I going to do that? Go to the public library? I'm going to hook up to the Internet before long." She gazed at the thing. Then she looked up.

"No, the first thing I'm going to do is write a letter to that school board about the way they treated you."

When neither of us responded, she said, "Well, thank you, James."

"I can help you when they've got you connected," said Pan. "We'll have to do it over the phone."

We all looked at the laptop, no one commenting on this reminder.

"I'm making lunch for us," Mom said, breaking the silence. "It's a special occasion. It's not often I have company bearing gifts."

Pan was right about my mom's cooking. She could make a savory chipped Formica if she had no other ingredients. We had pasta with cream sauce and bacon and some salad, and for dessert, a cake she had made with ricotta and brown sugar. Pan ate like he had been on a fast.

"I'm sending my own mother back here for lessons," he said. "She was driving sixty miles a week to spend two hundred dollars on natural foods, but it's nothing like this."

"We don't care about bugs or chemicals or genetic modifications here," I said. "We're a proud people."

"You ought to be. More cake, please."

"You realize, James," Mom said, "that I have no choice but to adopt you. If you won't be my son-in-law, you'll just have to be my son."

"I brought the papers," he said. "All you have to do is sign."

"I'm sure you'd love living in our chateau," I said.

"Your chateau is my chateau," Pan said, "but I don't think your father would be too happy about it."

Little bubbles of joy had poked their heads up during lunch. Now Dad, even absent, had popped them all at once. We ate our dessert for a few reflective moments.

Mom broke in with a grunt. "Her father," she said, "is responsible for Paolo. I decide on the next kid." She licked her fork. "Pass me that cake."

She cried when she told Pan good-bye, and he held her like he was leaving her at preschool the first day. She drove away, swiping at her eyes, waving, then shaking her head. Trying to be strong for Mom had made me feel more able to handle my own good-bye.

Pan and I sat on the porch for a while, not talking. I felt like I should say a million things, but nothing seemed important enough.

"I'll write," he said at last.

"No you won't. No one writes."

"True. But I will call. I'm good at calling. I will probably call before we've gotten out of Mohegan County, if not sooner."

But the calls would not be the same. He wouldn't be a few miles away, in the same dull town. He would be in Boston, which was as close to Mungers Mills as Hawaii.

"You'll have e-mail soon," he said. "And pages of

friends. Mom will not be able to resist. She may even start a business online, or find a lover or something."

"I don't want to think about that," I said, "although it would be nice if she found something to do that made her happy."

He put his arm around me. "She would have preferred that you brought out the hetero man in me."

"We both knew that wasn't going to happen."

"No."

"And she wouldn't have cared much for you if I had," I said. "She seems to have contempt for most straight guys."

"Your parents are truly a study in opposites."

"Yep."

"Can I get sickening for a minute, Joto?"

"Are you going to bring up Mom having an affair again?"

"No. I just want to be gooey. I don't like too many people, and since you're one of the few people I can honestly say I loves, I wanted you to know that I think you may have, on occasion . . ."

"What? Tell me. I'm eventually going to cry no matter what you say."

"Good. I would like quite a lot of mourning. Loud, loud mourning."

"Out with it."

"I just mean, I think you brought out . . . I think

you showed me. . . . I see it in you all the time and how you aren't fake about it. Kindness."

"I do love you, Pan," I said, and gulped back a sob.

"Even the part that tried to kill two people with a loaded tennis racket?"

"Even."

"If I had listened to you, I wouldn't be in this mess. What was the point of getting back at those reprobates? They won anyway. No, you always made me think about the right thing to do. I usually ignored you, but you made me think."

"It's okay."

"I am kind of sorry I'm not straight, just because we would have been great together."

That made tears shoot out almost horizontally. "Oh, don't say that."

"But you have Caspar, and you know what's deep, deep inside my heart, down past all the bitterness and disparagement and superiority? I am very happy you found each other."

"Was there something in my mom's cake?"

"Could be. But I really am."

"Yeah? You are?" I tried to breathe normally.

"Deep down, way deep. Mine-shaft deep."

"You were nice to him. We had fun, the three of us." Then I blubbered like my ice-cream cone had fallen straight into a dog's mouth. His arm was tight around me. I had to wipe my eyes and nose with the shoulder of my shirt. When that wave of grief pulled back, he relaxed his grip.

I watched him as he looked up at the sky. "Yeah." He took in a long breath. "He couldn't catch much of a break from me, at first."

He looked back at me, smiling like a grown-up giving comfort, and petted my hair a few strokes. "He is a good guy, Caspar, as guys go. And he's the only one good enough for my girl."

"You sound like the father of the bride," I managed before another spill of tears.

"That's the toast I'll give when you get married. Should we promise? Someday, for the bride and groom, whoever he turns out to be?"

A second wave was cresting, but I tried to inhale deep enough to fight it.

"Nah, let's not," he said. "Most promises don't age very well. We need an easier one. Let's promise to always remember our almost-year together. The tolerable parts. Oh, and our birthday. Those are easy. Promise?"

"I promise," I said, forcing my voice from the back of my throat. "But I am so afraid."

"Afraid of what?"

"I don't want you to be alone. I don't want anyone to hurt you again and again, like they did here."

"I'll be okay. I always am. Kiss from my best girl?"

"I'm snotty," I said, trying to wipe away the various emissions with my hand.

He tipped my head up with his finger. "You're beautiful. Always were. Always will be." He kissed my lips. "Loves ya."

"Loves ya," I squeaked.

He got up, moving with grace and rhythm to his mother's car. His beautiful blond hair disappeared inside.

I went back in the house, trying to keep from crying again which might give Paolo inspiration. But he was still sitting in front of the TV, mesmerized. He was so still, I thought about getting a mirror to check for breath. Then he moved his head and wheezed slightly.

It was risky, but I leaned down and gave him the lightest kiss. He smiled faintly, but didn't stir. I observed his profile. I could already see what he would look like as an old man. His little eyes bulged, his lips were too big, his shape was a bowling ball. So what if he was not going to win any cute baby contests? Fago would reach out from me like magic and wrap itself around him forever.

BK 823.912   M449C
CHRISTMAS HOLIDAY
C1939   15.00 FV

P9-APU-014

3000 436814 30019
St. Louis Community College

823.912 M449c   FV
MAUGHAM
 CHRISTMAS HOLIDAY
                        15.00

WITHDRAWN

 St. Louis Community
College

Library

5801 Wilson Avenue
St. Louis, Missouri 63110

THE WORKS OF
W. SOMERSET MAUGHAM

This is a volume in the Arno Press collection

THE WORKS OF
W. SOMERSET MAUGHAM

Introduction by Michael G. Wood

See last pages of this volume for a complete list of titles.

W. SOMERSET MAUGHAM

Christmas Holiday

ARNO PRESS

A New York Times Company

New York / 1977

Reprint Edition 1977 by Arno Press Inc.

Copyright © 1939 by W. Somerset Maugham.
All Rights Reserved.

Reprinted by permission of
  Doubleday & Company Inc.

THE WORKS OF W. SOMERSET MAUGHAM
ISBN for complete set: 0-405-07804-8
See last pages of this volume for titles.

Manufactured in the United States of America

————◆————

Library of Congress Cataloging in Publication Data

Maugham, William Somerset, 1874-1965.
    Christmas holiday.

    (The works of W. Somerset Maugham)
    Reprint of the ed. published by Doubleday, Doran,
Garden City, N. Y.
    I. Title. II. Series: Maugham, William
Somerset, 1874-1965. Works. 1976.
PZ3.M442Ch12 [PR6025.A86]   823'.9'12   75-25351
ISBN 0-405-07809-9

Introduction

"I have put the whole of my life into my books," Somerset Maugham wrote. The remark suggests a career of confession, and it is true that Maugham is the author of one long, intensely autobiographical novel: *Of Human Bondage*. He himself describes the writing of the book as an act of therapy and exorcism:

> My memories would not let me be. They became such a torment that I determined at last to have done with the theatre until I had released myself from them. My book took two years to write. I was disconcerted by its length, but I was not writing to please: I was writing to free myself from an intolerable obsession. I achieved the result I aimed at, for after I had corrected the proofs, I found all those ghosts were laid, and neither the people nor the incidents ever crossed my mind again.

The ghosts had their small revenge, however. When Maugham began to read *Of Human Bondage* for a recording company, some thirty years after the book was published, he broke down and cried, and the record was never made.

Maugham spoke often of the power of writing to allay a writer's sorrows:

> Whenever he has anything on his mind, whether it be a harassing reflection, grief at the death of a friend, unrequited love, wounded pride, anger at the treachery of someone to whom he has shown kindness, in short any emotion or any perplexing thought, he has only to put it down in black and white, using it as the theme of a story or the decoration of an essay, to forget all about it . . .

> . . . illness, privation, his hopes abandoned, his griefs, humiliations, everything is transformed by his power into material and by writing it he can overcome it . . . Nothing befalls him that he cannot transmute into a stanza, a song or a story, and having done this be rid of it. The artist is the only free man.

We may find the completeness and finality of some of those phrases — he has *only* to put it down to forget *all* about it, *nothing* befalls him that he cannot transmute into art — have a rather wishful ring, and of course we don't need Maugham's returning ghosts to remind us that the accounts of the heart are rarely so thoroughly and so easily settled. As Maugham himself says elsewhere, the imagination compensates us for all the things we have missed or lost in life. But if we hadn't missed or lost them we should not need the compensation: "To imagine is to fail; for it is the acknowledgement of defeat in the encounter with reality."

Still, there is nothing odd in Maugham's insistence on writing as exorcism, since the exorcism, at least once, worked well enough for him. It didn't defeat the ghosts for good, but it kept them quiet for a long spell. What is odd, in the light of Maugham's views, is that apart from *Of Human Bondage* there is scarcely an autobiographical work among all the novels, plays, stories, essays and travel books that Maugham wrote in a long and prolific life. Even his autobiography, he tells us in its opening words, is not an autobiography, and a phrase from the beginning of that book sheds some light on this curious puzzle. "In one way or another," Maugham says, "I have used in my writings whatever has happened to me in the course of my life." He means not that he has confessed all but that he hasn't wasted any of his material. It is in this sense that the whole of his life has gone into his books. His books have said as much about him as he is going to say. Before and after *Of Human Bondage* Maugham is not a writer who consoles himself in fiction for distresses suffered in reality. He is a writer who, in and out of fiction, cultivates a blend of irony and controlled curiosity which keeps reality's distresses at a comfortable distance. The ghosts are not exorcised. Where possible, they are headed off before they get a chance to do any haunting.

In spite of the considerable fame of *Of Human Bondage,* this second, more distant Maugham is undoubtedly the more famous one. This is the writer whose cherished themes, as Graham Greene once said, are usually thought to be adultery in China, murder in Malaya and suicide in the South Seas; whose chief subject is the ragged edge of the British Empire. He is Kipling turned inside out, as V. S. Pritchett suggested, discovering that the white man's burden is as often as not the white woman's infidelity, which is in turn a sort of infection by strange places and loneliness. Maugham writes of England too, of course, of country houses and upper-class London and the more respectable fringes of the literary life, but the constant feature of Maugham's stories and plays and novels, whether they are set in Batavia or in Belgrave Square, is Maugham's own wry, observing presence, the weary, witty, detached intelligence which directs the dialogue of the plays and frequently appears to comment on the goings-on in the novels and stories. It is a portrait of the artist as a man of the world, and it can produce a certain glibness. On the other hand, there is mostly an undercurrent of worry even in the glibness, a nervous streak in the man of the world, and it is the mixture that matters. Maugham speaks of ethics, for example. "It may be that in goodness we may see, not a reason for life nor an explanation, but an extenuation . . ." The idea is familiar enough, but the word *extenuation* gives a disconcerting twist to the tail of the sentence. Or again: "He was developing a sense of humor, and found he had a knack of saying bitter things, which caught people on the raw . . ." Is that what we usually mean by humor? Sometimes Maugham's irony is more carefully and consciously balanced: "I do not think a thought of self ever entered her untidy head. She was a miracle of unselfishness. It was really hardly human." Sometimes it is frankly comic: "Miss Jones was resolutely cheerful. She grimly looked on the bright side of things." Sometimes it conceals a subdued sense of outrage:

> When we went there (a missionary is speaking) they had no sense of sin at all. They broke the commandments one after the other and never knew they were doing wrong. And I think that was the most difficult part of my work, to instill into the natives the sense of sin.

And sometimes it brings off extraordinary, shifting combinations of denunciation and tribute, subtle praise and sharp blame:

> Hypocrisy is the most difficult and nerve-racking vice that any man can pursue; it needs an unceasing vigilance and a rare detachment of spirit. It cannot, like adultery or gluttony, be practised at spare moments; it is a whole-time job.

Maugham is not a difficult or complicated writer, and we can miss all the undercurrents in his prose and still enjoy him a great deal. But the undercurrents are likely to keep Maugham's writing alive when the simpler enjoyment has faded, and in any case I wonder whether anyone misses them entirely. They are like a nameless taste caught up in a taste we know well, a touch of bitterness in a sweet dish — or to be more precise, a touch of genuine bitterness in a bitter-seeming dish, a flavour of real, unnerving acrimony in the midst of a calm and worldly cynicism. Certainly a sense of these undercurrents is what separates Maugham's serious admirers from his serious detractors. Thus Edmund Wilson, seeing nothing of the sceptic within the popular writer, could say Maugham was "a half-trashy novelist, who writes badly, but is patronised by half-serious readers, who do not care much about writing", while Cyril Connolly, who could hardly be called a half-serious reader, saw mainly the scepticism, and insisted on Maugham's continuing dissatisfaction with the things that satisfy too many of us, on his discontent "with the banal routine of self-esteem and habit, with which most of us . . . fidget away our one-and-only lives." Both men are more or less right, because Maugham really had it both ways. He was one of the most successful writers of the century, and yet he seems to peer out at us from the heart of his success with a disappointed, dissenting face, seems to assure us in a whisper that money and fame are merely toys, ways of passing the time, better than most and certainly worth having, but not the secret of eternal life or even, when it comes down to it, of much temporal happiness.

Maugham's friends and family agree in finding him elusive. "I am indebted to him for nearly fifty years of kindness and hospitality," Noel Coward wrote, "but I cannot truthfully say that I really knew him intimately." "Looking back," Maugham's nephew Robin Maugham says, "I realize that though I sometimes feared him, I was fond of him; but I am afraid I never understood him." This is exactly the quality of Maugham's writing. He is present to the reader, an engaging, even a compelling story-teller — it is very hard to put down a Maugham story or novel once you have taken it up — but he is a man who is giving nothing away. Maugham's prose is lucid and musical, but above all it is remarkable for what it *doesn't* say. Consider this little story, one of Maugham's working notes:

> The peacock. We were driving through the jungle. It was not thick and presently we caught sight of a peacock among the trees with its beautiful tail outspread. It walked, a proud, magnificent object, treading the ground with a peculiar delicacy, with a sort of deliberation, and its walk was so elegant, so wonderfully graceful that it recalled to my memory Nijinsky stepping on to the stage at Covent Garden and walking with just such a delicacy, grace and elegance. I have seldom seen a sight more thrilling than that peacock threading its solitary way through the jungle. My companion told the driver to stop and seized his gun.
>
> "I'm going to have a shot at it."
>
> My heart stopped still. He fired, and I hoped he'd miss, but he didn't. The driver jumped out of the car and brought back the dead bird which a moment before had been so exultantly alive. It was a cruel sight.
>
> We ate the breast for dinner that night. The flesh was white, tender and succulent; it was a welcome change from the scraggy chickens which are brought to the table evening after evening in India.

Is there sarcasm there? A comment on the sudden switches of human feeling? A dark warning about the transience of beauty and the lure of food? No, there is just a vivid unsettling sequence: the bird is alive, the bird is dead, the bird is eaten. All interpretation, all attempts to say what such a sequence *means,* are left to us. Maugham merely records the sequence.

In his life and in his writing, Maugham appears to have found a tone which was a perfect disguise, which kept the world away. Even the malice which many often-told stories attribute to him can be seen as part of a role he is playing. "Tra-la-la-la," Maugham is supposed to have sung when he received the news of the death of his wife, divorced from him some twenty years earlier. "No more alimony. Tra-la-, tra-la." Perhaps Maugham's real feelings corresponded closely enough to the feelings he was expressing. But the expression itself still contains a large element of pose: there is a sense of the audience there. Somerset Maugham, seventy years old, is playing at being Somerset Maugham, the shocking, wicked old man. Behind that role, another Maugham, quite unknowable, entertaining who knows what complex configurations of guilt and joy and regret and relief and perfect indifference, lives his entirely private life. "I have put the whole of my life into my books." That innocent-seeming sentence turns into a sly joke. Both books and life for Maugham, apart from *Of Human Bondage* and the painful experiences that went into it, were a system of defences, high walls around a very secret self.

William Somerset Maugham was born in Paris in 1874, the youngest of six sons. His father was solicitor to the British Embassy, and his mother, generally acknowledged to have been a beautiful and charming woman, was well-known in Parisian high society. Maugham spoke only French until he was nine or ten years old. His mother died when he was eight, his father died two years later, and Maugham was sent to live with his uncle and aunt in Whitestable, on the coast of Kent, in England. He spent a number of miserable years there, interspersed in term-time with equally miserable periods at the King's School, Canterbury — all to be recorded with unforgiving anger in *Of Human Bondage*. The young Maugham had a stammer which he felt to be a severe handicap, and which never left him, although in later life he converted it into something of an asset in story-telling. Garson Kanin describes a speech made by Maugham, which began, "There are many . . . virtues in . . . growing old." A long pause followed, which lengthened into an uncomfortable silence. Finally Maugham continued, "I'm just . . . trying . . . to think what they are."

In 1890, Maugham contracted tuberculosis, and underwent a cure at Hyéres in the south of France. A year later he finished his secondary schooling and went to Heidelberg, in Germany, for a year, where he attended lectures at the university and began to take an interest in the theatre. In 1892, he entered St. Thomas' Medical School in London, and in 1897, having served as an intern and delivered some sixty-three babies, he qualified as a doctor, although he was never to practise. Maugham's first novel, *Liza of Lambeth*, based on his medical experiences in the slums and at the hospital, was published in 1897, and on the strength of its moderate success he decided to devote his life to writing. For the next few years he lived in Spain, Italy, London and Paris, published stories and novels, and wrote plays. These were the years of *The Making of a Saint* (1898), *The Hero* (1901), *Mrs. Craddock* (1902), *The Merry-Go-Round* (1904) and *The Magician* (1908) — all novels — and *Orientations* (1899), a collection of short stories. Maugham's first stage success was *Lady Frederick,* produced in London in 1907, and the following year saw two more hits — *Jack Straw* and *Mrs. Dot* — and one near-flop — *The Explorer* — so that four of Maugham's plays were then running in London at one time, and a cartoon published in *Punch* showed Shakespeare biting his nails and brooding in front of the boards which advertised Maugham's four productions. Not all his subsequent plays were to be resounding successes, but many of them were, with long runs both in England and America. Almost overnight, Maugham had become a playwright, with a major reputation, and that he remained until *Sheppey,* his last play, was performed in 1933, and for some time afterwards, of course.

When war came to Europe in 1914, Maugham joined a Red Cross unit, and it was in Belgium that he corrected the proofs of *Of Human Bondage,* published the following year. Soon, however, he was transferred to the Intelligence Service, on the grounds that the writer's trade was a good cover for a secret agent. "The work appealed," Maugham wrote later, "both to my sense of romance and my sense of the ridiculous." His missions took him to Switzerland, the South Seas and Russia — this last excursion involving an attempt to halt the Revolution of 1917. Much of his experience at this time found its way into *Ashenden,* a collection of short stories published in 1928, the first (and still one of the best) of the works of anti-romantic spy fiction, a portrait of the grubby, heartless world of espionage which points away from John Buchan's *The Thirty-nine Steps,* for example, and towards John Le Carré's *The Spy Who Came In From The Cold.*

In the midst of his activities as writer and spy, Maugham somehow found time to carry on an affair with, and then to marry Syrie Wellcome in 1916. The marriage was not a happy one; it ended in divorce in 1927. There was one child, Liza.

Towards the end of the war, Maugham's tuberculosis flared up again, and he spent two years in a sanatorium in Scotland. "He enjoyed his illness," Maugham's biographer Richard A. Cordell writes. And Maugham himself later said, "I had a grand time. I discovered for the first time in my life how very delightful it is to lie in bed . . . I delighted in the privacy of my room with the immense window wide open to the starry winter night. It gave me a delicious sense of security, aloofness and freedom."

In 1919, Maugham published *The Moon and Sixpence,* a novel suggested by the life of the painter Gauguin, and in 1925 he published *The Painted Veil,* a novel with a contemporary Chinese setting, but based on an incident in Dante. Several of Maugham's best-known plays — *The Circle* (1921), *East of Suez* (1922), *The Constant Wife* (1926), *The Sacred Flame* (1928) — were produced in the twenties, and there were also three volumes of short stories: *The Trembling of a Leaf* (1921), *The Casuarina Tree* (1926), and as already mentioned, *Ashenden* (1928). Maugham travelled a great deal in these years — to the Far East, the Near East, to America, to North Africa — and wrote two remarkable travel books: *On a Chinese Screen* (1922) and *The Gentleman in the*

Parlour (1930). In 1928 he bought the Villa Mauresque, a house in the south of France, at St. Jean-Cap-Ferrat, between Monaco and Nice, and it was there that he lived for the rest of his life when he wasn't travelling or uprooted by war. He spent the years of the second world war in America, mainly in North Carolina at the house of his publisher, Nelson Doubleday, and returned to the Villa Mauresque in 1946.

In 1930, Maugham published *Cakes and Ale,* a bitter and witty novel about a famous writer and his two successive, contrasting wives, and a work which many people, myself included, regard as Maugham's finest achievement. It was followed by eight more novels, the last of which is *Catalina* (1948) and the most important of which is *The Razor's Edge* (1944). There were five more collections of short stories, some essays and criticism and the literary last will and testament which is called *The Summing Up* (1938). In 1949 Maugham brought out *A Writer's Notebook,* a selection from his working notes taken over nearly sixty years — the first entry is dated 1892 — and in 1952, in a preface to the second volume of his collected short stories, he took his leave as a writer of fiction. If a writer is "so impudent," he wrote, "as to live to a ripe age," then "the time comes at last when, having given what he has to give, his powers fail . . . It is well then if he can bring himself to cease writing stories which might just as well have remained unwritten . . . I have written my last story." Maugham was seventy-eight years old. He continued to write essays, but in 1959 he had most of his remaining papers burned, although some, apparently, did survive the raid. At the age of ninety-one, seriously ill, his memory failing, this man who had once thought of committing suicide at sixty-five, but who now clung to life with the tenacity he had himself described, with some distaste, some fifty years before — "He was set upon one thing indomitably," he wrote of his hero's moribund uncle in *Of Human Bondage,* "and that was living, just living" — had a stroke, lost consciousness and soon died. His ashes were buried in the grounds of the King's School, Canterbury, which was home, of a sort, after all.

"For many years I have been described as a cynic." Maugham's supposed cynicism is partly a matter of his aloofness, of the careful privacy he preserved in his life and his work. This aloofness, as I suggested earlier, is a complicated affair, a game of mischief and masquerade as well as a means of self-protection. But it is also, at times, simply aloofness, absence. Maugham often seems to move his fictional characters around with a chilly, clinical indifference to their feelings, and while the following statement is impressively honest, it doesn't exactly warm the heart:

> I have been interested in men in general not for their own sakes, but for the sake of my work. I have not, as Kant enjoined, regarded each man as an end in himself, but as material that might be useful to me as a writer.

Maugham tended to see people as elements in a pattern, and when he glimpsed, or could invent, a pattern in the lives he observed or encountered, he had a story. One of his notes, for example, describes a successful and much-admired woman who is unhappy until she falls in love with a man much younger than herself, who subsequently dies in an air crash. "Her friends were afraid she would commit suicide. Not at all. She became happy, fat and contented. She had had her tragedy." Obviously there is an interesting human truth in such a reversal of what we would all expect, but above all there is a pattern, a marked neatness of design. Maugham looked for the same thing in his own life, thought of writing a last novel about the London slums because his first novel had been set there, spoke of completing the edifice of his life's works by writing *The Summing Up:*

> If I live I shall write other books, for my amusement and I hope for the amusement of my readers, but I do not think they will add anything essential to my design. The house is built.

There is a striking fidelity here to the philosophy developed by Philip Carey, the young hero of *Of Human Bondage.* Life has no meaning, Philip decides, so the best we can do is to treat life as if it were a rich carpet, and trace out the designs of our doings on it:

> There was one pattern, the most obvious, perfect, and beautiful, in which a man was born, grew to manhood, married, produced children, toiled for his bread, and died; but there were others, intricate and wonderful, in which happiness did not enter and in which success was not attempted; and in them might be discovered a troubling grace. Some lives . . . the blind indifference of chance cut off while the design was still imperfect; and then the solace was comfortable that it did not matter; other lives . . . offered a pattern which was difficult to follow: the point of view had to be shifted and old standards had to be altered before one could understand that such a life was its own justification.

The troubling grace of a life without happiness and without success is a powerful notion, and troubling grace is perhaps the chief quality of Maugham's best work, which creates the sense of a fragile order being rescued from an encroaching confusion. But the rest of the passage has an awkward complacency — "in such a philosophy there is consolation aplenty even for the least consolable of lives," — since everything is bound to make a pattern of some sort and suggests an instinct for tidiness rather than any large depth of sensibility or intellect. Maugham recognized this tendency in himself when he spoke of the "tightness of effect" and the "sensation of airlessness" provoked by fiction that is too well-made, and of course it is present in the remarks I quoted near the beginning of this piece, where literature is seen as too neat a solution to the upsets of life. Interestingly enough, one of the best of all Maugham's stories, *The Lotus Eater,* portrays a man who shapes his life perfectly, only to discover that his nerve is not as good as he thought it was. At the age of thirty-five Thomas Wilson has left England and the bank he worked in, and settled in Capri, where he leads a modest but pleasant and carefree existence. He has just enough money to last him until he is sixty, and then he intends to take his own life. "Don't you think after twenty-five years of perfect happiness one ought to be satisfied to call it a day?" he asks. When he reaches sixty, though, Wilson keeps postponing his final act, subsists on credit as long as his credit lasts, botches an attempt at suicide, and lives out the rest of his life, sick and poor and humiliated, on the charity of his old landlord. The story bears a disturbing, prophetic relation to Maugham's own end, serene at sixty-four ("I look forward to old age without dismay"), prepared for death at seventy-five ("I am on the wing"), but hanging on in angry senility by the time he was eighty-six, quarrelling with his family, and publishing a rancourous memoir about his marriage. As Maugham must have known all along, there are many things more important than patterns.

What seems to be Maugham's cynicism, then, is often merely his aloofness or his tidiness. But a question remains, which is not a question of Maugham's manner but of what he has to *say,* explicitly and implicitly. "I have been accused of making men out worse than they are," he said. "I do not think I have done this. All I have done is to bring into prominence certain traits that many writers shut their eyes to." Perhaps. There is a great deal of cruelty and violence and revenge in Maugham's fiction. Mackintosh, a British administrator in Samoa, so hates his superior that he leaves his gun lying around for a hostile native to use on the hated man. When the native does use it, Mackintosh, in an excess of guilt, walks out into the lagoon and shoots himself. Another administrator, in Borneo, has a subordinate who arouses such anger in the natives that they kill him. The administrator feels a great, quiet exultation: he had disliked the man, and is delighted to be rid of him. A husband finds out about his wife's infidelity, but creates no fuss and causes no trouble. He simply makes sure that she knows he knows. Another husband in the same situation takes his wife off with him to a cholera-infected town. When she asks him, later, whether he meant to kill her that way, he says, after a long hesitation, "At first." He himself dies of cholera, and she survives, to return to England.

Obviously popular fiction feeds on melodrama, which in turn feeds on acts of violence, but there is in Maugham an insistence on retaliation which goes well beyond the needs of the kind of fiction he is writing. There is a recurring pleasure in the sight of an enmity or a rancour which is actively satisfied, which finds a thorough, practical expression. We should not forget, either, that Maugham can take an almost aesthetic delight in random acts of mischief and malice. In the story *A Friend in Need* a kindly, respectable, humorous man sends another, younger man off on a long and dangerous swim, with the promise that he will give him a job when he gets back. The young man drowns in the offshore currents, and when asked whether he knew the young man would drown, the older man says, "Well, I hadn't got a vacancy in my office at the moment." Maugham also tells the story of Elizabeth Russell, who is said to have read out to her sick husband those passages in a book of hers where he appeared in a damaging light. When she finished, he turned his face to the wall and died. Maugham, with obvious relish, asks Mrs. Russell whether this terrible tale is true, and she looks blandly at him and says, "He was very ill. He would have died in any case."

A moralist may frown at all this, and a sentimentalist will be distressed. Maugham himself is being slightly disingenuous when he says he simply tells the truth in such matters, since he is clearly selecting, with great skill, those truths which have an ugly, malevolent glitter to them. Nevertheless, I think there is a genuine, uncompromising vision here, as well as a lot of gratuitous cruelty. At his best Maugham forces us to see that hatred has its own authentic joys and rewards, and I think of a line in Emily Brontë's *Wuthering Heights,* where Heathcliff is admonished to leave his revenge to God, and replies, "No, God won't have the satisfaction that I shall." The real question, perhaps, is not so much whether we have all felt such hatred at any time in our lives as whether we would be able to admit it if we did. There is a kind of courage in Maugham's allowing those grim and terminal revenges to have their day in his fiction.

The ground for most of these revenges in Maugham is humiliation, and Maugham's sourest and most famous contribution to the moral life of our century is probaly his diagnosis of love itself as above all, humiliation. Love in Maugham is either a helpless, unconditional surrender to instinct, an undignified collapse of all our best intentions; or it is a quest for disgrace, an infatuation with a creature we cannot respect and who will bring us only confused and ignoble pain. There is a sequence in *Of Human Bondage* which at first sight appears mismanaged, a clumsy attempt at pathos and suspense, but which then emerges as a strong portrait of love as masochism. Philip Carey introduces Mildred, the girl he loves, to his handsome and lively best friend, and Mildred and the best friend, predictably enough, go off together. It is only when we understand that Philip has not made a mistake, that indeed he has got just what he wanted, that things fall into place. Masochism, Maugham wrote much later, "is a sexual desire in a man to be subjected to ill treatment, physical and mental, by the woman he loves." Philip doesn't seek or receive physical ill treatment from Mildred, but he suffers mental unkindnesses constantly, eagerly. Having brought his friend and his girl together for his own anguish, he is soon offering them money so that they can spend a weekend in Oxford without him. Again, with this view of love as with Maugham's cases of satisfied hatred and cruelty, the question is not whether it is true in any complete sense, whether it is the whole story about human affections. Plainly it is not. The question, as with Proust, for example, is how we are to defend ourselves against a view of love which is obviously true *enough* to shake our most cherished assumptions about our relations with the people we care about.

Maugham was clear, even harsh, about his own limitations. He had some power of invention, he said, but only "small power of imagination."

> I have taken living people and put them into the situations, tragic or comic, that their characters suggested. I might well say that they invented their own stories . . .

> I knew that I had no lyrical quality. I had a small vocabulary and no efforts that I could make to enlarge it much availed me. I had little gift of metaphor; the original and striking simile seldom occurred to me.

The lucidity and simplicity of Maugham's style have often been praised. It is a style which does its job, but it is also the style of a man who has an ear for the flow and fall of a sentence, and occasionally there *is* a metaphor or a simile which stays in the mind. In the cholera epidemic in *The Painted Veil,* death is said to stand round the corner, "taking lives like a gardener digging up potatoes," and the casual, domestic image is perfect, just what is needed. Above all, of course, Maugham is a *readable* writer, a man who knows the art of keeping his audience with him, and the best test of his readability is to read him. A simple illustration of the way he makes himself readable, though, is his knack of suggesting exotic locations without brandishing foreign names or going in for that rather flashy familiarity with strange customs which is characteristic of Lawrence and Hemingway and Durrell and Lowry. A mention of the Pacific, of a Chinese cook, of hot weather, a reef and a lagoon, and we are in Samoa. Sunshine, coolies, rickshaws, a Chinese clerk, an electric fan, and we are in Singapore. These scenes are set with an immaculate discretion. And of course there is always a story being told.

This is true even of Maugham's non-fiction. His travel books are the notes of a man looking for stories. *On a Chinese Screen,* for example, is a set of jottings which Maugham decided to leave as jottings, but some of them were so close to fiction that he could include them, much later, among his *Complete Short Stories.* Similarly, Maugham's essays and criticism are composed mainly of anecdotes. Maugham looks at his favourite writers much as he looks at the people around him, and *The Art of Fiction,* an introduction to ten great novelists and their novels, spends most of its time telling the "stories," as it were, of Fielding and Jane Austen and Stendhal and Balzac and Melville and others. Maugham's criticism is limited by a rather depressing common sense — it may be true that obscurities arise in *Othello* because Shakespeare couldn't think of a better way of doing things, but I think a critic has to do better than that by way of interpretation all the same — and by the taste for tidiness I have already mentioned. I doubt whether many people would agree, for example, that *Wuthering Heights* is "clumsily constructed." Still, he has excellent taste and a gift for making fine and useful distinctions. He is a good companion rather than a provocative critic, and this is perhaps as it should be. Essays, travel books, over a hundred short stories: such works are the natural, continuing expression of the life of a writer who reads a lot and travels a great deal.

The plays and the novels are a slightly different matter, if only because they involve larger and more sustained excursions away from the pose of the casual story-teller. Maugham's plays are skillful and intelligent, but even the best of them — *Our Betters, The Circle, The Constant Wife* — seem rather brittle now, caught in a rather strange zone between nature and artifice. There is an air of elegant clockwork about them, which oddly enough tends to make them seem insufficiently artificial, makes them seem as if they were not quite acting on the strength of their own conventions, so that they have neither the force of naturalism nor the pace and folly of the plays of Congreve, say, or Wilde. Nevertheless, they are consistently playable and entertaining, and full of good lines:

— You have no heart, and you can't imagine that anyone else should have.

— I have plenty of heart, but it beats for people of my own class . . .

— If a man's unfaithful to his wife she's an object of sympathy, whereas if a woman's unfaithful to her husband he's merely an object of ridicule.

— That is one of those conventional prejudices that sensible people must strive to ignore . . .

Among the novels, *Of Human Bondage* is taken by many people to be Maugham's masterpiece, his "one great novel," according to Malcolm Cowley, who speculated on what he called the Somerset Maugham enigma: "Why has he never written another book that was half so good as *Of Human Bondage?*" The short answer, I would say, is that he has, and several of them at that. *Of Human Bondage* is a patient and precise account of a boy's growing up, and the story of Philip Carey's tortured, grovelling love for Mildred is intense and compelling. But otherwise there is a certain blandness about the novel which makes it easy to read but also easy to forget. It is not to be compared with its close contemporaries, Joyce's *Portrait of the Artist as a Young Man* or Lawrence's *Sons and Lovers. Cakes and Ale,* on the other hand, Maugham's own favourite among his novels, escapes blandness because it is so fiercely and unfailingly witty, and because Maugham is on his true home ground, talking not about his personal past but about the business of writing, which is the consuming interest of his present life. The book opens with a cruel portrait of Maugham's friends Hugh Walpole, but the portrait is also a mocking version of Maugham himself as the successful writer who has made a little talent go a very long way. People have been shocked by the book's disrespectful depiction of a figure much resembling Thomas Hardy, who had died only two years before the book appeared. But at this distance in time Maugham's view of Hardy seems extremely affectionate. Hardy is not the lofty and magisterial man of letters he is supposed to be, but he is something better. He is perky and alive and irreverent, the model of a man who has managed to survive his own greatness. Of Maugham's other novels, *The Moon and Sixpence, The Painted Veil* and *The Razor's Edge* are the most successful, although all three of them tend to alternate between masterly scenes and moments of glibness. But then even *Catalina* and *Then and Now,* which Maugham's admirers usually concede to the opposition, seem to me genuinely enjoyable, and that, perhaps, is the truest measure of Maugham's achievement. He never wrote an uninteresting book, and no doubt that is the right reward for knowing your own limitations so well.

Some critics rate Maugham's stories above his novels, but I think that only serves to displace the central question. It is true that the best of Maugham's stories are as good as the best of his novels, but the question is, How good is that? Maugham himself thought he had only "slender baggage" for his journey into posterity, and saw himself as standing "in the very front row of the second-raters." But then that judgement implies a view of who the other second-raters are. Richard A. Cordell puts Maugham alongside Thackeray, Gide, Hardy, Conrad, Bennett and Galsworthy in that category, which I think both subtly inflates Maugham's standing and confuses the issue. On the one hand at least three of those writers are first-rate by any standard, and on the other Maugham is almost certainly more important than Galsworthy, for example. His true peers, perhaps, to take an instance from each of three succeeding generations, are Arnold Bennett, Aldous Huxley and Graham Greene: honourable company, it seems to me. But such games are better not played too long. The names serve only as bearings, means of finding Maugham's domain on the map of modern literature.

Maugham's legacy to other writers is an ideal of perfect craftsmanship, and a reassurance that an author can be extremely popular without sacrificing either his intelligence or his culture. His larger, more general legacy to literature, I think, is the record of a lifelong exploration of a crippling respectability, of a sense of the pressure of opinion which is all the more painful because you know the pressure would vanish if you were brave enough to ignore it. "The Maughams had the intense respectability of the upper middle class," Maugham's nephew Robin writes. Maugham appears never to have felt that being a writer was a respectable profession, and of course his own homosexuality can't have helped much. He told Robin that his greatest mistake was to have persuaded himself that he was "three quarters normal and . . . only a quarter . . . queer — whereas really it was the other way round." Some of Maugham's heroes defeat respectability, flout convention and manage to live a life of their own. But his work contains far more victims than heroes, and most of his characters either succumb to propriety and regret their cowardice for the rest of their days, or they throw over the traces, and then sink further and further into disgrace and degradation, ending all too often in suicide. Maugham plays both roles in these stories, for all his aloofness and cynicism. He is the person who fails and the society which rules on the failure, he is respectability's enemy and the agent of respectability itself. V. S. Pritchett suggested that Maugham's fiction catered to our wish to be worldly and wise in the manner of Maugham's much-travelled, never-ruffled narrators, and that this accounted largely for his huge success. I think the fiction speaks to something more serious than that. It speaks to our profoundly divided social loyalties, to our mixed satisfaction and resentment at the lives we live, to our longing to drop out of it all like Paul Gauguin and to our knowledge that we are really not going to do it. It doesn't ask us to leave the world or change the world, and it doesn't invite us to indulge in regret. It does confront us with the long disappointment which is one of the costs of life in human society, and it reminds us how much of our time, even when we are quite alone, is spent in the confining stare of other people's eyes.

Michael Wood
Columbia University

W. SOMERSET MAUGHAM

Christmas Holiday

NEW YORK

Doubleday, Doran & Company, Inc.

1939

PRINTED AT THE *Country Life Press*, GARDEN CITY, N. Y., U. S. A.

CL

COPYRIGHT, 1939
BY W. SOMERSET MAUGHAM
ALL RIGHTS RESERVED

FIRST EDITION

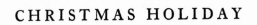
CHRISTMAS HOLIDAY

i

WITH A JOURNEY BEFORE HIM, Charley Mason's mother was anxious that he should make a good breakfast, but he was too excited to eat. It was Christmas Eve and he was going to Paris. They had got through the mass of work that quarter-day brought with it, and his father, having no need to go to the office, drove him to Victoria. When they were stopped for several minutes by a traffic block in Grosvenor Gardens Charley, afraid that he would miss the train, went white with anxiety. His father chuckled.

"You've got the best part of half an hour."

But it was a relief to arrive.

"Well, good-bye, old boy," his father said, "have a good time and don't get into more mischief than you can help."

The steamer backed into the harbour and the sight of the gray, tall, dingy houses of Calais filled him with elation. It was a raw day and the wind blew bitter. He strode along the platform as though he walked on air. The Golden Arrow, powerful, rich and impressive, which stood there waiting for him, was no ordinary

train, but a symbol of romance. While the light lasted
he looked out of the window and he laughed in his heart
as he recognized the pictures he had seen in galleries;
sand dunes, with patches of grass gray under the leaden
sky, cramped villages of poor persons' houses with slate
roofs, and then a broad, sad landscape of ploughed
fields and sparse bare trees; but the day seemed in a
hurry to be gone from the cheerless scene and in a short
while, when he looked out, he could see only his own
reflection and behind it the polished mahogany of the
Pullman. He wished he had come by air. That was what
he'd wanted to do, but his mother had put her foot
down; she'd persuaded his father that in the middle of
winter it was a silly risk to take, and his father, usually
so reasonable, had made it a condition of his going on
the jaunt that he should take the train.

Of course Charley had been to Paris before, half a
dozen times at least, but this was the first time that he
had ever gone alone. It was a special treat that his
father was giving him for a special reason: he had com-
pleted a year's work in his father's office and had passed
the necessary examinations to enable him to follow use-
fully his chosen calling. For as long as Charley could
remember, his father and mother, his sister Patsy and
he had spent Christmas at Godalming with their cousins
the Terry-Masons; and to explain why Leslie Mason,
after talking over the matter with his wife, had one
evening, a smile on his kindly face, asked his son
whether instead of coming with them as usual he would
like to spend a few days in Paris by himself, it is necessary to go back a little. It is necessary indeed to go back

to the middle of the nineteenth century, when an indus-
trious and intelligent man called Sibert Mason, who had
been head gardener at a grand place in Sussex and had
married the cook, bought with his savings and hers a
few acres north of London and set up as a market gardener. Though he was then forty and his wife not far
from it they had eight children. He prospered, and
with the money he made, bought little bits of land in
what was still open country. The city expanded and his
market garden acquired value as a building site; with
money borrowed from the bank he put up a row of
villas and in a short while let them all on lease. It would
be tedious to go into the details of his progress, and it
is enough to say that when he died, at the age of eighty-
four, the few acres he had bought to grow vegetables
for Covent Garden, and the properties he had continued to acquire whenever opportunity presented, were
covered with bricks and mortar. Sibert Mason took care
'that his children should receive the education that had
been denied him. They moved up in the social scale. He
made the Mason Estate, as he had somewhat grandly
named it, into a private company and at his death each
child received a certain number of shares as an inheri-
tance. The Mason Estate was well managed and though
it could not compare in importance with the Westmin-
ster or the Portman Estate, for its situation was modest
and it had long ceased to have any value as a residential
quarter, shops, warehouses, factories, slums, long rows
of dingy houses in two storeys, made it sufficiently prof-
itable to enable its proprietors, through no merit and
little exertion of their own, to live like the gentlemen

and ladies they were now become. Indeed, the head of
the family, the only surviving child of old Sibert's eldest
son, a brother having been killed in the war and a sister
by a fall in the hunting-field, was a very rich man. He
was a member of parliament and at the time of King
George the Fifth's Jubilee had been created a baronet.
He had tacked his wife's name on to his own and was
now known as Sir Wilfred Terry-Mason. The family
had hopes that his staunch allegiance to the Tory party
and the fact that he had a safe seat would result in his
being raised to the peerage.

Leslie Mason, youngest of Sibert's many grandchildren, had been sent to a public school and to Cambridge.
His share in the Estate brought him in two thousand
pounds a year, but to this was added another thousand
which he received as secretary of the company. Once a
year there was a meeting attended by such members
of the family as were in England, for of the third generation some were serving their country in distant parts
of the Empire, and some were gentlemen of leisure
who were often abroad, and with Sir Wilfred in the
chair, he presented the highly satisfactory statement
which the chartered accountants had prepared.

Leslie Mason was a man of varied interests. At this
time he was in the early fifties, tall, with a good figure,
and with his blue eyes, fine gray hair worn rather long,
and high colour, of an agreeable aspect. He looked
more like a soldier or a colonial governor home on
leave than a house agent and you would never have
guessed that his grandfather was a gardener and his
grandmother a cook. He was a good golfer, for which

pastime he had ample leisure, and a good shot. But Leslie Mason was more than a sportsman; he was keenly interested in the arts. The rest of the family had no such foibles and they looked upon Leslie's predilections with an amused tolerance, but when, for some reason or other, one of them wanted to buy a piece of furniture or a picture, his advice was sought and taken. It was natural enough that he should know what he was talking about, for he had married a painter's daughter. John Peron, his wife's father, was a member of the Royal Academy and for a long time, between the eighties and the end of the century, had made a good income by painting pictures of young women in eighteenth-century costume dallying with young men similarly dight. He painted them in gardens of old world flowers, in leafy bowers and in parlours furnished correctly with the chairs and tables of the period. But now when his pictures turned up at Christie's they were sold for thirty shillings or two pounds. Venetia Mason had inherited quite a number when her father died, but they had long stood in a box-room, covered with dust, their faces to the wall; for at this time of day even filial affection could not persuade her that they were anything but dreadful. The Leslie Masons were not in the least ashamed of the fact that his grandmother had been a cook, indeed with their friends they were apt to make a facetious point of it, but it embarrassed them to speak of John Peron. Some of the Mason relations still had on their walls examples of his work; they were a mortification to Venetia.

"I see you've still got father's picture there," she

said. "Don't you think it dates rather? Why don't you put it in one of the spare rooms?"

"My father-in-law was a very charming old man," said Leslie, "with beautiful manners, but I'm afraid he wasn't a very good painter."

"Well, my governor gave a tidy sum for it. It would be absurd to put a picture that cost three hundred pounds in a spare bedroom, but if you feel like that about it, I'll tell you what I'll do, I'll sell it you for a hundred and fifty."

For though in the course of three generations they had become ladies and gentlemen, the Masons had not lost their business acumen.

The Leslie Masons had gone a long way in artistic appreciation since their marriage and on the walls of the handsome new house they now inhabited in Porchester Close were pictures by Wilson Steer and Augustus John, Duncan Grant and Vanessa Bell. There was an Utrillo and a Vuillard, both bought while these masters were of moderate price, and there was a Derain, a Marquet and a Chirico. You could not enter their house, somewhat sparsely furnished, without knowing at once that they were in the movement. They seldom missed a private view and when they went to Paris made a point of going to Rosenberg's and the dealers in the Rue de Seine to have a look at what there was to be seen; they really liked pictures and if they did not buy any before the cultured opinion of the day had agreed on their merits this was due partly to a modest lack of confidence in their own judgement and partly to a fear that they might be making a bad bargain. After all, John Peron's pictures had been praised by the best critics and he had sold them for several hundred pounds apiece, and now what did they fetch? Two or three. It made you careful. But it was not only in painting that they were interested. They loved music; they went to Symphony Concerts throughout the winter; they had their favourite conductors and allowed no social engagements to prevent them from attending their performances. They went to hear the *Ring* once a year. To listen to music was a genuine delight to both of them. They had good taste and discrimination. They were regular first-nighters and they belonged to the societies that produce plays which are supposed to be above the comprehension of plain people. They read promptly the books that were talked about. They did this not only because they liked it, but because they felt it right to keep abreast of the times. They were honestly interested in art and it would be unjust even to hint a sneer because their taste lacked boldness and their appreciation originality. It may be that they were conventional in their judgements, but their conventionality was that of the highest culture of their day. They were incapable of making a discovery, but were quick to appreciate the discoveries of others. Though left to themselves they might never have seen anything very much to admire in Cézanne, no sooner was it borne in upon them that he was a great artist than in all sincerity they recognized the fact for themselves. They took no pride in their taste and there was no trace of snobbishness in their attitude.

"We're just very ordinary members of the public," said Venetia.

"Those objects of contempt to the artist, the people who know what they like," added Leslie.

It was a happy accident that they liked Debussy better than Arthur Sullivan and Virginia Woolf better than John Galsworthy.

This preoccupation with art left them little time for social life; they sought neither the great nor the distinguished, and their friends were very nice people who were well-to-do without being rich, and who took a judicious interest in the things of the mind. They did not much care for dinner parties and neither gave them often nor went to them more than civility required; but they were fond of entertaining their friends to supper on Sunday evenings when they could drop in dressed any way they liked and eat kedgeree and sausages and mash. There was good music and tolerable bridge. The conversation was intelligent. These parties were as pleasantly unpretentious as the Leslie Masons themselves, and though all the guests had their own cars and few of them less than five thousand a year, they flattered themselves that the atmosphere was quite bohemian.

But Leslie Mason was never happier than when, with no concert or first night to go to, he could spend the evening in the bosom of his family. He was fortunate in it. His wife had been pretty and now, a middle-aged woman, was still comely. She was nearly as tall as he, with blue eyes and soft brown hair only just streaked with gray. She was inclined to be stout, but her height enabled her to carry with dignity a corpulence which a strict attention to diet prevented from becoming uncomfortable. She had a broad brow, an open countenance and a diffident smile. Though she got her clothes in Paris, not from one of the fashionable dressmakers, but from a little woman 'round the corner', she never succeeded in looking anything but thoroughly English. She naturalized whatever she wore, and though she occasionally went to the extravagance of getting a hat at Reboux she had no sooner put it on her head than it looked as if it had come from the Army and Navy Stores. She always looked exactly what she was, an honest woman of the middle class in easy circumstances. She had loved her husband when she married him and she loved him still. With the community of interests that existed between them it was no wonder that they should live in harmony. They had agreed at the beginning of their married life that she knew more about painting than he and that he knew more about music than she, so that in these matters each bowed to the superior judgement of the other. When it came to Picasso's later work, for instance, Leslie said:

"Well, I don't mind confessing it took me some time before I learnt to like it, but Venetia never had a moment's doubt; with her flair she cottoned on to it like a flash of lightning."

And Mrs. Mason admitted that she'd had to listen to Sibelius' Second three or four times before she really understood what Leslie meant when he said that in its way it was as good as Beethoven.

"But of course he's got a real understanding of

music. Compared with him I'm almost a low-brow."

Leslie and Venetia Mason were not only fortunate in one another, but also in their children. They had two, which they thought the perfect number, since an only child might be spoiled, and three or four meant a great expense, so that they couldn't have lived as comfortably as they liked to, nor provided for them in such a way as to assure their future. They had taken their parental duties seriously. Instead of putting silly, childish pictures on the nursery walls they had decorated them with reproductions of pictures by Van Gogh, Gauguin and Marie Laurencin, so that from their earliest years their children's taste should be formed, and they had chosen the records for the nursery gramophone with equal care, with the result that before either of them could ride a bicycle they were familiar with Mozart and Haydn, Beethoven and Wagner. As soon as they were old enough they began to learn to play the piano, with very good teachers, and Charley especially showed great aptitude. Both children were ardent concert-goers. They would scramble in to a Sunday concert, where they followed the music with a score, or wait for hours to get a seat in the gallery at Covent Garden; for their parents, thinking that it proved a real enthusiasm if they had to listen to music in some discomfort, considered it unnecessary to buy expensive seats for them. The Leslie Masons did not very much care for Old Masters and seldom went to the National Gallery except when a new purchase was making a stir in the papers, but it had seemed to them only right to make their children acquainted with the great paintings of the

past, and as soon as they were old enough took them
regularly to the National Gallery, but they soon realized that if they wanted to give them a treat they must
take them to the Tate, and it was with gratification that
they found that what really excited them was the most
modern.

"It makes one think a bit," said Leslie to his wife, a
smile of pride shining in his kindly eyes, "to see two
young things like that taking to Matisse like a duck
takes to water."

She gave him a look that was partly amused and
partly rueful.

"They think I'm dreadfully old-fashioned because I
still like Monet. They say it's pure chocolate-box."

"Well, we trained their taste. We mustn't grouse if
they go ahead and leave us behind."

Venetia Mason gave a sweet and affectionate laugh.

"Bless their hearts, I don't grudge it them if they
think me hopelessly out of date. I shall go on liking
Monet and Manet and Degas whatever they say."

But it was not only to the artistic education of their
offspring that the Leslie Masons had given thought.
They were anxious that there should be nothing namby-
pamby about them and they saw to it that they should
acquire proficiency in games. They both rode well and
Charley was not half a bad shot. Patsy, who was just
eighteen, was studying at the Royal Academy of Music.
She was to come out in May and they were giving a
ball for her at Claridge's. Lady Terry-Mason was to
present her at Court. Patsy was so pretty, with her
blue eyes and fair hair, with her slim figure, her attrac-

tive smile and her gaiety, she would be snapped up all too soon. Leslie wanted her to marry a rising young barrister with political ambitions. For such a one, with the money she'd eventually inherit from the Mason Estate, with her culture, she'd make an admirable wife. But that would be the end of the united, cosy and happy family life which was so enjoyable. There would be no more of those pleasant, domestic evenings when they dined, the four of them, in the well-appointed dining-room with its Steer over the Chippendale sideboard, the table shining with Waterford glass and Georgian silver, waited on by well-trained maids in neat uniforms; simple English food perfectly cooked; and after dinner with its lively talk about art, literature and the drama, a glass of port, and then a little music in the drawing-room and a game of bridge. Venetia was afraid it was very selfish of her, but she couldn't help feeling glad that it would be some years at least before Charley could afford to marry too.

Charley was born during the war, he was twenty-three now, and when Leslie had been demobbed and gone down to Godalming to stay with the head of the family, already a member of parliament, but then only a knight, Sir Wilfred had suggested that he should be put down for Eton. Leslie would not hear of it. It was not the financial sacrifice he minded, but he had too much good sense to send his boy to a school where he would get extravagant tastes and acquire ideas unfitted to the station in life he would ultimately occupy.

"I went to Rugby myself and I don't believe I can do better than send him there too."

"I think you're making a mistake, Leslie. I've sent my boys to Eton. Thank God, I'm not a snob, but I'm not a fool either, and there's no denying it, it's a social asset."

"I daresay it is, but my position is very different from yours. You're a very rich man, Wilfred, and if things go well, you ought to end up in the House of Lords. I think it's quite right that you should give your sons the sort of start that'll enable them to take their proper place in society, but though officially I'm secretary of the Mason Estate and that sounds very respectable, when you come down to brass tacks I'm only a house agent, and I don't want to bring up my son to be a grand gentleman, I want him to be a house agent after me."

When Leslie spoke thus he was using an innocent diplomacy. By the terms of old Sibert's will and the accidents that have been already narrated, Sir Wilfred now possessed three-eighths of the Mason Estate, and it brought him in an income which was already large, and which, with leases falling in, the increasing value of the property, and good management, would certainly grow much larger. He was a clever, energetic man, and his position and his wealth gave him an influence with the rest of the family which none of its members questioned, but which it did not displease him to have acknowledged.

"You don't mean to say you'd be satisfied to let your boy take on your job?"

"It was good enough for me. Why shouldn't it be good enough for him? One doesn't know what the world's coming to and it may be that when he's grown up he'll be damned glad to step into a cushy billet at a thousand a year. But of course you're the boss."

Sir Wilfred made a gesture that seemed modestly to deprecate this description of himself.

"I'm a shareholder like the rest of you, but as far as I'm concerned, if you want it, he shall have it. Of course it's a long time ahead and I may be dead by then."

"We're a long-lived family and you'll live as long as old Sibert. Anyhow, there'll be no harm in letting the rest of them know that it's an understood thing that my boy should have my job when I'm through with it."

In order to enlarge their children's minds the Leslie Masons spent the holidays abroad, in winter at places where they ski and in summer at seaside resorts in the South of France; and once or twice with the same praiseworthy intention they made excursions to Italy and Holland. When Charley left school his father decided that before going to Cambridge he should spend six months at Tours to learn French. But the result of his sojourn in that agreeable town was unexpected and might very well have been disastrous, for when he came back he announced that he did not want to go to Cambridge, but to Paris, and that he wished to be a painter.. His parents were dumbfounded. They loved art, they often said it was the most important thing in their lives; indeed Leslie, not averse at times from philosophical reflection, was inclined to think that it was art only that redeemed human existence from meaninglessness, and he had the greatest respect for the persons who produced it; but he had never envisaged the possibility that any member of his family, let alone his own son, should adopt a career that was uncertain, to

some extent irregular, and in most cases far from lucrative. Nor could Venetia forget the fate that had befallen her father. It would be unjust to say that the
Leslie Masons were put out because their son had taken
their preoccupation with art more seriously than they
intended; their preoccupation couldn't have been more
serious, but it was from the patron's point of view;
though no two people could have been more bohemian,
they did have the Mason Estate behind them, and that,
as anyone could see, must make a difference. Their reaction to Charley's declaration was quite definite, but they
were aware that it would be difficult to put it in a way
that wouldn't make their attitude look a trifle insincere.

"I can't think what put the idea into his head," said
Leslie, talking it over with his wife.

"Heredity, I suppose. After all, my father was an
artist."

"A painter, darling. He was a great gentleman and
a wonderful raconteur, but no one in his senses could
call him an artist."

Venetia flushed and Leslie saw that he had hurt her
feelings. He hastened to make up for it.

"If he's inherited a feeling for art it's much more
likely to be from my grandmother. I know old Sibert
used to say you didn't know what tripe and onions were
until you tasted hers. When she gave up being a cook
to become a wife of a market gardener a great artist
was lost to the world."

Venetia chuckled and forgave him.

They knew one another too well to have need to
discuss their quandary. Their children loved them and

looked up to them; they were agreed that it would be a thousand pities by a false step to shake Charley's belief in his parents' wisdom and integrity. The young are intolerant and when you talk common sense to them are only too apt to think you are an old humbug.

"I don't think it would be wise to put one's foot down too decidedly," said Venetia. "Opposition might only make him obstinate."

"The situation's delicate. I don't deny that for a moment."

What made it more awkward was that Charley had brought back several canvases from Tours and when he had shown them they had expressed themselves in terms which it was difficult now to withdraw. They had praised as fond parents rather than as connoisseurs.

"You might take Charley up to the box-room one morning and let him have a look at your father's pictures. Don't make a point of it, you know, but let it seem accidental; and then when I get an opportunity I'll have a talk with him."

The opportunity came. Leslie was in the sitting-room they had arranged for the children so that they might have a place of their own. The reproductions of Gauguin and Van Gogh that had been in their nursery adorned the walls. Charley was painting a bunch of mixed flowers in a green vase.

"I think we'd better have those pictures you brought back from France framed and put up instead of these reproductions. Let's have another look at them."

There was one of three apples on a blue-and-white plate.

"I think it's damned good," said Leslie. "I've seen hundreds of pictures of three apples on a blue-and-white plate and it's well up to the average." He chuckled. "Poor old Cézanne, I wonder what he'd say if he knew how many thousands of times people had painted that picture of his."

There was another still life which represented a bottle of red wine, a packet of French tobacco in a blue wrapper, a pair of white gloves, a folded newspaper and a violin. These objects were resting on a table covered with a cloth in green and white squares.

"Very good. Very promising."

"D'you really think so, daddy?"

"I do indeed. It's not very original, you know, it's the sort of picture that every dealer has a dozen of in his store-room, but you've never had a lesson in your life and it's a very creditable piece of work. You've evidently inherited some of your grandfather's talent. You have seen his pictures, haven't you?"

"I hadn't for years. Mummy wanted to find something in the box-room and she showed them to me. They're awful."

"I suppose they are. But they weren't thought so in his own day. They were highly praised and they were bought. Remember that a lot of stuff that we admire now will be thought just as awful in fifty years' time. That's the worst of art; there's no room for the second-rate."

"One can't tell what one'll be till one tries."

"Of course not, and if you want to take up painting professionally your mother and I are the last people who'd stand in your way. You know how much art means to us."

"There's nothing I want to do in the world more than paint."

"With the share of the Mason Estate that'll come to you eventually you'll always have enough to live on in a modest way, and there've been several amateurs who've made quite a nice little reputation for themselves."

"Oh, but I don't want to be an amateur."

"It's not so easy to be anything else with a thousand to fifteen hundred a year behind you. I don't mind telling you it'll be a bit of a disappointment to me. I was keeping this job as secretary to the Estate warm for you, but I daresay some of the cousins will jump at it. I should have thought myself it was better to be a competent business man than a mediocre painter, but that's neither here nor there. The great thing is that you should be happy and we can only hope that you'll turn out a better artist than your grandfather."

There was a pause. Leslie looked at his son with kindly eyes.

"There's only one thing I'm going to ask you to do. My grandfather started life as a gardener and his wife was a cook. I only just remember him, but I have a notion that he was a pretty rough diamond. They say it takes three generations to make a gentleman, and at all events I don't eat peas with a knife. You're a member of the fourth. You may think it's just snobbishness on my part, but I don't much like the idea of you sinking in the social scale. I'd like you to go to Cambridge and take your degree, and after that if you want to go to Paris and study painting you shall go with my blessing."

That seemed a very generous offer to Charley and he accepted it with gratitude. He enjoyed himself very much at Cambridge. He did not find much opportunity to paint, but he got into a set interested in the drama and in his first year wrote a couple of one-act plays. They were acted at the A.D.C. and the Leslie Masons went to Cambridge to see them. Then he made the acquaintance of a don who was a distinguished musician. Charley played the piano better than most undergraduates, and he and the don played duets together. He studied harmony and counterpoint. After consideration he decided that he would rather be a musician than a painter. His father with great good humour consented to this, but when Charley had taken his degree, he carried him off to Norway for a fortnight's fishing. Two or three days before they were due to return Venetia Mason received a telegram from Leslie containing the one word Eureka. Notwithstanding their culture neither of them knew what it meant, but its significance was perfectly clear to the recipient and that is the primary use of language. She gave a sigh of relief. In September Charley went for four months into the firm of accountants employed by the Mason Estate to learn something of book-keeping and at the New Year joined his father in Lincoln's Inn Fields. It was to reward the application he had shown during his first year in business that his father was now sending him, with twenty-five pounds in his pocket, to have a lark in Paris. And a great lark Charley was determined to have.

ii

THEY WERE NEARLY THERE. The attendants were
collecting the luggage and piling it up inside the door
so that it could be conveniently handed down to the
porters. Women put a last dab of lipstick on their
mouths and were helped into their furs. Men struggled
into their great-coats and put on their hats. The pro-
pinquity in which these persons had sat for a few hours,
the pleasant warmth of the Pullman, had made a cor-
porate unity of them, separated as occupants of a coach
with its own number from the occupants of other
coaches; but now they fell asunder, and each one, or
each group of two or three, regained the discreet indi-
viduality which for a while had been merged in that
of all the others. In the smoke-laden air, rank with stale
tobacco, strong scent, the odour of human bodies and
the frowst of steam-heating, they acquired on a sudden
an air of mystery. Strangers once more, they looked at
one another with preoccupied, unseeing eyes. Each one
felt in himself a vague hostility to his neighbour. Some
were already queuing up in the passage so that they
might get out quickly. The heat of the Pullman had

coated the windows with vapour and Charley wiped them a bit clean with his hand to look out. He could see nothing.

The train ran into the station. Charley gave his bag to a porter and with long steps walked up the platform; he was expecting his friend Simon Fenimore to meet him. He was disappointed not to see him at once; but there was a great mob at the barrier and he supposed that he was waiting there. He scanned eagerly the eager faces; he passed through; persons struggled through the crowd to seize a new arrival's hand; women kissed one another; he could not see his friend. He was so convinced he must be there that he lingered for a little, but he was intimidated by his porter's obvious impatience and presently followed him out to the courtyard. He felt vaguely let down. The porter got him a taxi and Charley gave the driver the name of the hotel where Simon had taken a room for him. When the Leslie Masons went to Paris they always stayed at an hotel in the Rue St. Honoré. It was exclusively patronized by English and Americans, but after twenty years they still cherished the delusion that it was a discovery of their own, essentially French, and when they saw American luggage on a landing or went up in the lift with persons who could be nothing but English, they never ceased to be surprised.

"I wonder how on earth *they* happen to be here," they said.

For their own part they had always been careful never to speak about it to their friends; when they had hit upon a little bit of old France they weren't going to risk its being spoilt. Though the director and the porter talked English fluently they always spoke to them in their own halting French, convinced that this was the only language they knew. But the mere fact that he had so often been to this hotel with his family was a sufficient reason for Charley not to stay there when he was going to Paris by himself. He was bent on adventure, and a respectable family hotel, where, according to his parents, nobody went but the French provincial nobility, was hardly the right place for the glorious, wild and romantic experiences with which his imagination for the last month had been distracting his mind. So he had written to Simon asking him to get him a room somewhere in the Latin Quarter; he wasn't particular about sanitary conveniences and didn't mind how grubby it was so long as it had the right atmosphere; and Simon in due course had written back to tell him that he had engaged a room at a hotel near the Gare Montparnasse. It was in a quiet street just off the Rue de Rennes and conveniently near the Rue Campagne Première where he himself lived.

Charley quickly got over his disappointment that Simon had not come to meet him, he was sure either to be at the hotel or to have telephoned to say that he would be round immediately, and driving through the crowded streets that lead from the Gare du Nord to the Seine his spirits rose. It was wonderful to arrive in Paris by night. A drizzling rain was falling and it gave the streets an exciting mystery. The shops were brightly lit. The pavements were multitudinous with umbrellas and the water dripping on them glistened dimly under the street lamps. Charley remembered one of Renoir's pictures. Sometimes a gust of wind made women crouch under their umbrellas and their skirts swirled round their legs. His taxi drove furiously to his prudent English idea and he gasped whenever with a screeching of brakes it pulled up suddenly to avoid a collision. The red lights held them up at a crossing and in both directions a great stream of persons surged over like a panic-stricken mob flying before a police charge. To Charley's excited gaze they seemed quite different from an English crowd, more alert, more eager; when by chance his eyes fell on a girl walking by herself, a sempstress or a typist going home after the day's work, it delighted him to fancy that she was hurrying to meet her lover; and when he saw a pair walking arm in arm under an umbrella, a young man with a beard, in a broad-brimmed hat, and a girl with a fur round her neck, walking as though it were such bliss to be together they did not mind the rain and were unconscious of the jostling throng, he thrilled with a poignant and sympathetic joy. At one corner owing to a block his taxi was side by side with a handsome limousine. There sat in it a woman in a sable coat, with painted cheeks and painted lips, and a profile of incredible distinction. She might have been the Duchesse de Guermantes driving back after a tea party to her house in the Boulevard St. Germain. It was wonderful to be twenty-three and in Paris on one's own.

"By God, what a time I'm going to have."

The hotel was grander than he had expected. Its façade, with its architectural embellishments, suggested the flamboyant taste of the late Baron Haussmann. He found that a room had been engaged for him, but Simon had left neither letter nor message. He was taken upstairs not as he had anticipated by a slovenly boots in a dirty apron, with a sinister look on his ill-shaven face, but by an affable director who spoke perfect English and wore a morning coat. The room was furnished with hygienic severity, and there were two beds in it, but the director assured him that he would only charge him for the use of one. He showed Charley with pride the communicating bath-room. Left to himself Charley looked about him. He had expected a little room with heavy curtains of dull rep, a wooden bed with a huge eiderdown and an old mahogany ward-robe with a large mirror; he had expected to find used hairpins on the dressing-table and in the drawer of the table de nuit half a lipstick and a broken comb in which a few dyed hairs were still entangled. That was the idea his romantic fancy had formed of a student's room in the Latin Quarter. A bath-room! That was the last thing he had bargained for. This room might have been a room in one of the cheaper hotels in Switzerland to which he had sometimes been with his parents. It was clean, threadbare and sordid. Not even Charley's ardent imagination could invest it with mystery. He unpacked his bag disconsolately. He had a bath. He thought it rather casual of Simon, even if he could not be bothered to meet him, not to have left a message. If he made no sign of life he would have to dine by himself. His father and mother and Patsy would have got down to Godalming by now; there was going to be a jolly party, Sir Wilfred's two sons and their wives and two nieces of Lady Terry-Mason's. There would be music, games and dancing. He half wished now that he hadn't jumped at his father's offer to spend the holiday in Paris. It suddenly occurred to him that Simon had perhaps had to go off somewhere for his paper and in the hurry of an unexpected departure had forgotten to let him know. His heart sank.

Simon Fenimore was Charley's oldest friend and indeed it was to spend a few days with him that he had been so eager to come to Paris. They had been at a private school together and together at Rugby; they had been at Cambridge together too, but Simon had left without taking a degree, at the end of his second year in fact, because he had come to the conclusion that he was wasting time; and it was Charley's father who had got him on to the London newspaper for which for the last year he had been one of the Paris correspondents. Simon was alone in the world. His father was in the Indian Forest Department and while Simon was still a young child had divorced his mother for promiscuous adultery. She had left India and Simon, by order of the court in his father's custody, was sent to England and put into a clergyman's family till he was old enough to go to school. His mother vanished into obscurity. He had no notion whether she was alive or dead. His father died of cirrhosis of the liver when Simon was twelve and he had but a vague recollection of a thin, slightly-built man with a sallow, lined face and a tight-lipped mouth. He left only just enough money to educate his son. The Leslie Masons had been touched by

the poor boy's loneliness and had made a point of asking him to spend a good part of his holidays with them.
As a boy he was thin and weedy, with a pale face in
which his black eyes looked enormous, a great quantity
of straight dark hair which was always in need of a
brush, and a large, sensual mouth. He was talkative,
forward for his age, a great reader, and clever. He
had none of the diffidence which was in Charley such an
engaging trait. Venetia Mason, though from a sense of
duty she tried hard, could not like him. She could not
understand why Charley had taken a fancy to someone
who was in every way so unlike him. She thought Simon
pert and conceited. He was insensible to kindness and
took everything that was done for him as a matter of
course. She had a suspicion that he had no very high
opinion either of her or of Leslie. Sometimes when Leslie was talking with his usual good sense and intelligence
about something interesting Simon would look at him
with a glimmer of irony in those great black eyes of his
and his sensual lips pursed in a sarcastic pucker. You
would have thought Leslie was being prosy and a trifle
stupid. Now and then when they were spending one of
their pleasant quiet evenings together, chatting of one
thing and another, he would go into a brown study; he
would sit staring into vacancy, as though his thoughts
were miles away, and perhaps, after a while, take up a
book and start reading as though he were by himself.
It gave you the impression that their conversation
wasn't worth listening to. It wasn't even polite. But
Venetia Mason chid herself.

"Poor lamb, he's never had a chance to learn manners. I *will* be nice to him. I *will* like him."

Her eyes rested on Charley, so good-looking, with his slim body, ("it's awful the way he grows out of his clothes, the sleeves of his dinner-jacket are too short for him already,") his curling brown hair, his blue eyes, with long lashes, and his clear skin. Though perhaps he hadn't Simon's showy brilliance, he was good, and he was artistic to his fingers' ends. But who could tell what he might have become if she had run away from Leslie and Leslie had taken to drink, and if instead of enjoying a cultured atmosphere and the influence of a nice home he had had, like Simon, to fend for himself? Poor Simon! Next day she went out and bought him half a dozen ties. He seemed pleased.

"I say, that's jolly decent of you. I've never had more than two ties at one time in my life."

Venetia was so moved by the spontaneous generosity of her pretty gesture that she was seized with a sudden wave of sympathy.

"You poor lonely boy," she cried, "it's so dreadful for you to have no parents."

"Well, as my mother was a whore, and my father a drunk, I daresay I don't miss much."

He was seventeen when he said this.

It was no good, Venetia simply couldn't like him. He was harsh, cynical and unscrupulous. It exasperated her to see how much Charley admired him; Charley thought him brilliant and anticipated a great career for him. Even Leslie was impressed by the extent of his reading and the clearness with which even as a boy he expressed himself. At school he was already an ardent socialist and at Cambridge he became a communist. Leslie listened to his wild theories with good-humoured tolerance. To him it was all talk, and talk, he had an instinctive feeling, was just talk; it didn't touch the essential business of life.

"And if he does become a well-known journalist or gets into the House, there'll be no harm in having a friend in the enemy's camp."

Leslie's ideas were liberal, so liberal that he didn't mind admitting the Socialists had several notions that no reasonable man could object to; theoretically he was all in favour of the nationalization of the coal-mines, and he didn't see why the state shouldn't run the public services as well as private companies; but he didn't think they should go too far. Ground rents, for instance, that was a matter that was really no concern of the state; and slum property; in a great city you had to have slums, in point of fact the lower classes preferred them to model dwelling-houses, not that the Mason Estate hadn't done what it could in this direction, but you couldn't expect a landlord to let people live in his houses for nothing, and it was only fair that he should get a decent return on his capital.

Simon Fenimore had decided that he wanted to be a foreign correspondent for some years so that he could gain a knowledge of Continental politics which would enable him when he entered the House of Commons to be an expert on a subject of which most Labour members were necessarily ignorant; but when Leslie took him to see the proprietor of the newspaper who was prepared to give a brilliant young man his chance, he warned him that the proprietor was a very rich man, and that he could not expect to create a favourable impression if he delivered himself of revolutionary sentiments. Simon, however, made a very good impression on the magnate by the modesty of his demeanour, his air of energy and his easy conversation.

"He was as good as gold," Leslie told his wife afterwards. "He's got his head screwed on his shoulders all right, that young fellow. It's what I always told you, talk doesn't amount to anything really. When it comes down to getting a job with a living wage attached to it, like every sensible man he's prepared to put his theories in his pocket."

Venetia agreed with him. It was quite possible, their own experience proved it, to have a real love for beauty and at the same time to realize the importance of material things. Look at Lorenzo de' Medici; he'd been a successful banker and an artist to his finger-tips. She thought it very good of Leslie to have taken so much trouble to do a service for someone who was incapable of gratitude. Anyhow the job he had got him would take Simon to Vienna and thus remove Charley from an influence which she had always regarded with misgiving. It was that wild talk of his that had put it into the boy's head that he wanted to be an artist. It was all very well for Simon, he hadn't a penny in the world and no connections; but Charley had a snug berth to go into. There were enough artists in the world. Her consolation had been that Charley had so much candour of soul and a disposition of such sweetness that no evil communications could corrupt his good manners.

At this moment Charley was dressing himself and wondering, forlorn, how he should spend the evening. When he had got his trousers on he rang up the office of Simon's newspaper, and it was Simon himself who answered.

"Simon."

"Hulloa, have you turned up? Where are you?"

Simon seemed so casual that Charley was taken aback.

"At the hotel."

"Oh, are you? Doing anything to-night?"

"No."

"We'd better dine together, shall we? I'll stroll around and fetch you."

He rang off. Charley was dashed. He had expected Simon to be as eager to see him as he was to see Simon, but from Simon's words and from his manner you would have thought that they were casual acquaintances and that it was a matter of indifference to him if they met or not. Of course it was two years since they'd seen one another and in that time Simon might have changed out of all recognition. Charley had a sudden fear that his visit to Paris was going to be a failure and he awaited Simon's arrival with a nervousness that annoyed him. But when at last he walked into the room there was in his appearance at least little alteration. He was now twenty-three and he was still the lanky fellow, though only of average height, that he had always been. He was shabbily dressed in a brown jacket and gray flannel trousers and wore neither hat nor great coat. His long face was thinner and paler than ever and his black eyes seemed larger. They were never still. Hard, shining, inquisitive, suspicious, they seemed to indicate the quality of the brain behind. His mouth was large and ironical, and he had small irregular teeth that somewhat reminded you of one of the smaller beasts of prey. With his pointed chin and prominent cheek-bones he was not good-looking, but his expression was so high-strung, there was in it so strange a disquiet, that you could hardly have passed him in the street without taking notice of him. At fleeting moments his face had a sort of tortured beauty, not a beauty of feature but the beauty of a restless, striving spirit. A disturbing thing about him was that there was no gaiety in his smile, it was a sardonic grimace, and when he laughed his face was contorted as though he were suffering from an agony of pain. His voice was high-pitched; it did not seem to be quite under his control, and when he grew excited often rose to shrillness.

Charley, restraining his natural impulse to run to the door and wring his hand with the eager friendliness of his happy nature, received him coolly. When there was a knock he called "Come in," and went on filing his nails. Simon did not offer to shake hands. He nodded as though they had met already in the course of the day.

"Hulloa!" he said. "Room all right?"

"Oh, yes. The hotel's a bit grander than I expected."

"It's convenient and you can bring anyone in you like. I'm starving. Shall we go along and eat?"

"O.K."

"Let's go to the Coupole."

They sat down opposite one another at a table up-stairs and ordered their dinner. Simon gave Charley an appraising look.

"I see you haven't lost your looks, Charley," he said with his wry smile.

"Luckily they're not my fortune."

Charley was feeling a trifle shy. The separation had for the moment at all events destroyed the old intimacy there had so long been between them. Charley was a good listener, he had indeed been trained to be so from early childhood, and he was never unwilling to sit silent while Simon poured out his ideas with eloquent confu-sion. Charley had always disinterestedly admired him; he was convinced he was a genius so that it seemed quite natural to play second fiddle to him. He had an affec-tion for Simon because he was alone in the world and nobody much liked him, whereas he himself had a happy home and was in easy circumstances; and it gave him a sense of comfort that Simon, who cared for so few people, cared for him. Simon was often bitter and sar-castic, but with him he could also be strangely gentle. In one of his rare moments of expansion he had told him that he was the only person in the world that he gave a damn for. But now Charley felt with malaise that there was a barrier between them. Simon's restless eyes darted from his face to his hands, paused for an instant on his new suit and then glanced rapidly at his collar and tie; he felt that Simon was not surrendering himself as he had to him alone in the old days, but was holding back, critical and aloof; he seemed to be taking stock of him as if he were a stranger and he were making up his mind what sort of a person this was. It made Charley uncomfortable and he was sore at heart.

"How d'you like being a business man?" asked Simon.

Charley faintly coloured. After all the talks they had had in the past he was prepared for Simon to treat him with derision because he had in the end fallen in with his father's wishes, but he was too honest to conceal the truth.

"I like it much better than I expected. I find the work very interesting and it's not hard. I have plenty of time to myself."

"I think you've shown a lot of sense," Simon answered, to his surprise. "What did you want to be a painter or a pianist for? There's a great deal too much art in the world. Art's a lot of damned rot anyway."

"Oh, Simon!"

"Are you still taken in by the artistic pretensions of your excellent parents? You must grow up, Charley. Art! It's an amusing diversion for the idle rich. Our world, the world we live in, has no time for such nonsense."

"I should have thought . . ."

"I know what you would have thought; you would have thought it gave a beauty, a meaning to existence; you would have thought it was a solace to the weary and heavy-laden and an inspiration to a nobler and fuller life. Balls! We may want art again in the future, but it won't be your art, it'll be the art of the people."

"Oh, Lord!"

"The people want dope and it may be that art is the best form in which we can give it them. But they're not ready for it yet. At present it's another form they want."

"What is that?"

"Words."

It was extraordinary, the sardonic vigour he put into the monosyllable. But he smiled, and though his lips grimaced Charley saw in his eyes for a moment that same look of good-humoured affection that he had been accustomed to see in them.

"No, my boy," he continued, "you have a good time, go to your office every day and enjoy yourself. It can't last very long now and you may just as well get all the fun out of it that you can."

"What d'you mean by that?"

"Never mind. We'll talk about it some other time. Tell me, what have you come to Paris for?"

"Well, chiefly to see you."

Simon flushed darkly. You would have thought that a word of kindness, and when Charley spoke you could never doubt that it was from the heart, horribly embarrassed him.

"And besides that?"

"I want to see some pictures, and if there's anything good in the theatre I'd like to go. And I want to have a bit of a lark generally."

"I suppose you mean by that that you want to have a woman."

"I don't get much opportunity in London, you know."

"Later on I'll take you to the Sérail."

"What's that?"

"You'll see. It's not bad fun."

They began to talk of Simon's experiences in Vienna, but he was reticent about them.

"It took me some time to find my feet. You see, I'd never been out of England before. I learnt German. I read a great deal. I thought. I met a lot of people who interested me."

"And since then, in Paris?"

"I've been doing more or less the same thing; I've been putting my ideas in order. I'm young. I've got plenty of time. When I'm through with Paris I shall go to Rome, Berlin or Moscow. If I can't get a job with the paper, I shall get some other job; I can always teach English and earn enough to keep body and soul together. I wasn't born in the purple and I can do without things. In Vienna, as an exercise in self-denial, I lived for a month on bread and milk. It wasn't even a hardship. I've trained myself now to do with one meal a day."

"D'you mean to say this is your first meal to-day?"

"I had a cup of coffee when I got up and a glass of milk at one."

"But what's the object of it? You're adequately paid in your job, aren't you?"

"I get a living wage. Certainly enough to have three meals a day. Who can achieve mastery over others unless he first achieves mastery over himself?"

Charley grinned. He was beginning to feel more at his ease.

"That sounds like a tag out of a dictionary of quotations."

"It may be," Simon replied indifferently. "Je prends mon bien où je le trouve. A proverb distils the wisdom of the ages and only a fool is scornful of the commonplace. You don't suppose I intend to be a foreign correspondent for a London paper or a teacher of English all my life. These are my Wanderjahre. I'm going to spend them in acquiring the education I never got at the stupid school we both went to or in that suburban cemetery they call the University of Cambridge. But it's not only knowledge of men and books that I want to acquire; that's only an instrument; I want to acquire something much harder to come by and more important: an unconquerable will. I want to mould myself as the Jesuit novice is moulded by the iron discipline of the Order. I think I've always known myself; there's nothing that teaches you what you are, like being alone in the world, a stranger everywhere, and living all your life with people to whom you mean nothing. But my knowledge was instinctive. In these two years I've been abroad I've learnt to know myself as I know the fifth proposition of Euclid. I know my strength and my weakness and I'm ready to spend the next five or six years cultivating my strength and ridding myself of my weakness. I'm going to take myself as a trainer takes an athlete to make a champion of him. I've got a good brain. There's no one in the world who can see to the end of his nose with such perspicacity as I can, and believe me, in the world we live in that's a great force. I can talk. You have to persuade men to action not by

reasoning, but by rhetoric. The general idiocy of mankind is such that they can be swayed by words, and however mortifying, for the present you have to accept the
fact as you accept it in the cinema that a film to be a
success must have a happy ending. Already I can do
pretty well all I like with words; before I'm through
I shall be able to do anything."

Simon took a long draught of the white wine they
were drinking and sitting back in his chair began to
laugh. His face writhed into a grimace of intolerable
suffering.

"I must tell you an incident that happened a few
months ago here. They were having a meeting of the
British Legion or something like that, I forget what
for, war graves or something; my chief was going to
speak, but he had a cold in the head and he sent me
instead. You know what our paper is, bloody patriotic
as long as it helps our circulation, all the dirt we can
get, and a high moral tone. My chief's the right man
in the right place. He hasn't had an idea in his head
for twenty years. He never opens his mouth without
saying the obvious and when he tells a dirty story it's
so stale that it doesn't even stink any more. But he's
as shrewd as they make 'em. He knows what the proprietor wants and he gives it to him. Well, I made the
speech he would have made. Platitudes dripped from
my mouth. I made the welkin ring with claptrap. I gave
them jokes so hoary that even a judge would have
been ashamed to make them. They roared with laughter. I gave them pathos so shaming that you would have
thought they would vomit. The tears rolled down their

cheeks. I beat the big drum of patriotism like a Salvation Lass sublimating her repressed sex. They cheered me to the echo. It was the speech of the evening. When it was all over the big-wigs wrung my hand still overwhelmed with emotion. I got them all right. And d'you know, I didn't say a single word that I didn't know was contemptible balderdash. Words, words, words! Poor old Hamlet."

"It was a damned unscrupulous thing to do," said Charley. "After all, I daresay they were just a lot of ordinary, decent fellows who were only wanting to do what they thought was the right thing, and what's more they were probably prepared to put their hands in their pockets to prove the sincerity of their convictions."

"You would think that. In point of fact more money was raised for whatever the damned cause was than had ever been raised before at one of their meetings and the organizers told my chief it was entirely due to my brilliant speech."

Charley in his candour was distressed. This was not the Simon he had known so long. Formerly, however wild his theories were, however provocatively expressed, there was a sort of nobility in them. He was disinterested. His indignation was directed against oppression and cruelty. Injustice roused him to fury. But Simon did not notice the effect he had on Charley or if he did was indifferent to it. He was absorbed in himself.

"But brain isn't enough and eloquence, even if it's necessary, is after all a despicable gift. Kerensky had them both and what did they avail him? The important

thing is character. It's my character I've got to mould.
I'm sure one can do anything with oneself if one tries.
It's only a matter of will. I've got to train myself so
that I'm indifferent to insult, neglect and ridicule. I've
got to acquire a spiritual aloofness so complete that if
they put me in prison I shall feel myself as free as a
bird in the air. I've got to make myself so strong that
when I make mistakes I am unshaken, but profit by
them to act rightly. I've got to make myself so hard
that not only can I resist the temptation to be pitiful,
but I don't even feel pity. I've got to wring out of my
heart the possibility of love."

"Why?"

"I can't afford to let my judgement be clouded by
any feeling that I might have for a human being. You
are the only person I've ever cared for in the world,
Charley. I shan't rest till I know in my bones that if
it were necessary to put you against a wall and shoot
you with my own hands I could do it without a moment's hesitation and without a moment's regret."

Simon's eyes had a dark opaqueness which reminded
you of an old mirror, in a deserted house, from which
the quick-silver was worn away, so that when you
looked in it you saw, not yourself, but a sombre depth
in which seemed to lurk the reflections of long past
events and passions long since dead and yet in some
terrifying way tremulous still with a borrowed and
mysterious life.

"Did you wonder why I didn't come to the station
to meet you?"

"It would have been nice if you had. I supposed you couldn't get away."

"I knew you'd be disappointed. It's our busy time at the office, we have to be on tap then to telephone to London the news that's come through in the course of the day, but it's Christmas Eve, the paper doesn't come out to-morrow and I could have got away easily. I didn't come because I wanted to so much. Ever since I got your letter saying you were coming over I've been sick with the desire to see you. When the train was due and I knew you'd be wandering up the platform looking for me and rather lost in that struggling crowd, I took a book and began to read. I sat there, forcing myself to attend to it, and refusing to let myself listen for the telephone that I expected every moment to ring. And when it did and I knew it was you, my joy was so intense that I was enraged with myself. I almost didn't answer. For more than two years now I've been striving to rid myself of the feeling I have for you. Shall I tell you why I wanted you to come over? One idealizes people when they're away, it's true that absence makes the heart grow fonder, and when one sees them again one's often surprised that one saw anything in them at all. I thought that if there were anything left in me of the old feeling I had for you the few days you're spending here now would be enough to kill it."

"I'm afraid you'll think me very stupid," said Charley, with his engaging smile, "but I can't for the life of me see why you want to."

"I do think you're very stupid."

"Well, taking that for granted, what is the reason?"

Simon frowned a little and his restless eyes darted here and there like a hare trying to escape a pursuer.

"You're the only person who ever cared for me."

"That's not true. My father and mother have always been very fond of you."

"Don't talk such nonsense. Your father was as indifferent to me as he is to art, but it gave him a warm, comfortable feeling of benevolence to be kind to the orphan penniless boy whom he could patronize and impress. Your mother thought me unscrupulous and self-seeking. She hated the influence she thought I had over you and she was affronted because she saw that I thought your father an old humbug, the worst sort of humbug, the one who humbugs himself; the only satisfaction I ever gave her was that she couldn't look at me without thinking how nice it was that you were so very different from me."

"You're not very flattering to my poor parents," said Charley, mildly.

Simon took no notice of the interruption.

"We clicked at once. What that old bore Goethe would have called elective affinity. You gave me what I'd never had. I, who'd never been a boy, could be a boy with you. I could forget myself in you. I bullied you and ragged you and mocked you and neglected you, but all the time I worshipped you. I felt wonderfully at home with you. With you I could be just myself. You were so unassuming, so easily pleased, so gay and so good-natured, merely to be with you rested my tortured nerves and released me for a moment from that driving force that urged me on and on. But I don't want rest and I don't want release. My will falters when I look at your sweet and diffident smile. I can't afford to be soft, I can't afford to be tender. When I look into those blue eyes of yours, so friendly, so confiding in human nature, I waver, and I daren't waver. You're my enemy and I hate you."

Charley had flushed uncomfortably at some of the things that Simon had said to him, but now he chuckled good-humouredly.

"Oh, Simon, what stuff and nonsense you talk."

Simon paid no attention. He fixed Charley with his glittering, passionate eyes as though he sought to bore into the depths of his being.

"Is there anything there?" he said, as though speaking to himself. "Or is it merely an accident of expression that gives the illusion of some quality of the soul?" And then to Charley: "I've often asked myself what it was that I saw in you. It wasn't your good looks, though I daresay they had something to do with it; it wasn't your intelligence, which is adequate without being remarkable; it wasn't your guileless nature or your good temper. What is it in you that makes people take to you at first sight? You've won half your battle before ever you take the field. Charm? What is charm? It's one of the words we all know the meaning of, but we can none of us define. But I know if I had that gift of yours, with my brain and my determination there's no obstacle in the world I couldn't surmount. You've got vitality and that's part of charm. But I have just as much vitality as you; I can do with four hours' sleep for days on end and I can work for sixteen hours a day without getting tired. When people first meet me they're antagonistic, I have to conquer them by sheer brain-power, I have to play on their weaknesses, I have to make myself useful to them, I have to flatter them. When I came to Paris my chief thought me the most disagreeable young man and the most conceited he'd ever met. Of course he's a fool. How can a man be conceited when he knows his defects as well as I know mine? Now he eats out of my hand. But I've had to work like a dog to achieve what you can do with a flicker of your long eyelashes. Charm is essential. In the last two years I've got to know a good many prominent politicians and they've all got it. Some more and some less. But they can't all have it by nature. That shows it can be acquired. It means nothing, but it arouses the devotion of their followers so that they'll do blindly all they're bidden and be satisfied with the reward of a kind word. I've examined them at work. They can turn it on like water from a tap. The quick, friendly smile; the hand that's so ready to clasp yours. The warmth in the voice that seems to promise favours, the show of interest that leads you to think your concerns are your leader's chief preoccupation, the intimate manner which tells you nothing, but deludes you into thinking you are in your master's confidence. The clichés, the hundred varieties of dear old boy that are so flattering on influential lips. The ease and naturalness, the perfect acting that imitates nature, and the sensitiveness that discerns a fool's vanity and takes care never to affront it. I can learn all that, it only means a little more effort and a little more self-control. Sometimes of course they overdo it, the pros, their charm becomes so mechanical that it ceases to work; people see through it, and feeling they've been duped are resentful." He gave Charley another of his piercing glances. "Your charm is natural, that's why it's so devastating. Isn't it absurd that a tiny wrinkle should make life so easy for you?"

"What on earth do you mean?"

"One of the reasons why I wanted you to come over was to see exactly in what your charm consisted. As far as I can tell it depends on some peculiar muscular formation of your lower orbit. I believe it to be due to a little crease under your eyes when you smile."

It embarrassed Charley to be thus anatomized, and to divert the conversation from himself, he asked:

"But all this effort of yours, what is it going to lead you to?"

"Who can tell? Let's go and have our coffee at the Dôme."

"All right. I'll get hold of a waiter."

"I'm going to stand you your dinner. It's the first meal that we've had together that I've ever paid for."

When he took out of his pocket some notes to settle up with he found with them a couple of cards.

"Oh, look, I've got a ticket for you for the Midnight Mass at St. Eustache. It's supposed to be the best church music in Paris and I thought you'd like to go."

"Oh, Simon, how nice of you. I should love to. You'll come with me, won't you?"

"I'll see how I feel when the time comes. Anyhow take the tickets."

Charley put them in his pocket. They walked to the Dôme. The rain had stopped, but the pavement was still wet and when the light of a shop window or a street lamp fell upon it, palely glistened. A lot of people were wandering to and fro. They came out of the shadow of the leafless trees as though from the wings of a theatre, passed across the light and then were lost again in another patch of night. Cringing but persistent, the Algerian peddlers, their eyes alert for a possible buyer, passed with a bundle of Eastern rugs and cheap furs over their arms. Coarse-faced boys, a fez on their heads, carried baskets of monkey-nuts and monotonously repeated their raucous cry: cacaouettes, cacaouettes. At a corner stood two negroes, their dark faces pinched with cold, as though time had stopped and they waited because there was nothing in the world to do but wait. The two friends reached the Dôme. The terrace where in summer the customers sat in the open was glassed in. Every table was engaged, but as they came in a couple got up and they took the empty places. It was none too warm, and Simon wore no coat.

"Won't you be cold?" Charley asked him. "Wouldn't you prefer to sit inside?"

"No, I've taught myself not to mind cold."

"What happens when you catch one?"

"I ignore it."

Charley had often heard of the Dôme, but had never been there, and he looked with eager curiosity at the people who sat all round them. There were young men in turtle-neck sweaters, some of them with short beards, and girls bare-headed, in raincoats; he supposed they

were painters and writers, and it gave him a little thrill
to look at them.

"English or American," said Simon, with a scornful
shrug of the shoulders. "Wasters and rotters most of
them, pathetically dressing up for a role in a play that
has long ceased to be acted."

Over there was a group of tall, fair-haired youths
who looked like Scandinavians, and at another table a
swarthy, gesticulating, loquacious band of Levantines.
But the greater number were quiet French people,
respectably dressed, shopkeepers from the neighbour-
hood who came to the Dôme because it was convenient,
with a sprinkling of provincials who, like Charley, still
thought it the resort of artists and students.

"Poor brutes, they haven't got the money to lead the
Latin Quarter life any more. They live on the edge of
starvation and work like galley-slaves. I suppose you've
read the *Vie de Bohême?* Rodolphe now wears a neat
blue suit that he's bought off the nail and puts his
trousers under his mattress every night to keep them
in shape. He counts every penny he spends and takes
care to do nothing to compromise his future. Mimi and
Musette are hard-working girls, trade unionists, who
spend their spare evenings attending party meetings,
and even if they lose their virtue, keep their heads."

"Don't you live with a girl?"

"No."

"Why not? I should have thought it would be very
pleasant. In the year you've been in Paris you must
have had plenty of chances of picking someone up."

"Yes, I've had one or two. Strange when you come to

think of it. D'you know what my place consists of?
A studio and a kitchen. No bath. The concierge is
supposed to come and clean up every day, but she has
varicose veins and hates climbing the stairs. That's
all I have to offer and yet there've been three girls who
wanted to come and share my squalor with me. One
was English, she's got a job here in the International
Communist Bureau, another was a Norwegian, she's
working at the Sorbonne, and one was French—you'd
have thought she had more sense; she was a dressmaker
and out of work. I picked her up one evening when
I was going out to dinner, she told me she hadn't had
a meal all day and I stood her one. It was a Saturday
night and she stayed till Monday. She wanted to stay
on, but I told her to get out and she went. The Norwegian was rather a nuisance. She wanted to darn my
socks and cook for me and scrub the floor. When I
told her there was nothing doing she took to waiting
for me at street corners, walking beside me in the street
and telling me that if I didn't relent she'd kill herself.
She taught me a lesson that I've taken to heart. I had
to be rather firm with her in the end."

"What d'you mean by that?"

"Well, one day I told her that I was sick of her
pestering. I told her that next time she addressed me
in the street I'd knock her down. She was rather stupid
and she didn't know I meant it. Next day when I came
out of my house, it was about twelve and I was just
going to the office, she was standing on the other side
of the street. She came up to me, with that hang-dog
look of hers, and began to speak. I didn't let her get

more than two or three words out, I hit her on the chin and she went down like a ninepin."

Simon's eyes twinkled with amusement.

"What happened then?"

"I don't know. I suppose she got up again. I walked on and didn't look round to see. Anyhow she took the hint and that's the last I saw of her."

The story made Charley very uncomfortable and at the same time made him want to laugh. But he was ashamed of this and remained silent.

"The comic one was the English communist. My dear, she was the daughter of a dean. She'd been to Oxford and she'd taken her degree in economics. She was terribly genteel, oh, a perfect lady, but she looked upon promiscuous fornication as a sacred duty. Every time she went to bed with a comrade she felt she was helping the Cause. We were to be good pals, fight the good fight together, shoulder to shoulder, and all that sort of thing. The dean gave her an allowance and we were to pool our resources, make my studio a Centre, have the comrades in to afternoon tea and discuss the burning questions of the day. I just told her a few home truths and that finished her."

He lit his pipe again, smiling to himself quietly, with that painful smile of his, as though he were enjoying a joke that hurt him. Charley had several things to say, but did not know how to put them so that they should not sound affected and so arouse Simon's irony.

"But is it your wish to cut human relations out of your life altogether?" he asked, uncertainly.

"Altogether. I've got to be free. I daren't let another

person get a hold over me. That's why I turned out the little sempstress. She was the most dangerous of the lot. She was gentle and affectionate. She had the meekness of the poor who have never dreamt that life can be other than hard. I could never have loved her, but I knew that her gratitude, her adoration, her desire to please, her innocent cheerfulness, were dangerous. I could see that she might easily become a habit of which I couldn't break myself. Nothing in the world is so insidious as a woman's flattery; our need for it is so enormous that we become her slave. I must be as impervious to flattery as I am indifferent to abuse. There's nothing that binds one to a woman like the benefits one confers on her. She would have owed me everything, that girl, I should never have been able to escape from her."

"But, Simon, you have human passions like the rest of us. You're twenty-three."

"And my sexual desires are urgent? Less urgent than you imagine. When you work from twelve to sixteen hours a day and sleep on an average six, when you content yourself with one meal a day, much as it may surprise you, your desires are much attenuated. Paris is singularly well arranged for the satisfaction of the sexual instinct at moderate expense and with the least possible waste of time, and when I find that my appetite is interfering with my work I have a woman just as when I'm constipated I take a purge."

Charley's clear blue eyes twinkled with amusement and a charming smile parting his lips displayed his strong white teeth.

"Aren't you missing a lot of fun? You know, one's young for such a little while."

"I may be. I know one can do nothing in the world unless one's single-minded. Chesterfield said the last word about sexual congress: the pleasure is momentary, the position is ridiculous, and the expense is damnable. It may be an instinct that one can't suppress, but the man's a pitiful fool who allows it to divert him from his chosen path. I'm not afraid of it any more. In a few more years I shall be entirely free from its temptation."

"Are you sure you can prevent yourself from falling in love one of these days? Such things do happen, you know, even to the most prudent men."

Simon gave him a strange, one might even have thought a hostile, look.

"I should tear it out of my heart as I'd wrench out of my mouth a rotten tooth."

"That's easier said than done."

"I know. Nothing that's worth doing is done easily, but that's one of the odd things about man, if his self-preservation is concerned, if he has to do something on which his being depends, he can find in himself the strength to do it."

Charley was silent. If anyone else had spoken to him as Simon had done that evening he would have thought it a pose adopted to impress. Charley had heard during his three years at Cambridge enough extravagant talk to be able, with his common sense and quiet humour, to attach no more importance to it than it deserved. But he knew that Simon never talked for effect. He

was too contemptuous of his fellows' opinion to extort
their admiration by taking up an attitude in which he
did not believe. He was fearless and sincere. When he
said that he thought this and that, you could be certain
that he did, and when he said he had done that and the
other you need not hesitate to believe that he had. But
just as the manner of life that Simon had described
seemed to Charley morbid and unnatural, so the ideas
he expressed with a fluency that showed they were well
considered seemed to him outrageous and horrible. He
noticed that Simon had avoided saying what was the
end for which he was thus so sternly disciplining himself; but at Cambridge he had been violently communist and it was natural to suppose that he was training himself to play his part in the revolution they had
then, all of them, anticipated in the near future.
Charley, much more concerned with the arts, had listened with interest, but without feeling that the matter
was any particular affair of his, to the heated arguments
he heard in Simon's rooms. If he had been obliged to
state his views on a subject to which he had never given
much thought, he would have agreed with his father:
whatever might happen on the Continent there was no
danger of communism in England; the hash they'd
made in Russia showed it was impracticable; there
always had been rich and poor in the world and there
always would be; the English working man was too
shrewd to let himself be led away by a lot of irresponsi-
ble agitators; and after all he didn't have a bad time.

Simon went on. He was eager to deliver himself of
thoughts that he had bottled up for many months and

he had been used to impart them to Charley for as long as he could remember. Though he reflected upon them with the intensity which was one of his great gifts, he found that they gained in clearness and force when he had this perfect listener to put them to.

"An awful lot of hokum is talked about love, you know. An importance is ascribed to it that is entirely at variance with fact. People talk as though it were self-evidently the greatest of human values. Nothing is less self-evident. Until Plato dressed his sentimental sensuality in a captivating literary form the ancient world laid no more stress on it than was sensible; the healthy realism of the Muslims has never looked upon it as anything but a physical need; it was Christianity, buttressing its emotional claims with neo-Platonism, that made it into the end an aim, the reason, the justification of life. But Christianity was the religion of slaves. It offered the weary and the heavy-laden heaven to compensate them in the future for their misery in this world and the opiate of love to enable them to bear it in the present. And like every drug it enervated and destroyed those who became subject to it. For two thousand years it's suffocated us. It's weakened our wills and lessened our courage. In this modern world we live in we know that almost everything is more important to us than love, we know that only the soft and the stupid allow it to affect their actions, and yet we pay it a foolish lip-service. In books, on the stage, in the pulpit, on the platform the same old sentimental rubbish is talked that was used to hoodwink the slaves of Alexandria."

"But, Simon, the slave population of the ancient world was just the proletariat of to-day."

Simon's lips trembled with a smile and the look he fixed on Charley made him feel that he had said a silly thing.

"I know," said Simon quietly.

For a while his restless eyes were still, but though he looked at Charley his gaze seemed fixed on something in the far distance. Charley did not know of what he thought, but he was conscious of a faint malaise.

"It may be that the habit of two thousand years has made love a human necessity and in that case it must be taken into account. But if dope must be administered the best person to do so is surely not a dope-fiend. If love can be put to some useful purpose it can only be by someone who is himself immune to it."

"You don't seem to want to tell me what end you expect to attain by denying yourself everything that makes life pleasant. I wonder if any end can be worth it."

"What have you been doing with yourself for the last year, Charley?"

The sudden question seemed inconsequent, but he answered it with his usual modest frankness.

"Nothing very much, I'm afraid. I've been going to the office pretty well every day; I've spent a certain amount of time on the Estate getting to know the properties and all that sort of thing: I've played golf with father. He likes to get in a round two or three days a week. And I've kept up with my piano-playing. I've been to a good many concerts. I've seen most of the picture shows. I've been to the opera a bit and seen a certain number of plays."

"You've had a thoroughly good time?"

"Not bad. I've enjoyed myself."

"And what d'you expect to do next year?"

"More or less the same, I should think."

"And the year after, and the year after that?"

"I suppose in a few years I shall get married and then my father will retire and hand over his job to me. It brings in a thousand a year, not so bad in these days, and of course eventually I shall get my half of my father's share in the Mason Estate."

"And then you'll lead the sort of life your father has led before you?"

"Unless the Labour party confiscate the Mason Estate. Then of course I shall be in the cart. But until then I'm quite prepared to do my little job and have as much fun as I can on the income I've got."

"And when you die will it have mattered a damn whether you ever lived or not?"

For a moment the unexpected question disconcerted Charley and he flushed.

"I don't suppose it will."

"Are you satisfied with that?"

"To tell you the truth I've never thought about it. But if you ask me point-blank, I think I should be a fool if I weren't. I could never have become a great artist. I talked it over with father that summer after I came down when we went fishing in Norway. He put it awfully nicely. Poor old dear, he was very anxious not to hurt my feelings, but I couldn't help admitting that what he said was true. I've got a natural facility for doing things, I can paint a bit and write a bit and play a bit, perhaps I might have had a chance if I'd only been able to do one thing; but it was only a facility. Father was quite right when he said that wasn't enough, and I think he was right too when he said it was better to be a pretty good business man than a second-rate artist. After all, it's a bit of luck for me that old Sibert Mason married the cook and started growing vegetables on a bit of land that the growth of London turned into a valuable property. Don't you think it's enough if I do my duty in that state of life in which providence or chance, if you like, has placed me?"

Simon gave him a smile more indulgent than any that had tortured his features that evening.

"I daresay, Charley. But not for me. I would sooner be smashed into a mangled pulp by a bus when we cross the street than look forward to a life like yours."

Charley looked at him calmly.

"You see, Simon, I have a happy nature and you haven't."

Simon chuckled.

"We must see if we can't change that. Let's stroll along. I'll take you to the Sérail."

iii

THE FRONT DOOR, a discreet door in a house of respectable appearance, was opened for them by a negro
in Turkish dress and as they entered a narrow ill-lit
passage a woman came out of an ante-room. She took
them in with a quick, cool glance, but then recognizing
Simon, immediately assumed an air of geniality. They
shook hands warmly.

"This is Mademoiselle Ernestine," he said to
Charley and then to her: "My friend has arrived from
London this evening. He wishes to see life."

"You've brought him to the right place."

She gave Charley an appraising look. Charley saw
a woman who might have been in the later thirties,
good-looking in a cold, hard way, with a straight nose,
thin painted lips and a firm chin; she was neatly dressed
in a dark suit of somewhat masculine cut. She wore a
collar and tie and as a pin the crest of a famous English
regiment.

"He's good-looking," she said. "These ladies will
be pleased to see him."

"Where is Madame to-night?"

"She's gone home to spend the holidays with her family. I am in charge."

"We'll go in, shall we?"

"You know your way."

The two young men passed along the passage and opening a door found themselves in a vast room garishly decorated in the pinchbeck style of a Turkish bath. There were settees round the walls and in front of them little tables and chairs. A fair sprinkling of people were sitting about, mostly in day clothes, but a few in dinner-jackets; men in twos and threes; and at one table a mixed party, the women in evening frocks, who had evidently come to see one of the sights of Paris. Waiters in Turkish dress stood about and attended to orders. On a platform was an orchestra consisting of a pianist, a fiddler and a man who played the saxophone. Two benches facing one another jutted out on to the dance floor and on these sat ten or twelve young women. They wore Turkish slippers, but with high heels, baggy trousers of some shimmering material that reached to their ankles, and small turbans on their heads. The upper part of their bodies was naked. Other girls similarly dressed were seated with men who were standing a drink. Simon and Charley sat down and ordered a bottle of champagne. The band started up. Three or four men rose to their feet and going over to the benches chose partners to dance with. The rest of the girls listlessly danced together. They talked in a desultory way to one another and threw inquisitive glances at the men who were sitting at the various tables. It was apparent that the party of sight-seers, with the smart women from a different world, excited their curiosity. On the face of it, except that the girls were half naked, there was nothing to distinguish the place from any night club but the fact that there was room to dance in comfort. Charley noticed that at a table near theirs two men with dispatch-cases, from which in the course of conversation they extracted papers, were talking business as unconcernedly as if they were in a café. Presently one of the men from the group of sight-seers went and spoke to two girls who were dancing together, whereupon they stopped and went up to the table from which he had come; one of the women, beautifully dressed in black, with a string of emeralds round her neck, got up and began dancing with one of the two girls. The other went back to the bench and sat down. The sous-maîtresse, the woman in the coat and skirt, came up to Simon and Charley.

"Well, does your friend see any of these ladies who takes his fancy?"

"Sit down with us a minute and have a drink. He's having a look round. The night's young yet."

She sat down and when Simon called the waiter ordered an orangeade.

"I'm sorry he's come here for the first time on such a quiet night. You see, on Christmas Eve a lot of people have to stay at home. But it'll get more lively presently. A crowd of English have come over to Paris for the holidays. I saw in the paper that they're running the Golden Arrow in three sections. They're a great nation, the English; they have money."

Charley, feeling rather shy, was silent, and she asked
Simon if he understood French.

"Of course he does. He spent six months in Touraine
to learn it."

"What a beautiful district! Last summer when I took
my holiday I motored all through the Châteaux country.
Angèle comes from Tours. Perhaps your friend would
like to dance with her." She turned to Charley. "You
do dance, don't you?"

"Yes, I like it."

"She's very well educated and she comes from an
excellent family. I went to see them when I was in
Tours and they thanked me for all that I had done for
their daughter. They were persons of the greatest
respectability. You mustn't think that we take anyone
here. Madame is very particular. We have our name
and we value it. All these ladies here come from families
who are highly esteemed in their own town. That is
why they like to work in Paris. Naturally they don't
want to cause embarrassment to their relations. Life
is hard and one has to earn one's living as best one can.
Of course I don't pretend that they belong to the
aristocracy, but the aristocracy in France is thoroughly
corrupt, and for my part I set much greater value on
the good French bourgeois stock. That is the backbone
of the country."

Mademoiselle Ernestine gave you the impression
of a sensible woman of sound principle. You could not
but feel that her views on the social questions of the
day would be well worth listening to. She patted
Simon's hand and again speaking to Charley said:

"It always gives me pleasure to see Monsieur Simon. He's a good friend of the house. He doesn't come very often, but when he does he behaves like a gentleman. He is never drunk like some of your compatriots and one can talk to him of interesting subjects. We are always glad to see journalists here. Sometimes I think the life we lead is a little narrow and it does one good to talk to someone who is in the centre of things. It takes one out of one's rut. He's sympathetic."

In those surroundings, as though he felt himself strangely at home, Simon was easy and genial. If he was acting it was a very good performance that he was giving. You would have thought that he felt some queer affinity between himself and the sous-maîtresse of the brothel.

"Once he took me to a répétition générale at the Français. All Paris was there. Academicians, ministers, generals. I was dazzled."

"And I may add that not one of the women looked more distinguished than you. It did my reputation a lot of good to be seen with you."

"You should have seen the faces of some of the bigwigs who come here, when they saw me in the foyer walking on the arm of Monsieur Simon."

Charley knew that to go to a great social function with such a companion was the kind of joke that appealed to Simon's sardonic humour. They talked a little more and then Simon said:

"Listen, my dear, I think we ought to do our young friend proud as it's the first time he's been here. What about introducing him to the Princess? Don't you think he'd like her?"

Mademoiselle Ernestine's strong features relaxed into a smile and she gave Charley an amused glance.

"It's an idea. It would at least be an experience that he hasn't had before. She has a pretty figure."

"Let's have her along and stand her a drink."

Mademoiselle Ernestine called a waiter.

"Tell the Princess Olga to come here." Then to Charley: "She's Russian. Of course since the revolution we have been swamped with Russians, we're fed to the teeth with them and their Slav temperament; for a time the clients were amused by it, but they're tired of them now. And then they're not serious. They're noisy and quarrelsome. The truth is, they're barbarians, and they don't know how to behave. But Princess Olga is different. She has principles. You can see that she's been well brought up. She has something, there's no denying it."

While she was speaking Charley saw the waiter go up to a girl who was sitting on one of the benches and speak to her. His eyes had been wandering and he had noticed her before. She sat strangely still, and you would have thought that she was unconscious of her surroundings. She got up now, gave a glance in their direction, and walked slowly towards them. There was a singular nonchalance in her gait. When she came up she gave Simon a slight smile and they shook hands.

"I saw you come in just now," she said, as she sat down.

Simon asked her if she would drink a glass of champagne.

"I don't mind."

"This is a friend of mine who wants to know you."

"I'm flattered." She turned an unsmiling glance on Charley. She looked at him for a time that seemed to him embarrassingly long, but her eyes held neither welcome nor invitation; their perfect indifference was almost nettling. "He's handsome." Charley smiled shyly and then the faintest suspicion of a smile trembled on her lips. "He looks good-natured."

Her turban, her baggy trousers were of gauze, pale blue and thickly sprinkled with little silver stars. She was not very tall; her face was heavily made up, her cheeks extravagantly rouged, her lips scarlet and her eyelids blue; eyebrows and eyelashes were black with mascara. She was certainly not beautiful, she was only prettyish, with rather high cheek-bones, a fleshy little nose and eyes not set deep in their sockets, not prominent either, but on a level as it were with her face, like windows set flush with a wall. They were large and blue, and their blue, emphasized both by the colour of her turban and by the mascara, was like a flame. She had a neat, trim, slight figure, and the skin of her body, pale amber in hue, had a look of silky softness. Her breasts were small and round, virginal, and the well-shaped nipples were rosy.

"Why don't you ask the Princess to dance with you, Charley?" said Simon.

"Will you?" said he.

She gave the very faintest shrug of one shoulder and

without a word rose to her feet. At the same time Mademoiselle Ernestine, saying she had affairs to attend to, left them. It was a new and thrilling experience for Charley to dance with a girl with nothing on above the waist. It made him rather breathless to put his hand on her naked body and to feel her bare breasts against him. The hand which he held in his was small and soft. But he was a well-brought-up young man, with good manners, and feeling it was only decent to make polite conversation, talked in the same way as he would have to any girl at a dance in London whom he did not know. She answered civilly enough, but he had a notion that she was not giving much heed to what he said. Her eyes wandered vaguely about the room, but there was no indication that they found there anything to excite her interest. When he clasped her a little more closely to him she accepted the more intimate hold without any sign that she noticed it. She acquiesced. The band stopped playing and they returned to their table. Simon was sitting there alone.

"Well, does she dance well?" he asked.

"Not very."

Suddenly she laughed. It was the first sign of animation she had given and her laugh was frank and gay.

"I'm sorry," she said, speaking English, "I wasn't attending. I can dance better than that and next time I will."

Charley flushed.

"I didn't know you spoke English. I wouldn't have said that."

"But it was quite true. And you dance so well, you deserve a partner who can dance too."

Hitherto they had spoken French. Charley's was not very accurate, but it was fluent enough, and his accent was good. She spoke it very well, but with the sing-song Russian intonation which gives the language an alien monotony. Her English was not bad.

"The Princess was educated in England," said Simon.

"I went there when I was two and stayed till I was fourteen. I haven't spoken it much since then and I've forgotten."

"Where did you live?"

"In London. In Ladbroke Grove. In Charlotte Street. Wherever it was cheap."

"I'm going to leave you young things now," said Simon. "I'll see you to-morrow, Charley."

"Aren't you going to the Mass?"

"No."

He left them with a casual nod.

"Have you known Monsieur Simon long?" asked the Princess.

"He's my oldest friend."

"Do you like him?"

"Of course."

"He's very different from you. I should have thought he was the last person you would have taken to."

"He's brilliantly clever. He's been a very good friend to me."

She opened her mouth to speak, but then seemed to think better of it, and kept silent. The music began to play once more.

"Will you dance with me again?" she asked. "I want to show you that I *can* dance when I want to."

Perhaps it was because Simon had left them and she felt less constraint, perhaps it was something in Charley's manner, maybe his confusion when he had realized that she spoke English, that had made her take notice of him, there was a difference in her attitude. It had now a kindliness which was unexpected and attractive. While they danced she talked with something approaching gaiety. She went back to her childhood and spoke with a sort of grim humour of the squalor in which she and her parents had lived in cheap London lodgings. And now, taking the trouble to follow Charley's steps, she danced very well. They sat down again and Charley glanced at his watch; it was getting on towards midnight. He was in a quandary. He had often heard them speak at home of the church music at St. Eustache, and the opportunity of hearing Mass there on Christmas Eve was one that he could not miss. The thrill of arriving in Paris, his talk with Simon, the new experience of the Sérail and the champagne he had drunk, had combined to fill him with a singular exaltation and he had an urgent desire to hear music; it was as strong as his physical desire for the girl he had been dancing with. It seemed silly to go at this particular juncture and for such a purpose; but there it was, he wanted to, and after all nobody need know.

"Look," he said, with an engaging smile, "I've got a date. I must go away now, but I shall be back in an hour. I shall still find you here, shan't I?"

"I'm here all night."

"But you won't get fixed up with anybody else?"

"Why have you got to go away?"

He smiled a trifle shyly.

"I'm afraid it sounds absurd, but my friend has given me a couple of tickets for the Mass at St. Eustache, and I may never have another opportunity of hearing it."

"Who are you going with?"

"Nobody."

"Will you take me?"

"You? But how could you get away?"

"I can arrange that with Mademoiselle. Give me a couple of hundred francs and I'll fix it."

He gave her a doubtful glance. With her naked body, her powder-blue turban and trousers, her painted face, she did not look the sort of person to go to church with. She saw his glance and laughed.

"I'd give anything in the world to go. Do, do. I can change in ten minutes. It would give me so much pleasure."

"All right."

He gave her the money and telling him to wait for her in the entrance, she hurried away. He paid for the wine and after ten minutes, counted on his watch, went out.

As he stepped into the passage a girl came up to him.

"I haven't kept you waiting, you see. I've explained to Mademoiselle. Anyway she thinks Russians are mad."

Until she spoke he had not recognized her. She wore a brown coat and skirt and a felt hat. She had taken off her make-up, even the red on her lips, and her eyes under the thin fair line of her shaven eyebrows looked neither so large nor so blue. In her brown clothes, neat but cheap, she looked nondescript. She might have been a workgirl such as you see pouring along side streets from the back door of a department store at the luncheon hour. She was hardly even pretty, but she looked very young; and there was something humble in her bearing that gave Charley a pang.

"Do you like music, Princess?" he asked, when they got into a taxi.

He did not quite know what to call her. Even though she was a prostitute, he felt it would be rude, with her rank, on so short an acquaintance to call her Olga, and if she had been reduced to so humiliating a position by the stress of circumstances it behoved him all the more to treat her with respect.

"I'm not a princess, you know, and my name isn't Olga. They call me that at the Sérail because it flatters the clients to think they are going to bed with a princess and they call me Olga because it's the only Russian name they know besides Sasha. My father was a professor of economics at the University at Leningrad and my mother was the daughter of a customs official."

"What is your name then?"

"Lydia."

They arrived just as the Mass was beginning. There were crowds of people and no chance of getting a seat. It was bitterly cold and Charley asked her if she would like his coat. She shook her head without answering. The aisles were lit by naked electric globes and they threw harsh beams on the vaulting, the columns and

the dark throng of worshippers. The choir was brilliantly lit. They found a place by a column where,
protected by its shadow, they could feel themselves
isolated. There was an orchestra on a raised platform.
At the altar were priests in splendid vestments. The
music seemed to Charley somewhat florid, and he listened to it with a faint sense of disappointment. It did
not move him as he had expected it would and the
soloists, with their metallic, operatic voices, left him
cold. He had a feeling that he was listening to a performance rather than attending a religious ceremony,
and it excited in him no sensation of reverence. But
for all that he was glad to have come. The darkness
into which the light from the electric globes cut like a
bright knife, making the Gothic lines grimmer; the soft
brilliance of the altar, with its multitude of candles,
with the priests performing actions whose meaning was
unknown to him; the silent crowd that seemed not to
participate but to wait anxiously like a crowd at a
station barrier waiting for the gate to open; the stench
of wet clothes and the aromatic perfume of incense;
the bitter cold that lowered like a threatening unseen
presence; it was not a religious emotion that he got
from all this, but the sense of a mystery that had its
roots far back in the origins of the human race. His
nerves were taut, and when on a sudden the choir to the
full accompaniment of the orchestra burst with a great
shout into the Adeste Fideles he was seized with an exultation over he knew not what. Then a boy sang a
canticle; the thin, silvery voice rose in the silence and
the notes trickled, with a curious little hesitation at

first, as though the singer were not quite sure of himself, trickled like water crystal-clear trickling over the white stones of a brook; and then, the singer gathering assurance, the sounds were caught up, as though by great dark hands, and borne into the intricate curves of the arches and up to the night of the vaulted roof. Suddenly Charley was conscious that the girl by his side, Lydia, was crying. It gave him a bit of a turn, but with his polite English reticence he pretended not to notice; he thought that the dark church and the pure sound of the boy's voice had filled her with a sudden sense of shame. He was an imaginative youth and he had read many novels. He could guess, he fancied, what she was feeling and he was seized with a great pity for her. He found it curious, however, that she should be so moved by music that was not of the best quality. But now she began to be shaken by heavy sobs and he could pretend no longer that he did not know she was in trouble. He put out a hand and took hers, thinking to offer her thus the comfort of his sympathy, but she snatched away her hand almost roughly. He began to be embarrassed. She was now crying so violently that the bystanders could not but notice it. She was making an exhibition of herself and he went hot with shame.

"Would you like to go out?" he whispered.

She shook her head angrily. Her sobbing grew more and more convulsive and suddenly she sank down on her knees and, burying her face in her hands, gave herself up to uncontrolled weeping. She was heaped up on herself strangely, like a bundle of cast-off clothes, and except for the quivering shoulders you would have thought her in a dead faint. She lay crouched at the foot of the tall pillar, and Charley, miserably self-conscious, stood in front of her trying to protect her from view. He saw a number of persons cast curious glances at her and then at him. It made him angry to think what they must suppose. The musicians were hushed, the choir was mute, and the silence had a thrilling quality of awe. Communicants, serried row upon row, pressed up to the altar steps to take in their mouths the Sacred Host that the priest offered them. Charley's delicacy prevented him from looking at Lydia and he kept his eyes fixed on the bright-lit chancel. But when she raised herself a little he was conscious of her movement. She turned to the pillar and putting her arm against it hid her face in the crook of her elbow. The passion of her weeping had exhausted her, but the way in which she now sprawled, leaning against the hard stone, her bent legs on the stone paving, expressed such a hopelessness of woe that it was even more intolerable than to see her crushed and bowed on the floor like a person thrown into an unnatural attitude by a violent death.

The service reached its close. The organ joined with the orchestra for the voluntary, and an increasing stream of people, anxious to get to their cars or to find taxis, streamed to the doors. Then it was finished, and a great throng swept down the length of the church. Charley waited till they were alone in the place they had chosen and the last thick wedge of people seemed to be pressing to the doors. He put his hand on her shoulder.

"Come. We must go now."

He put his arm round her and lifted her to her feet. Inert, she let him do what he liked. She held her eyes averted. Linking her arm in his he led her down the aisle and waited again a little till all but a dozen people had gone out.

"Would you like to walk a few steps?"

"No, I'm so tired. Let's get into a taxi."

But they had to walk a little after all, for they could not immediately find one. When they came to a street lamp she stopped and taking a mirror from her bag looked at herself. Her eyes were swollen. She took out a puff and dabbed it over her face.

"There's not much to be done," he said, with a kindly smile. "We'd better go and have a drink somewhere. You can't go back to the Sérail like that."

"When I cry my eyes always swell. It'll take hours to go down."

Just then a taxi passed and Charley hailed it.

"Where shall we go?"

"I don't care. The Select. Boulevard Montparnasse."

He gave the address and they drove across the river. When they arrived he hesitated, for the place she had chosen seemed crowded, but she stepped out of the taxi and he followed her. Notwithstanding the cold a lot of people were sitting on the terrace. They found a table within.

"I'll go into the ladies' room and wash my eyes."

In a few minutes she returned and sat down by his side. She had pulled down her hat as far as she could to hide her swollen lids and had powdered herself, but she had put on no rouge and her face was white. She was quite calm. She said nothing about the passion of weeping that had overcome her and you might have thought she took it as a natural thing that needed no excuse.

"I'm very hungry," she said. "You must be hungry, too."

Charley was ravenous and while he waited for her had wondered whether in the circumstances it would seem very gross if he ordered himself bacon and eggs. Her remark relieved his mind. It appeared that bacon and eggs were just what she fancied. He wanted to order a bottle of champagne, thinking she needed the stimulant, but she would not let him.

"Why should you waste your money? Let's have some beer."

They ate their simple meal with appetite. They talked little. Charley, with his good manners, tried to make polite conversation, but she did not encourage him and presently they fell into silence. When they had finished and had had coffee, he asked Lydia what she would like to do.

"I should like to sit here. I'm fond of this place. It's cosy and intimate. I like to look at the people who come here."

"All right, we'll sit here."

It was not exactly how he had proposed to pass his first night in Paris. He wished he hadn't been such a fool as to take her to the Midnight Mass. He had not the heart to be unkind to her. But perhaps there was some intonation in his reply that struck her, for she turned a little to look him in the face. She gave him once more the smile he had already seen two or three times on her. It was a queer sort of smile. It hardly moved the lips; it held no gaiety, but was not devoid of kindliness; there was more irony in it than amusement and it was rare and unwilling, patient and disillusioned.

"This can't be very amusing for you. Why don't you go back to the Sérail and leave me here?"

"No, I won't do that."

"I don't mind being alone, you know. I sometimes come here by myself and sit for hours. You've come to Paris to enjoy yourself. You'd be a fool not to."

"If it doesn't bore you I'd like to sit here with you."

"Why?" She gave him on a sudden a disdainful glance. "Do you look upon yourself as being noble and self-sacrificing? Or are you sorry for me or only curious?"

Charley could not imagine why she seemed angry with him or why she said these wounding things.

"Why should I feel sorry for you? Or curious?"

He meant her to understand that she was not the first prostitute he had met in his life and he was not likely to be impressed with a life-story which was probably sordid and in all likelihood untrue. Lydia stared at him with an expression which to him looked like incredulous surprise.

"What did your friend Simon tell you about me?"

"Nothing."

"Why do you redden when you say that?"

"I didn't know I reddened," he smiled.

In fact Simon had told him that she was not a bad

romp, and would give him his money's worth, but that was not the sort of thing he felt inclined to tell her just then. With her pale face and swollen eyelids, in that poor brown dress and the black felt hat, there was nothing to remind one of the creature, in her blue Turkish trousers, with a naked body, who had had a curious, exotic attractiveness. It was another person altogether, quiet, respectable, demure, with whom Charley could as little think of going to bed as with one of the junior mistresses at Patsy's old school. Lydia relapsed into silence. She seemed to be sunk in reverie. When at last she spoke it was as though she were continuing her train of thought rather than addressing him.

"If I cried just now in church it wasn't for the reason that you thought. I've cried enough for that, heaven knows, but just then it was for something different. I felt so lonely. All those people, they have a country, and in that country, homes; to-morrow they'll spend Christmas Day together, father and mother and children; some of them, like you, went only to hear the music, and some have no faith, but just then, all of them, they were joined together by a common feeling; that ceremony, which they've known all their lives, and whose meaning is in their blood, every word spoken, every action of the priests, is familiar to them, and even if they don't believe with their minds, the awe, the mystery, is in their bones and they believe with their hearts; it is part of the recollections of their childhood, the gardens they played in, the countryside, the streets of the towns. It binds them together, it makes them one, and some deep instinct tells them that they belong to one another. But I am a stranger. I have no country, I have no home, I have no language. I belong nowhere. I am outcast."

She gave a mournful little chuckle.

"I'm a Russian and all I know of Russia is what I've read. I yearn for the broad fields of golden corn and the forests of silver beech that I've read of in books and though I try and try, I can't see them with my mind's eye. I know Moscow from what I've seen of it at the cinema. I sometimes rack my brain to picture to myself a Russian village, the straggling village of log houses with their thatched roofs that you read about in Chekov, and it's no good, I know that what I see isn't that at all. I'm a Russian and I speak my native language worse than I speak English and French. When I read Tolstoi and Dostoievsky it is easier for me to read them in a translation. I'm just as much a foreigner to my own people as I am to the English and French. You who've got a home and a country, people who love you, people whose ways are your ways, whom you understand without knowing them—how can you tell what it is to belong nowhere?"

"But have you no relations at all?"

"Not one. My father was a socialist, but he was a quiet, peaceable man absorbed in his studies, and he took no active part in politics. He welcomed the revolution and thought it was the opening of a new era for Russia. He accepted the Bolsheviks. He only asked to be allowed to go on with his work at the university. But they turned him out and one day he got news that he was going to be arrested. We escaped through Finland, my father, my mother and me. I was two. We lived in England for twelve years. How, I don't know. Sometimes my father got a little work to do, sometimes people helped us, but my father was homesick. Except when he was a student in Berlin he'd never been out of Russia before; he couldn't accustom himself to English life, and at last he felt he had to go back. My mother implored him not to. He couldn't help himself, he had to go, the desire was too strong for him; he got into touch with people at the Russian embassy in London, he said he was prepared to do any work the Bolsheviks gave him; he had a good reputation in Russia, his books had been widely praised, and he was an authority on his subject. They promised him everything and he sailed. When the ship docked he was taken off by the agents of the Cheka. We heard that he'd been taken to a cell on the fourth floor of the prison and thrown out of the window. They said he'd committed suicide."

She sighed a little and lit another cigarette. She had been smoking incessantly since they finished supper.

"He was a mild gentle creature. He never did anyone harm. My mother told me that all the years they'd been married he'd never said a harsh word to her. Because he'd made his peace with the Bolsheviks the people who'd helped us before wouldn't help us any more. My mother thought we'd be better off in Paris. She had friends there. They got her work addressing letters. I was apprenticed to a dressmaker. My mother died because there wasn't enough to eat for both of us and she denied herself so that I shouldn't go hungry. I found a job with a dressmaker who gave me half the usual wages because I was Russian. If those friends of my mother's, Alexey and Evgenia, hadn't given me a bed to sleep in I should have starved too. Alexey played the violin in an orchestra at a Russian restaurant and Evgenia ran the ladies' cloak-room. They had three children and the six of us lived in two rooms. Alexey was a lawyer by profession, he'd been one of my father's pupils at the university."

"But you have them still?"

"Yes, I have them still. They're very poor now. You see, everyone's sick of the Russians, they're sick of Russian restaurants and Russian orchestras. Alexey hasn't had a job for four years. He's grown bitter and quarrelsome and he drinks. One of the girls has been taken charge of by an aunt who lives at Nice, and another has gone into service, the son has become a gigolo and he does the night clubs at Montmartre; he's often here, I don't know why he isn't here this evening, perhaps he's clicked. His father curses him and beats him when he's drunk, but the hundred francs he brings home when he's found a friend helps to keep things going. I live there still."

"Do you?" said Charley in surprise.

"I must live somewhere. I don't go to the Sérail till night and when trade is slack I often get back by four or five. But it's terribly far away."

For a while they sat in silence.

"What did you mean when you said just now you hadn't been crying for the reason I thought?" asked Charley at length.

She gave him once more a curious, suspicious look.

"Do you really mean that you don't know who I am? I thought that was why your friend Simon sent for me."

"He told me nothing except—except that you'd give me a good time."

"I'm the wife of Robert Berger. That is why, although I'm a Russian, they took me at the Sérail. It gives the clients a kick."

"I'm afraid you'll think me very stupid, but I honestly don't know what you're talking about."

She gave a short, hard laugh.

"Such is fame. A day's journey and the name that's on every lip means nothing. Robert Berger murdered an English bookmaker called Teddie Jordan. He was condemned to fifteen years' penal servitude. He's at St. Laurent in French Guiana."

She spoke in such a matter-of-fact way that Charley could hardly believe his ears. He was startled, horrified and thrilled.

"And you really didn't know?"

"I give you my word I didn't. Now you speak of it I remember reading about the case in the English papers. It created rather a sensation because the—the victim was English, but I'd forgotten the name of the— of your husband."

"It created a sensation in France, too. The trial lasted three days. People fought to get to it. The papers gave it the whole of their front page. No one talked of anything else. Oh, it was a sensation all right. That was when I first saw your friend Simon, at least that's when he first saw me, he was reporting the case for his paper and I was in court. It was an exciting trial, it gave the journalists plenty of opportunity. You must get him to tell you about it. He's proud of the articles he wrote. They were so clever, bits of them got translated and were put in the French papers. It did him a lot of good."

Charley did not know what to say. He was angry with Simon; he recognized his puckish humour in putting him in the situation in which he now found himself.

"It must have been awful for you," he said lamely.

She turned a little and looked into his eyes. He, whose life had been set in pleasant places, had never before seen on a face a look of such hideous despair. It hardly looked like a human face, but like one of those Japanese masks which an artist has fashioned to portray a certain emotion. He shivered. Lydia till now, for Charley's sake, had been talking mostly in English, breaking into French now and then when she found it too difficult to say what she wanted in the unfamiliar language, but now she went on in French. The sing-song of her Russian accent gave it a strange plaintiveness, but at the same time lent a sense of unreality to what she said. It gave you the impression of a person talking in a dream.

"I'd only been married six months. I was going to have a baby. Perhaps it was that that saved his neck. That and his youth. He was only twenty-two. The baby was born dead. I'd suffered too much. You see, I loved him. He was my first love and my last love. When he was sentenced they wanted me to divorce him, transportation is a sufficient reason in French law; they told me that the wives of convicts always divorced and they were angry with me when I wouldn't. The lawyer who defended him was very kind to me. He said that I'd done everything I could, and that I'd had a bad time, but I'd stood by him to the end and now I ought to think of myself, I was young and must remake my life, I was making it even more difficult if I stayed tied to a convict. He was impatient with me when I said that I loved Robert and Robert was the only thing in the world that mattered to me, and that whatever he did I'd love him, and that if ever I could go out to him, and he wanted me, I'd go and gladly. At last he shrugged his shoulders and said there was nothing to be done with us Russians, but if ever I changed my mind and wanted a divorce I was to come to him and he'd help me. And Evgenia and Alexey, poor drunken, worthless Alexey, they gave me no peace. They said Robert was a scoundrel, they said he was wicked, they said it was disgraceful that I should love him. As if one could stop loving because it's disgraceful to love! It's so easy to call a man a scoundrel. What does it mean? He murdered and he suffered for his crime. None of them knew him as I knew him. You see, he loved me. They didn't know how tender he was, how charming, how gay, how boyish. They said he came near killing me as he killed Teddie Jordan; they didn't see that it only made me love him more."

It was almost impossible for Charley, knowing nothing of the circumstances, to get anything coherent out of what she was saying.

"Why should he have killed you?" he asked.

"When he came home—after he'd killed Jordan, it was very late and I'd gone to bed, but his mother was waiting up for him. We lived with her. He was in high spirits, but when she looked at him she knew he'd done something terrible. You see, for weeks she'd been expecting it and she'd been frantic with anxiety.

" 'Where have you been all this time?' she asked him.

" 'I? Nowhere,' he said. 'Round with the boys.' He chuckled and gently patted her cheek. 'It's so easy to kill a man, mother,' he said. 'It's quite ridiculous, it's so easy.'

"Then she knew what he'd done and she burst out crying.

" 'Your poor wife,' she said. 'Oh, how desperately unhappy you're going to make her.'

"He looked down and sighed.

" 'Perhaps it would be better if I killed her too,' he said.

" 'Robert!' she cried.

"He shook his head.

" 'Don't be afraid, I shouldn't have the courage,' he said. 'And yet, if I did it in her sleep, she'd know nothing.'

" 'My God, why did you do it?' she cried.

"Suddenly he laughed. He had a wonderfully gay, infectious laugh. You couldn't hear it without feeling happy.

" 'Don't be so silly, mother, I was only joking,' he said. 'I've done nothing. Go to bed and to sleep.'

"She knew he was lying. But that's all he would say.

At last she went to her room. It was a tiny house, in Neuilly, but it had a bit of garden and there was a little pavilion at the end of it. When we married she gave us the house and moved in there so that she could be with her son and yet not on the top of us. Robert came up to our room and he waked me with a kiss on my lips. His eyes were shining. He had blue eyes, not so blue as yours, gray rather, but they were large and very brilliant. There was almost always a smile in them. They were wonderfully alert."

But Lydia had gradually slowed down the pace of her speech as she came to these sentences. It was as though a thought had struck her and she was turning it over in her mind while she talked. She looked at Charley with a curious expression.

"There *is* something in your eyes that reminds me of him, and your face is the same shape as his. He wasn't so tall as you and he hadn't got your English complexion. He was very good-looking." She was silent for a moment. "What a malicious fool that Simon of yours is."

"What do you mean by that?"

"Nothing."

She leant forward, with her elbows on the table, her face in her hands, and went on, in a rather monotonous voice, as though she were reciting under hypnosis something that was passing before her vacant eyes.

"I smiled when I woke.

" 'How late you are,' I said. 'Be quick and come to bed.'

" 'I can't sleep now,' he said. 'I'm too excited. I'm hungry. Are there any eggs in the kitchen?'

"I was wide awake by then. You can't think how charming he looked sitting on the side of the bed in his new gray suit. He was always well-dressed and he wore his clothes wonderfully well. His hair was very beautiful, dark brown and waving, and he wore it long, brushed back on his head.

" 'I'll put on a dressing-gown and we'll go and see,' I said.

"We went into the kitchen and I found eggs and onions. I fried the onions and scrambled them with the eggs. I made some toast. Sometimes when we went to the theatre or had been to a concert we used to make ourselves something to eat when we got home. He loved scrambled eggs and onions, and I cooked them just in the way he liked. We used to love those modest suppers that we had by ourselves in the kitchen. He went into the cellar and brought out a bottle of champagne. I knew his mother would be cross, it was the last of half a dozen bottles that Robert had had given him by one of his racing friends, but he said he felt like champagne just then and he opened the bottle. He ate the eggs greedily and he emptied his glass at a gulp. He was in tearing spirits. When we first got into the kitchen I'd noticed that though his eyes were shining so brightly his face was pale, and if I hadn't known that nothing was more unlikely I should have thought he'd been drinking, but now the colour came back to his cheeks. I thought he'd been just tired and hungry. He'd been out all day, tearing about, I was sure, and it might be that he hadn't had a bite to eat. Although we'd only been parted a few hours he was almost crazy with joy at being with me again. He couldn't stop kissing me and while I was scrambling the eggs I had to push him away because he wanted to hug me and I was afraid he'd spoil the cooking. But I couldn't help laughing. We sat side by side at the kitchen table as close as we could get. He called me every sweet, endearing name he could think of, he couldn't keep his hands off me, you would have thought we'd only been married a week instead of six months. When we'd finished I wanted to wash everything up so that when his mother came in for breakfast she shouldn't find a mess, but he wouldn't let me. He wanted to get to bed quickly.

"He was like a man possessed of a god. I never thought it was possible for a man to love a woman as he loved me that night. I never knew a woman was capable of such adoration as I was filled with. He was insatiable. It seemed impossible to slake his passion. No woman ever had such a wonderful lover as I had that night. And he was my husband. Mine! Mine! I worshipped him. If he'd let me I would have kissed his feet. When at last he fell asleep exhausted, the dawn was already peeping through a chink in the curtains. But I couldn't sleep. I looked at his face as the light grew stronger; it was the unlined face of a boy. He slept, holding me in his arms, and there was a tiny smile of happiness on his lips. At last I fell asleep too.

"He was still sleeping when I woke and I got out of bed very quietly so as not to disturb him. I went into the kitchen to make his coffee for him. We were very poor. Robert had worked in a broker's office, but he'd had a quarrel with his employer and had walked out on him, and since then he hadn't found anything regular to do. He was crazy about racing and sometimes he made a bit that way, though his mother hated it, and occasionally he earned a little money by selling second-hand cars on commission, but all we really had to depend on was his mother's pension, she was the widow of an army doctor, and the little money she had besides. We didn't keep a servant and my mother-in-law and I did the housework. I found her in the kitchen, peeling potatoes for lunch.

" 'How is Robert?' she asked me.

" 'He's still asleep. I wish you could see him. With his hair all tousled he looks as if he was sixteen.'

"The coffee was on the hob and the milk was warm. I put it on to boil and had a cup, then I crept upstairs to get Robert's clothes. He was a dressy fellow and I'd learnt how to press them. I wanted to have them all ready for him and neatly laid out on a chair when he woke. I brought them down into the kitchen and gave them a brush and then I put an iron on to heat. When I put the trousers on the kitchen table I noticed there were stains on one of the legs.

" 'What on earth is that?' I cried. 'Robert *has* got his trousers in a mess.'

"Madame Berger got up from her chair so quickly that she upset the potatoes. She snatched up the trousers and looked at them. She began to tremble.

" 'I wonder what it is,' I said. 'Robert will be furious. His new suit.'

"I saw she was upset, but you know, the French are funny in some ways, they don't take things like that as casually as we Russians do. I don't know how many hundred francs Robert had paid for the suit, and if it was ruined she wouldn't sleep for a week thinking of all the money that had been wasted.

" 'It'll clean,' I said.

" 'Take Robert up his coffee,' she said sharply. 'It's after eleven and quite time he woke. Leave me the trousers. I know what to do with them.'

"I poured him out a cup and was just going upstairs with it when we heard Robert clattering down in his slippers. He nodded to his mother and asked for the paper.

" 'Drink your coffee while it's hot,' I said to him.

"He paid no attention to me. He opened the paper and turned to the latest news.

" 'There's nothing,' said his mother.

"I didn't know what she meant. He cast his eyes down the columns and then took a long drink of coffee. He was unusually silent. I took his coat and began to give it a brush.

" 'You made your trousers in an awful mess last night,' I said. 'You'll have to wear your blue suit to-day.'

"Madame Berger had put them over the back of a chair. She took them to him and showed him the stains. He looked at them for a minute while she watched him in silence. You would have thought he couldn't take his eyes off them. I couldn't understand their silence. It was strange. I thought they were taking a trivial accident in an absurdly tragic way. But of course the French have thrift in their bones.

" 'We've got some petrol in the house,' I said. 'We can get the stains out with that. Or they can go to the cleaner's.'

"They didn't answer. Robert, frowning, looked down. His mother turned the trousers round, I suppose to look if there were stains on the back, and then, I think, felt that there was something in the pockets.

" 'What have you got here?'

"He sprang to his feet.

" 'Leave it alone. I won't have you look in my pockets.'

"He tried to snatch the trousers from her, but before he could do so she had slipped her hand into the hip-pocket and taken out a bundle of bank-notes. He stopped dead when he saw she had them. She let the trousers drop to the ground and with a groan put her hand to her breast as though she'd been stabbed. I saw then that they were both of them as pale as death. A sudden thought seized me; Robert had often said to me that he was sure his mother had a little hoard hidden away somewhere in the house. We'd been terribly short of money lately. Robert was crazy to go down to the Riviera; I'd never been there and he'd been saying for weeks that if we could only get a bit of cash we'd go down and have a honeymoon at last. You see, at the time we married, he was working at that broker's and couldn't get away. The thought flashed through my mind that he'd found his mother's hoard. I blushed to the roots of my hair at the idea that he'd stolen it and yet I wasn't surprised. I hadn't lived with him for six months without knowing that he'd think it rather a lark. I saw that they were thousand-franc notes that she held in her hand. Afterwards I knew there were seven of them. She looked at him as though her eyes would start out of her head.

" 'When did you get them, Robert?' she asked.

"He gave a laugh, but I saw he was nervous.

" 'I made a lucky bet yesterday,' he answered.

" 'Oh, Robert,' I cried, 'you promised your mother you'd never play the horses again.'

" 'This was a certainty,' he said, 'I couldn't resist. We shall be able to go down to the Riviera, my sweet. You take them and keep them or they'll just slip through my fingers.'

" 'No, no, she mustn't have them,' cried Madame Berger. She gave Robert a look of real horror, so that I was astounded, then she turned to me. 'Go and do your room. I won't have the rooms left unmade all day long.'

"I saw she wanted to get rid of me and I thought I'd be better out of the way if they were going to quarrel. The position of a daughter-in-law is delicate. His mother worshipped Robert, but he was extravagant and it worried her to death. Now and then she made a scene. Sometimes they'd shut themselves up in her pavilion at the end of the garden and I'd hear their voices raised in violent discussions. He would come away sulky and irritable and when I saw her I knew she'd been crying. I went upstairs. When I came down again they stopped talking at once and Madame Berger told me to go out and buy some eggs for lunch. Generally Robert went out about noon and didn't come back till night, often very late, but that day he stayed in. He read and played the piano. I asked him what had passed between him and his mother, but he wouldn't tell me, he told me to mind my own business. I think neither of them spoke more than a dozen sentences all day. I thought it would never end. When we went to bed I snuggled up to Robert and put my arms round his neck, for of course I knew he was worried and I wanted to console him, but he pushed me away.

" 'For God's sake leave me alone,' he said. 'I'm in no mood for love-making to-night. I've got other things to think about.'

"I was bitterly wounded, but I didn't speak. I moved away from him. He knew he'd hurt me, for in a little while he put out his hand and lightly touched my face.

" 'Go to sleep, my sweet,' he said. 'Don't be upset because I'm in a bad humour to-day. I drank too much yesterday. I shall be all right to-morrow.'

" 'Was it your mother's money?' I whispered.

"He didn't answer at once.

" 'Yes,' he said at last.

" 'Oh, Robert, how could you?' I cried.

"He paused again before he said anything. I was wretched. I think I began to cry.

" 'If anyone should ask you anything you never saw me with the money. You never knew that I had any.'

" 'How can you think I'd betray you?' I cried.

" 'And the trousers. Maman couldn't get the stains out. She's thrown them away.'

"I suddenly remembered that I'd smelt something burning that afternoon while Robert was playing and I was sitting with him. I got up to see what it was.

" 'Stay here,' he said.

" 'But something's burning in the kitchen,' I said.

" 'Maman's probably burning old rags. She's in a dirty temper to-day, she'll bite your head off if you go and interfere with her.'

"I knew now that it wasn't old rags she was burning; she hadn't thrown the trousers away, she'd burnt them. I began to be horribly frightened, but I didn't say anything. He took my hand.

" 'If anyone should ask you about them,' he said, 'you must say that I got them so dirty cleaning a car that they had to be given away. My mother gave them to a tramp the day before yesterday. Will you swear to that?'

" 'Yes,' I said, but I could hardly speak.

"Then he said a terrifying thing.

" 'It may be that my head depends on it.'

"I was too stunned, I was too horrified, to say anything. My head began to ache so that I thought it would burst. I don't think I closed my eyes all night. Robert slept fitfully. He was restless even in his sleep and turned from side to side. We went downstairs early, but my mother-in-law was already in the kitchen. As a rule she was very decently dressed and when she went out she looked quite smart. She was a doctor's widow and the daughter of a staff officer; she had a feeling about her position and she would let no one know to what economies she was reduced to make the show she did when she went to pay visits on old army friends. Then, with her waved hair and her manicured hands, with rouge on her cheeks, she didn't look more than forty; but now, her hair tousled, without any make-up, in a dressing-gown, she looked like an old procuress who'd retired to live on her savings. She didn't say good morning to Robert. Without a word she handed him the paper. I watched him while he read it and I saw his expression change. He felt my eyes upon him and looked up. He smiled.

" 'Well, little one,' he said gaily, 'what about this coffee? Are you going to stand there all the morning looking at your lord and master or are you going to wait on him?'

"I knew there was something in the paper that would tell me what I had to know. Robert finished his breakfast and went upstairs to dress. When he came down again, ready to go out, I had a shock, for he was wearing the light gray suit that he had worn two days before, and the trousers that went with it. But then of course I remembered that he'd had a second pair made when he ordered the suit. There had been a lot of discussion about it. Madame Berger had grumbled at the expense, but he had insisted that he couldn't hope to get a job unless he was decently dressed and at last she gave in as she always did, but she insisted that he should have a second pair of trousers, she said it was always the trousers that grew shabby first and it would be an economy in the end if he had two pairs. Robert went out and said he wouldn't be in to lunch. My mother-in-law went out soon afterwards to do her marketing and the moment I was alone I seized the paper. I saw that an English bookmaker, called Teddie Jordan, had been found dead in his flat. He had been stabbed in the back. I had often heard Robert speak of him. I knew it was he who had killed him. I had such a sudden pain in my heart that I thought I should die. I was terrified. I don't know how long I sat there. I couldn't move. At last I heard a key in the door and I knew it was Madame Berger coming in again. I put the paper back where she'd left it and went on with my work."

Lydia gave a deep sigh. They had not got to the restaurant till one or after and it was two by the time they finished supper. When they came in the tables were full and there was a dense crowd at the bar. Lydia had been talking a long time and little by little people had been going. The crowd round the bar thinned out. There were only two persons sitting at it now and only one table besides theirs was occupied. The waiters were getting restive.

"I think we ought to be going," said Charley. "I'm sure they want to be rid of us."

At that moment the people at the other table got up to go. The woman who brought their coats from the cloak-room brought Charley's too and put it on the table beside him. He called for the bill.

"I suppose there's some place we could go to now?"

"We could go to Montmartre. Graaf's is open all night. I'm terribly tired."

"Well, if you like I'll drive you home."

"To Alexey and Evgenia's? I can't go there to-night.

He'll be drunk. He'll spend the whole night abusing Evgenia for bringing up the children to be what they are and weeping over his own sorrows. I won't go to the Sérail. We'd better go to Graaf's. At least it's warm there."

She seemed so woebegone, and really so exhausted, that Charley with hesitation made a proposal. He remembered that Simon had told him that he could take anyone into the hotel.

"Look here, I've got two beds in my room. Why don't you come back with me there?"

She gave him a suspicious look, but he shook his head smiling.

"Just to sleep, I mean," he added. "You know, I've had a journey to-day and what with the excitement and one thing and another I'm pretty well all in."

"All right."

There was no cab to be found when they got out into the street, but it was only a little way to the hotel and they walked. A sleepy night watchman opened the door for them and took them upstairs in the lift. Lydia took off her hat. She had a broad, white brow. He had not seen her hair before. It was short, curling round the neck, and pale brown. She kicked off her shoes and slipped out of her dress. When Charley came back from the bathroom, having got into his pyjamas, she was not only in bed but asleep. He got into his own bed and put out the light. They had not exchanged a word since they left the restaurant.

Thus did Charley spend his first night in Paris.

iv

IT WAS LATE when he woke. For a moment he had no notion where he was. Then he saw Lydia. They had not drawn the curtains and a gray light filtered through the shutters. The room with its pitchpine furniture looked squalid. She lay on her back in the twin bed with her eyes open, staring up at the dingy ceiling. Charley glanced at his watch. He felt shy of the strange woman in the next bed.

"It's nearly twelve," he said. "We'd better just have a cup of coffee and then I'll take you to lunch somewhere if you like."

She looked at him with grave, but not unkindly, eyes.

"I've been watching you sleep. You were sleeping as peacefully, as profoundly, as a child. You had such a look of innocence on your face, it was shattering."

"My face badly needs a shave," said he.

He telephoned down to the office for coffee and it was brought by a stout, middle-aged maid, who gave Lydia a glance, but whose expression heavily conveyed nothing. Charley smoked a pipe and Lydia one cigarette after another. They talked little. Charley did not know how to deal with the singular situation in which he found himself and Lydia seemed lost in thoughts unconcerned with him. Presently he went into the bathroom to shave and bath. When he came back he found Lydia sitting in an armchair at the window in his dressing-gown. The window looked into the courtyard and all there was to see was the windows, storey above storey, of the rooms opposite. On the gray Christmas morning it looked incredibly cheerless. She turned to him.

"Couldn't we lunch here instead of going out?"

"Downstairs, d'you mean? If you like. I don't know what the food's like."

"The food doesn't matter. No, up here, in the room. It's so wonderful to shut out the world for a few hours. Rest, peace, silence, solitude. You would think they were luxuries that only the very rich can afford, and yet they cost nothing. Strange that they should be so hard to come by."

"If you like I'll order you lunch here and I'll go out."

Her eyes lingered on him and there was a slightly ironic smile in them.

"I don't mind you. I think probably you're very sweet and nice. I'd rather you stayed; there's something cosy about you that I find comforting."

Charley was not a youth who thought very much about himself, but at that moment he could not help a slight sense of irritation because really she seemed to be using him with more unconcern than was reasonable. But he had naturally good manners and did not betray his feeling. Besides, the situation was odd, and though it was not to find himself in such a one that he had come to Paris, it could not be denied that the experience was interesting. He looked round the room. The beds were unmade; Lydia's hat, her coat and skirt, her shoes and stockings were lying about, mostly on the floor; his own clothes were piled up untidily on a chair.

"The place looks terribly frowsy," he said. "D'you think it would be very nice to lunch in all this mess?"

"What does it matter?" she answered, with the first laugh he had heard from her. "But if it upsets your prim English sense of decorum, I'll make the beds, or the maid can while I'm having a bath."

She went into the bathroom and Charley telephoned for a waiter. He ordered some eggs, some meat, cheese and fruit, and a bottle of wine. Then he got hold of the maid. Though the room was heated there was a fire-place and he thought a fire would be cheerful. While the maid was getting the logs he dressed himself, and then, when she got busy setting things to rights, he sat down and looked at the grim courtyard. He thought disconsolately of the jolly party at the Terry-Masons'. They would be having a glass of sherry now before sitting down to their Christmas dinner of turkey and plum pudding, and they would all be very gay, pleased with their Christmas presents, noisy and jolly. After a while Lydia came back. She had no make-up on her face, but she had combed her hair neatly, the swelling of her eyelids had gone down, and she looked young and pretty; but her prettiness was not the sort that excites carnal desires and Charley, though naturally susceptible, saw her come in without a flutter of his pulse.

"Oh, you've dressed," she said. "Then I can keep on your dressing-gown, can't I? Let me have your slippers. I shall float about in them, but it doesn't matter."

The dressing-gown had been a birthday present from his mother, and it was of blue patterned silk; it was much too long for her, but she arranged herself in it so that it was not unbecoming. She was glad to see the fire and sat down in the chair he had drawn up for her. She smoked a cigarette. What seemed to him strange was that she took the situation as though there were nothing strange in it. She was as casual in her behaviour as though she had known him all her life; if anything more was needed to banish any ideas he might have cherished about her, nothing could have been more efficacious than the impression he so clearly got from her that she had put out of her mind for good and all the possibility of his wanting to go to bed with her. He was surprised to see with what good appetite she ate. He had a notion after what she had told him the night before that she was too distraught to eat but sparingly, and it was a shock to his romantic sensibility to see that she ate as much as he did and with obvious satisfaction.

They were drinking their coffee when the telephone rang. It was Simon.

"Charley? Would you like to come round and have a talk?"

"I'm afraid I can't just now."

"Why not?" Simon asked sharply.

It was characteristic of him to think that everyone

should be ready to drop whatever he was doing if he wanted him. However little something mattered to him, if he had a whim for it and he was crossed, it immediately assumed consequence.

"Lydia's here."

"Who the devil's Lydia?"

Charley hesitated an instant.

Well, Princess Olga."

There was a pause and then Simon burst into a harsh laugh.

"Congratulations, old boy. I knew you'd click. Well, when you have a moment to spare for an old friend, let me know."

He rang off. When Charley turned back to Lydia she was staring into the fire. Her impassive face gave no sign that she had heard the conversation. Charley pushed back the little table at which they had lunched and made himself as comfortable as he could in a shallow armchair. Lydia leaned over and put another log on the fire. There was a sort of intimacy in the action that did not displease Charley. She was settling herself down as a small dog turns round two or three times on a cushion and, having made a suitable hollow, curls up in it. They stayed in all the afternoon. The joyless light of the winter day gradually failed and they sat by the light of the wood-fire. In the rooms on the opposite side of the court lights were turned on here and there, and the pale, uncurtained windows had a false strange look like lighted windows in the stage-set of a street. But they were not more unreal than the position in which he found himself seemed to Charley, sitting in that sordid bedroom, by the fitful blazing of the log fire, while that woman whom he did not know told him her terrible story. It seemed not to occur to her that he might be unwilling to listen. So far as he could tell she had no inkling that he might have anything else to do, nor that in baring her heart to him, in telling him her anguish, she was putting a burden on him that a stranger had no right to exact. Was it that she wanted his sympathy? He wasn't even sure of that. She knew nothing about him and wanted to know nothing. He was only a convenience, and but for his sense of humour, he would have found her indifference exasperating. Towards evening she fell silent, and presently by her quiet breathing Charley knew she had fallen asleep. He got up from his chair, for he had sat in it so long that his limbs ached, and went to the window, on tiptoe so as not to wake her, and sitting down on a stool looked out into the courtyard. Now and again he saw someone pass behind the lighted windows; he saw an elderly woman watering a flower-pot; he saw a man in his shirt-sleeves lying on his bed reading; he wondered who and what these people were. They looked like ordinary middle-class persons in modest circumstances, for after all the hotel was cheap and the quarter dowdy; but seen like that, through the windows, as though in a peep-show, they looked strangely unreal. Who could tell what people were really and what grim passions, what crimes, their commonplace aspect concealed? In some of the rooms the curtains were drawn and only a chink of light between them showed that there was anyone there. Some of the windows were black; they were not empty, for the hotel was full, but their occupants were out. On what mysterious errands? Charley's nerves were shaken and he had a sudden feeling of horror for all those unknown persons whose lives were so strange to him; below the smooth surface he seemed to sense something confused, dark, monstrous and terrible.

He pondered, his brow knit in concentration, the long, unhappy story to which he had listened all the afternoon. Lydia had gone back and forth, now telling him of her struggle to live when she was working for a pittance at a dressmaker's and after that some incident of her poverty-stricken childhood in London; then more of those agonizing days that followed the murder, the terror of the arrest and the anguish of the trial. He had read detective stories, he had read the papers, he knew that crimes were committed, he knew that people lived in penury, but he had known it all, as it were from the outside; it gave him a strange, a frightening sensation to find himself thrown into personal contact with someone to whom horrible things had actually happened. He remembered suddenly, he did not know why, a picture of Manet's of somebody's execution—was it Maximilian's?—by a shooting squad. He had always thought it a striking picture. Now it came to him as a shock to realize that it portrayed an incident that had occurred. The Emperor had in fact stood in that place, and as the soldiers levelled their rifles, it must have seemed incredible to him that he should stand there and in a moment cease to live.

And now that he knew Lydia, now that he had

listened to her last night and that day, now that he had eaten with her, and danced with her, now that for so many hours they had lived together in such close proximity, it seemed unbelievable that such things should have befallen her.

If ever anything looked like pure chance it was that Lydia and Robert Berger met at all. Through the friends she lived with, who worked in a Russian restaurant, Lydia sometimes got a ticket for a concert, and when she couldn't and there was something she very much wanted to hear, she scraped together out of her weekly earnings enough to buy herself standing-room. This was her only extravagance and to go to a concert her only recreation. It was chiefly Russian music she liked. Listening to that she felt that somehow she was getting to the heart of the country she had never seen, but which drew her with a yearning that must ever remain unsatisfied. She knew nothing of Russia but what she had heard from the lips of her father and mother, from the conversation between Evgenia and Alexey when they talked of old times, and from the novels she had read. It was when she was listening to the music of Rimsky-Korsakov and Glazounov, to the racy and mordant compositions of Stravinsky, that the impressions she had thus gained gathered form and substance. Those wild melodies, those halting rhythms, in which there was something so alien from Europe, took her out of herself and her sordid existence and overwhelmed her with such a passion of love that happy, releasing tears flowed down her cheeks. But because nothing of what she saw with the mind's eye had she

seen with a bodily eye, because it was a product of hear-
say and a fevered imagination, she saw it in a strangely
distorted fashion; she saw the Kremlin, with its gilt
and star-sprinkled domes, the Red Square and the Kitai
Gorod, as though they were the setting of a fairy tale;
for her Prince Andrey and the charming Natasha still
went their errands in the busy streets of Moscow,
Dmitri Karamazov, after a wild night with the gipsies,
still met the sweet Alyosha on the Mostbaretsk Bridge,
the merchant Rogozhin dashed past in his sled with
Nastasya Filippovna by his side, and the wan characters of Chekov's stories drifted hither and yon at the
breath of circumstance like dead leaves before the
wind; the Summer Garden and the Nevsky Prospekt
were magic names, and Anna Karenina still drove in
her carriage, Vronsky elegant in his new uniform
climbed the stairs of the great houses on the Fontanka
Canal, and the misbegotten Raskolnikov walked the
Liteiny. In the passion and nostalgia of that music, with
Turgeniev at the back of her mind, she saw the spa-
cious, dilapidated country houses where they 'talked
through the scented night, and the marshes, pale in
the windless dawn, where they shot the wild duck;
with Gorki, the wretched villages where they drank
furiously, loved brutally and killed; the turbid flow of
the Volga, the interminable steppes of the Caucasus,
and the enchanting garish Crimea. Filled with longing,
filled with regret for a life that had passed for ever,
homesick for a home she had never known, a stranger
in a hostile world, she felt at that moment one with the
great, mysterious country. Even though she spoke its

language haltingly, she was Russian, and she loved her native land; at such moments she felt that there was where after all she belonged and she understood how it was that her father, despite the warnings, was obliged, even at the risk of death, to return to it.

It was at a concert, one where all the music was Russian, that she found herself standing next to a young man who, she noticed, now and then looked at her curiously. Once she happened to turn her eyes on him and was struck by the passionate absorption with which he seemed to be listening; his hands were clasped and his mouth slightly open as though he were out of breath. He was rapt in ecstasy. He had clean-cut features and looked well-bred. Lydia gave him but a passing glance and once more returned to the music and the crowding dreams it awoke in her. She too was carried away and she was hardly aware that a little sob broke from her lips. She was startled when she felt a small, soft hand take hers and give it a slight pressure. She quickly drew her hand away. The piece was the last before the interval and when it ended the young man turned to her. He had lovely eyes, gray under bushy eyebrows, and they were peculiarly gentle.

"You're crying, Mademoiselle."

She had thought he might be Russian like herself, but his accent was purely French. She understood that that quick pressure of her hand was one of instinctive sympathy, and was touched by it.

"Not because I am unhappy," she answered, with a faint smile.

He smiled back and his smile was charming.

"I know. This Russian music, it's strangely thrilling and yet it tears one's heart to pieces."

"But you're French. What can it mean to you?"

"Yes. I'm French. I don't know what it means to me. It's the only music I want to listen to. It is power and passion, blood and destruction. It makes every nerve in my body tingle." He gave a little laugh at himself. "Sometimes when I listen to it I feel there is nothing that man is capable of that I cannot do."

She did not answer. It was singular that the same music could say such different things to different people. To her the music they had just heard spoke of the tragedy of human destiny, the futility of striving against fate, and the joy, the peace of humility and resignation.

"Are you coming to next week's concert?" he asked then. "That's to be all Russian too."

"I don't think so."

"Why not?"

He was very young, he could be no older than herself, and there was an ingenuousness in him that made it impossible for her to answer too stiffly a question which in a stranger was indiscreet. There was something in his manner that made her sure he was not trying to pick her up. She smiled.

"I'm not a millionaire. They're rare now, you know, the Russians who are."

"I know some of the people who are running these concerts. I have a pass that admits two. If you like to meet me next Sunday in the doorway, you can come in on it."

"I don't think I could quite do that."

"Do you think it would be compromising?" he smiled. "The crowd would surely be a sufficient chaperon."

"I work in a dressmaker's shop. It would be hard to compromise me. I don't know that I can put myself under an obligation to a total stranger."

"I am sure you are a very well-brought-up young lady, but you should not have unreasonable prejudices."

She did not want to argue the point.

"Well, we'll see. In any case I thank you for the suggestion."

They talked of other things till the conductor once more raised his baton. At the end of the concert he turned to say good-bye to her.

"Till next Sunday then?" he said.

"We'll see. Don't wait for me."

They lost one another in the crowd that thronged towards the exits. During the next week she thought from time to time of the good-looking young man with the large gray eyes. She thought of him with pleasure. She had not arrived at her age without having had to resist now and then the advances of men. Both Alexey and his son the gigolo had made a pass at her, but she had not found it difficult to deal with them. A smart box on the ear had made the lachrymose drunkard understand that there was nothing doing, and the boy she had kept quiet by a judicious mingling of ridicule and plain speech. Often enough men had tried to pick her up in the street, but she was always too tired and often too hungry to be tempted by their advances; it caused her a grim amusement to reflect that the offer of a square meal would have tempted her much more than the offer of a loving heart. She had felt, with her woman's instinct, that the young man of the concert was not quite like that. Doubtless, like any other youth of his age, he would not miss an opportunity for a bit of fun if he could get it, but it was not for the sake of that that he had offered to take her to the concert on Sunday. She had no intention of going, but she was touched that he had asked her. There was something very nice about him, something ingenuous and frank. She felt that she could trust him. She looked at the programme. They were giving the Symphonie Pathétique, she didn't much care about that, Tchaikovsky was too Europeanized for her taste, but they were giving also the *Sacre du Printemps* and Borodin's string quartet. She wondered whether the young man had really meant what he said. It might very well be that his invitation had been issued on the spur of the moment and in half an hour completely forgotten. When Sunday came she had half a mind to go and see, she did very much want to hear the concert, and she had not a penny more in her pocket than she needed for her Metro and her lunches during the week, she had had to give everything else to Evgenia to provide the household with food; if he was not there no harm would have been done, and if he was and really had a pass for two, well, it would cost him nothing and committed her to nothing.

Finally an impulse took her to the Salle Pleyel and

there he was, where he had said he would be, waiting
for her. His eyes lit up and he shook her warmly by
the hand as though they were old friends.

"I'm so glad you've come," he said. "I've been waiting for twenty minutes. I was so afraid I'd miss you."

She blushed and smiled. They went into the concert
room and she found he had seats in the fifth row.

"Did you get these given you?" she asked with
surprise.

"No, I bought them. I thought it would be nice to
be comfortable."

"What folly! I'm so used to standing."

But she was flattered by his generosity and when
presently he took her hand did not withdraw it. She
felt that if it gave him pleasure to hold it, it did her
no harm, and she owed him that. During the interval
he told her his name, Robert Berger, and she told him
hers. He added that he lived with his mother at Neuilly
and that he worked in a broker's office. He talked in
an educated way, with a boyish enthusiasm that made
her laugh, and there was an animation about him that
Lydia could not but feel attractive. His shining eyes,
the mobility of his face, suggested an ardent nature.
To sit next to him was like sitting in front of a fire;
his youth glowed with a physical warmth. When the
concert was over they walked along the Champs-
Élysées together and then he asked her if she would
like some tea. He would not let her refuse. It was a
luxury Lydia had never known to sit in a smart tea-
shop among well-dressed people, and the appetizing

smell of cakes, the heady smell of women's perfume, the warmth, the comfortable chairs, the noisy talk, went to her head. They sat there for an hour. Lydia told him about herself, what her father had been and what had happened to him, how she lived now and how she earned her living; he listened as eagerly as he talked. His gray eyes were tender with sympathy. When it was time for her to go he asked her whether she would come to a cinema one evening. She shook her head.

"Why not?"

"You are a rich young man, and . . ."

"Oh, no, I'm not. Far from it. My mother has little more than her pension and I have only the little I make."

"Then you shouldn't have tea at expensive tea-rooms. Anyhow I am a poor working girl. Thank you for all your kindness to me, but I am not a fool; you have been sweet to me, I don't think it would be very nice of me to accept more of your kindness when I can make no return for it."

"But I don't want a return. I like you. I like to be with you. Last Sunday, when you were crying, you looked so touching, it broke my heart. You're alone in the world, and I—I'm alone too in my way. I was hoping we could be friends."

She looked at him coolly for a moment. They were the same age, but of course really she was years older than he; his mien was so candid she had no doubt that he believed what he said, but she was wise enough to know that he was talking nonsense.

"Let me be quite frank with you," she said. "I know

I'm not a raving beauty, but after all I'm young and there are people who think me prettyish, people who like the Russian type, it's asking too much of me to believe that you are seeking my society just for the pleasure of my conversation. I've never been to bed with a man. I don't think it would be very honest of me if I let you go on wasting your time and your money on me when I have no intention of going to bed with you."

"That is frank enough in all conscience," he smiled, oh, so charmingly, "but you see, I knew that. I haven't lived in Paris all my life without learning something. I know instinctively whether a girl is ready for a little fun or if she isn't. I saw at once that you were good. If I held your hand at the concert it was because you were feeling the music as deeply as I was, and the touch of your hand—I hardly know how to explain it—I felt that your emotion flowed into me and gave mine a richer intensity. Anyhow there was in my feeling nothing of desire."

"And yet we were feeling very different things," she said thoughtfully. "Once I looked at your face and I was startled by its expression. It was cruel and ruthless. It was not like a human face any more, it was a mask of triumphant malice. It frightened me."

He laughed gaily and his laugh was so young, so musical and care-free, the look of his eyes so tenderly frank, it was impossible to believe that for a moment under the influence of that emotional music his features had borne an expression of such cold ferocity.

"What fancies you have! You don't think I am a

white-slaver, like at the cinema, and that I am trying to get you into my clutches and shall then ship you out to Buenos Aires?"

"No," she smiled, "I don't think that."

"How can it hurt you to come to the pictures with me? You've made the position quite clear and I accept it."

She laughed now. It was absurd to make so much fuss. She had little enough amusement in her life, and if he liked to give her a treat and was content merely to sit beside her and to talk, she would be a fool to forgo it. After all, she was nothing. She need answer for her actions to nobody. She could take care of herself and she had given him full warning.

"Oh, very well," she said.

They went to the pictures several times and after the show Robert accompanied Lydia to whichever was the nearest station for her to get a train home. During the little walk he took her arm and for a part of the performance he held her hand, once or twice when they parted he kissed her lightly on both cheeks, but these were the only familiarities he permitted himself. He was good company. He had a chaffing, ironic way of talking about things that pleased her. He did not pretend to have read very much, he had no time, he said, and life was more entertaining than books, but he was not stupid and he could speak intelligently of such books as he had read. It interested Lydia to discover that he had a peculiar admiration for André Gide. He was an enthusiastic tennis-player and he told her that at one time he had been encouraged to take it seriously;

people of importance in the game, thinking he had the making of a champion, had interested themselves in him. But nothing came of it.

"One needs more money and more time to get into the first rank than I could dispose of," he said.

Lydia had a notion that he was in love with her, but she would not allow herself to be certain of it, for she could not but fear that her own feelings made her no safe judge of his. He occupied her thoughts more and more. He was the first friend of her own age that she had ever had. She owed him happy hours at the concerts he took her to on Sunday afternoons, and happy evenings at the cinema. He gave her life an interest and excitement it had never had before. For him she took pains to dress more prettily. She had never been in the habit of making up, but on the fourth or fifth time she met him she rouged her cheeks a little and made up her eyes.

"What have you done to yourself?" he said, when they got into the light. "Why have you been putting all that stuff on your face?"

She laughed and blushed under her rouge.

"I wanted to be a little more of a credit to you. I couldn't bear that people should think you were with a little kitchen-maid who'd just come up to Paris from her native province."

"But almost the first thing I liked in you was that you were so natural. One gets so tired of all these painted faces. I don't know why, I found it touching that you had nothing on your pale cheeks, nothing on your lips, nothing on your eyebrows. It was refreshing, like a little

wood that you come into after you've been walking in
the glare of the road. Having no make-up on gives you
a look of candour and one feels it is a true expression
of the uprightness of your soul."

Her heart began to beat almost painfully, but it was
that curious sort of pain which is more blissful than
pleasure.

"Well, if you don't like it, I'll not do it again. After
all, I only did it for your sake."

She looked with an inattentive mind at the picture
he had brought her to see. She had mistrusted the
tenderness in his musical voice, the smiling softness of
his eyes, but after this it was almost impossible not to
believe that he loved her. She had been exercising all
the self-control she possessed to prevent herself from
falling in love with him. She had kept on saying to
herself that it was only a passing fancy on his part and
that it would be madness if she let her feelings run away
with her. She was determined not to become his mistress. She had seen too much of that sort of thing
among the Russians, the daughters of refugees who
had so much difficulty in making any sort of a living;
often enough, because they were bored, because they
were sick of grinding poverty, they entered upon an
affair, but it never lasted; they seemed to have no
capacity for holding a man, at least not the Frenchmen
whom they generally fell for; their lovers grew tired
of them, or impatient, and chucked them; then they
were even worse off than they had been before, and
often nothing remained but the brothel. But what else
was there that she could hope for? She knew very well

he had no thought of marriage. The possibility of such
a thing would never have crossed his head. She knew
French ideas. His mother would not consent to his
marrying a Russian sewing-woman, which was all she
was really, without a penny to bless herself with.
Marriage in France was a serious thing; the position
of the respective families must be on a par and the
bride had to bring a dowry conformable with the bride-
groom's situation. It was true that her father had been
a professor of some small distinction at the university,
but in Russia, before the revolution, and since then
Paris swarmed with princes and counts and guardsmen
who were driving taxis or doing manual labour. Everyone looked upon the Russians as shiftless and unde-
pendable. People were sick of them. Lydia's mother,
whose grandfather had been a serf, was herself hardly
more than a peasant, and the professor had married
her in accordance with his liberal principles; but she was
a pious woman and Lydia had been brought up with
strict principles. It was in vain that she reasoned with
herself; it was true that the world was different now
and one must move with the times: she could not help
it, she had an instinctive horror of becoming a man's
mistress. And yet. And yet. What else was there to
look forward to? Wasn't she a fool to miss the opportunity that presented itself? She knew that her prettiness was only the prettiness of youth, in a few years
she would be drab and plain; perhaps she would never
have another chance. Why shouldn't she let herself go?
Only a little relaxation of her self-control and she
would love him madly, it would be a relief not to keep

that constant rein on her feelings, and he loved her, yes, he loved her, she knew it, the fire of his passion was so hot it made her gasp, in the eagerness of his mobile face she read his fierce desire to possess her; it would be heavenly to be loved by someone she loved to desperation, and if it didn't last, and of course it couldn't, she would have had the ecstasy of it, she would have the recollection, and wouldn't that be worth all the anguish, the bitter anguish she must suffer when he left her? When all was said and done, if it was intolerable there was always the Seine or the gas oven.

But the curious, the inexplicable, thing was that he didn't seem to want her to be his mistress. He used her with a consideration that was full of respect. He could not have behaved differently if she had been a young girl in the circle of his family acquaintance whose situation and fortune made it reasonable to suppose that their friendship would eventuate in a marriage satisfactory to all parties. She could not understand it. She knew that the notion was absurd, but in her bones she had a queer inkling that he wished to marry her. She was touched and flattered. If it was true he was one in a thousand, but she almost hoped it wasn't, for she couldn't bear that he should suffer the pain that such a wish must necessarily bring him; whatever crazy ideas he harboured, there was his mother in the background, the sensible, practical, middle-class French-woman, who would never let him jeopardize his future and to whom he was devoted as only a Frenchman can be to his mother.

But one evening, after the cinema, when they were walking to the Metro station he said to her:

"There's no concert next Sunday. Will you come and have tea at home? I've talked about you so much to my mother that she'd like to make your acquaintance."

Lydia's heart stood still. She realized the situation at once. Madame Berger was getting anxious about this friendship that her son had formed, and she wanted to see her, the better to put an end to it.

"My poor Robert, I don't think your mother would like me at all. I think it's much wiser we shouldn't meet."

"You're quite wrong. She has a great sympathy for you. The poor woman loves me, you know, I'm all she has in the world, and it makes her happy to think that I've made friends with a young girl who is well brought up and respectable."

Lydia smiled. How little he knew women if he imagined that a loving mother could feel kindly towards a girl that her son had casually picked up at a concert! But he pressed her so strongly to accept the invitation, which he said he issued on his mother's behalf, that at last she did. She thought indeed that it would only make Madame Berger look upon her with increased suspicion if she refused to meet her. They arranged that he should pick her up at the Porte St. Denis at four on the following Sunday and take her to his mother's. He drove up in a car.

"What luxury!" said Lydia, as she stepped in.

"It's not mine, you know. I borrowed it from a friend."

Lydia was nervous of the ordeal before her and not even Robert's affectionate friendliness sufficed to give her confidence.

They drove to Neuilly.

"We'll leave the car here," said Robert, drawing up to the kerb in a quiet street. "I don't want to leave it outside our house. It wouldn't do for the neighbours to think I had a car and of course I can't explain that it's only lent."

They walked a little.

"Here we are."

It was a tiny detached villa, rather shabby from want of paint and smaller than, from the way Robert had talked, she expected. He took her into the drawing-room. It was a small room crowded with furniture and ornaments, with oil pictures in gold frames on the walls, and opened by an archway on to the dining-room in which the table was set for tea. Madame Berger put down the novel she was reading and came forward to greet her guest. Lydia had pictured her as a rather stout, short woman in widow's weeds, with a mild face and the homely, respectable air of a person who has given up all thought of earthly vanity; she was not at all like that; she was thin, and in her high-heeled shoes as tall as Robert; she was smartly dressed in black flowered silk and she wore a string of false pearls round her neck; her hair, permanently waved, was very dark brown and though she must have been hard on fifty there was not a white streak in it. Her sallow skin was somewhat heavily powdered. She had fine eyes, Robert's delicate, straight nose, and the same thin lips,

but in her, age had given them a certain hardness. She
was in her way and for her time of life a good-looking
woman, and she evidently took pains over her appearance, but there was in her expression nothing of the
charm that made Robert so attractive. Her eyes, so
bright and dark, were cool and watchful. Lydia felt
the sharp, scrutinizing look with which Madame Berger
took her in from head to foot as she entered the room,
but it was immediately superseded by a cordial and
welcoming smile. She thanked Lydia effusively for coming so long a distance to see her.

"You must understand how much I wanted to see
a young girl of whom my son has talked to me so much.
I was prepared for a disagreeable surprise. I have, to
tell you the truth, no great confidence in my son's
judgement. It is a relief to me to see that you are as
nice as he told me you were."

All this she said with a good deal of facial expression, with smiles and little nods of the head, flatteringly,
in the manner of a hostess accustomed to society trying
to set a stranger at her ease. Lydia, watchful too,
answered with becoming diffidence. Madame Berger
gave an emphatic, slightly forced laugh and made an
enthusiastic little gesture.

"But you are charming. I'm not surprised that this
son of mine should neglect his old mother for your
sake."

Tea was brought in by a stolid-looking young maid
whom Madame Berger, while continuing her gesticu-
lative, complimentary remarks, watched with sharp,
anxious eyes, so that Lydia guessed that a tea-party

was an unusual event in the house and the hostess was not quite sure that the servant knew how to set about things. They went into the dining-room and sat down. There was a small grand piano in it.

"It takes up room," said Madame Berger, "but my son is passionately devoted to music. He plays for hours at a time. He tells me that you are a musician of the first class."

"He exaggerates. I'm very fond of it, but very ignorant."

"You are too modest, mademoiselle."

There was a dish of little cakes from the confectioner's and a dish of sandwiches. Under each plate was a doyley and on each a tiny napkin. Madame Berger had evidently taken pains to do things in a modish way. With a smile in her cold eyes she asked Lydia how she would like her tea.

"You Russians always take lemon, I know, and I got a lemon for you specially. Will you begin with a sandwich?"

The tea tasted of straw.

"I know you Russians smoke all through your meals. Please do not stand on any ceremony with me. Robert, where are the cigarettes?"

Madame Berger pressed sandwiches on Lydia, she pressed cakes; she was one of those hostesses who look upon it as a mark of hospitality to make their guests eat however unwilling they may be. She talked without ceasing, well, in a high-pitched, metallic voice, smiling a great deal, and her politeness was effusive. She asked Lydia a great many questions, which had a casual air so that on the face of it they looked like the civil inquiries a woman of the world would put out of sympathy for a friendless girl, but Lydia realized that they were cleverly designed to find out everything she could about her. Lydia's heart sank; this was not the sort of woman who for love of her son would allow him to do an imprudent thing; but the certainty of this gave her back her own assurance. It was obvious that she had nothing to lose; she certainly had nothing to hide; and she answered the questions with frankness. She told Madame Berger, as she had already told Robert, about her father and mother, and what her life had been in London and how she had lived since her mother's death. It even amused her to see behind Madame Berger's warm sympathy, through her shocked commiserating answers, the shrewdness that weighed every word she heard and drew conclusions upon it. After two or three unavailing attempts to go, which Madame Berger would not hear of, Lydia managed to tear herself away from so much friendliness. Robert was to see her home. Madame Berger seized both her hands when she said good-bye to her and her fine dark eyes glittered with cordiality.

"You are delicious," she said. "You know your way now, you must come and see me often, often; you will be always sure of a hearty welcome."

When they were walking along to the car Robert took her arm with an affectionate gesture which seemed to ask for protection rather than to offer it and which charmed her.

"Well, my dear one, it went off very well. My mother

liked you. You made a conquest of her at once. She'll adore you."

Lydia laughed.

"Don't be so silly. She detested me."

"No, no, you're wrong. I promise you. I know her, I saw at once that she took to you."

Lydia shrugged her shoulders, but did not answer. When they parted they arranged to go to the cinema on the following Tuesday. She agreed to his plan, but she was pretty sure that his mother would put a stop to it. He knew her address now.

"If anything should happen to prevent you, you'll send me a petit bleu?"

"Nothing will happen to prevent me," he said fondly.

She was very sad that evening. If she could have got by herself she would have cried. But perhaps it was just as well that she couldn't; it was no good making oneself bad blood. It had been a foolish dream. She would get over her unhappiness; after all, she was used to it. It would have been much worse if he had been her lover and thrown her over.

Monday passed, Tuesday came; but no petit bleu. She was certain that it would be there when she got back from work. Nothing. She had an hour before she need think of getting ready, and she passed it waiting with sickening anxiety for the bell to ring; she dressed with the feeling that she was foolish to take the trouble, for the message would arrive before she was finished. She wondered if it were possible that he would let her go to the cinema and not turn up. It would be heartless, it would be cruel, but she knew that he was under his mother's thumb, she suspected he was weak, and it might be that to let her go to a meeting-place and not come himself would seem to him the best way, brutal though it was, to show her that he was done with her. No sooner had this notion occurred to her than she was sure of it and she nearly decided not to go. Nevertheless she went. After all, if he could be so beastly it would prove that she was well rid of him.

But he was there all right and when he saw her walking along he came towards her with the springy gait which marked his eager vitality. On his face shone his sweet smile. His spirits seemed even higher than usual.

"I'm not in the mood for the pictures this evening," he said. "Let us have a drink at Fouquet's and then go for a drive. I've got a car just round the corner."

"If you like."

It was fine and dry, though cold, and the stars in the frosty night seemed to laugh with a good-natured malice at the gaudy lights of the Champs-Élysées. They had a glass of beer, Robert meanwhile talking nineteen to the dozen, and then they walked up the Avenue George V to where he had parked his car. Lydia was puzzled. He talked quite naturally, but she had no notion what were his powers of dissimulation, and she could not help asking herself whether he proposed the drive in order to break unhappy news to her. He was an emotional creature, sometimes, she had discovered, even a trifle theatrical, (but that amused rather than offended her), and she wondered whether he were setting the stage for an affecting scene of renunciation.

"This isn't the same car that you had on Sunday," she said, when they came to it.

"No. It belongs to a friend who wants to sell. I said I wanted to show it to a possible purchaser."

They drove to the Arc de Triomphe and then along the Avenue Foch till they came to the Bois. It was dark there except when they met the head-lights of a car coming towards them, and deserted except for a car parked here and there in which one surmised a couple was engaged in amorous conversation. Presently Robert drew up at the kerb.

"Shall we stop here and smoke a cigarette?" he said. "You're not cold?"

"No."

It was a solitary spot and in other circumstances Lydia might have felt a trifle nervous. But she thought she knew Robert well enough to know that he was incapable of taking advantage of the situation. He had too nice a nature. Moreover she had an intuition that he had something on his mind, and was curious to know what it was. He lit her cigarette and his and for a moment kept silent. She realized that he was embarrassed and did not know how to begin. Her heart began to beat anxiously.

"I've got something to say to you, my dear," he said at last.

"Yes?"

"Mon Dieu, I hardly know how to put it. I'm not

often nervous, but at the moment I have a curious sensation that is quite new to me."

Lydia's heart sank, but she had no intention of showing that she was suffering.

"If one has something awkward to say," she answered lightly, "it's better to say it quite plainly, you know. One doesn't do much good by beating about the bush."

"I'll take you at your word. Will you marry me?"

"Me?"

It was the last thing she had expected him to say.

"I love you passionately. I think I fell in love with you at first sight, when we stood side by side at that concert, and the tears poured down your pale cheeks."

"But your mother?"

"My mother is delighted. She's waiting now. I said that if you consented I would take you to her. She wants to embrace you. She's happy at the thought that I'm settling down with someone she entirely approves of, and the idea is that after we've all had a good cry together we should crack a bottle of champagne."

"Last Sunday when you took me to see your mother, had you told her that you wished to marry me?"

"But of course. She very naturally wanted to see what you were like. She's not stupid, my mother; she made up her mind at once."

"I had an idea she didn't like me."

"You were wrong."

They smiled into one another's eyes, and she raised her face to his. For the first time he kissed her on the lips.

"There's no doubt," he said, "that a right-hand drive is much more convenient for kissing a girl than a left-hand."

"You fool," she laughed.

"Then you do care for me a little?"

"I've worshipped you ever since I first saw you."

"But with the reserve of a well-brought-up young woman who will not give free rein to her emotions until she's quite sure it's prudent?" he answered, tenderly chaffing her.

But she answered seriously:

"I've suffered so much in my short life, I didn't want to expose myself to a suffering perhaps greater than I could bear."

"I adore you."

She had never known such happiness; indeed, she could hardly bring herself to believe it: at that moment her heart overflowed with gratitude to life. She would have liked to sit there, nestling in his arms, for ever; at that moment she would have liked to die. But she bestirred herself.

"Let us go to your mother," she said.

She felt on a sudden warm with love for that woman who but just knew her, and yet, contrary to all expectation, because her son loved her, because with her sharp eyes she had seen that she deeply loved her son, had consented, even gladly, to their marriage. Lydia did not think there could be another woman in France who was capable of such a sacrifice.

They drove off. Robert parked the car in a street parallel to the one in which he lived. When they reached the little house he opened the front door with his latch-key and excitedly preceded Lydia into the sitting-room.

"O.K., mother."

Lydia immediately followed him in and Madame Berger, in the same black dress of flowered silk as she had worn on Sunday, came forward and took her in her arms.

"My dear child," she cried. "I'm so happy."

Lydia burst into tears. Madame Berger kissed her tenderly.

"There, there, there! You mustn't cry. I give you my son with all my heart. I know you'll make him a good wife. Come, sit down. Robert will open a bottle of champagne."

Lydia composed herself and dried her eyes.

"You are too good to me, Madame. I don't know what I've done to deserve so much kindness."

Madame Berger took her hand and gently patted it.

"You have fallen in love with my son and he has fallen in love with you."

Robert had gone out of the room. Lydia felt that she must at once state the facts as they were.

"But, Madame, I don't feel sure that you realize the circumstances. The little money that my father was able to get out of Russia went years ago. I have nothing but what I earn. Nothing, absolutely nothing. And only two dresses besides the one I'm wearing."

"But, my dear child, what does that matter? Oh, I don't deny it, I should have been pleased if you had been able to bring Robert a reasonable dot, but money isn't everything. Love is more important. And nowadays what is money worth? I flatter myself that I am a good judge of character and it didn't take me long to discover that you have a sweet and honest nature. I saw that you had been well brought up and I judged that you had good principles. After all that is what one wants in a wife, and you know, I know my Robert, he would never have been happy with a little French bourgeoise. He has a romantic disposition and it says something to him that you are Russian. And it isn't as if you were nobody; it is after all something one need not be ashamed of to be the daughter of a professor."

Robert came in with glasses and a bottle of champagne. They sat talking late into the night. Madame Berger had her plan cut and dried and they could do nothing but accept it; Lydia and Robert should live in the house while she would make herself comfortable in the little pavilion at the back of the garden. They would have their meals in common, but otherwise she would keep to her own quarters. She was decided that the young couple must be left to themselves and not exposed to interference from her.

"I don't want you to look upon me as a mother-in-law," she told Lydia. "I want to be the mother to you that you've lost, but I also want to be your friend."

She was anxious that the marriage should take place without delay. Lydia had a League of Nations passport and a Carte de Séjour; her papers were in order; so they had only to wait the time needed for notification to be made at the Mairie. Since Robert was Catholic and Lydia Orthodox, they decided, notwithstanding Madame Berger's reluctance, to waive a religious ceremony that neither of them cared about. Lydia was too excited and too confused to sleep that night.

The marriage took place very quietly. The only persons present were Madame Berger and an old friend of the family, Colonel Legrand, an army doctor who had been a brother officer of Robert's father; Evgenia and Alexey and their children. It took place on a Friday and since Robert had to go to work on the Monday morning their honeymoon was brief. Robert drove Lydia to Dieppe in a car that he had been lent and drove her back on Sunday night.

Lydia did not know that the car, like the cars in which he had on other occasions driven her, was not lent, but stolen; that was why he had always parked them a street or two from that in which he lived; she did not know that Robert had a few months before been sentenced to two years' imprisonment with sursis, that is, with a suspended sentence because it was his first conviction; she did not know that he had since been tried on a charge of smuggling drugs and had escaped conviction by the skin of his teeth; she did not know that Madame Berger had welcomed the marriage because she thought it would settle Robert and that it was indeed the only chance he had of leading an honest life.

v

CHARLEY HAD NO IDEA how long he had been sitting at the window, absent-mindedly gazing out into the dark court, when he was called back from the perplexed welter of his thoughts by the sound of Lydia's voice.

"I believe I've been asleep," she said.

"You certainly have."

He turned on the light, which he had not done before for fear of waking her. The fire was almost out and he put on another log.

"I feel so refreshed. I slept without dreaming."

"D'you have bad dreams?"

"Fearful."

"If you'll dress we might go out to dinner."

There was an ironic, but not unkindly, quality in the smile she gave him.

"I don't suppose this is the way you usually spend Christmas Day."

"I'm bound to say it isn't," he answered, with a cheerful grin.

She went into the bathroom and he heard her having a bath. She came back still wearing his dressing-gown.

"Now if you'll go in and wash, I'll dress."

Charley left her. He accepted it as quite natural that

though she had slept all night in the next bed to his she should not care to dress in his presence.

Lydia took him to a restaurant she knew in the Avenue du Maine where she said the food was good. Though a trifle self-consciously old-world, with its panelled walls, chintz curtains and pewter plates, it was a friendly little place, and there was no one there but two middle-aged women in collars and ties and three young Indians who ate in moody silence. You had a feeling that, lonely and friendless, they dined there that evening because they had no place to go.

Lydia and Charley sat in a corner where their conversation could not be overheard. Lydia ate with hearty appetite. When he offered her a second helping of one of the dishes they had ordered she pushed forward her plate.

"My mother-in-law used to complain of my appetite. She used to say that I ate as though I had never had enough in my life. Which was true, of course."

It gave Charley a turn. It was a queer sensation to sit down to dinner with someone who year in and year out had never had quite enough to eat. And another thing: it disturbed his preconceived ideas to discover that one could undergo all the misery she had undergone and yet eat voraciously. It made her tragedy a little grotesque; she was not a romantic figure, but just a quite ordinary young woman, and that somehow made all that had happened to her more horrible.

"Did you get on well with your mother-in-law?" he asked.

"Yes. Reasonably. She wasn't a bad woman. She was

hard, scheming, practical and avaricious. She was a good housekeeper and she liked everything in the house to be just so. I used to infuriate her with my Russian sloppiness, but she had a great control over her temper and never allowed an irritable word to escape her. After Robert, her great passion was for respectability. She was proud of her father having been a staff officer and her husband a colonel in the Medical Service. They were both officers in the Legion of Honour. Her husband had lost a leg in the war. She was very proud of their distinguished record, and she had a keen sense of the social importance their position gave her. I suppose you'd say she was a snob, but in such a pretty way that it didn't offend you, it only made you laugh. She had notions of morality that foreigners often think are unusual in France. For instance, she had no patience with women who were unfaithful to their husbands, but she looked upon it as natural enough that men should deceive their wives. She would never have dreamt of accepting an invitation unless she had the power to return it. Once she'd made a bargain she'd stick to it even though it turned out to be a bad one. Though she counted every penny she spent she was scrupulously honest, honest by principle and honest from loyalty to her family. She had a deep sense of justice. She knew she'd acted dishonourably in letting me marry Robert in the dark, and should at least have given me the chance of deciding whether, knowing all, I would marry him or not—and of course I would never have hesitated; but she didn't know that, and she thought that I should have good cause to blame her when I found out and all she could answer was that where Robert was concerned she was prepared to sacrifice anyone else; and because of that she forced herself to be tolerant of a great deal in me that she didn't like. She put all her determination, all her self-control, all her tact, into the effort of making the marriage a success. She felt it was the only chance that Robert had of reforming and her love was so great that she was prepared to lose him to me. She was even prepared to lose her influence over him, and that I think is what a woman values, whether it's a son or a husband or a lover or anything, even more than his love for her. She said that she wouldn't interfere with us and she never did. Except in the kitchen, later on when we gave up the maid, and at meal times, we hardly saw her. When she wasn't out she spent the whole time in her little pavilion at the end of the garden and when, thinking she was lonely, we asked her to come and sit with us, she refused on the excuse that she had work to do, letters to write, or a book she wanted to finish. She was a woman whom it was difficult to love, but impossible not to respect."

"What has happened to her now?" asked Charley.

"The cost of the trial ruined her. Most of her small fortune had already gone to keep Robert out of prison and the rest went on lawyers. She had to sell the house which was the mainstay of her pride in her position as an officer's widow and she had to mortgage her pension. She was always a good cook, she's gone as general servant in the apartment of an American who has a studio at Auteuil."

"D'you ever see her?"

"No. Why should I? We have nothing in common. Her interest in me ceased when I could be no further use in keeping Robert straight."

Lydia went on to tell him about her married life. It was a pleasure for her to have a house of her own and heaven not to have to go to work every morning. She soon discovered that there was no money to waste, but compared with what she had been used to, the circumstances in which she now lived were affluent. And at least she had security. Robert was sweet to her, he was easy to live with, inclined to let her wait on him, but she loved him so much that this was a delight to her, gay with an impudent, happy-go-lucky cynicism that made her laugh, and brim-full of vitality. He was generous to a fault considering how poor they were. He gave her a gold wrist-watch and a vanity case that must have cost at least a couple of thousand francs and a bag in crocodile skin. She was surprised to find a tram ticket in one of the pockets, and when she asked Robert how it got there, he laughed. He said he had bought the bag off a girl who had had a bad day at the races. Her lover had only just given it her and it was such a bargain that he had not been able to resist buying it. Now and then he took her to the theatre and then they went to Montmartre to dance. When she wanted to know how he had the money for such extravagance he answered gaily that with the world full of fools it would be absurd if a clever man couldn't get on to a good thing now and again. But these excursions they kept secret from Madame Berger. Lydia would have thought it impossible to love Robert more than when she married him, but every day increased her passion. He was not only a charming lover, but also a delightful companion.

About four months after their marriage Robert lost his job. This created a disturbance in the household that she failed to understand, for his salary had been negligible; but he and his mother shut themselves up in the pavilion for a long time, and when Lydia saw her mother-in-law next it was obvious that she had been crying. Her face was haggard and she gave Lydia a look of sullen exasperation as though she blamed her. Lydia could not make it out. Then the old doctor, the friend of the family, Colonel Legrand, came and the three of them were again closeted in Madame Berger's room. For two or three days Robert was silent and for the first time since she had known him somewhat irritable; when she asked him what was the matter he told her sharply not to bother. Then, thinking perhaps that he must offer some explanation, he said the whole trouble was that his mother was so avaricious. Lydia knew that though she was sparing, she was never so where her son was concerned, for him nothing was too good; but seeing that Robert was in a highly nervous state, she felt it better to say nothing. For two or three days Madame Berger looked dreadfully worried, but then, whatever the difficulty was, it was settled; she dismissed, however, the maid to keep whom had been almost a matter of principle, for so long as she had a servant Madame Berger could look upon herself as a lady. But now she told Lydia that it was a useless waste;

the two of them could easily run the little house between them, and doing the marketing herself she could be sure of not being robbed; and besides, with nothing to do really, she would enjoy cooking. Lydia was only too willing to do the housework.

Life went on pretty much as it had before. Robert quickly regained his good humour and was as gay, loving and delightful as he had ever been. He got up late in the morning and went out to hunt for a job, and often he did not come back till late in the night. Madame Berger always had a good meal for Robert, but when the two women were alone they ate sparingly; a bowl of thin soup, a salad and a bit of cheese. It was plain that Madame Berger was harassed. More than once Lydia came into the kitchen and found her standing there, doing nothing, with her face distraught, as though an intolerable anxiety possessed her, but on Lydia's approach she chased the expression away and busied herself with the work upon which she was engaged. She still kept up appearances, and on the 'days' of old friends dressed herself in her best, faintly rouged her cheeks, and sallied forth, very upright and a pattern of middle-class respectability, to pay her visit. After a short while, though he was still without a job, Robert seemed to have no less spending-money than he had before. He told Lydia that he had managed to sell one or two secondhand cars on commission; and then that he had got in with some racing men at a bar he went to and got tips from them. Lydia did not know why a suspicion insinuated itself into her unwilling mind that something was going on that was not above board. On one occasion an incident occurred which troubled her. One Sunday Robert told his mother that a man who, he hoped, was going to give him a job had asked him to bring Lydia to lunch at his house near Chartres and he was going to drive her down; but when they had started, picking up the car two streets off the one in which they lived, he told Lydia that this was an invention. He had had a bit of luck at the races on the previous Thursday and was taking her to lunch at Jouy. He had told his mother this story because she would look upon it as an unjustified extravagance to go and spend money at a restaurant. It was a warm and beautiful day. Luncheon was served in the garden and the place was crowded. They found two seats at a table that was already occupied by a party of four. This party were finishing their meal and left while they were but half through theirs.

"Oh, look," said Robert, "one of those ladies has left her bag behind."

He took it and, to Lydia's surprise, opened it. She saw there was money inside. He looked quickly right and left and then gave her a sharp, cunning, malicious glance. Her heart stood still. She had a conviction that he was just about to take the money out and put it in his pocket. She gasped with horror. But at that moment one of the men who had been at the table came back and saw Robert with the bag in his hands.

"What are you doing with that bag?" he asked.

Robert gave him his frank and charming smile.

"It was left behind. I was looking to see if I could find out to whom it belonged."

The man looked at him with stern, suspicious eyes. "You had only to give it to the proprietor."

"And do you think you would ever have got it back?" Robert answered blandly, returning him the bag.

Without a word the man took it and went away.

"Women are criminally careless with their bags," said Robert.

Lydia gave a sigh of relief. Her suspicion was absurd. After all, with people all around, no one could have the effrontery to steal money out of a bag; the risk was too great. But she knew every expression of Robert's face and, unbelievable as it was, she was certain that he had intended to take it. He would have looked upon it as a capital joke.

She had resolutely put the occurrence out of her mind, but on that dreadful morning when she read in the paper that the English bookmaker, Teddie Jordan, had been murdered it returned to her. She remembered the look in Robert's eyes. She had known then, in a horrible flash of insight, that he was capable of anything. She knew now what the stain was on his trousers. Blood! And she knew where those thousand-franc notes had come from. She knew also why, when he had lost his job, Robert had worn that sullen look, why his mother had been distracted and why Colonel Legrand, the doctor, had been closeted with mother and son for hours of agitated colloquy. Because Robert had stolen money. And if Madame Berger had sent away the maid and since then had skimped and saved it was because she had had to pay a sum she could ill afford to save him from prosecution. Lydia read once more the account of the crime. Teddie Jordan lived alone in a ground-floor flat which the concierge kept clean for him. He had his meals out, but the concierge brought him his coffee every morning at nine. It was thus she had found him. He was lying on the floor, in his shirt-sleeves, a knife wound in his back, near the gramophone, with a broken record under him so that it looked as if he had been stabbed while changing it. His empty pocket-book was on the chimney-piece. There was a half-finished whiskey and soda on a table by the side of an armchair and another glass, unused, on a tray with the bottle of whiskey, a syphon and an uncut cake. It was obvious that he had been expecting a visitor, but the visitor had refused to drink. Death had taken place some hours before. The reporter had apparently conducted a small investigation of his own, but how much fact there was in what he narrated and how much fiction, it was hard to say. He had questioned the concierge, and from her learnt that so far as she knew no women ever came to the apartment, but a certain number of men, chiefly young, and from this she had drawn her own conclusions. Teddie Jordan was a good tenant, gave no trouble, and when in funds, was generous. The knife had been thrust into his back with such violence that, according to the reporter, the police were convinced that the murderer must have been a man of powerful physique. There were no signs of disorder in the room, which indicated that Jordan had been attacked suddenly and had had no chance to defend himself. The knife was not found, but stains on the window curtain showed that it had been wiped on it. The reporter went on to say that, though the police had looked with care, they had discovered no fingerprints; from this he concluded that the murderer had either wiped them away or worn gloves. In the first case it showed great coolness and in the second premeditation.

The reporter had then gone on to Jojo's Bar. This was a small bar in a back street behind the Boulevard de la Madeleine, frequented by jockeys, bookmakers and betting men. You could get simple fare, bacon and eggs, sausages and chops, and it was here that Jordan regularly had his meals. It was here too that he did much of his business. The reporter learnt that Jordan was popular among the bar's frequenters. He had his ups and downs, but when he had had a good day was open-handed. He was always ready to stand anyone a drink and was hail-fellow-well-met with everyone. All the same he had the reputation of being a pretty wily customer. Sometimes he was up against it and then would run up a fairly heavy bill, but in the end he always paid up. The reporter mentioned the concierge's suspicions to Jojo, the proprietor of the bar, but was assured by him that there was no foundation for them. He ended his graphic story by saying that the police were actively engaged in making inquiries and expected to make an arrest within twenty-four hours.

Lydia was terrified. She did not doubt for a moment that Robert was guilty of the crime; she was as sure of that as if she had seen him commit it.

"How could he? How could he?" she cried.

But she was startled at the sound of her own voice. Even though the kitchen was empty she must not let her thoughts find expression. Her first, her only feeling was that he must be saved from the terrible danger that faced him. Whatever he had done, she loved him; nothing he could do would ever make her love him less. When it occurred to her that they might take him from her she could have screamed with anguish. Even at that moment she was intoxicated by the thought of his soft lips on hers and the feel of his slim body, still a boy's body, in her arms. They said the knife-thrust had shown great violence, and they were looking for a big, powerful man. Robert was strong and wiry, but he was neither big nor powerful. And then there was what the concierge suspected. The police would hunt in the night-clubs and the cafés, in Montmartre and the Rue de Lappe, which the homosexuals frequented. Robert never went to such places and no one knew better than she how far he was from any abnormal inclination. It was true that he went a good deal to Jojo's Bar, but so did many others; he went to get tips from the jockeys and better odds from the bookmakers than he was likely to get at the tote. It was all above board. There was no reason why suspicion should ever fall on him. The trousers had been destroyed, and who would ever think that Madame Berger, with her thrift, had persuaded Robert to buy a second pair? If the police discovered that Robert knew Jordan (and Jordan knew masses of people) and made an examination of the house (it was unlikely, but it might be that they would make enquiries of everyone with whom the

bookmaker was known to have been friendly) they
would find nothing. Except that little packet of thousand-franc notes. At the thought of them Lydia was
panic-stricken. It would be easy to ascertain that they
had been in straitened circumstances. Robert and she
had always thought that his mother had a little hoard
hidden away somewhere in her pavilion, but that doubtless had gone at the time Robert lost his job; if suspicion once fell on him it was inevitable that the police
should discover what the trouble had been; and how
then could she explain that she had several thousand
francs? Lydia did not know how many notes there had
been in the packet. Perhaps eight or ten. It was a substantial sum to poor people. It was a sum that Madame
Berger, even though she knew how Robert had got the
notes, would never have the courage to part with. She
would trust in her own cunning to hide them where no
one would think of looking. Lydia knew it would be
useless to talk to her. No argument would move her in
such a case. The only thing was to get at them herself
and burn them. She would never have a moment's peace
till then. Then the police might come and no incriminat-
ing evidence could be discovered. With frenzied
anxiety she set her mind to think where Madame Berger
would have been most likely to put them. She did not
often go into the pavilion, for Madame Berger did the
room herself, but she had in her mind's eye a pretty
clear picture of it, and in her thought now she examined
minutely every piece of furniture and every likely place
of concealment. She determined to take the first opportunity to make a search.

The opportunity presented itself sooner than she could have foreseen. That very afternoon, after the meagre lunch which the two women had eaten in silence, Lydia was sitting in the parlour, sewing. She could not read, but she had to do something to calm the frightful disquietude that gnawed at her heart-strings. She heard Madame Berger come into the house and supposed she was going into the kitchen, but the door was opened.

"If Robert comes back tell him I shall be in soon after five."

To Lydia's profound astonishment she saw that her mother-in-law was dressed in all her best. She wore her black dress of flowered silk and a black satin toque and she had a silver fox round her neck.

"Are you going out?" Lydia cried.

"Yes, it's the last day of la générale. She would think it very ill-mannered of me if I did not put in an appearance. Both she and the general had a great affection for my poor husband."

Lydia understood. She saw that in view of what might happen Madame Berger was determined that on that day of all others she must behave as she naturally would. To omit a social duty might be ascribed to fear that her son was implicated in the murder of the book-maker. To fulfil it, on the other hand, was proof that the possibility had never entered her head. She was a woman of indomitable courage. Beside her, Lydia could only feel herself weak and womanish.

As soon as she was gone Lydia bolted the front door so that no one could come in without ringing and crossed the tiny garden. She gave it a cursory glance; there was a patch of weedy grass surrounded by a gravel walk, and in the middle of the grass a bed in which chrysanthemums had been planted to flower in the autumn. She had a conviction that her mother-in-law was more likely to have hidden the notes in her own apartment than there. The pavilion consisted of one largish room with a closet adjoining which Madame Berger had made into her dressing-room. The larger room was furnished with a highly carved bedroom suite in mahogany, a sofa, an armchair and a rosewood desk. On the walls were enlarged photographs of herself and her deceased husband, a photograph of his grave, under which hung his medals and his Legion of Honour, and photographs of Robert at various ages. Lydia considered where a woman of that sort would naturally hide something. She had doubtless a place that she always used, since for years she had had to keep her money where Robert could not find it. She was too cunning to choose such an obvious hiding-place as the bed, a secret drawer in the writing-desk, or the slits in the armchair and the sofa. There was no fireplace in the room, but a gas stove with an iron pipe. Lydia looked at it. She saw no possibility of concealing anything there; besides, in winter it was used, and Lydia thought her mother-in-law the sort of woman who, having found a safe place, would stick to it. She stared about her with perplexity. Because she could think of nothing better to do she unmade the bed and took the pillow out of its slip. She looked at it carefully and felt it over. The mattress was covered with a material so

hard that she felt sure Madame Berger could not have
cut one of the seams and re-sewn it. If she had used
the same hiding-place for a long period it must be one
that she could get at conveniently and such that, if she
wanted to take money out, she could quickly efface
all trace of her action. For form's sake Lydia looked
through the chest of drawers and the writing-desk.
Nothing was locked and everything was carefully
arranged. She looked into the wardrobe. Her mind
had been working busily all the time. She had heard
innumerable stories of how the Russians hid things,
money and jewels, so that they might save them from
the Bolsheviks. She had heard stories of extreme in-
genuity that had been of no avail and of others in
which by some miracle discovery had been averted.
She remembered one of a woman who had been
searched in the train between Moscow and Leningrad.
She had been stripped to the skin, but she had sewn
a diamond necklace in the hem of her fur-coat, and
though it had been carefully examined the diamonds
were overlooked. Madame Berger had a fur-coat too,
an old astrakhan that she had had for years, and this
was in the wardrobe. Lydia took it out and made a
thorough search, but she could neither see nor feel
anything. There was no sign of recent stitching. She
replaced it and one by one took out the three or four
dresses that Madame Berger possessed. There was no
possibility that the notes could have been sewn up in
any of them. Her heart sank. She was afraid that her
mother-in-law had hidden the notes so well that she
would never find them. A new idea occurred to her.

People said that the best way to hide something was in a place so conspicuous that no one would think of looking there. A work-basket, for instance, like the one Madame Berger had on a little table beside the armchair. Somewhat despondently, with a look at her watch, for time was passing and she could not afford to stay too long, she turned the things in it over. There was a stocking that Madame Berger had been mending, scissors, needles, various odds and ends, and reels of cotton and silk. There was a half-finished tippet in black wool that Madame Berger was making to put over her shoulders when she came from the pavilion to the house. Among the reels of black and white cotton Lydia was surprised to find one of yellow thread. She wondered what her mother-in-law used that for. Her heart gave a great leap as her eyes fell on the curtains. The only light in the room came from the glass door, and one pair hung there; another pair served as a portière for the door that led to the dressing-room. Madame Berger was very proud of them, they had belonged to her father the colonel and she remembered them from her childhood. They were very rich and heavy, with a fringed and festooned pelmet, and they were of yellow damask. Lydia went up first to those at the window and turned back the lining. They had been made for a higher room than that in which they now were, and since Madame Berger had not had the heart to cut them, had been turned up at the bottom. Lydia examined the deep hem; it had been sewn by a professional sempstress and the thread was faded. Then she looked at the curtains on each side of the door. She gave a deep sigh. At the corner nearest to the front wall, and so in darkness, there was a little piece about four inches long which the clean thread showed to have been recently stitched. Lydia got the scissors out of the work-basket and quickly cut; she slipped her hand through the opening and pulled out the notes. She put them in her dress and then it did not take her more than a few minutes to get a needle and the yellow thread and sew up the seam so that no one could tell it had been touched. She looked round the room to see that no trace of her interference remained. She went back to the house, upstairs into the bathroom, and tore the notes into little pieces; she threw them into the pan of the closet and pulled the plug. Then she went downstairs again, drew back the bolt on the front door, and sat down once more to her sewing. Her heart was beating so madly that she could hardly endure it; but she was infinitely relieved. Now the police could come and they would find nothing.

Presently Madame Berger returned. She came into the drawing-room and sank down on a sofa. The effort she had made had taken it out of her and she was all in. Her face sagged and she looked an old woman. Lydia gave her a glance, but said nothing. In a few minutes, with a sigh of weariness, she raised herself to her feet and went to her room. When she came back she had taken off her smart clothes and wore felt slippers and a shabby black dress. Notwithstanding the marcelled hair, the paint on her lips and the rouge on her face, she looked like an old charwoman.

"I'll see about preparing dinner," she said.

"Shall I come and help you?" asked Lydia.

"No, I prefer to be alone."

Lydia went on working. The silence in the little house was sinister. It was so intense that the sound after a while of Robert inserting his latch-key in the lock had all the effect of a frightening noise. Lydia clenched her hands to prevent herself from crying out. He gave his little whistle as he entered the house, and Lydia, gathering herself together, went out into the passage. He had two or three papers in his hand.

"I've brought you the evening papers," he cried gaily. "They're full of the murder."

He went into the kitchen where he knew his mother would be and threw the papers on the table. Lydia followed him in. Without a word Madame Berger took one of them and began to read it. There were big headlines. It was front-page news.

"I've been to Jojo's Bar. They can talk of nothing else. Jordan was one of their regular clients and everybody knew him. I talked to him myself on the night he was murdered. He'd not done so badly on the day's racing and he was standing everybody drinks."

His conversation was so easy and natural, you would have thought he had not a care in the world. His eyes glittered and there was a slight flush on the cheeks that were usually rather pasty. He was excited, but showed no sign of nervousness. Trying to make her tone as unconcerned as his, Lydia asked him:

"Have they any idea who the murderer was?"

"They suspect it was a sailor. The concierge says she saw Jordan come in with one about a week ago. But of course it may just as well have been someone disguised as a sailor. They're rounding up the frequenters of the notorious bars in Montmartre. From the condition of the skin round the wound it appears that the blow was struck with great force. They're looking for a husky, big man of powerful physique. Of course there are one or two boxers who have a funny reputation."

Madame Berger put down the paper without remark.

"Dinner will be ready in a few minutes," she said. "Is the cloth laid, Lydia?"

"I'll go and lay it."

When Robert was there they took the two principal meals of the day in the dining-room, even though it gave more work. But Madame Berger said:

"We can't live like savages. Robert has been well brought up and he's accustomed to having things done properly."

Robert went upstairs to change his coat and put on his slippers. Madame Berger could not bear him to sit about the house in his best clothes. Lydia set about laying the table. Suddenly a thought occurred to her, and it was such a violent shock that she staggered and to support herself had to put her hand on the back of a chair. It was two nights before that Teddie Jordan had been murdered, and it was two nights before that Robert had awakened her, made her cook supper for him, and then hurried her to bed. He had come to her arms straight from committing the horrible crime; and his passion, his insatiable desire, the frenzy of his lust had their source in the blood of a human being.

"And if I conceived that night?"

Robert clattered downstairs in his slippers.

"I'm ready, mummy," he cried.

"I'm coming."

He entered the dining-room and sat down in his usual place. He took his napkin out of the ring and stretched over to take a piece of bread from the platter on which Lydia had put it.

"Is the old woman giving us a decent dinner to-night? I've got a beautiful appetite. I had nothing but a sandwich at Jojo's for lunch."

Madame Berger brought in the bowl of soup and taking her seat at the head of the table ladled out a couple of spoonfuls for the three of them. Robert was in high spirits. He talked gaily. But the two women hardly answered. They finished the soup.

"What's coming next?" he asked.

"Cottage pie."

"Not one of my favourite dishes."

"Be thankful you have anything to eat at all," his mother answered sharply.

He shrugged his shoulders and gave Lydia a gay wink. Madame Berger went into the kitchen to fetch the cottage pie.

"The old woman doesn't seem in a very good humour to-night. What's she been doing with herself?"

"It was the générale's last day of the season. She went there."

"The old bore! That's enough to put anyone out of temper."

Madame Berger brought in the dish and served it. Robert helped himself to some wine and water. He went on talking of one thing and another, in his usual ironical and rather amusing way, but at last he could ignore no longer the taciturnity of his companions.

"But what is the matter with you both to-night?" he interrupted himself angrily. "You sit there as glum as two mutes at a funeral."

His mother, forcing herself to eat, had been sitting with her eyes glued to her plate, but now she raised them and, silently, looked him full in the face.

"Well, what is it?" he cried flippantly.

She did not answer, but continued to stare at him. Lydia gave her a glance. In those dark eyes, as full of expression as Robert's, she read reproach, fear, anger, but also an unhappiness so poignant that it was intolerable. Robert could not withstand the intensity of that anguished gaze and dropped his eyes. They finished the meal in silence. Robert lit a cigarette and gave one to Lydia. She went into the kitchen to fetch the coffee. They drank it in silence.

There was a ring at the door. Madame Berger gave a little cry. They all sat still as though they were paralysed. The ring was repeated.

"Who is that?" whispered Madame Berger.

"I'll go and see," said Robert. Then, with a hard look on his face: "Pull yourself together, mother. There's nothing to get upset about."

He went to the front door. They heard strange voices, but he had closed the parlour door after him and they could not distinguish what was said. In a minute or two he came back. Two men followed him into the room.

"Will you both go into the kitchen," he said. "These gentlemen wish to talk to me."

"What do they want?"

"That is precisely what they are going to tell me," Robert answered coolly.

The two women got up and went out. Lydia stole a glance at him. He seemed perfectly self-possessed. It was impossible not to guess that the two strangers were detectives. Madame Berger left the kitchen door open, hoping she would be able to hear what was being said, but across the passage, through a closed door, the words spoken were inaudible. The conversation went on for the best part of an hour, then the door was opened.

"Lydia, go and fetch me my coat and my shoes," cried Robert. "These gentlemen want me to accompany them."

He spoke in his light, gay voice, as though his assurance were unperturbed, but Lydia's heart sank. She went upstairs to do his bidding. Madame Berger said never a word. Robert changed his coat and put on his shoes.

"I shall be back in an hour or two," he said. "But don't wait up for me."

"Where are you going?" asked his mother.

"They want me to go to the Commissariat. The Commissaire de Police thinks I may be able to throw some light on the murder of poor Teddie Jordan."

"What has it got to do with you?"

"Only that, like many others, I knew him."

Robert left the house with the two detectives.

"You'd better clear the table and help me to wash up," said Madame Berger.

They washed up and put everything in its place. Then they sat on each side of the kitchen table to wait. They did not speak. They avoided one another's eyes. They sat for an interminable time. The only sound that broke the ominous silence was the striking of the cuckoo clock in the passage. When it struck three Madame Berger got up.

"He won't come back to-night. We'd better go to bed."

"I couldn't sleep. I'd rather wait here."

"What is the good of that? It's only wasting the electric light. You've got something to make you sleep, haven't you? Take a couple of tablets."

With a sigh Lydia rose to her feet. Madame Berger gave her a frowning glance and burst out angrily:

"Don't look as if the world was coming to an end. You've got no reason to pull a face like that. Robert's done nothing that can get him into trouble. I don't know what you suspect."

Lydia did not answer, but she gave her a look so charged with pain that Madame Berger dropped her eyes.

"Go to bed! Go to bed!" she cried angrily.

Lydia left her and went upstairs. She lay awake all night waiting for Robert, but he did not come. When in the morning she came down, Madame Berger had already been out to get the papers. The Jordan murder was still front-page news, but there was no mention of an arrest; the Commissaire was continuing his investi-

gations. As soon as she had drunk her coffee Madame
Berger went out. It was eleven before she came back.
Lydia's heart sank when she saw her drawn face.

"Well?"

"They won't tell me anything. I got hold of the
lawyer and he's gone to the Commissariat."

They were finishing a miserable luncheon when there
was a ring at the front door. Lydia opened it and found
Colonel Legrand and a man she had not seen before.
Behind them were two other men, whom she at once
recognized as the police officers who had come the
night before, and a grim-faced woman. Colonel Legrand asked for Madame Berger. Her anxiety had
brought her to the kitchen door, and seeing her, the
man who was with him pushed past Lydia.

"Are you Madame Léontine Berger?"

"I am."

"I am Monsieur Lukas, Commissaire de Police. I
have an order to search this house." He produced a
document. "Colonel Legrand has been designated by
your son, Robert Berger, to attend the search on his
behalf."

"Why do you want to search my house?"

"I trust that you will not attempt to prevent me from
fulfilling my duty."

She gave the Commissaire an angry, scornful look.

"If you have an order I have no power to prevent
you."

Accompanied by the Colonel and the two detectives
the Commissaire went upstairs, while the woman who
had come with them remained in the kitchen with

Madame Berger and Lydia. There were two rooms on the upper floor, a fairly large one which Robert and his wife used, and a smaller one in which he had slept as a bachelor. There was besides only a bathroom with a geyser. They spent nearly two hours there and when they came down the Commissaire had in his hand Lydia's vanity-case.

"Where did you get this?" he asked.

"My husband gave it me."

"Where did he get it?"

"He bought it off a woman who was down and out."

The Commissaire gave her a searching look. His eyes fell on the wrist-watch she was wearing and he pointed to it.

"Did your husband also give you that?"

"Yes."

He made no further observation. He put the vanity-case down and rejoined his companions who had gone into the double room which was part dining-room and part parlour. But in a minute or two Lydia heard the front door slam and looking out of the window saw one of the police officers go to the gate and drive off in the car that was standing at the kerb. She looked at the pretty vanity-case with sudden misgiving. Presently, so that a search might be made of the kitchen, Lydia and Madame Berger were invited to go into the parlour. Everything there was in disorder. It was plain that the search had been thorough. The curtains had been taken down and they lay on the floor. Madame Berger winced when her eyes fell on them, and she opened her mouth to speak, but by an effort of will kept silence. But when, after some time in the kitchen, the men crossed the tiny patch of garden to the pavilion, she could not prevent herself from going to the window and looking at them. Lydia saw that she was trembling and was afraid the woman who was with them would see it too. But she was idly looking at a motor paper. Lydia went up to the window and took her mother-in-law's hand. She dared not even whisper that there was no danger. When Madame Berger saw the yellow brocade curtains being taken down she clutched Lydia's hand violently, and all Lydia could do was by an answering pressure to attempt to show her that she need not fear. The men remained in the room nearly as long as they had remained upstairs.

While they were there the officer who had gone away returned. After a little he went out again and fetched two shovels from the waiting car. The two underlings, with Colonel Legrand watching, proceeded to dig up the flower bed. The Commissaire came into the sitting-room.

"Have you any objection to letting this lady search you?" he asked.

"None."

"None."

He turned to Lydia.

"Then perhaps Madame would go to her room with this person."

When Lydia went upstairs she saw why they had been so long. It looked as though the room had been ransacked by burglars. On the bed were Robert's clothes and she guessed that they had been subjected to very careful scrutiny. The ordeal over, the Commissaire asked Lydia questions about her husband's wardrobe. They were not difficult to answer, for it was not extensive: two pairs of tennis trousers, two suits besides the one he had on, a dinner-jacket and plus-fours; and she had no reason not to reply truthfully. It was past seven o'clock when the search was at last concluded. But the Commissaire had not yet done. He took up Lydia's vanity-case which she had brought in from the kitchen and which was lying on a table.

"I am going to take this away with me and also your watch, Madame, if you will kindly give it me."

"Why?"

"I have reason to suspect that they are stolen goods."

Lydia stared at him in dismay. But Colonel Legrand stepped forward.

"You have no right to take them. Your warrant to search the house does not permit you to remove a single thing from it."

The Commissaire smiled blandly.

"You are quite right, Monsieur, but my colleague has, on my instructions, secured the necessary authority."

He made a slight gesture, whereupon the man who had gone away in the car—on an errand which was now patent—produced from his pocket a document which he handed to him. The Commissaire passed it on to Colonel Legrand. He read it and turned to Lydia.

"You must do as Monsieur le Commissaire desires."

She took the watch off her wrist. The Commissaire put it with the vanity-case in his pocket.

"If my suspicions prove to be unfounded the objects will of course be returned to you."

When at last they all left and Lydia had bolted the door behind them, Madame Berger hurried across the garden. Lydia followed her. Madame Berger gave a cry of consternation when she saw the condition in which the room was.

"The brutes!"

She rushed to the curtains. They were lying on the floor. She gave a piercing scream when she saw that the seams had been ripped up. She flopped on to the ground and turned on Lydia a face contorted with horror.

"Don't be afraid," said Lydia. "They didn't find the notes. I found them and destroyed them. I knew you'd never have the courage."

She gave her hand to Madame Berger and helped her to her feet. Madame Berger stared at her. They had never spoken of the subject that for forty-eight hours had obsessed their tortured thoughts. But now the time for silence was passed. Madame Berger seized Lydia's arm with a cruel grip and in a harsh, intense voice said:

"I swear to you by all the love I bear him that Robert didn't murder the Englishman."

"Why do you say that when you know as certainly as I do that he did?"

"Are you going to turn against him?"

"Does it look like it? Why do you suppose I destroyed those notes? You must have been mad to think they wouldn't find them. Could you think a trained detective would miss such an obvious hiding-place?"

Madame Berger released her hold of Lydia's arm. Her expression changed and a sob burst from her throat. Suddenly she stretched out her arms, took Lydia in them, and pressed her to her breast.

"Oh, my poor child, what trouble, what unhappiness I've brought upon you."

It was the first time Lydia had ever seen Madame Berger betray emotion. It was the first time she had ever known her show an uncalculated, disinterested affection. Hard, painful sobs rent her breast and she clung desperately to Lydia. Lydia was deeply moved. It was horrible to see that self-controlled woman, with her pride and her iron will, break down.

"I ought never to have let him marry you," she wailed. "It was a crime. It was unfair to you. It seemed his only chance. Never, never, never should I have allowed it."

"But I loved him."

"I know. But will you ever forgive him? Will you ever forgive me? I'm his mother, it doesn't matter to me, but you're different; how can your love survive this?"

Lydia snatched herself away and seized Madame Berger by the shoulders. She almost shook her.

"Listen to me. I don't love for a month or a year. I love for always. He's the only man I've loved. He's the only man I shall ever love. Whatever he's done, whatever the future has in store, I love him. Nothing can make me love him less. I adore him."

Next day the evening papers announced that Robert

Berger had been arrested for the murder of Teddie
Jordan.

A few weeks later Lydia knew that she was with child
and she realized with horror that she had received the
fertilizing seed on the very night of the brutal murder.

Silence fell between Lydia and Charley. They had
long since finished their dinner and the other diners
had gone. Charley, listening without a word, absorbed
as he had never been in his life, to Lydia's story, had,
all the same, been conscious that the restaurant was
empty and that the waitresses were anxious for them
to go, and once or twice he had been on the point of
suggesting to Lydia that they should move. But it was
difficult, for she spoke as if in a trance, and though
often her eyes met his he had an uncanny sensation
that she did not see him. But then a party of Americans
came in, six of them, three men and three girls, and
asked if it was too late to have dinner. The patronne,
foreseeing a lucrative order, since they were all very
lively, assured them that her husband was the cook
and if they didn't mind waiting, would cook them whatever they wished. They ordered champagne cocktails.
They were out to enjoy themselves and their gaiety
filled the little restaurant with laughter. But Lydia's
tragic story seemed to encompass the table at which
she and Charley sat with a mysterious and sinister
atmosphere which the high spirits of that happy crowd
could not penetrate; and they sat in their corner, alone,
as though they were surrounded by an invisible wall.

"And do you love him still?" asked Charley at last.

"With all my heart."

She spoke with such a passionate sincerity that it was impossible not to believe her. It was strange, and Charley could not prevent the slight shiver of dismay that passed through him. She did not seem to belong to quite the same human species as he did. That violence of feeling was rather terrifying, and it made him a little uncomfortable to be with her. He might have felt like that if he had been talking quite casually to someone for an hour or two and then suddenly discovered it was a ghost. But there was one thing that troubled him. It had been on his mind for the last twenty-four hours, but not wishing her to think him censorious, he had not spoken of it.

"In that case I can't help wondering how you can bear to be in a place like the Sérail. Couldn't you have found some other means of earning your living?"

"I tried to. I'm a good needle-woman, I was apprenticed to a dress-maker. You'd have thought I could have got work in that business; when they found out who I was no one would have me. It meant that or starvation."

There seemed nothing more to say, and Charley was silent. She planted her elbows on the red-and-white checkered table-cloth and rested her face on her hands. Charley was sitting opposite to her and she gazed into his eyes with a long reflective look that seemed to bore into the depths of his being.

"I didn't mind as much as you might have thought I would." She hesitated for an instant. "I wanted to atone."

Charley stared at her uncomprehendingly. Her words, spoken hardly above a whisper, gave him a shock. He had a sensation that he had never had before; it seemed to him that a veil that painted the world in pleasant, familiar colours had been suddenly rent and he looked into a convulsed and writhing darkness.

"What in God's name do you mean?"

"Though I love Robert with all my heart, with all my soul, I know that he sinned. I felt that the only way I could serve Robert now was by submitting to a degradation that was the most horrible I could think of. At first I thought I would go to one of those brothels where soldiers go, and workmen, and the riff-raff of a great city, but I feared I should feel pity for those poor people whose hurried, rare visits to such places afford the only pleasure of their cruel lives. The Sérail is frequented by the rich, the idle, the vicious. There was no chance there that I should feel anything but hatred and contempt for the beasts who bought my body. There my humiliation is like a festering wound that nothing can heal. The brutal indecency of the clothes I have to wear is a shame that no habit can dull. I welcome the suffering. I welcome the contempt these men have for the instrument of their lust. I welcome their brutality. I'm in hell as Robert is in hell and my suffering joins with his, and it may be that my suffering makes it more easy for him to bear his."

"But he's suffering because he committed a crime. You suffered enough for no fault of yours. Why should you expose yourself to suffering unnecessarily?"

"Sin must be paid for by suffering. How can you with your cold English nature know what the love is that is all my life? I am his and he is mine. I should be as vile as his crime was if I hesitated to share his suffering. I know that my suffering as well as his is necessary to expiate his sin."

Charley hesitated. He had no particular religious feelings. He had been brought up to believe in God, but not to think of him. To do that would be—well, not exactly bad form, but rather priggish. It was difficult for him now to say what he had in mind, but he found himself in a situation where it seemed almost natural to say the most unnatural things.

"Your husband committed a crime and was punished for it. I daresay that's all right. But you can't think that a—a merciful God demands atonement from you for somebody else's misdeeds."

"God? What has God to do with it? Do you suppose I can look at the misery in which the vast majority of the people live in the world and believe in God? Do you suppose I believe in God who let the Bolsheviks kill my poor, simple father? Do you know what I think? I think God has been dead for millions upon millions of years. I think when he took infinity and set in motion the process that has resulted in the universe, he died, and for ages and ages men have sought and worshipped a being who ceased to exist in the act of making existence possible for them."

"But if you don't believe in God I can't see the point of what you're doing. I could understand it if you believed in a cruel God who exacted an eye for an eye and a tooth for a tooth. Atonement, the sort of atonement you want to make, is meaningless if there's no God."

"You would have thought so, wouldn't you? There's no logic in it. There's no sense. And yet, deep down in my heart, no, much more than that, in every fibre of my body, I know that I must atone for Robert's sin. I know that that is the only way he can gain release from the evil that racks him. I don't ask you to think I'm reasonable. I only ask you to understand that I can't help myself. I believe that somehow—how I don't know —my humiliation, my degradation, my bitter, ceaseless pain, will wash his soul clean, and even if we never see one another again he will be restored to me."

Charley sighed. It was all strange to him, strange, morbid and disturbing. He did not know what to make of it. He felt more than ever ill-at-ease with that alien woman with her crazy fancies; and yet she looked ordinary enough, a prettyish little thing, not very well dressed; a typist or a girl in the post-office. Just then, at the Terry-Masons', they would probably have started dancing; they would be wearing the paper caps they'd got out of the crackers at dinner. Some of the chaps would be a bit tight, but hang it all, on Christmas Day no one could mind. There'd have been a lot of kissing under the mistletoe, a lot of fun, a lot of ragging, a lot of laughter; they were all having a grand time. It seemed very far away, but thank God, it was there, normal, decent, sane and real; this was a nightmare. A nightmare? He wondered if there was anything in what she said, this woman with her tragic history and her miserable life, that God had died when he created the wide world; and was he lying dead on some vast mountain range on a dead star or was he absorbed into the universe he had caused to be? It was rather funny, if you came to think of it, Lady Terry-Mason rounding up all the house party to go to church on Christmas morning. And his own father backing her up.

"I don't pretend I'm much of a church-goer myself, but I think one ought to go on Christmas Day. I mean, I think it sets a good example."

That's what he would say.

"Don't look so serious," said Lydia. "Let's go."

They walked along the forbidding, sordid street that leads from the Avenue du Maine to the Place de Rennes, and there Lydia suggested that they should go to the news reel for an hour. It was the last performance of the day. Then they had a glass of beer and went back to the hotel. Lydia took off her hat and the fur she wore round her neck. She looked at Charley thoughtfully.

"If you want to come to bed with me you can, you know," she said in just the same tone as she might have used if she had asked him if he would like to go to the Rotonde or the Dôme.

Charley caught his breath. All his nerves revolted from the idea. After what she had told him he could not have touched her. His mouth for a moment went grim with anger; he really was not going to have her mortify her flesh at his expense. But his native politeness prevented him from uttering the words that were on the tip of his tongue.

"Oh, I don't think so, thank you."

"Why not? I'm there for that and that's what you came to Paris for, isn't it? Isn't that why all you English come to Paris?"

"I don't know. Anyhow I didn't."

"What else did you come for?"

"Well, partly to see some pictures."

She shrugged her shoulders.

"It's just as you like."

She went into the bathroom. Charley was a trifle piqued that she accepted his refusal with so much unconcern. He thought at least she might have given him credit for his delicacy. Because perhaps she owed him something, at least board and lodging for twenty-four hours, he might well have looked upon it as a right to take what she offered; it wouldn't have been unbecoming if she had thanked him for his disinterestedness. He was inclined to sulk. He undressed, and when she came in from the bathroom, in his dressing-gown, he went in to wash his teeth. She was in bed when he returned.

"Will it bother you if I read a little before I go to sleep?" he asked.

"No. I'll turn my back to the light."

He had brought a Blake with him. He began to read. Presently from Lydia's quiet breathing in the next bed he knew she was asleep. He read on for a little and switched off the light.

Thus did Charley Mason spend Christmas Day in Paris.

vi

THEY DID NOT WAKE till so late next morning that by the time they had had their coffee, read the papers (like a domestic couple who had been married for years), bathed and dressed, it was nearly one.

"We might go along and have a cocktail at the Dôme and then lunch," he said. "Where would you like to go?"

"There's a very good restaurant on the boulevard in the other direction from the Coupole. Only it's rather expensive."

"Well, that doesn't matter."

"Are you sure?" She looked at him doubtfully. "I don't want you to spend more than you can afford. You've been very sweet to me. I'm afraid I've taken advantage of your kindness."

"Oh, rot!" he answered, flushing.

"You don't know what it's meant to me, these two days. Such a rest. Last night's the first night for months that I've slept without waking and without dreams. I feel so refreshed. I feel quite different."

She did indeed look much better this morning. Her

skin was clearer and her eyes brighter. She held her head more alertly.

"It's been a wonderful little holiday you've given me. It's helped me so much. But I mustn't be a burden to you."

"You haven't been."

She smiled with gentle irony.

"You've been very well brought up, my dear. It's nice of you to say that, and I'm so unused to having people say nice things to me that it makes me want to cry. But after all you've come to Paris to have a good time; you know now you're not likely to have it with me. You're young and you must enjoy your youth. It lasts so short a while. Give me lunch to-day if you like and this afternoon I'll go back to Alexey's."

"And to-night to the Sérail?"

"I suppose so."

She sighed, but she checked the sigh and with a little gay shrug of the shoulders gave him a bright smile. Frowning slightly in his uncertainty Charley looked at her with pained eyes. He felt awkward and big, and his radiant health, his sense of well-being, the high spirits that bubbled inside him, seemed to himself in an odd way an offence. He was like a rich man vulgarly displaying his wealth to a poor relation. She looked very frail, a slim little thing in a shabby brown dress, and after that good night so much younger that she seemed almost a child. How could you help being sorry for her? And when you thought of her tragic story, when you thought—oh, unwillingly, for it was ghastly and senseless, yet troubling so that it haunted you—of that crazy idea of hers of atoning for her husband's crime by her own degradation, your heart-strings were wrung. You felt that you didn't matter at all, and if your holiday in Paris, to which you'd looked forward with such excitement, was a wash-out—well, you just had to put up with it. It didn't seem to Charley that it was he who was uttering the halting words he spoke, but a power within him that acted independently of his will. When he heard them issue from his lips he didn't even then know why he said them.

"I don't have to get back to the office till Monday morning and I'm staying till Sunday. If you care to stay on here till then, I don't see why you shouldn't."

Her face lit up so that you might have thought a haphazard ray of the winter sun had strayed into the room.

"Do you mean that?"

"Otherwise I wouldn't have suggested it."

It looked as though her legs suddenly gave way, for she sank on to a chair.

"Oh, it would be such a blessing. It would be such a rest. It would give me new courage. But I can't, I can't."

"Why not? On account of the Sérail?"

"Oh, no, not that. I could send them a wire to say I had influenza. It's not fair to you."

"That's my business, isn't it?"

It seemed a bit grim to Charley that he should have to persuade her to do what it was quite plain she was only too anxious to do, and what he would just as soon she didn't. But he didn't see how else he could act now. She gave him a searching look.

"Why should you do this? You don't want me, do you?" He shook his head. "What can it matter to you if I live or die, what can it matter to you if I'm happy or not? You've not known me forty-eight hours yet. Friendship? I'm a stranger to you. Pity? What has one got to do with pity at your age?"

"I wish you wouldn't ask me embarrassing questions," he grinned.

"I suppose it's just natural goodness of heart. They always say the English are kind to animals. I remember one of our landladies who used to steal our tea took in a mangy mongrel because it was homeless."

"If you weren't so small I'd give you a smack on the face for that," he retorted cheerfully. "Is it a go?"

"Let's go out and have lunch. I'm hungry."

During luncheon they spoke of indifferent things, but when they had finished and Charley, having paid the bill, was waiting for his change, she said to him:

"Did you really mean it when you said I could stay with you till you went away?"

"Definitely."

"You don't know what a boon it would be to me. I can't tell you how I long to take you at your word."

"Then why don't you?"

"It won't be much fun for you."

"No, it won't," he answered frankly, but with a charming smile. "But it'll be interesting."

She laughed.

"Then I'll go back to Alexey's and get a few things. At least a toothbrush and some clean stockings."

They separated at the station and Lydia took the

Metro. Charley thought that he would see if Simon was in. After asking his way two or three times he found the Rue Campagne Première. The house in which Simon lived was tall and dingy, and the wood of the shutters showed gray under the crumbling paint. When Charley put in his head at the concierge's loge he was almost knocked down by the stink of fug, food and human body that assailed his nostrils. A little old woman in voluminous skirts, with her head wrapped in a dirty red muffler, told him in rasping, angry tones, as though she violently resented his intrusion, where exactly Simon lived, and when Charley asked if he was in bade him go and see. Charley, following her directions, went through the dirty courtyard and up a narrow staircase smelling of stale urine. Simon lived on the second floor and in answer to Charley's ring opened the door.

"H'm. I wondered what had become of you."

"Am I disturbing you?"

"No. Come in. You'd better keep on your coat. It's not very warm in here."

That was true. It was icy. It was a studio, with a large north light, and there was a stove in it, but Simon, who had apparently been working, for the table in the middle was littered with papers, had forgotten to keep it up and the fire was almost out. Simon drew a shabby armchair up to the stove and asked Charley to sit down.

"I'll put some more coke on. It'll soon get warmer. I don't feel the cold myself."

Charley found that the armchair, having a broken spring, was none too comfortable. The walls of the studio were a cold slate-gray, and they too looked as though they hadn't been painted for years. Their only ornament was large maps tacked up with drawing-pins. There was a narrow iron bed which hadn't been made.

"The concierge hasn't been up to-day yet," said Simon, following Charley's glance.

There was nothing else in the studio but the large dining-table, bought second-hand, which Simon wrote at, some shelves with books in them, a desk-chair such as they use in offices, two or three kitchen chairs piled up with books, and a strip of worn carpet by the bed. It was cheerless and the cold winter light coming in through the north window added its moroseness to the squalid scene. A third-class waiting-room at a wayside station could not have seemed more unfriendly.

Simon drew a chair up to the stove and lit a pipe. With his quick wits he guessed the impression his surroundings were making on Charley and smiled grimly.

"It's not very luxurious, is it? But then I don't want luxury." Charley was silent and Simon gave him a coolly disdainful look. "It's not even comfortable, but then I don't want comfort. No one should be dependent on it. It's a trap that's caught many a man who you would have thought had more sense."

Charley was not without a streak of malice and he was not inclined to let Simon put it over on him.

"You look cold and peaked and hungry, old boy. What about taking a taxi to the Ritz Bar and having some scrambled eggs and bacon in warmth and comfortable armchairs?"

"Go to hell. What have you done with Olga?"

"Her name's Lydia. She's gone home to get a tooth-brush. She's staying with me at the hotel till I go back to London."

"The devil she is. Going some, aren't you?" The two young men stared at one another for a moment. Simon leant forward. "You haven't fallen for her, have you?"

"Why did you bring us together?"

"I thought it would be rather a joke. I thought it would be a new experience for you to go to bed with the wife of a notorious murderer. And to tell you the truth, I thought she might fall for you. I should laugh like a hyena if she has. After all, you're rather the same type as Berger, but a damned sight better-looking."

Charley suddenly remembered a remark that Lydia had made when they were having supper together after the Midnight Mass. He had not understood what she meant at the time, but now he did.

"It may surprise you to learn that she tumbled to that. I'm afraid you won't be able to laugh like a hyena."

"Have you been together ever since I left you with her on Christmas Eve?"

"Yes."

"It seems to agree with you. You look all right. A bit pale, perhaps."

Charley tried not to look self-conscious. He would not for the world have had Simon know that his relations with Lydia had been entirely platonic. It would only have aroused his derisive laughter. He would have

looked upon Charley's behaviour as despicably sentimental.

"I don't think it was a very good joke to get me off
with her without letting me know what I was in for,"
said Charley.

Simon gave him a tortured smile.

"It appealed to my sense of humour. It'll be something to tell your parents when you go home. Anyhow
you've got nothing to grouse about. It's all panned out
very well. Olga knows her job and will give you a
damned good time in that way, and she's no fool; she's
read a lot and she can talk much more intelligently than
most women. It'll be a liberal education, my boy. D'you
think she's as much in love with her husband as ever
she was?"

"I think so."

"Curious, human nature is, isn't it? He was an awful
rotter, you know. I suppose you know why she's at
the Sérail? She wants to make enough money to pay
for his escape; then she'll join him in Brazil."

Charley was disconcerted. He had believed her when
she told him that she was there because she wanted to
atone for Robert's sin, and even though the notion had
seemed to him extravagant there was something about
it that had strangely moved him. It was a shock to think
that she might have lied to him. If what Simon said
were true she had just been making a fool of him.

"I covered the trial for our paper, you know," Simon
went on. "It caused rather a sensation in England because the fellow that Berger killed was an Englishman,
and they gave it a lot of space. It was a snip for me;

I'd never been to a murder trial in France before and I was pretty keen to see one. I've been to the Old Bailey, and I was curious to compare their methods with ours. I wrote a very full account of it; I've got it here; I'll give it you to read if you like."

"Yes, I would."

"The murder created a great stir in France. You see, Robert Berger wasn't an apache or anything like that. He was by way of being a gent. His people were very decent. He was well-educated and he spoke English quite passably. One of the papers called him the Gentleman Gangster and it caught on; it took the public fancy and made him quite a celebrity. He was good-looking too, in his way, and young, only twenty-two, and that helped. The women all went crazy over him. God, the crush there was to get into the trial! It was a real thrill when he came into the court-room. He was brought in between two warders for the press photographers to have a go at him before the judges came in. I never saw anyone so cool. He was quite nicely dressed and he knew how to wear his clothes. He was freshly shaved and his hair was very neat. He had a fine head of dark brown hair. He smiled at the photographers and turned this way and that, as they asked him to, so that they could all get a good view of him. He looked like any young chap with plenty of money that you might see at the Ritz Bar having a drink with a girl. It tickled me to think that he was such a rogue. He was a born criminal. Of course his people weren't rich, but they weren't starving, and I don't suppose he ever really wanted for a hundred francs. I wrote a rather pretty article about him for one of the weekly papers, and the French press printed extracts from it. It did me a bit of good over here. I took the line that he engaged in crime as a form of sport. See the idea? It worked up quite amusingly. He'd been almost a first-class tennis-player and there was some talk of training him for championship play, but oddly enough, though he played a grand game in ordinary matches, he had a good serve and was quick at the net, when it came to tournaments he always fell down. Something went wrong then. He hadn't got power of resistance, determination or whatever it is, that the great tennis-player has got to have. An interesting psychological point, I thought. Anyhow his career as a tennis-player came to an end because money began to be missed from the changing-room when he was about, and though it was never actually proved that he'd taken it everyone concerned was pretty well convinced that he was the culprit."

Simon relit his pipe.

"One thing that peculiarly struck me in Robert Berger was his combination of nerve, self-possession and charm. Of course charm is an invaluable quality, but it doesn't often go with nerve and self-possession. Charming people are generally weak and irresolute, charm is the weapon nature gives them to cope with their disadvantages; I would never set much trust in anyone who had it."

Charley gave his friend a slightly amused glance; he knew that Simon was belittling a quality he did not think he possessed in order to assure himself that it was of no great consequence beside those he was convinced he had. But he did not interrupt.

"Robert Berger was neither weak nor irresolute. He very nearly got away with his murder. It was a damned smart bit of work on the part of the police that they got him. There was nothing sensational or spectacular in the way they went about the job; they were just thorough and patient. Perhaps accident helped them a little, but they were clever enough to take advantage of it. People must always be prepared to do that, you know, and they seldom are."

An absent look came into Simon's eyes, and once more Charley was aware that he was thinking of himself.

"What Lydia didn't tell me was how the police first came to suspect him," said Charley.

"When first they questioned him they hadn't the ghost of an idea that he had anything to do with the murder. They were looking for a much bigger man."

"What sort of a chap was Jordan?"

"I never ran across him. He was a bad hat, but he was all right in his way. Everybody liked him. He was always ready to stand you a drink, and if you were down and out he never minded putting his hand in his pocket. He was a little fellow, he'd been a jockey, but he'd got warned off in England, and it turned out later that he'd done nine months at Wormwood Scrubs for false pretences. He was thirty-six. He'd been in Paris ten years. The police had an idea that he was mixed up in the drug traffic, but they'd never been able to get the goods on him."

"But how did the police come to question Berger at all?"

"He was one of the frequenters of Jojo's Bar. That's where Jordan used to have his meals. It's rather a shady place patronized by bookmakers and jockeys, touts, runners and the sort of people with the reputation that we journalists describe as unsavoury, and naturally the police interviewed as many of them as they could get hold of. You see, Jordan had a date with someone that night, that was shown by the fact that there were a couple of glasses on the tray and a cake, and they thought he might have dropped a hint about whom he was going to meet. They had a pretty shrewd suspicion that he was queer, and it was just possible one of the chaps at Jojo's had seen him about with someone. Berger had been rather pally with Jordan, and Jojo, the owner of the bar, told the police he'd seen him touch the bookie for money several times. Berger had been tried on a charge of smuggling heroin into France from Belgium, and the two men who were up with him went to jug, but he got off somehow. The police knew he was as guilty as hell, and if Jordan had been mixed up with dope and had met his death in connection with that, they thought Berger might very well know who was responsible. He was a bad lot. He'd been convicted on another charge, stealing motor-cars, and got a suspended sentence of two years."

"Yes, I know that," said Charley.

"His system was as simple as it was ingenious. He used to wait till he saw someone drive up to one of the big stores, the Printemps or the Bon Marché, in a

Citroën, and go in, leaving it at the kerb. Then he'd walk up, as bold as brass, as though he'd just come out of the store, jump in and drive off."

"But didn't they lock the cars?"

"Seldom. And he had some Citroën keys. He always stuck to the one make. He'd use the car for two or three days and then leave it somewhere, and when he wanted another, he'd start again. He stole dozens. He never tried to sell them, he just borrowed them when he wanted one for a particular purpose. That was what gave me the idea for my article. He pinched them for the fun of the thing, for the pleasure of exercising his audacious cleverness. He had another ingenious dodge that came out at the trial. He'd hang around in his car about the bus stops just at the time the shops closed, and when he saw a woman waiting for a bus he'd stop and ask her if she'd like a lift. I suppose he was a pretty good judge of character and knew the sort of woman who'd be likely to accept a ride from a good-looking young man. Well, the woman got in and he'd drive off in the direction she wanted to go, and when they came to a more or less deserted street he stalled the car. He pretended he couldn't get it to start and he would ask the woman to get out, lift the hood and tickle the carburettor while he pressed the self-starter. The woman did so, leaving her bag and her parcels in the car, and just as she was going to get in again, when the engine was running, he'd shoot off and be out of sight before she realized what he was up to. Of course a good many women went and complained to the police, but they'd only seen him in the dark, and all they could say was that he was a good-looking, gentlemanly young man in a Citroën, with a pleasant voice, and all the police could do was to tell them that it was very unwise to accept lifts from good-looking, gentlemanly young men. He was never caught. At the trial it came out that he must often have done very well out of these transactions.

"Anyhow a couple of police officers went to see him. He didn't deny that he'd been at Jojo's Bar on the evening of the murder and had been with Jordan, but he said he'd left about ten o'clock and hadn't seen him after that. After some conversation they invited him to accompany them to the Commissariat. The Commissaire de Police who was in charge of the preliminary proceedings had no notion, mind you, that Berger was the murderer. He thought it was a toss-up whether Jordan had been killed by some tough that he'd brought to his flat or by a member of the drugring whom he might have double-crossed. If the latter, he thought he could wheedle, jockey, bully or frighten Berger into giving some indication that would enable the police to catch the man they were after.

"I managed to get an interview with the Commissaire. He was a chap called Lukas. He was not at all the sort of type you'd expect to find in a job like that. He was a big, fat, hearty fellow, with red cheeks, a heavy moustache and great shining black eyes. He was a jolly soul and you'd have bet a packet that there was nothing he enjoyed more than a good dinner and a bottle of wine. He came from the Midi and he had an accent that you could cut with a knife. He had a fat,

jovial laugh. He was a friendly, back-slapping, good-
natured man to all appearances and you felt inclined to
confide in him. In point of fact he'd had wonderful
success in getting confessions out of suspects. He had
great physical endurance and was capable of conducting an examination for sixteen hours at a stretch.
There's no third degree in France of the American sort,
no knocking about, I mean, or tooth-drilling or anything like that, to extort a confession; they just bring a
man into the room and make him stand, they don't let
him smoke and they don't give him anything to eat, they
just ask him questions; they go on and on, they smoke,
and when they're hungry they have a meal brought in
to them; they go on all night, because they know that
at night a man's powers of resistance are at their low-
est; and if he's guilty he has to be very strong-minded if
by morning for the sake of a cup of coffee and a cigarette he won't confess. The Commissaire got nothing
out of Berger. He admitted that at one time he'd been
friendly with the heroin smugglers, but he asserted his
innocence of the charge on which he'd been tried and
acquitted. He said he'd done stupid things in his youth,
but he'd had his lesson; after all, he'd only borrowed
cars for two or three days to take girls out, it wasn't a
very serious crime, and now that he was married he was
going straight. As far as the drug traffickers were concerned he'd had nothing to do with them since his trial
and he had had no idea that Teddie Jordan was mixed
up with them. He was very frank. He told the Commissaire that he was very much in love with his wife,
and his great fear was that she would discover his past.

For her sake as well as for his own and his mother's, he was determined to lead in future a decent and honourable life. The fat, jolly man went on asking questions, but in a friendly, sympathetic way so that you felt, I think, that he couldn't wish you any harm. He applauded Berger's good resolutions, he congratulated him on marrying a penniless girl for love, he hoped they would have children which were not only an ornament to a home, but a comfort to their parents. But he had Berger's dossier; he knew that in the heroin case, though the jury had refused to convict, he was undoubtedly guilty, and from enquiries he had made that day, that he had been discharged from the broker's firm and had only escaped prosecution because his mother had made restitution of the money he had embezzled. It was a lie that since his marriage he had been leading an honest life. He asked him about his financial circumstances. Berger confessed that they were difficult, but his mother had a little and soon he was bound to get a job and then they would be all right. And pocket money? Now and then he made a bit racing and he introduced clients to bookmakers, that was how he'd become friendly with Jordan, and got a commission. Sometimes he just went without.

" 'En effet,' said the Commissaire, 'the day before he was killed you said you were penniless and you borrowed fifty francs from Jordan.'

" 'He was good to me. Poor chap. I shall miss him.'

"The Commissaire was looking at Berger with his friendly, twinkling eyes, and it occurred to him that the young man was not ill-favoured. Was it possible?

But no, that was nonsense. He had a notion that Berger was lying when he said he had given up all relations with the drug traffickers. After all, he was hard up and there was good money to be made there; Berger went about among the sort of people who were addicted to dope. The Commissaire had an impression, though he had no notion on what he founded it, that Berger, if he didn't know for certain who'd committed the murder, had his suspicions: of course he wouldn't tell, but if they found heroin hidden away in the house at Neuilly they might be able to force him to. The Commissaire was a shrewd judge of character and he was pretty sure that Berger would give a friend away to save his own skin. He made up his mind that he would hold Berger and have the house searched before he had any chance of disposing of anything that was there. With the same idea in his mind he asked him about his movements on the night of the murder. Berger stated that he had come in from Neuilly rather late and had walked to Jojo's Bar; he had found a lot of men there who had come in after the races. He got two or three drinks stood him, and Jordan, who'd had a good day, said he'd pay for his dinner. After he'd eaten he hung about for a bit, but it was very smoky and it made his head ache, so he went for a stroll on the boulevard. Then about eleven he went back to the bar and stayed there till it was time to catch the last Metro back to Neuilly.

" 'You were away just long enough to kill the Englishman in point of fact,' said the Commissaire in a joking sort of way.

"Berger burst out laughing.

" 'You're not going to accuse me of that?' he said.

" 'No, not that,' laughed the other.

" 'Believe me, Jòrdan's death is a loss to me. The fifty francs he lent me the day before he was murdered wasn't the first I'd had from him. I don't say it was very scrupulous, but when he'd had a few drinks it wasn't hard to get money out of him.'

" 'Still, he'd made a lot that day, and though he wasn't drunk when he left the bar, he was in a happy mood. You might have thought it worth while to make sure of a few thousand francs at one go rather than get it in fifties from time to time.'

"The Commissaire said this more to tease than because he thought there was anything in it. And he didn't think it a bad thing to let Berger suppose he was a possible object of suspicion. It would certainly not make him less disinclined to tell the culprit's name if he had an inkling of it. Berger took out the money in his pocket and put it on the table. It amounted to less than ten francs.

" 'If I'd robbed poor Jordan of his money y,ou don't suppose I'd only have that in my pocket now.'

" 'My dear boy, I suppose nothing. I only pointed out that you had the time to kill Jordan and that money would have been useful to you.'

"Berger gave him his frank and disarming smile.

" 'Both those things, I admit,' he said.

" 'I will be perfectly open with you,' said the other. 'I don't think you murdered Jordan, but I'm fairly certain that if you don't know who did, you have at least a suspicion.'

"Berger denied this, and though the Commissaire pressed him, persisted in his denial. It was late by now and the Commissaire thought it would be better to resume the conversation next day, he thought also that a night in the cells would give Berger an opportunity to consider his position. Berger, who had been arrested twice before, knew that it was useless to protest.

"You know that the dope traffickers are up to every sort of trick to conceal their dope. They hide it in hollow walking-sticks, in the heels of shoes, in the lining of old clothes, in mattresses and pillows, in the frames of bedsteads, in every imaginable place, but the police know all their dodges, and you can bet your boots that if there'd been anything in the house at Neuilly they'd have found it. They found nothing. But when the Commissaire had been going through Lydia's bedroom he'd come across a vanity-case, and it struck him that it was an expensive one for a woman of that modest class to have. She had a watch on that looked as if it had cost quite a lot of money. She said that her husband had given her both the watch and the vanity-case, and it occurred to the Commissaire that it might be interesting to find out how he had got the money to buy them. On getting back to his office he had inquiries made and in a very short while learnt that several women had reported that they had had bags stolen by a young man who had offered them lifts in a Citroën. One woman had left a description of a vanity-case which she had thus lost and it corresponded with that which the Commissaire had found in Lydia's possession; another stated that there had been in her bag a gold watch from such and such a maker. The same maker's name was on Lydia's. It was plain that the mysterious young man whom the police had never been able to lay their hands on was Robert Berger. That didn't seem to bring the solution of the Jordan murder any nearer, but it gave the Commissaire an additional weapon to induce Berger to spill the beans. He had him brought into his room and asked him to explain how he had come by the vanity-case and the watch. Berger said he'd bought one of them from a tart who wanted money and the other from a man he'd met in a bar. He could give the name of neither. They were casual persons whom he'd got into conversation with and had neither seen before nor since. The Commissaire then formally arrested him on a charge of theft, and telling him that he would be confronted next morning with the two women to whom he was convinced the articles belonged, tried to persuade him to save trouble by making a confession. But Berger stuck to his story and refused to answer any more questions till he had the assistance of a lawyer, which by French law, now that he was arrested, he was entitled to have at an examination. The Commissaire could do nothing but acquiesce, and that finished the proceedings for the night.

"On the followng morning the two women in question came to the Commissariat and immediately they were shown the objects recognized them. Berger was brought in and one of them at once identified him as the obliging young man who had given her a lift.

The other was doubtful; it was night when she had accepted his offer to drive her home and she had not seen his face very well, but she thought she would recognize his voice. Berger was told to read out a couple of sentences from a paper and he had not read half a dozen words before the woman cried out that she was certain it was the same man. I may tell you that Berger had a peculiarly soft and caressing voice. The women were dismissed and Berger taken back to the cell. The vanity-case and the watch were on the table before him and the Commissaire looked at them idly. Suddenly his expression grew more intent."

Charley interrupted.

"Simon, how could you know that? You're romancing."

Simon laughed.

"I'm dramatizing a little. I'm telling you what I said in my first article. I had to make as good a story out of it as I could, you know."

"Go on then."

"Well, he sent for one of his men, and asked him if Berger had on a wrist-watch when he was arrested, and if he had, to bring it. Remember, all this came out at the trial afterwards. The cop got Berger's watch. It was an imitation gold thing, in a metal that I think's called aureum, and it had a round face. The press had given a lot of details about Jordan's murder; they'd said, for instance, that the knife with which the blow had been inflicted hadn't been found, and, incidentally, it never was; and they'd said that the police hadn't discovered any finger-prints. You'd have expected to

find some either on the leather note-case in which
Jordan had kept his money or on the door handle; and
of course they deduced from that that the murderer had
worn gloves. But what they didn't say, because the
police had taken care to keep it dark, was that when
they had gone through Jordan's room with a fine comb
they had found fragments of a broken watch-glass. It
couldn't have belonged to Jordan's watch, and it
needn't necessarily have belonged to the murderer's, but
there was just a chance that somehow or other, in his
nervousness or haste, by an accidental knock against
a piece of furniture, the murderer had broken the glass
of his watch. It wasn't a thing he would be likely to
notice at such a moment. Not all the pieces had been
found, but enough to show that the watch they had belonged to was small and oblong. The Commissaire had
the pieces in an envelope, carefully wrapped up in
tissue-paper, and he now laid them out before him.
They would have exactly fitted Lydia's watch. It might
be only a coincidence; there were in use thousands
of watches of just that size and shape. Lydia's had a
glass. But the Commissaire pondered. He turned over
in his mind various possibilities. They seemed so far-
fetched that he shrugged his shoulders. Of course
during the period, three-quarters of an hour at least,
that Berger claimed he'd been strolling along the boulevard, he would have had plenty of time to get to
Jordan's apartment, a ten minutes' walk from Jojo's
Bar, commit the murder, wash his hands, tidy himself
up, and walk back again; but why should he have been
wearing his wife's watch? He had one of his own. His

own, of course, might have been out of order. The Commissaire nodded his head thoughtfully."

Charley giggled.

"Really, Simon."

"Shut up. He gave instructions that plain-clothes men should go to every watchmaker's within a radius of two miles round the house in Neuilly where the Bergers lived. They were to ask if within the last week any watchmaker had repaired a watch in imitation gold or had put a glass in a small lady's-watch with an oblong face. Within a few hours one of the men came back and said that a watchmaker, not more than a quarter of a mile from the Bergers' house, said that he had repaired a watch corresponding to the description and it had been called for, and at the same time the customer had brought another watch to have a glass put in. He had done it on the spot and she had come in for it half an hour later. He couldn't remember what the customer looked like, but he thought she had a Russian accent. The two watches were taken for the watchmaker to look at and he claimed that they were those he had repaired. The Commissaire beamed as he might have beamed if he had a great plate of bouillabaisse set before him in the Old Port at Marseilles. He knew he'd got his man."

"What was the explanation?" asked Charley.

"Simple as A B C. Berger had broken his watch and borrowed the one he'd given to Lydia. She hardly ever went out and didn't need it. You must remember that in those days she was a quiet, modest, rather shy girl with few friends of her own, and I should say some-

what lethargic. At the trial two men swore that they'd
noticed Berger wearing it. Jojo, who was a police
informer, knew that Berger was a crook and wondered
how he had got it. In a casual way he mentioned to
Berger that he had a new watch on and Berger told
him it was his wife's. Lydia went to the watchmaker's
to get her husband's watch the morning after the murder, and very naturally, since she was there, had a new
glass put in her own. It never occurred to her to mention it and Berger never knew that he had broken it."

"But you don't mean to say that he was convicted
on that?"

"No. But it was enough to justify the Commissaire
charging him with the murder. He thought, quite
rightly as it turned out, that new evidence would be
forthcoming. All through his interrogations Berger
conducted himself with amazing adroitness and self-
possession. He admitted everything that could be
proved and no longer attempted to deny that it was
he who had robbed all those women of their handbags,
he admitted that even after his conviction he had gone
on pinching cars whenever he wanted one; he said the
ease with which it could be done was too much for
him and the risk appealed to his adventurousness; but
he denied absolutely that he'd had anything to do with
the murder. He claimed that the fact of the pieces of
glass fitting Lydia's watch proved nothing, and she
swore black and blue that she'd broken the glass herself. The juge d'instruction in whose charge the case
was of course eventually placed was puzzled because
no trace could be found of the money Berger must have

stolen, and actually it never was found. Another odd
thing was that there was no trace of blood on the
clothes that Berger was wearing on that particular
night. The knife wasn't found either. It was proved that
Berger had one, in the circles he moved in that was
usual enough, but he swore that he'd lost it a month
before. I told you that the detectives' work was pretty
good. There'd been no finger-prints on the stolen cars
nor on the stolen handbags, which when he'd emptied
he'd apparently just thrown into the street and some of
which had eventually got into the hands of the police,
so it was pretty obvious that he had worn gloves. They
found a pair of leather gauntlets among his things, but
it was unlikely that he would have kept them on when
he went to see Jordan, and from the place in which the
body was found, which suggested that Jordan had been
changing a record when he was struck, it was plain that
Berger hadn't murdered him the moment Jordan let
him into the room. Besides, they were too large to go
in his pocket and if he had had them at the bar someone would have noticed them. Of course Berger's
photo had been published in all the papers, and in their
difficulty the police got the press to help them. They
asked anyone who could remember having sold about
such-and-such a date a pair of gloves, probably gray,
to a young man in a gray suit, to come forward. The
papers made rather a thing about it; they put his photo
in again with the caption: 'Did you sell him the gloves
he wore to kill Teddie Jordan?'

"You know, a thing that has always struck me is
people's fiendish eagerness to give anyone away. They

pretend it's public spirit, I don't believe a word of it, I don't believe it's even, as a rule anyway, the desire for notoriety; I believe it's just due to the baseness of human nature that gets a kick out of injuring others. You know, of course, that in England the Treasury and the King's Proctor are supposed to have a wonderful system of espionage to detect income-tax evasions, and collusion and so forth in divorce cases. Well, there's not a word of truth in it. They depend entirely on anonymous letters. There are a whole mass of people who can't wait if they have the chance of doing down someone who's trying to get away with anything."

"It's a grim thought," said Charley, but added cheerfully: "I can only hope you're exaggerating."

"Well, anyhow, a woman from the glove department at the Trois Quartiers came forward and said she remembered selling a young man a pair of gray suède gloves on the day of the murder. She was a woman of about forty and she'd liked the look of him. He was particularly anxious that they should match his gray suit and he wanted them rather large so that he shouldn't have any difficulty in slipping into them. Berger was paraded with a dozen other young men and she picked him out at once, but, as his lawyer pointed out, that was easy since she had only just seen his picture in the paper. Then they got hold of one of Berger's crooked friends who said he'd met him on the night of the murder, not walking towards the boulevard, but in a direction that would have taken him to Jordan's apartment. He'd shaken hands with him and had noticed that he was wearing gloves. But that par-

ticular witness was a thorough scamp. He had a foul
record, and Berger's counsel at the trial attacked him
violently. Berger denied that he had seen him on that
particular evening and his counsel tried to persuade
the jury that it was a cooked-up story that the man had
invented in order to ingratiate himself with the police.
The damning thing was the trousers. There'd been a
lot of stuff in the papers about Berger's smart clothes,
the well-dressed gangster and all that sort of thing;
you'd have thought, to read it, that he got his suits in
Savile Row and his haberdashery at Charvet's. The
prosecution was anxious to prove that he was in desperate need of money and they went round to all the
shops that supplied things both to him and for the
household to find out if there had been any pressure
put to settle unpaid accounts. But it appeared that
everything bought for the house was paid for on the
nail and there were no outstanding debts. So far as
clothes were concerned Berger, it turned out, had
bought nothing since he lost his job but one gray suit.
The detective who was interviewing the tailor asked
when this had been paid for and the tailor turned up
his books. He was an advertising tailor in a large way
of business who made clothes to measure at a lowish
price. It was then discovered that Berger had ordered
an extra pair of trousers with the suit. The police had
a list of every article in his wardrobe, and this pair
of trousers didn't figure on it. They at once saw the
importance of the fact and they made up their minds
to keep it dark till the trial.

"It was a thrilling moment, believe me, when the

prosecution introduced the subject. There could be no doubt that Berger had had two pairs of trousers to his new gray suit and that one of the pairs was missing. When he was asked about it he never even attempted to explain. He didn't seem flummoxed. He said he didn't know they were missing. He pointed out that he had had no opportunity of going over his wardrobe for some months, having been in prison awaiting trial, and when he was asked how he could possibly account for their disappearance suggested flippantly that perhaps one of the police officers who had searched the house was in need of a pair of new trousers and had sneaked them. But Madame Berger had her explanation pat, and I'm bound to say I thought it a very ingenious one. She said that Lydia had been ironing the trousers, as she always did after Robert had worn them, and the iron was too hot and she had burnt them. He was fussy about his clothes and it had been something of a struggle to find the money to pay for the suit, they knew he would be angry with his wife, and Madame Berger, wishing to spare her his reproaches and seeing how scared she was, proposed that they shouldn't tell him; she would get rid of the trousers and Robert perhaps would never notice that they had disappeared. Asked what she had done with them she said that a tramp had come to the door, asking for money, and she had given him the trousers instead. The size of the burn was gone into. She claimed that it made the trousers unwearable, and when the public prosecutor pointed out that invisible mending would have repaired the damage, she answered that it would have

cost more than the trousers were worth. Then he suggested that in their impoverished circumstances Berger
might well have worn them in the house; it would
surely have been better to risk his displeasure than to
throw away a garment which might still be useful.
Madame Berger said she never thought of that, she
gave them to the tramp on an impulse, to get rid of
them. The prosecutor put it to her that she had to get
rid of them because they were blood-stained and that
she hadn't given them to a tramp who had so conveniently presented himself, but had herself destroyed
them. She hotly denied this. Then where was the tramp?
He would read of the incident in the papers and knowing that a man's life was at stake would surely present
himself. She turned to the press, throwing out her arms
with a dramatic gesture.

" 'Let all these gentlemen,' she cried, 'spread it far
and wide. Let them beseech him to come forward and
save my son.'

"She was magnificent on the witness stand. The
public prosecutor subjected her to a merciless examination; she fought like a fury. He took her through
young Berger's life and she admitted all his misdeeds,
from the episode at the tennis club to his thefts from
the broker who after his conviction had, out of charity,
given him another chance. She took all the blame of
them on herself. A French witness is allowed much
greater latitude than is allowed to a witness in an
English criminal trial, and with bitter self-reproach she
confessed that his errors were due to the indulgence
with which she had brought him up. He was an only

child and she had spoilt him. Her husband had lost a leg in the war, while attending to the wounded under fire, and his ill health had made it necessary for her to give him unremitting attention to the detriment of her maternal duties. His untimely end had left the wretched boy without guidance. She appealed to the emotions of the jury by dwelling on the grief that had afflicted them both when death robbed their little family of its head. Then her son had been her only consolation. She described him as high-spirited, headstrong, easily led by bad companions, but deeply affectionate and, whatever else he was guilty of, incapable of murdering a man who had never shown him anything but kindness.

"But somehow she didn't create a favourable impression. She insisted on her own unimpeachable respectability in a way that grated on you. Even though she was defending the son she adored she missed no opportunity to remind the Court that she was the daughter of a staff officer. She was smartly dressed, in black, perhaps too smartly, she gave you the impression of a woman who was trying to live above her station; and she had a calculating expression on her hard, decided features; you couldn't believe that she'd have given a crust of bread, much less a pair of trousers, even though damaged, to a beggar."

"And Lydia?"

"Lydia was rather pathetic. She was very much in the family way. Her face was swollen with tears and her voice hardly rose above a whisper, so that you could only just hear what she said. No one believed her story that she had broken the glass of the watch herself, but the prosecutor wasn't hard on her as he'd been on her mother-in-law; she was too obviously the innocent victim of a cruel fate. Madame Berger and Robert had used her unmercifully for their own ends. The Court took it as natural enough that she should do everything in her power to save her husband. It was even rather touching when she told how kind and sweet he had always been to her. It was quite clear that she was madly in love with him. The look she gave him when she came on to the witness stand was very moving. Out of all that crowd of witnesses, policemen and detectives, jailors, bar-loungers, informers, crooks, mental experts—they called a couple of experts who had made a psychological examination of Berger and a pretty picture they painted of his character—out of all that crowd, I say, she was the only one who appeared to have any human feeling.

"They'd got Maître Lemoine, one of the best criminal lawyers at the French bar, to defend Berger; he was a very tall, thin man, with a long sallow face, immense black eyes and very black thick hair. He had the most eloquent hands I've ever seen. He was a striking figure in his black gown, with the white of his lawyer's bands under his chin. He had a deep, powerful voice. He reminded you, I hardly know why, of one of those mysterious figures in a Longhi picture. He was an actor as well as an orator. By a look he could express his opinion of a man's character and by a pause the improbability of his statements. I wish you could have seen the skill with which he treated the hostile wit-

nesses, the suavity with which he inveigled them into
contradicting themselves, the scorn with which he exposed their baseness, the ridicule with which he treated
their pretensions. He could be winningly persuasive and
brutally harsh. When the mental experts deposed that
on repeated examinations of Berger in prison they had
formed the opinion that he was vain, arrogant and
mendacious, ruthless, devoid of moral sense, unscrupulous and insensible to remorse, he reasoned with them
as though he were a trained psychologist. It was a
delight to watch the working of his subtle brain. He
spoke generally in an easy, conversational tone, but
enriched by his lovely voice and with a beautiful choice
of words; you felt that everything he said could have
gone straight down in a book without alteration; but
when he came to his final speech and used all the
resources at his disposal the effect was stupendous. He
insisted on the flimsiness of the evidence; he poured
contempt on the credibility of the disreputable witnesses; he drew red herrings across the path; he con-
tended that the prosecution hadn't made out a case
upon which it was possible to convict. Now he was
chatty and seemed to talk to the jury as man to man,
now he worked up to a flight of impassioned pleading
and his voice grew and grew in volume till it rang
through the court-room like the pealing of thunder.
Then a pause so dramatic that you felt your skin go
all goosy. His peroration was magnificent. He told
the jury that they must do their duty and decide
according to their conscience, but he besought them
to put out of their minds all the prejudice occasioned by

the young man's admitted crimes, and his voice low and tremulous with emotion—by God! it was effective —he reminded them that the man the public prosecutor asked them to sentence to death was the son of a widow, herself the daughter of a soldier who had deserved well of his country, and the son of an officer who had given his life in its defence; he reminded them that he was recently married, and had married for love, and his young wife now bore in her womb the fruits of their union. Could they let this innocent child be brought into the world with the stigma that his father was a convicted murderer? Claptrap? Of course it was claptrap, but if you'd been there and heard those thrilling, grave accents you wouldn't have thought so. Gosh! how people cried. I nearly did myself, only I saw the tears coursing down Berger's cheeks and him wiping his eyes with a handkerchief, and that seemed to me so comic that I kept my head. But it was a fine effort, and not all the huissiers in the world could have prevented the applause that burst from the crowd when he sat down.

"The prosecuting counsel was a stout, rubicund fellow of thirty-five, I should say, or forty, who looked like a North Country farmer. He oozed self-satisfaction. You felt that for him the case was a wonderful chance to make a splash and so further his career. He was verbose and confused, so that, if the presiding judge hadn't come to his help now and then, the jury would hardly have known what he was getting at. He was cheaply melodramatic. On one occasion he turned to Berger who had just made some remark aside to one of the warders who sat in the dock with him, and said:

" 'You may smile now, but you won't smile when, with your arms pinioned behind your back, you walk in the cold gray light of dawn and see the guillotine rear its horror before your eyes. No smile then will break on your lips, but your limbs will shake with terror, and remorse for your monstrous crime wring your heart.'

"Berger gave the warder an amused look, but so contemptuous of what the public prosecutor had said, that if he hadn't been eaten up with vanity he couldn't have failed to be disconcerted. It was grand to see the way Lemoine treated him. He paid him extravagant compliments, but charged with such corrosive irony that, for all his conceit, the public prosecutor couldn't help seeing he was made a fool of. Lemoine was so malicious, but with such perfect courtesy and with such a condescending urbanity, that you could see in the eyes of the presiding judge a twinkle of appreciation. I very much doubt if the prosecuting counsel advanced his career by his conduct of this case.

"The three judges sat in a row on the bench. They were rather impressive in their scarlet robes and black squarish caps. Two were middle-aged men and never opened their mouths. The presiding judge was a little old man, with the wrinkled face of a monkey, and a tired, flat voice, but he was very observant; he listened attentively, and when he spoke it was without severity, but with a passionless calm that was rather frightening. He had the exquisite reasonableness of a man who has no illusions about human nature, but having long since learnt that man is capable of any vileness accepts the fact as just as much a matter of course as that he has two arms and two legs. When the jury went out to consider their verdict we journalists scattered to have a chat, a drink or a cup of coffee. We all hoped they wouldn't be too long, because it was getting late and we wanted to get our stuff in. We had no doubt that they'd find Berger guilty. One of the odd circumstances I've noticed in the murder trials I've attended is how unlike the impression is you get about things in court to that which you get by reading about them in the paper. When you read the evidence you think that after all it's rather slight, and if you'd been on the jury you'd have given the accused the benefit of the doubt. But what you've left out of account is the general atmosphere, the feeling that you get; it puts an entirely different colour on the evidence. After about an hour we were told that the jury had arrived at a decision and we trooped in again. Berger was brought up from the cells and we all stood up as the three judges trailed in one after the other. The lights had been lit and it was rather sinister in that crowded court. There was a tremor of apprehension. Have you ever been to the Old Bailey?"

"No, in point of fact, I haven't," said Charley.

"I go often when I'm in London. It's a good place to learn about human nature. There's a difference in feeling between that and a French court that made a most peculiar impression on me. I don't pretend to understand it. At the Old Bailey you feel that a prisoner is confronted with the majesty of the law. It's something impersonal that he has to deal with, Justice in the abstract. An idea, in fact. It's awful in the literal sense of the word. But in that French court, during the two days I spent there, I was beset by a very different feeling, I didn't get the impression that it was permeated by a grandiose abstraction, I felt that the apparatus of law was an arrangement by which a bourgeois society protected its safety, its property, its privileges from the evil-doer who threatened them. I don't mean the trial wasn't fair or the verdict unjustified, what I mean is that you got the sensation of a society that was outraged because it feared, rather than of a principle that must be upheld. The prisoner was up against men who wanted to safeguard themselves rather than, as with us, up against an idea that must prevail though the heavens fall. It was terrifying rather than awful. The verdict was guilty of murder with extenuating circumstances."

"What were the extenuating circumstances?"

"There were none, but French juries don't like to sentence a man to death, and by French law when there are extenuating circumstances capital punishment can't be inflicted. Berger got off with fifteen years' penal servitude."

Simon looked at his watch and got up.

"I must be going. I'll give you the stuff I wrote about the trial and you can read it at your leisure. And look, here's the article I wrote on crime as a form of sport. I showed it to your girl friend, but I don't think she liked it very much; anyhow, she returned it without a word of comment. As an exercise in sardonic humour it's not so dusty."

vii

SINCE HE HAD NO WISH to read Simon's articles in Lydia's presence, Charley, on parting from his friend, went to the Dôme, ordered himself a cup of coffee, and settled himself down to their perusal. He was glad to read a connected account of the murder and the trial, for Lydia's various narratives had left him somewhat confused. She had told him this and that, not in the order in which it had occurred, but as her emotion dictated. Simon's three long articles were coherent, and though there were particulars which Charley had learnt from Lydia and of which he was ignorant, he had succeeded in constructing a graphic story which it was easy to follow. He wrote almost as he spoke, in a fluent journalistic style, but he had managed very effectively to present the background against which the events he described had been enacted. You got a sinister impression of a world, sordid, tumultuous, in which these gangsters, dope traffickers, bookies and racecourse touts lived their dark and hazardous lives. Dregs of the population of a great city, living on their wits, suspicious of one another, ready to betray their best friend if it could be of advantage to themselves, open-handed, sociable, gaily cynical, even good-humoured, they seemed to enjoy that existence, with all its dangers and vicissitudes, which kept you up to the mark and made you feel that you really were living. Each man's hand was against his neighbour's, but the alertness which this forced upon you was exhilarating. It was a world in which a man would shoot another for a trifle, but was just as ready to take flowers and fruit, bought at no small sacrifice, to a third who was sick in hospital. The atmosphere with which Simon had not unskilfully encompassed his story filled Charley with a strange unease. The world he knew, the peaceful happy world of the surface, was like a pretty lake in which were reflected the dappled clouds and the willows that grew on its bank, where care-free boys paddled their canoes and the girls with them trailed their fingers in the soft water. It was terrifying to think that below, just below, dangerous weeds waved tentacles to ensnare you and all manner of strange, horrible things, poisonous snakes, fish with murderous jaws, waged an unceasing and hidden warfare. From a word here, a word there, Charley got the impression that Simon had peered fascinated into those secret depths, and he asked himself whether it was merely curiosity, or some horrible attraction, that led him to observe those crooks and blackguards with a cynical indulgence.

In this world Robert Berger had found himself wonderfully at home. Of a higher class and better educated than most of its inhabitants, he had enjoyed a certain prestige. His charm, his easy manner and his social position attracted his associates, but at the same time put them on their guard against him. They knew he was a crook, but curiously enough, because he was a garçon de bonne famille, a youth of respectable parentage, took it somewhat amiss that he should be. He worked chiefly alone, without confederates, and kept his own counsel. They had a notion that he despised them, but they were impressed when he had been to a concert and talked enthusiastically ánd, for all they could tell, with knowledge of the performance. They did not realize that he felt himself wonderfully at ease in their company. In his mother's house, with his mother's friends, he felt lonely and oppressed; he was irritated by the inactivity of the respectable life. After his conviction on the charge of stealing a motor car he had said to Jojo in one of his rare moments of confidence:

"Now I needn't pretend any more. I wish my father were alive, he would have turned me out of the house and then I should be free to lead the only life I like. Evidently I can't leave my mother. I'm all she has."

"Crime doesn't pay," said Jojo.

"You seem to make a pretty good thing out of it," Robert laughed. "But it's not the money, it's the excitement and the power. It's like diving from a great height. The water looks terribly far away, but you make the plunge, and when you rise to the surface, gosh! you feel pleased with yourself."

Charley put the newspaper cuttings back in his pocket, and, his brow slightly frowning with the effort,

tried to piece together what he now knew of Robert
Berger in order to get some definite impression of the
sort of man he really was. It was all very well to say
he was a worthless scamp of whom society was well
rid; that was true of course, but it was too simple and
too sweeping a judgement to be satisfactory; the idea
dawned in Charley's mind that perhaps men were more
complicated than he had imagined, and if you just said
that a man was this or that you couldn't get very far.
There was Robert's passion for music, especially Russian music, which, so unfortunately for her, had brought
Lydia and him together. Charley was very fond of
music. He knew the delight it gave him, the pleasure,
partly sensual, partly intellectual, when intoxicated by
the loveliness that assailed his ears, he remained yet
keenly appreciative of the subtlety with which the composer had worked out his idea. Looking into himself,
as perhaps he had never looked before, to find out what
exactly it was he felt when he listened to one of the
greater symphonies, it seemed to him that it was a
complex of emotions, excitement and at the same time
peace, love for others and a desire to do something
for them, a wish to be good and a delight in goodness,
a pleasant languor and a funny detachment as though
he were floating above the world and whatever happened there didn't very much matter; and perhaps if
you had to combine all those feelings into one and give
it a name, the name you'd give it was happiness. But
what was it that Robert Berger got when he listened
to music? Nothing like that, that was obvious. Or was
it unjust to dismiss such emotions as music gave *him*

as vile and worthless? Might it not be rather that in music he found release from the devil that possessed him, that devil which was stronger than himself so that he neither could be delivered, nor even wanted to be delivered, from the urge that drove him to crime because it was the expression of his warped nature, because by throwing himself into antagonism with the forces of law and order he realized his personality— might it not be that in music he found peace from that impelling force and for a while, resting in heavenly acquiescence, saw as though through a rift in the clouds a vision of love and goodness?

Charley knew what it was to be in love. He knew that it made you feel friendly to all men, he knew that you wanted to do everything in the world for the girl you loved, he knew that you couldn't bear the thought of hurting her and he knew that you couldn't help wondering what she saw in you, because of course she was wonderful, definitely, and if you were honest with yourself you were bound to confess that you couldn't hold a candle to her. And Charley supposed that if he felt like that everyone else must feel like that and therefore Robert Berger had too. There was no doubt that he loved Lydia with passion, but if love filled him with a sense of—Charley jibbed at the word that came to his mind, it made him almost blush with embarrassment to think of it—well, with a sense of holiness, it was strange that he could commit sordid and horrible crimes. There must be two men in him. Charley was perplexed, which can hardly be considered strange, for he was but twenty-three, and older, wiser men have failed to understand how a scoundrel can love as purely and disinterestedly as a saint. And was it possible for Lydia to love her husband even now with an all-forgiving devotion if he were entirely worthless?

"Human nature wants a bit of understanding," he muttered to himself.

Without knowing it, he had said a mouthful.

But when he came to consider the love that consumed Lydia, a love that was the cause of her every action, the inspiration of her every thought, so that it was like a symphonic accompaniment that gave depth and significance to the melodic line which was her life from day to day, he could only draw back in an almost horrified awe as he might have drawn back, terrified but fascinated, at the sight of a forest on fire or a river in flood. This was something with which his experience could not cope. By the side of this he knew that his own little love affairs had been but trivial flirtations and the emotion which had from time to time brought charm and gaiety into his somewhat humdrum life no more than a boy's sentimentality. It was incomprehensible that in the body of that commonplace, drab little woman there should be room for a passion of such intensity. It was not only what she said that made you realize it, you felt it, intuitively as it were, in the aloofness which, for all the intimacy with which she treated you, kept you at a distance; you saw it in the depths of her transparent eyes, in the scorn of her lips when she didn't know you were looking at her, and you heard it in the undertones of her sing-song voice. It was not like any of the civilized feelings that Charley was familiar with, there was something wild and brutal in it, and notwithstanding her high-heeled shoes, her silk stockings, and her coat and skirt, Lydia did not seem a woman of to-day, but a savage with elemental instincts who still harboured in the darkest recesses of her soul the ape-like creature from which the human being is descended.

"By God! what have I let myself in for?" said Charley.

He turned to Simon's article. Simon had evidently taken pains over it for the style was more elegant than that of his reports of the trial. It was an exercise in irony written with detachment, but beneath the detachment you felt the troubled curiosity with which he had considered the character of this man who was restrained neither by scruple nor by the fear of consequences. It was a clever little essay, but so callous that you could not read it without discomfort. Trying to make the most of his ingenious theme, Simon had forgotten that human beings, with feelings, were concerned; and if you smiled, for it was not lacking in a bitter wit, it was with malaise. It appeared that Simon had somehow gained admittance to the little house at Neuilly, and in order to give an impression of the environment in which Berger had lived, he described with acid humour the tasteless, stuffy and pretentious room into which he had been ushered. It was furnished with two drawing-room suites, one Louis Quinze and the other Empire. The Louis Quinze suite was in carved wood, gilt and covered in blue silk with little pink flowers on

it; the Empire suite was upholstered in light yellow
satin. In the middle of the room was an elaborately-
carved gilt table with a marble top. Both suites had
evidently come from one of those shops in the Boulevard St. Antoine that manufacture period furniture
wholesale, and had been then bought at auction when
their first owners had wanted to get rid of them. With
two sofas and all those chairs it was impossible to move
without precaution and there was nowhere you could
sit in comfort. On the walls were large oil paintings
in heavy gold frames, which, it was obvious, had been
bought at sale-rooms because they were going for
nothing.

The prosecution had reconstructed the story of the
murder with plausibility. It was evident that Jordan
had taken a fancy to Robert Berger. The meals he had
stood him, the winners he had given him and the money
he had lent him, proved that. At last Berger had consented to come to his apartment, and so that their leaving the bar together should not attract attention they
had arranged for one to go some minutes after the
other. They met according to plan, and since the concierge was certain she had admitted that night no one
who asked for Jordan, it was plain that they had
entered the house together. Jordan lived on the ground
floor. Berger, still wearing his smart new gloves, sat
down and smoked a cigarette while Jordan busied himself getting the whiskey and soda and bringing in the
cake from his tiny kitchen. He was the sort of man who
always sat in his shirt-sleeves at home, and he took off
his coat. He put on a record. It was a cheap, old-

fashioned gramophone, without an automatic change, and it was while Jordan was putting on a new record that Berger, coming up behind him as though to see what it was, had stabbed him in the back. To claim, as the defence did, that he had not the strength to give a blow of such violence as the post-mortem indicated, was absurd. He was very wiry. Persons who had known him in his tennis days testified that he had been known for the power of his forehand drive. If he had never got into the first rank it was not due to an inadequate physique, but to some psychological failing that defeated his will to win.

Simon accepted the view of the prosecution. He thought they had got the facts pretty accurately, and that the reason they gave for Jordan's asking the young man to come to his apartment was correct, but he was convinced they were wrong in supposing that Berger had murdered him for the money he knew he had made during the day. For one thing, the purchase of the gloves showed that he had decided upon the deed before he knew that Jordan would be in possession that night of an unusually large sum. Though the money had never been found Simon was persuaded that he had taken it, but that was by the way; it was there for the taking and he was glad enough to get it, but to do so was not the motive of the murder. The police claimed that he had stolen between fifty and sixty cars; he had never even attempted to sell one of them; he abandoned them sometimes after a few hours, at the most after a few days. He purloined them for the convenience of having one when he needed it, but much more to exercise his daring and resource. His robberies from women, by means of the simple trick he had devised, brought him little profit; they were practical jokes that appealed to his sense of humour. To carry them out required the charm which he loved to exert. It made him giggle to think of those women left speechless and gaping in an empty street while he sped on. The thing was, in short, a form of sport, and each time he had successfully brought it off he was filled with the self-satisfaction that he might have felt when by a clever lob or by a drop shot he won a point off an opponent at tennis. It gave him confidence. And it was the risk, the coolness that was needed, the power to make a quick decision if it looked as though discovery were inevitable, much more than the large profits, that had induced him to engage in the business of smuggling dope into France. It was like rock-climbing; you had to be sure of foot, you had to keep your head; your life depended on your nerve, your strength, your instinct; but when you had surmounted every difficulty and achieved your aim, how wonderful after that terrific strain was the feeling of deliverance and how intoxicating the sense of victory! Certainly for a man of his slender means he had got a good deal of money out of the broker who had employed him; but it had come in driblets and he had spent it on taking Lydia to night clubs and for excursions in the country, or with his friends at Jojo's Bar. Every penny had gone by the time he was caught; and it was only a chance that he was; the method he had conceived for robbing his employer was so adroit that he might very well have got away with it indefinitely. Here again it looked as though it were much more for the fun of the thing, than for profit, that he had committed a crime. He told his lawyer quite frankly that the broker was so confident of his own cleverness, he could not resist making a fool of him.

But by now, Simon went on, pursuing his idea, Robert Berger had exhausted the amusement he was capable of getting out of the smaller varieties of evil-doing. During one of the periods he spent in jail await-ing trial he had made friends with an old lag, and had listened to his stories with fascinated interest. The man was a cat burglar who specialized in jewellery and he made an exciting tale of some of his exploits. First there was the marking down of the prey, then the pa-tient watching to discover her habits, the examination of the premises; you had to find out not only where the jewels were kept and how to get into the house, but also what were the chances of making a quick get-away if necessary; and after you had made sure of everything there was the long waiting for the suitable opportunity. Often months elapsed between the time when you made up your mind to go after the stuff and the time when at last you had a whack at it. That was what choked Berger off; he had the nerve, the agility and the pres-ence of mind that were needed, but he would never have had the patience for the complicated business that must precede the burglary.

Simon likened Robert Berger to a man who has shot partridge and pheasant for years, and having ceased to find diversion in the exercise of his skill, craves for a sport in which there is an element of danger and so turns his mind to big game. No one could say when Berger began to be obsessed with the idea of murder, but it might be supposed that it took possession of him gradually. Like an artist heavy with the work demanding expression in his soul, who knows that he will not find peace till he has delivered himself of the burden, Berger felt that by killing he would fulfil himself. After that, having expressed his personality to its utmost, he would be at rest and then could settle down with Lydia to a life of humdrum respectability. His instincts would have been satisfied. He knew that it was a monstrous crime, he knew that he risked his neck, but it was the monstrousness of it that tempted him and the risk that made it worth the attempt.

Here Charley put the article down. He thought that Simon was really going too far. He could just fancy himself committing murder in a moment of ungovernable rage, but by no effort of imagination could he conceive of anyone doing such a thing—doing it not even for money, but for sport as Simon put it—because he was driven to it by an urge to destroy and so assert his own being. Did Simon really believe there was anything in his theory, or was it merely that he thought it would make an effective article? Charley, though with a slight frown on his handsome face, went on reading.

Perhaps, Simon continued, Robert Berger would have been satisfied merely to toy with the idea if circumstances had not offered him the predestined victim. He may often, when drinking with one of his boon com-

panions, have considered the feasibility of killing him
and put the notion aside because the difficulties were
too great or detection too certain. But when chance
threw him in contact with Teddie Jordan he must have
felt that here was the very man he had been looking
for. He was a foreigner, with a large acquaintaince,
but no close friends, who lived alone in a blind alley.
He was a crook; he was connected with the dope traffic;
if he were found dead one day the police might well
suppose that his murder was the result of a gangsters'
quarrel. If they knew nothing of his sexual habits, they
would be sure to find out about them after his death
and likely enough to assume that he had been killed
by some rough who wanted more money than he was
prepared to give. Among the vast number of bullies,
blackmailers, dope-peddlers and bad hats who might
have done him in, the police would not know where to
look, and in any case he was an undesirable alien and
they would think he was just as well out of the way.
They would make enquiries and if results were not soon
obtained quietly shelve the case. Berger saw that Jordan had taken a fancy to him and he played him like
an angler playing a trout. He made dates which he
broke. He made half-promises which he did not keep.
If Jordan, thinking he was being made a fool of, threatened to break away, he exercised his charm to induce
him to have patience. Jordan thought it was he who
pursued and the other who fled. Berger laughed in his
sleeve. He tracked him as a hunter day after day tracks
a shy and suspicious beast in the jungle, waiting for
his opportunity, with the knowledge that, for all its

instinctive caution, the brute will at last be delivered into his hands. And because Berger had no feeling of animosity for Jordan, neither liking him nor disliking him, he was able to devote himself without hindrance to the pleasure of the chase. When at length the deed was done and the little bookmaker lay dead at his feet, he felt neither fear nor remorse, but only a thrill so intense that he was transported.

Charley finished the essay. He shuddered. He did not know whether it was Robert Berger's brutal treachery and callousness that more horrified him or the cool relish with which Simon described the workings of the murderer's depraved and tortuous mind. It was true that this description was the work of his own invention, but what fearful instinct was it in him that found delight in peering into such vile depths? Simon leaned over to look into Berger's soul, as one might lean over the edge of a fearful precipice, and you had the impression that what he saw filled him with envy. Charley did not know how he had got the impression (because there was nothing in those careful periods or in that half-flippant irony actually to suggest it) that while he wrote he asked himself whether there was in him, Simon Fenimore, the courage and the daring to do a deed so shocking, cruel and futile. Charley sighed.

"I've known Simon for nearly fifteen years. I thought I knew him inside out. I'm beginning to think I don't know the first thing about him."

But he smiled happily. There were his father and his mother and Patsy. They would be leaving the Terry-Masons next day, tired after those strenuous days of

fun and laughter, but glad to get back to their bright,
artistic and comfortable house.

"Thank God, they're decent, ordinary people. You
know where you are with them."

He suddenly felt a wave of affection for them sweep
over him.

But it was growing late; Lydia would be getting back
and he did not want to keep her waiting, she would be
lonely, poor thing, by herself in that sordid room; he
stuffed the essay into his pocket with the other cuttings
and walked back to the hotel. He need not have fashed
himself. Lydia was not there. He took Mansfield Park,
which with Blake's Poems was the only book he had
brought with him, and began to read. It was a delight
to move in the company of those well-mannered persons
who after the lapse of more than a hundred years
seemed as much alive as anyone you met to-day. There
was a gracious ease in the ordered course of their lives,
and the perturbations from which they suffered were not
so serious as to distress you. It was true that Cinderella
was an awful little prig and Prince Charming a monstrous pedant; it was true that you could not but wish
that instead of setting her prim heart on such an owl she
had accepted the proposals of the engaging and witty
villain; but you accepted with indulgence Jane Austen's
determination to reward good sense and punish levity.
Nothing could lessen the delight of her gentle irony
and caustic humour. It took Charley's mind off that
story of depravity and crime in which he seemed to have
got so strangely involved. He was removed from the
dingy, cheerless room and in fancy saw himself sitting

on a lawn, under a great cedar, on a pleasant summer evening; and from the fields beyond the garden came the scent of hay. But he began to feel hungry and looked at his watch. It was half-past eight. Lydia had not returned. Perhaps she had no intention of doing so? It wouldn't be very nice of her to leave him like that, without a word of explanation or farewell, and the possibility made him rather angry, but then he shrugged his shoulders.

"If she doesn't want to come back, let her stay away."

He didn't see why he should wait any longer, so he went out to dinner, leaving word at the porter's desk where he was going so that if she came she could join him. Charley wasn't quite sure if it amused, flattered or irritated him, that the staff should treat him with a sort of confidential familiarity as though they got a vicarious satisfaction out of the affair which, naturally enough, they were convinced he was having. The porter was smilingly benevolent and the young woman at the cashier's desk excited and curious. Charley chuckled at the thought of their shocked surprise if they had known how innocent were his relations with Lydia. He came back from his solitary dinner and she was not yet there. He went up to his room and went on reading, but now he had to make a certain effort to attend. If she didn't come back by twelve he made up his mind to give her up and go out on the loose. It was absurd to spend the best part of a week in Paris and not have a bit of fun. But soon after eleven she opened the door and entered, carrying a small and very shabby suitcase.

"Oh, I'm tired," she said. "I've brought a few things with me. I'll just have a wash and then we'll go out to dinner."

"Haven't you dined? I have."

"Have you?"

She seemed surprised.

"It's past eleven."

She laughed.

"How English you are! Must you always dine at the same hour?"

"I was hungry," he answered rather stiffly.

It seemed to him that she really might express some regret for having kept him waiting so long. It was plain, however, that nothing was farther from her thoughts.

"Oh, well, it doesn't matter, I don't want any dinner. What a day I've had! Alexey was drunk; he had a row with Paul this morning, because he didn't come home last night, and Paul knocked him down. Evgenia was crying, and she kept on saying: 'God has punished us for our sins. I have lived to see my son strike his father. What is going to happen to us all?' Alexey was crying too. 'It is the end of everything,' he said. 'Children no longer respect their parents. Oh, Russia, Russia!' "

Charley felt inclined to giggle, but he saw that Lydia was taking the scene in all seriousness.

"And did you cry too?"

"Naturally," she answered, with a certain coldness.

She had changed her dress and now wore one of black silk. It was plain enough but well cut. It suited her. It made her clear skin more delicate and deepened the colour of her blue eyes. She wore a black hat, rather saucy in shape, with a feather in it, and much more becoming than the old black felt. The smarter clothes had had an effect on her; she wore them more elegantly and carried herself with a graceful assurance. She no longer looked like a shop-girl, but like a young woman of some distinction, and prettier than Charley had ever seen her, but she gave you less than ever the impression that there was anything doing, as the phrase goes; if she had given before the effect of a respectable work-girl who knew how to take care of herself, she gave now that of a modish young woman perfectly capable of putting a too enterprising young man in his place.

"You've got a different frock on," said Charley, who was already beginning to get over his ill humour.

"Yes, it's the only nice one I've got. I thought it was too humiliating for you to have to be seen with such a little drab as I was looking. After all, the least a handsome young man in beautiful clothes can ask is that when he goes into a restaurant with a woman people shouldn't say: how can he go about with a slut who looks as though she were wearing the cast-off clothes of a maid of all work? I must at least try to be a credit to you."

Charley laughed. There was really something rather likeable about her.

"Well, we'd better go out and get you something to eat. I'll sit with you. If I know anything about your appetite you could eat a horse."

They started off in high spirits. He drank a whiskey and soda and smoked his pipe while Lydia ate a dozen oysters, a beefsteak and some fried potatoes. She told him at greater length of her visit to her Russian friends. She was greatly concerned at their situation. There was no money except the little the children earned. One of these days Paul would get sick of doing his share and would disappear into that equivocal night life of Paris, to end up, if he was lucky, when he had lost his youth and looks, as a waiter in a disreputable hotel. Alexey was growing more and more of a soak and even if by chance he got a job would never be able to hold it. Evgenia had no longer the courage to withstand the difficulties that beset her; she had lost heart. There was no hope for any of them.

"You see, it's twenty years since they left Russia. For a long time they thought there'd be a change there and they'd go back, but now they know there's no chance. It's been hard on people like that, the revolution; they've got nothing to do now, they and all their generation, but to die."

But it occurred to Lydia that Charley could not be much interested in people whom he had not even seen. She could not know that while she was talking to him about her friends he was telling himself uneasily that, if he guessed aright what was in Simon's mind, it was just such a fate that he was preparing for him, for his father, mother and sister, and for their friends. Lydia changed the subject.

"And what have you been doing with yourself this afternoon? Did you go and see any pictures?"

"No. I went to see Simon."

Lydia was looking at him with an expression of indulgent interest, but when he answered her question, she frowned.

"I don't like your friend Simon," she said. "What is it that you see in him?"

"I've known him since I was a kid. We were at school together and at Cambridge. He's been my friend always. Why don't you like him?"

"He's cold, calculating and inhuman."

"I think you're wrong there. No one knows better than I do that he's capable of great affection. He's a lonely creature. I think he hankers for a love that he can never arouse."

Lydia's eyes shone with mockery, but, as ever, there was in it a rueful note.

"You're very sentimental. How can anyone expect to arouse love who isn't prepared to give himself? In spite of all the years you've known him I wonder if you know him as well as I do. He comes a lot to the Sérail; he doesn't often go up with a girl and then not from desire, but from curiosity. Madame makes him welcome, partly because he's a journalist and she likes to keep in with the press, and partly because he sometimes brings foreigners who drink a lot of champagne. He likes to talk to us and it never enters his head that we find him repulsive."

"Remember that if he knew that he wouldn't be offended. He'd only be curious to know why. He has no vanity."

Lydia went on as though Charley had said nothing.

"He hardly looks upon us as human beings, he

despises us and yet he seeks our company. He's at ease with us. I think he feels that our degradation is so great, he can be himself, whereas in the outside world he must always wear a mask. He's strangely insensitive. He thinks he can permit himself anything with us and he asks us questions that put us to shame and never sees how bitterly he wounds us."

Charley was silent. He knew well enough how Simon, with his insatiable curiosity, could cause people profound embarrassment and was only surprised and scornful when he found that they resented his inquiries. He was willing enough to display the nakedness of his soul and it never occurred to him that the reserves of others could be due, not to stupidity as he thought, but to modesty. Lydia continued:

"Yet he's capable of doing things that you'd never expect of him. One of our girls was suddenly taken ill. The doctor said she must be operated on at once, and Simon took her to a nursing home himself so that she shouldn't have to go to the hospital, and paid for the operation; and when she got better he paid her expenses to go away to a convalescent home. And he'd never even slept with her."

"I'm not surprised. He attaches no importance to money. Anyhow it shows you that he's capable of a disinterested action."

"Or do you think he wanted to examine in himself what the emotion of goodness exactly was?"

Charley laughed.

"It's obvious that you haven't got much use for poor Simon."

"He's talked to me a great deal. He wanted to find out all I could tell him about the Russian Revolution, and he wanted me to take him to see Alexey and Evgenia so that he could ask them. You know he reported Robert's trial. He tried to make me tell him all sorts of things that he wanted to know. He went to bed with me because he thought he could get me to tell him more. He wrote an article about it. All that pain, all that horror and disgrace, were no more to him than an occasion to string clever, flippant words together; and he gave it me to read to see how I would take it. I shall never forgive him that. Never."

Charley sighed. He knew that Simon, with his amazing insensitiveness to other people's feelings, had shown her that cruel essay with no intention of hurting, but from a perfectly honest desire to see how she reacted to it and to discover how far her intimate knowledge would confirm his fanciful theory.

"He's a strange creature," said Charley. "I daresay he has a lot of traits which one would rather he hadn't, but he has great qualities. There's one thing at all events that you can say about him: if he doesn't spare others, he doesn't spare himself. After not seeing him for two years, and he's changed a lot in that time, I can't help finding his personality rather impressive."

"Frightening, I should have said."

Charley moved uneasily on his plush seat, for that also, somewhat to his dismay, was what he had found it.

"He lives an extraordinary life, you know. He works sixteen hours a day. The squalor and discomfort of his surroundings are indescribable. He's trained himself to eat only one meal a day."

"What is the object of that?"

"He wants to strengthen and deepen his character. He wants to make himself independent of circumstances. He wants to prepare himself for the role he expects one day to be called upon to play."

"And has he told you what that role is?"

"Not precisely."

"Have you ever heard of Dzerjinsky?"

"No."

"Simon has talked to me about him a great deal. Alexey was a lawyer in the old days, a clever one with liberal principles, and he defended Dzerjinsky at one of his trials. That didn't prevent Dzerjinsky from having Alexey arrested as a counter-revolutionary and sending him for three years to Alexandrovsk. That was one of the reasons why Simon wanted me so much to take him to see Alexey. And when I wouldn't, because I couldn't bear that he should see to what depths that poor, broken-down man had sunk, he charged me with questions to put to him."

"But who was Dzerjinsky?" asked Charley.

"He was the head of the Cheka. He was the real master of Russia. He had an unlimited power over the life and death of the whole population. He was monstrously cruel; he imprisoned, tortured and killed thousands upon thousands of people. At first I thought it strange that Simon should be so interested in that abominable man, he seemed to be fascinated by him, and then I guessed the reason. That is the role he means to play when the revolution he's working for takes place. He knows that the man who is master of the police is master of the country."

Charley's eyes twinkled.

"You make my flesh creep, dear. But you know, England isn't like Russia; I think Simon will have to wait a hell of a long time before he's dictator of England."

But this was a matter upon which Lydia could brook no flippancy. She gave him a dark look.

"He's prepared to wait. Didn't Lenin wait? Do you still think the English are made of different clay from other men? Do you think the proletariat, which is growing increasingly conscious of its power, is going to leave the class you belong to indefinitely in possession of its privileges? Do you think that a war, whether it results in your defeat or your victory, is going to result in anything but a great social upheaval?"

Charley was not interested in politics. Though, like his father, of liberal views, with mildly socialistic tendencies so long as they were not carried beyond the limits of prudence, by which, though he didn't know it, he meant so long as they didn't interfere with his comfort and his income, he was quite prepared to leave the affairs of the country to those whose business it was to deal with them; but he could not let these provocative questions of Lydia's go without an answer.

"You talk as though we did nothing for the working classes. You don't seem to know that in the last fifty years their condition has changed out of all recognition. They work fewer hours than they did and get higher

wages for what they do. They have better houses to
live in. Why, on our own estate we're doing away with
slums as quickly as it's economically possible. We've
given them old age pensions and we provide them with
enough to live on when they're out of work. They get
free schooling, free hospitals, and now we're beginning
to give them holidays with pay. I really don't think
the British working man has much to complain of."

"You must remember that the views of a benefactor
and the views of a beneficiary on the value of a bene-
faction are apt to differ. Do you really expect the working man to be grateful to you for the advantages he's
extracted from you at the point of a pistol? Do you
think he doesn't know that he owes the favours you've
conferred on him to your fear rather than to your
generosity?"

Charley was not going to let himself be drawn into
a political discussion if he could help it, but there was
one more thing he couldn't refrain from saying.

"I shouldn't have thought that the condition in which
you and your Russian friends now find yourselves would
lead you to believe that mob-rule was a great success."

"That is the bitterest part of our tragedy. However
much we may deny it, we know in our hearts that whatever has happened to us, we've deserved it."

Lydia said this with a tragic intensity that somewhat
disconcerted Charley. She was a difficult woman; she
could take nothing lightly. She was the sort of woman
who couldn't even ask you to pass the salt without
giving you the impression that it was no laughing matter. Charley sighed; he supposed he must make allow-

ances, for she had had a rotten deal, poor thing; but was the future really so black?

"Tell me about Dzerjinsky," he said, stumbling a little over the pronunciation of the difficult name.

"I can only tell you what Alexey has told me. He says the most remarkable thing about him was the power of his eyes; he had a curious gift, he was able to fix them upon you for an immensely long time, and the glassy stare of them, with their dilated pupils, was simply terrifying. He was extremely thin, he'd contracted tuberculosis in prison, and he was tall; not bad-looking, with good features. He was absolutely single-minded, that was the secret of his power, he had a cold, arid temperament; I don't suppose he'd ever given himself up with a whole heart to a moment's pleasure. The only thing he cared about was his work; he worked day and night. At the height of his career he lived in one small room with nothing in it but a desk and an old screen, and behind the screen a narrow iron bed. They say that in the year of famine, when they brought him decent food instead of horseflesh, he sent it away, demanding the same rations as were given to the other workers in the Cheka. He lived for the Cheka and nothing else. There was no humanity in him, neither pity nor love, only fanaticism and hatred. He was terrible and implacable."

Charley shuddered a little. He could not but see why Lydia had told him about the terrorist, and in truth it was startling to note how close the resemblance was between the sinister man she had described and the man he had so surprisingly discovered that Simon was be-

come. There was the same asceticism, the same indifference to the pleasant things of life, the same power of
work, and perhaps the same ruthlessness. Charley
smiled his good-natured smile.

"I daresay Simon has his faults like the rest of us.
One has to be tolerant with him because he hasn't had
a very happy or a very easy life. I think perhaps he
craves for affection, and there's something that people
find repellent in his personality which prevents him
from getting it. He's frightfully sensitive and things
which wouldn't affect ordinary people wound him to
the quick. But at heart I think he's kind and generous."

"You're deceived in him. You think he has your own
good nature and unselfish consideration. I tell you, he's
dangerous. Dzerjinsky was the narrow idealist who for
the sake of his ideal could bring destruction upon his
country without a qualm. Simon isn't even that. He
has no heart, no conscience, no scruple, and if the
occasion arises he will sacrifice you who are his dearest
friend without hesitation and without remorse."

viii

THEY WOKE next day at what was for them an early hour. They had breakfast in bed, each with his tray, and after breakfast, while Charley, smoking his pipe read the *Mail*, Lydia, a cigarette between her lips, did her hands. You would have thought, to see them, each engaged on his respective occupation, that they were a young married couple whose first passion had dwindled into an easy friendship. Lydia painted her nails and spread out her fingers on the sheet to let them dry. She gave Charley a mischievous glance.

"Would you like to go to the Louvre this morning? You came to Paris to see pictures, didn't you?"

"I suppose I did."

"Well, let's get up then and go."

When the maid who brought them their coffee drew the curtains the day that filtered into the room from the courtyard had looked as gray and bleak as on the mornings that had gone before; and they were surprised, on stepping into the street, to see that the weather had suddenly changed. It was cold still, but the sun was bright and the clouds, high up in the heavens, were white and shining. The air had a frosty bite that made your blood tingle.

"Let's walk," said Lydia.

In that gay, quivering light the Rue de Rennes lost its dinginess, and the gray, shabby houses no longer wore the down-at-heel, despondent air they usually do, but had a mellow friendliness as though, like old women in reduced circumstances, they felt less forlorn now that the unexpected sunshine smiled on them as familiarly as on the grand new buildings on the other side of the river. When they crossed the Place St. Germain-des-Prés and there was a confusion of buses and trams, recklessly-speeding taxis, lorries and private cars, Lydia took Charley's arm; and like lovers, or a grocer and his wife taking a walk of a Sunday afternoon, they sauntered arm in arm, stopping now and then to look into the window of a picture-dealer, down the narrow Rue de Seine. Then they came on to the quay. Here the Paris day burst upon them in all its winter beauty and Charley gave a little exclamation of delight.

"You like this?" smiled Lydia.

"It's a picture by Raffaelli." He remembered a line in a poem that he had read at Tours: "Le vierge, le vivace et le bel aujourd'hui."

The air had a sparkle so that you felt you could take it up in your hands and let it run through your fingers like the water of a fountain. To Charley's eyes, accustomed to the misty distances and soft haze of London, it seemed amazingly transparent. It outlined the buildings, the bridge, the parapet by the side of the river, with an elegant distinctness, but the lines, as though drawn by a sensitive hand, were tender and gracious. Tender too was the colour, the colour of sky and cloud, the colour of stone; they were the colours of the eighteenth-century pastelists; and the leafless trees, their slim branches a faint mauve against the blue, repeated with exquisite variety a pattern of delicate intricacy. Because he had seen pictures of just that scene Charley was able to take it in, without any sense of surprise, but with a loving, understanding recognition; its beauty did not shatter him by its strangeness, nor perplex him by its unexpectedness, but filled him with a sense of familiar joy such as a countryman might feel when after an absence of years he sees once more the dear, straggling street of his native village.

"Isn't it lovely to be alive?" he cried.

"It's lovely to be as young and enthusiastic as you are," said Lydia, giving his arm a little squeeze, and if she choked down a sob he did not notice it.

Charley knew the Louvre well, for every time his parents spent a few days in Paris (to let Venetia get her clothes from the little dressmaker who was just as good as those expensive places in the Rue Royale and the Rue Cambon) they made a point of taking their children there. Leslie Mason made no bones at confessing that he preferred new pictures to old.

"But after all, it's part of a gentleman's education to have done the great galleries of Europe, and when people talk about Rembrandt and Titian and so on, you look a bit of a fool if you can't put your word in. And I don't mind telling you that you couldn't have a better guide than your mother. She's very artistic, and she knows what's what, and she won't waste your time over a lot of tripe."

"I don't claim that your grandfather was a great artist," said Mrs. Mason, with the modest self-assurance of someone who is without conceit aware that he knows his subject, "but he knew what was good. All I know about art he taught me."

"Of course you had a flair," said her husband.

Mrs. Mason considered this for a moment.

"Yes, I suppose you're right, Leslie. I had a flair."

What made it easier to do the Louvre with expedition and spiritual profit was that in those days they had not rearranged it, and the Salon Carré contained most of the pictures which Mrs. Mason thought worthy of her children's attention. When they entered that room they walked straight to Leonardo's Gioconda.

"I always think one ought to look at that first," she said. "It puts you in the right mood for the Louvre."

The four of them stood in front of the picture and with reverence gazed at the insipid smile of that prim and sex-starved young woman. After a decent interval for meditation Mrs. Mason turned to her husband and her two children. There were tears in her eyes.

"Words fail me to express what that picture always makes me feel," she said, with a sigh. "Leonardo was a Great Artist. I think everybody's bound to acknowledge that."

"I don't mind admitting that I'm a bit of a philistine when it comes to old masters," said Leslie, "but that's got a je ne sais quoi that gets you, there's no denying that. Can you remember that bit of Pater's, Venetia? He hit the nail on the head and no mistake."

"You mean the bit that begins: 'Hers is the head

upon which all the ends of the world are come.' I used to know it by heart years ago; I'm afraid I've forgotten it now."

"That's a pity."

"Well, my memory isn't what it was. Let's go and look at the Raphael now, shall we?"

But it was impossible to avoid seeing the two vast canvases of Paolo Veronese that faced one another on opposite walls.

"It's worth while giving them a glance," she said. "Your grandfather had a very high opinion of them. Of course Veronese was neither subtle nor profound. He had no soul. But he certainly had a gift of composition, and you must remember that there's no one now who could arrange so great a number of figures in a harmonious, and yet natural, design. You must admire them if for no other reason because of their vitality and for the sheer physical vigour Veronese must have had to paint such enormous pictures. But I think there's more in them than that. They do give you an impression of the abundant, multicoloured life of the period and of the pleasure-loving, pagan spirit which was characteristic of patrician Venice in the heyday of its glory."

"I've often tried to count the number of figures in the Marriage of Cana," said Leslie Mason, "but every time I make it different."

The four of them began to count, but none of the results they reached agreed. Presently they strolled into the Grande Galerie.

"Now here is L'Homme au Gant," said Mrs. Mason. "I'm not sorry you looked at the Veroneses first, because they do bring out very clearly the peculiar merit of Titian. You remember what I said about Veronese having no soul; well, you've only got to look at L'Homme au Gant to see that soul is just what Titian had."

"He was a remarkable old buffer," said Leslie Mason. "He lived to the age of ninety-nine and then it needed the plague to kill him."

Mrs. Mason smiled slightly.

"I have no hesitation," she continued, "in saying that I consider this one of the finest portraits that's ever been painted. Of course one can't compare it with a portait by Cézanne or even by Manet."

"We mustn't forget to show them the Manet, Venetia."

"No, we won't do that. We'll come to that presently. But what I mean to say is that you must accept the idiom of the time at which it was painted, and bearing that in mind I don't think anyone can deny that it's a masterpiece. Of course just as a piece of painting it's beyond praise, but it's got a distinction and an imaginative quality which are very unique. Don't you think so, Leslie?"

"Definitely."

"When I was a girl I used to spend hours looking at it. It's a picture that makes you dream. Personally I think it's a finer portrait than Velasquez's Pope, the one in Rome, you know, just because it's more suggestive. Velasquez was a very great painter, I admit that, and he had an enormous influence on Manet, but what I miss in him is exactly what Titian had—Soul."

Leslie Mason looked at his watch.

"We mustn't waste too much time here, Venetia," he said, "or we shall be late for lunch."

"All right. We'll just go and look at the Ingres and the Manet."

They walked on, glancing right and left at the pictures that lined the walls, but there was nothing that Mrs. Mason thought worth lingering over.

"It's no good burdening their minds with a lot of impressions that'll only confuse them," she told her husband. "It's much better that they should concentrate on what's really important."

"Definitely," he answered.

They entered the Salle des États, but at the threshold Mrs. Mason stopped.

"We won't bother about the Poussins to-day," she said. "You have to come to the Louvre to see them, and there's no doubt that he was a Great Artist. But he was more of a painter's painter than a layman's, and I think you're a little young to appreciate him. One day when you're both of you a bit older we'll come and have a good go at him. I mean you have to be rather sophisticated to thoroughly understand him. The room that we're coming to now is nineteenth century. But I don't think we need bother about Delacroix either. He was a painter's painter too, and I wouldn't expect you to see in him what I do; you must take my word for it that he was a very considerable artist. He was no mean colourist and he had a strong romantic feeling. And you certainly needn't trouble your heads with the Barbizon School. In my young days they were very much admired, but that was before we understood the Impressionists even, and of course we hadn't so much as heard of Cézanne or Matisse; they don't amount to anything and they can be safely ignored. I want you to look first at the Odalisque of Ingres and then at the Olympia of Manet. They're wonderfully placed, opposite one another, so that you can look at both of them at the same time, compare them and draw your own conclusions."

Having said this Mrs. Mason advanced into the room with her husband by her side, while Charley and Patsy followed together a step or two behind. On reaching the exact spot where she thought the two pictures which she particularly wanted her offspring to admire could be seen to best advantage, she stopped with the triumphant air with which a conjurer extracts a rabbit from a hat and cried:

"There!"

They stood in a row for some minutes and Mrs. Mason gazed at the two nudes with rapture. Then she turned to the children.

"Now let's go and examine them close at hand."

They stood in front of the Odalisque.

"It's no good, Venetia," said Leslie. "You may say I'm a philistine, but I don't like the colour. The pink of that body is just the pink of that face cream you used to put on at night till I made you stop it."

"You needn't reveal the secrets of the alcove to these innocent children," said Venetia with a prim and at the same time roguish smile. "But I would never claim for a moment that Ingres was a great colourist; all the same I do think that blue is a very sweet colour and I've often thought I'd like an evening dress just like it. D'you think it would be too young, Patsy?"

"No, darling. Not a bit."

"But that's neither here nor there. Ingres was probably the greatest draughtsman who ever lived. I don't know how anyone can look at those firm and lovely lines and not feel he's in the presence of one of the great manifestations of the human spirit. I remember my father telling me that once he came here with one of his fellow-students from Julien's who'd never seen it, and when his eyes fell on it he was so overcome with its beauty of line that he actually fainted."

"I think it's much more likely that it was long past the hour at which reasonable people have lunch and that he fainted with hunger."

"Isn't your father awful?" smiled Mrs. Mason. "Well, let's just have five minutes more for the Olympia, Leslie, and then I'm ready to go."

They marched up to Manet's great picture.

"When you come to a masterpiece like this," said Mrs. Mason, "you can do nothing but keep your mouth shut and admire. The rest, as Hamlet said, is silence. No one, not even Renoir, not even El Greco, has ever painted flesh like that. Look at that right breast. It's a miracle of loveliness. One is simply left gasping. Even my poor father, who couldn't bear the moderns, was forced to admit that the painting of that breast was pretty good. Pretty good? I ask you. Now I suppose you see a black line all round the figure. You do, Charley, don't you?"

Charley acknowledged that he did.

"And you, Patsy?"

"Yes."

"Well, I don't," she cried triumphantly. "I used to see it, I know it's there, but I give you my word, I don't see it any more."

After that they went to lunch.

Through his long-standing acquaintance with the famous gallery and the useful information he had acquired from his mother, Charley, with Lydia by his side, entered the Salon Carré now with something of the confidence of a good tennis-player stepping on to the court. He was eager to show Lydia his favourite pictures and ready to explain to her exactly what was admirable in them. It was, however, something of a surprise to discover that the room had been rearranged and the Gioconda, to which he would naturally have taken her first, was nowhere to be seen. They spent but ten minutes there. When Charley went with his parents it took them an hour to do that room and even then, his mother said, they hadn't exhausted its treasures. But L'Homme au Gant was in its old place and he gently led her up to it. They looked at it for a while.

"Stunning, isn't it?" he said then, giving her arm an affectionate pressure.

"Yes, it's all right. What business is it of yours?"

Charley turned his head sharply. No one had ever asked him a question like that about a picture before.

"What on earth d'you mean? It's one of the great portraits of the world. Titian, you know."

"I daresay. But what's it got to do with you?"

Charley didn't quite know what to say.

"Well, it's a very fine picture and it's beautifully painted. Of course it doesn't tell a story if that's what you mean."

"No, I don't," she smiled.

"I don't suppose it's got anything to do with me really."

"Then why should you bother about it?"

Lydia moved on and Charley followed her. She gave other pictures an indifferent glance. Charley was troubled by what she had said and he puzzled his brains to discover what could be at the back of her mind. She gave him an amused smile.

"Come," she said. "I'll show you some pictures."

She took his arm and they walked on. Suddenly he caught sight of the Gioconda.

"There she is," he cried. "I must stop and have a good look at that. I make a point of it when I come to the Louvre."

"Why?"

"Hang it all, it's Leonardo's most celebrated picture. It's one of the most important pictures in the world."

"Important to you?"

Charley was beginning to find her a trifle irritating; he couldn't make out what she was getting at; but he was a good-humoured youth, and he wasn't going to lose his temper.

"A picture may be important even if it isn't very important to me."

"But it's only you who count. So far as you're concerned the only meaning a picture has is the meaning it has for you."

"That seems an awfully conceited way of looking at it."

"Does that picture say anything to you really?"

"Of course it does. It says all sorts of things, but I don't suppose I could put them any better than Pater did. He wrote a piece about it that's in all the anthologies."

But even as he spoke he recognized that his answer was lame. He was beginning to have a vague inkling of what Lydia meant, and then the uneasy feeling came to him that there was something in art that he'd never been told about. But he fortunately remembered what his mother had said about Manet's Olympia.

"In point of fact I don't know why you should say anything about a picture at all. You either like it or you don't."

"And you really like that one?" she asked in a tone of mild interrogation.

"Very much."

"Why?"

He thought for a moment.

"Well, you see, I've known it practically all my life."

"That's why you like your friend Simon, isn't it?" she smiled.

He felt it was an unfair retort.

"All right. You take me and show me the pictures you like."

The position was reversed. It was not he, as he had expected, who was leading the way and with such information as would add interest to the respective canvases, sympathetically drawing her attention to the great masterpieces he had always cared for; but it was she who was conducting him. Very well. He was quite ready to put himself in her hands and see what it was all about.

"Of course," he said to himself, "she's Russian. One has to make allowances for that."

They trudged past acres of canvas, through one room after another, for Lydia had some difficulty in finding her way; but finally she stopped him in front of a small picture that you might easily have missed if you had not been looking for it.

"Chardin," he said. "Yes, I've seen that before."

"But have you ever looked at it?"

"Oh, yes. Chardin wasn't half a bad painter in his way. My mother thinks a lot of him. I've always rather liked his still lifes myself."

"Is that all it means to you? It breaks my heart."

"That?" cried Charley with astonishment. "A loaf of bread and a flagon of wine? Of course it's very well painted."

"Yes, you're right; it's very well painted; it's painted with pity and love. It's not only a loaf of bread and a flagon of wine; it's the bread of life and the blood of Christ, but not held back from those who starve and thirst for them and doled out by priests on stated occasions; it's the daily fare of suffering men and women. It's so humble, so natural, so friendly; it's the bread and wine of the poor who ask no more than that they should be left in peace, allowed to work and eat their simple food in freedom. It's the cry of the despised and rejected. It tells you that whatever their sins men

at heart are good. That loaf of bread and that flagon
of wine are symbols of the joys and sorrows of the
meek and lowly. They ask for your mercy and your
affection; they tell you that they're of the same flesh
and blood as you. They tell you that life is short and
hard and the grave is cold and lonely. It's not only a
loaf of bread and a flagon of wine; it's the mystery of
man's lot on earth, his craving for a little friendship
and a little love, the humility of his resignation when
he sees that even they must be denied him."

Lydia's voice was tremulous and now the tears
flowed from her eyes. She brushed them away impatiently.

"And isn't it wonderful that with those simple
objects, with his painter's exquisite sensibility, moved
by the charity in his heart, that funny, dear old man
should have made something so beautiful that it breaks
you? It was as though, unconsciously perhaps, hardly
knowing what he was doing, he wanted to show you
that if you only have enough love, if you only have
enough sympathy, out of pain and distress and unkind-
ness, out of all the evil of the world, you can create
beauty."

She was silent and for long stood looking at the little
picture. Charley looked at it too, but with perplexity.
It was a very good picture; he hadn't really given it
more than a glance before, and he was glad Lydia had
drawn his attention to it; in some odd way it was rather
moving; but of course he could never have seen in it all
she saw. Strange, unstable woman! It was rather
embarrassing that she should cry in a public gallery;

they did put you in an awkward position, these Russians; but who would have thought a picture could affect anyone like that? He remembered his mother's story of how a student friend of his grandfather's had fainted when he first saw the Odalisque of Ingres; but that was away back in the nineteenth century, they were very romantic and emotional in those days. Lydia turned to him with a sunny smile on her lips. It disconcerted him to see with what suddenness she could go from tears to laughter.

"Shall we go now?" she said.

"But don't you want to see any more pictures?"

"Why? I've seen one. I feel happy and peaceful. What could I get if I saw another?"

"Oh, all right."

It seemed a very odd way of doing a picture gallery. After all, they hadn't looked at the Watteaus or the Fragonards. His mother was bound to ask him if he'd seen the Embarkation for Cythera. Someone had told her they'd cleaned it and she'd want to know how the colours had come out.

They did a little shopping and then lunched at a restaurant on the quay on the other side of the river and Lydia as usual ate with a very good appetite. She liked the crowd that surrounded them and the traffic that passed noisily in the roadway. She was in a good humour. It was as though the violent emotion from which she had suffered had rinsed her spirit clean, and she talked of trivial things with a pleasant cheerfulness. But Charley was thoughtful. He did not find it so easy to dismiss the disquietude that affected him. She did not usually notice his moods, but the trouble of his mind was so clearly reflected on his face that at last she could not but be struck by it.

"Why are you so silent?" she asked him, with a kindly, sympathetic smile.

"I was thinking. You see, I've been interested in art all my life. My parents are very artistic, I mean some people might even say they were rather highbrow, and they were always keen on my sister and me having a real appreciation of art; and I think we have. It rather worries me to think that with all the pains I've taken, and the advantages I've had, I don't seem really to know so much about it as you do."

"But I know nothing about art," she laughed.

"But you do seem to feel about it very strongly, and I suppose art is really a matter of feeling. It's not as though I didn't like pictures. I get an enormous kick out of them."

"You mustn't be worried. It's very natural that you should look at pictures differently from me. You're young and healthy, happy and prosperous. You're not stupid. They're a pleasure to you among a lot of other pleasures. It gives you a feeling of warmth and satisfaction to look at them. To walk through a gallery is a very agreeable way of passing an idle hour. What more can you want? But you see, I've always been poor, often hungry, and sometimes terribly lonely. They've been riches to me, food and drink and company. When I was working and my employer had nagged me to distraction I used to slip into the Louvre at the luncheon hour and her scolding didn't matter any more. And

when my mother died and I had nobody left, it com-
forted me. During those long months when Robert
was in prison before the trial and I was pregnant, I
think I should have gone mad and killed myself if it
hadn't been that I could go there, where nobody knew
me and nobody stared at me, and be alone with my
friends. It was rest and peace. It gave me courage. It
wasn't so much the great well-known masterpieces
that helped me, it was the smaller, shyer pictures that
no one noticed, and I felt they were pleased that I
looked at them. I felt that nothing really mattered so
very much, because everything passed. Patience!
Patience! That's what I learnt there. And I felt that
above all the horror and misery and cruelty of the
world, there was something that helped you to bear it,
something that was greater and more important than
all that, the spirit of man and the beauty he created.
Is it really strange that that little picture I showed you
this morning should mean so much to me?"

To make the most of the fine weather they walked
up the busy Boulevard St. Michel and when they got to
the top turned into the gardens of the Luxembourg.
They sat down and, talking little, idly watched the
nurses, no longer, alas, wearing the long satin streamers
of a generation ago, trundling prams, the old ladies in
black who walked with sober gait in charge of little
children, and the elderly gentlemen, with thick scarves
up to their noses, who paced up and down immersed in
thought; with friendly hearts they looked at the long-
legged boys and girls who ran about playing games, and
when a pair of young students passed wondered what it

was they so earnestly discussed. It seemed not a public park, but a private garden for the people on the left bank, and the scene had a moving intimacy. But the chilly rays of the waning sun gave it withal a certain melancholy, for within the iron grille that separated it from the bustle of the great city, the garden had a singular air of unreality, and you had a feeling that those old people who trod the gravel paths, those children whose cries made a cheerful hubbub, were ghosts taking phantom walks or playing phantom games, who at dusk would dissolve, like the smoke of a cigarette, into the oncoming darkness. It was growing very cold, and Charley and Lydia wandered back, silent friendly companions, to the hotel.

When they got to their room Lydia took out of her suit-case a thin sheaf of piano pieces.

"I brought some of the things Robert used to play. I play so badly and we haven't got a piano at Alexey's. D'you think you could play them?"

Charley looked at the music. It was Russian. Some of the pieces were familiar to him.

"I think so," he said.

"There's a piano downstairs and there'll be nobody in the salon now. Let's go down."

The piano badly wanted tuning. It was an upright. The keyboard was yellow with age and because it was seldom played on the notes were stiff. There was a long music stool and Lydia sat down by Charley's side. He put on the rack a piece by Scriabin that he knew and after a few resounding chords to try the instrument began to play. Lydia followed the score and turned the pages for him. Charley had had as good masters as could be found in London, and he had worked hard. He had played at concerts at school and afterwards at Cambridge, so that he had acquired confidence. He had a light, pleasant touch. He enjoyed playing.

"There," he said when he came to the end of the piece.

He was not displeased with himself. He knew that he had played it according to the composer's intention and with the clear, neat straightforwardness that he liked in piano-playing.

"Play something else," said Lydia.

She chose a piece. It was an arrangement for the piano of folk songs and folk dances by a composer of whom Charley had never heard. It startled him to see the name of Robert Berger written in a firm, bold hand on the cover. Lydia stared at it in silence and then turned the page. He looked at the music he was about to play and wondered what Lydia was thinking now. She must have sat by Robert's side just as she was sitting by his. Why did she want to torture herself by making him play those pieces that must recall to her bitter memories of her short happiness and the misery that followed it?

"Well, begin."

He played well at sight and the music was not difficult. He thought he acquitted himself of his task without discredit. Having struck the last chord he waited for a word of praise.

"You played it very nicely," said Lydia, "but where does Russia come in?"

"What exactly d'you mean by that?" he asked, somewhat affronted.

"You play it as if it was about a Sunday afternoon in London with people in their best clothes walking around those great empty squares and wishing it was time for tea. But that's not what it is at all. It's the old, old song of peasants who lament the shortness and the hardness of their life, it's the wide fields of golden corn and the labour of gathering in the harvest, it's the great forest of beech-trees, and the nostalgia of the workers for an age when peace and plenty reigned on the earth, and it's the wild dance that for a brief period brings them forgetfulness of their lot."

"Well, you play it better."

"I can't play," she answered, but she edged him along the bench and took his seat.

He listened. She played badly, but for all that got something out of the music that he hadn't seen in it. She managed, though at a price, to bring out the tumult of its emotion and the bitterness of its melancholy; and she infused the dance rhythms with a barbaric vitality that stirred the blood. But Charley was put out.

"I must confess I don't see why you should think you get the Russian atmosphere better by playing false notes and keeping your foot firmly on the loud pedal," he said, acidly, when she finished.

She burst out laughing and flinging both her arms round his neck kissed him on the cheeks.

"You are a sweet," she cried.

"It's very nice of you to say so," he answered coldly, disengaging himself.

"Have I offended you?"

"Not at all."

She shook her head and smiled at him with soft
tenderness.

"You play very well and your technique is excellent,
but it's no good thinking you can play Russian music;
you can't. Play me some Schumann. I'm sure you can."

"No, I'm not going to play any more."

"If you're angry with me, why don't you hit me?"

Charley couldn't help chuckling.

"You fool. It never occurred to me. Besides, I'm
not angry."

"You're so big and strong and handsome, I forget
that you're only a young boy." She sighed. "And you're
so unprepared for life. Sometimes when I look at you
I get such a pang."

"Now don't get all Russian and emotional."

"Be nice to me and play some Schumann."

When Lydia liked she could be very persuasive. With
a diffident smile Charley resumed his seat. Schumann, in
point of fact, was the composer he liked best and he
knew a great deal by heart. He played to her for an
hour, and whenever he wanted to stop she urged him to
go on. The young woman at the cashier's desk was
curious to see who was playing the piano and peeped
in. When she went back to her counter she murmured
to the porter with an arch and meaning smile:

"The turtle doves are having a good time."

When at last Charley stopped, Lydia gave a little
sigh of contentment.

"I knew that was the music to suit you. It's like you,

healthy and comfortable and wholesome. There's fresh
air in it and sunshine and the delicious scent of pine-
trees. It's done me good to listen to it and it's done
me good to be with you. Your mother must love you
very much."

"Oh, come off it."

"Why are you so good to me? I'm tiresome, dull and
exasperating. You don't even like me very much, do
you?"

Charley considered this for a moment.

"Well, I don't very much, to tell you the truth."

She laughed.

"Then why do you bother about me? Why don't you
just turn me out into the street?"

"I can't imagine."

"Shall I tell you? Goodness. Just pure, simple, stupid
goodness."

"Go to hell."

They dined in the Quarter. It had not escaped
Charley's notice that Lydia took no interest in him as
an individual. She accepted him as you might accept a
person with whom you find yourself on a ship for a
few days and so forced to a certain intimacy, but it does
not matter to you where he came from and what sort of
a man he is; he emerged from non-existence when he
stepped on board and will return to it when, on reaching
port, you part company with him. Charley was modest
enough not to be piqued by this, for he could not but
realize that her own troubles and perplexities were so
great that they must absorb her attention; and he was
not a little surprised now when she led him to talk about

himself. He told her of his artistic inclinations and of
the wish he had so long harboured to be an artist, and
she approved his common sense which in the end had
persuaded him to prefer the assured life of a business
man. He had never seen her more cheerful and more
human. Knowing English domestic life only through
Dickens, Thackeray and H. G. Wells, she was curious
to hear how existence was pursued in those prosperous,
sober houses in Bayswater that she knew but from their
outside. She asked him about his home and his family.
These were subjects on which he was always glad to
talk. He spoke of his father and mother with a faintly
mocking irony which Lydia saw well enough he assumed only to conceal the loving admiration with
which he regarded them. Without knowing it he drew
a very pleasant picture of an affectionate, happy family
who lived unpretentiously in circumstances of moderate
affluence at peace with themselves and the world and
undisturbed by any fear that anything might happen to
affect their security. The life he described lacked neither
grace nor dignity; it was healthy and normal, and
through its intellectual interests not entirely material;
the persons who led it were simple and honest, neither
ambitious nor envious, prepared to do their duty by
the state and by their neighbours according to their
lights; and there was in them neither harm nor malice.
If Lydia saw how much of their good nature, their
kindliness, their not unpleasing self-complacency depended on the long-established and well-ordered prosperity of the country that had given them birth; if she
had an inkling that, like children building castles on

the sea sand, they might at any moment be swept away by a tidal wave, she allowed no sign of it to appear on her face.

"How lucky you English are," she said.

But Charley was a trifle surprised at the impression his own words made on him. In the course of his recital he had for the first time seen himself from the standpoint of an observer. Until now, like an actor who says his lines, but never having seen the play from the front, has but a vague idea of what it is all about, he had played his part without asking himself whether it had any meaning. It would be too much to say that it made him uneasy, it slightly perplexed him, to realize that while they were all, his father, his mother, his sister, himself, busy from morning till night, so that the days were not long enough for what they wanted to do; yet when you came to look upon the life they led from one year's end to another it gave you an uncomfortable feeling that they, none of them, did anything at all. It was like one of those comedies where the sets are good and the clothes pretty, where the dialogue is clever and the acting competent, so that you pass an agreeable evening, but a week later cannot remember a thing about it.

When they had finished dinner they took a taxi to a cinema on the other side of the river. It was a film of the Marx brothers and they rocked with laughter at the extravagant humour of the marvellous clowns; but they laughed not only at Groucho's wise-cracks and at Harpo's comic quandaries, they laughed at one another's laughter. The picture finished at midnight, but

Charley was too excited to go quietly to bed and he asked Lydia if she would come with him to some place where they could dance.

"Where would you like to go?" asked Lydia. "Montmartre?"

"Wherever you like as long as it's gay." And then, remembering his parents' constant, but seldom achieved, desire when they came to Paris: "Where there aren't a lot of English people."

Lydia gave him the slightly mischievous smile that he had seen on her lips once or twice before. It surprised him, but at the same time was sympathetic to him. It surprised him because it went so strangely with what he thought he knew of her character; and it was sympathetic to him because it suggested that, for all her tragic history, there was in her a vein of high spirits and of a rather pleasing, teasing malice.

"I'll take you somewhere. It won't be gay, but it may be interesting. There's a Russian woman who sings there."

They drove a long way, and when they stopped Charley saw that they were on the quay. The twin towers of Notre-Dame were distinct against the frosty, starry night. They walked a few steps up a dark street and then went through a narrow door; they descended a flight of stairs and Charley, to his astonishment, found himself in a large cellar with stone walls; from these jutted out wooden tables large enough to accommodate ten or twelve persons, and there were wooden benches on each side of them. The heat was stifling and the air gray with smoke. In the space left by the tables a dense throng was dancing to a melancholy tune. A slatternly waiter in shirt-sleeves found them two places and took their order. People sitting here and there looked at them curiously and whispered to one another; and indeed Charley in his well-cut English blue serge, Lydia in her black silk and her smart hat with the feather in it, contrasted violently with the rest of the company. The men wore neither collars nor ties, and they danced with their caps on, the end of a cigarette stuck to their lips. The women were bare-headed and extravagantly painted.

"They look pretty tough," said Charley.

"They are. Most of them have been in jug and those that haven't should be. If there's a row and they start throwing glasses or pulling knives, just stand against the wall and don't move."

"I don't think they much like the look of us," said Charley. "We seem to be attracting a good deal of attention."

"They think we're sight-seers and that always puts their backs up. But it'll be all right. I know the patron."

When the waiter brought the two beers they had ordered Lydia asked him to get the landlord along. In a moment he came, a big fellow with the naked look of a fat priest, and immediately recognized Lydia. He gave Charley a shrewd, suspicious stare, but when Lydia introduced him as a friend of hers, shook hands with him warmly and said he was glad to see him. He sat down and for a few minutes talked with Lydia in an undertone. Charley noticed that their neighbours watched the scene and he caught one man giving another a wink. They were evidently satisfied that it was all right. The dance came to an end and the other occupants of the table at which they sat came back. They gave the strangers hostile looks, but the patron explained that they were friends, whereupon one of the party, a sinister-looking chap, with the scar of a razor wound on his face, insisted on offering them a glass of wine. Soon they were all talking merrily together. They were plainly eager to make the young Englishman at home, and a man sitting by his side explained to him that though the company looked a bit rough they were all good fellows with their hearts in the right place. He was a little drunk. Charley, having got over his first uneasiness, began to enjoy himself.

Presently the saxophone player got up and advanced his chair. The Russian singer of whom Lydia had spoken came forward with a guitar in her hand and sat down. There was a burst of applause.

"C'est La Marishka," said Charley's drunken friend, "there's no one like her. She was the mistress of one of the commissars, but Stalin had him shot and if she hadn't managed to get out of Russia he'd have shot her too."

A woman on the other side of the table overheard him.

"What nonsense you're telling him, Loulou," she cried. "La Marishka was the mistress of a grand duke before the revolution, everyone knows that, and she had diamonds worth millions, but the Bolsheviks took everything from her. She escaped disguised as a peasant."

La Marishka was a woman of forty, haggard and sombre, with gaunt, masculine features, a brown skin, and enormous, blazing eyes under black, heavy, arching brows. In a raucous voice, at the top of her lungs, she sang a wild, joyless song, and though Charley could not understand the Russian words a cold feeling ran down his spine. She was loudly applauded. Then she sang a sentimental ballad in French, the lament of a girl for her lover who was to be executed next morning, which roused her audience to frenzy. She finished, for the time being, with another Russian song, lively this time, and her face lost its tragic cast; it took on a look of rude and brutal gaiety, and her voice, deep and harsh, acquired a rollicking quality; your blood was stirred and you could not but exult, but at the same time you were moved, for below the bacchanalian merriment was the desolation of futile tears. Charley looked at Lydia and caught her mocking glance. He smiled good-naturedly. That grim woman got something out of the music which he was conscious now was beyond his reach. Another burst of applause greeted the end of the number, but La Marishka, as though she did not hear it, without a sign of acknowledgement, rose from her chair and came over to Lydia. The two women began to talk in Russian. Lydia turned to Charley.

"She'll have a glass of champagne if you'll offer it to her."

"Of course."

He signalled to a waiter and ordered a bottle; then, with a glance at the half-dozen people sitting at the table, changed his order.

"Two bottles and some glasses. Perhaps these gentlemen and ladies will allow me to offer them a glass too."

There was a murmur of polite acceptance. The wine was brought and Charley filled a number of glasses and passed them down the table. There was a great deal of health drinking and clinking of glasses together.

"Vive l'Entente Cordiale."

"À nos alliés."

They all got very friendly and merry. Charley was having a grand time. But he had come to dance, and when the orchestra began once more to play he pulled Lydia to her feet. The floor was soon crowded and he noticed that a lot of curious eyes were fixed upon her; he guessed that it had spread through the company who she was; it made her to those bullies and their women, somewhat to Charley's embarrassment, an object of interest, but she did not seem even to be aware that anyone looked at her.

Presently the patron touched her on the shoulder.

"I have a word to say to you," he muttered.

Lydia released herself from Charley's arms and going to one side with the fat landlord listened to what he said. Charley could see that she was startled. He was evidently trying to point someone out to her, for Charley saw her craning her neck; but with the thick mass of dancers in the way she could see nothing, and in a moment she followed the patron to the other end of the long cellar. She seemed to have forgotten Charley. Somewhat piqued, he went back to his table. Two couples were sitting there comfortably enjoying his champagne, and they greeted him heartily. They were all very familiar now and they asked him what he had done with his little friend. He told them what had happened. One of the men was a short thick-set fellow with a red face and a magnificent moustache. His shirt open at the neck showed his hairy chest, and his arms, for he had taken off his coat in that stifling heat and turned up his shirt-sleeves, were profusely tattooed. He was with a girl who might have been twenty years younger than he. She had very sleek black hair, parted in the middle, with a bun on her neck, a face dead-white with powder, scarlet lips and eyes heavy with mascara. The man nudged her with his elbow.

"Now then, why don't you dance with the English-man? You've drunk his bubbly, haven't you?"

"I don't mind," she said.

She danced clingingly. She smelt strongly of scent, but not so strongly as to disguise the fact that she had eaten at dinner a dish highly flavoured with garlic. She smiled alluringly at Charley.

"He must be rotten with vice, this pretty little Englishman," she gurgled, with a squirm of a lithe body in her black, but dusty, velvet gown.

"Why do you say that?" he smiled.

"To be with the wife of Berger, what's that if it isn't vice?"

"She's my sister," said Charley gaily.

She thought this such a good joke that when the band stopped and they went back to the table she repeated it to the assembled company. They all thought it very funny, and the thick-set man with the hairy chest slapped him on the back.

"Farceur, va !"

Charley was not displeased to be looked upon as a humorist. It was nice to be a success. He realized that as the lover of a notorious murderer's wife he was something of a personage there. They urged him to come again.

"But come alone next time," said the girl he had just danced with.

"We'll find you a girl. What d'you want to get mixed up with one of the Russians for? The wine of the country, that's what you want."

Charley ordered another bottle of champagne. He was far from tight, but he was merry. He was seeing life with a vengeance. When Lydia came back he was talking and laughing with his new friends as if he had known them all his life. He danced the next dance with her. He noticed that she was not keeping step with him and he gave her a little shake.

"You're not attending."

She laughed.

"I'm sorry. I'm tired. Let's go."

"Has something happened to upset you?"

"No. It's getting very late and the heat's awful."

Having warmly shaken hands with their new friends, they left and got into a taxi. Lydia sank back exhausted. He was feeling happy and affectionate and he took her hand and held it. They drove in silence.

They went to bed, and in a few minutes Charley became aware from her regular breathing that Lydia had fallen asleep. But he was too excited to sleep. The evening had amused him and he was keenly alert. He thought it all over for a while and chuckled at the grand story he would make of it when he got home. He turned on the light to read. But he could not give his attention to the poems of Blake just then. Disordered notions flitted across his mind. He switched off the light and presently fell into a light doze, but in a little while awoke. He was tingling with desire. He heard the quiet breathing of the sleeping woman in the bed by his side and a peculiar sensation stirred his heart. Except on that first evening at the Sérail no feeling for Lydia had touched him except pity and kindliness. Sexually she did not in the least attract him. After seeing her for several days all day long he did not even think her pretty; he did not like the squareness of her face, her high cheek-bones, and the way her pale eyes were set flat in their orbits; sometimes, indeed, he thought her really plain. Notwithstanding the life she had adopted—for what strange, unnatural reason—she gave him a sense of such deadly respectability that it choked him off. And then her indifference to sexual congress was chilling. She looked with contempt and loathing on the men who for money sought their pleasure of her. The passionate love she bore for Robert gave her an aloofness from all human affections that killed desire. But besides all that Charley didn't think he liked her very much for herself; she was sometimes sullen, almost always indifferent; she took whatever he did for her as her right; it was all very well to say that she asked for nothing, it would have been graceful if she had shown, not gratitude, but a glimmering recognition of the fact that he was trying to

do his best for her. Charley had an uneasy fear that
she was making a mug of him; if what Simon said was
true and she was making money at the brothel in order
to help Robert to escape, she was nothing but a callous
liar; he flushed hotly when it occurred to him that she
was laughing behind his back at his simplicity. No, he
didn't admire her, and the more he thought of her the
less he thought he liked her. And yet at that moment
he was so breathless with desire of her that he felt he
would choke. He thought of her not as he saw her
every day, rather drab, like a teacher at a Sunday
school, but as he had first seen her in those baggy
Turkish trousers and the blue turban spangled with
little stars, her cheeks painted and her lashes black with
mascara; he thought of her slender waist, her clear,
soft, honey-coloured skin, and her small firm breasts
with their rosy nipples. He tossed on his bed. His desire
now was uncontrollable. It was anguish. After all, it
wasn't fair; he was young and strong and normal; why
shouldn't he have a bit of fun when he had the chance?
She was there for that, she'd said so herself. What did
it matter if she thought him a dirty swine? He'd done
pretty well by her, he deserved something in return.
The faint sound of her quiet breathing was strangely
exciting and it quickened his own. He thought of the
feel of her soft lips when he pressed his mouth to hers
and the feel of her little breasts when he took them in
his hands; he thought of the feel of her lissom body in
his arms and the feel of his long legs lying against hers.
He put on the light, thinking it might wake her, and
got out of bed. He leaned over her. She lay on her

back, her hands crossed over her breast like a stone figure on a tomb; tears were running out of her closed eyes and her mouth was distorted with grief. She was crying in her sleep. She looked like a child, lying there, and her face had a child's look of hopeless misery, for a child does not know that sorrow, like all other things, will pass. Charley gave a gasp. The unhappiness of that sleeping woman was intolerable to see, and all his passion, all his desire, were extinguished by the pity that overcame him. She had been gay during the day, easy to talk to and companionable, and it had seemed to him that she was free, at least for a while, from the pain that, he was conscious, lurked always in the depths of her being; but in sleep it had returned to her and he knew only too well what unhappy dreams distraught her. He gave a deep sigh.

But he felt more disinclined for sleep than ever, and he could not bear the thought of getting into bed again. He turned the shade down so that the light should not disturb Lydia, and going to the table filled his pipe and lit it. He drew the heavy curtain that was over the window and sitting down looked out into the court. It was in darkness but for one lighted window, and this had a sinister look. He wondered whether someone lay ill in that room or, simply sleepless like himself, brooded over the perplexity of life. Or perhaps some man had brought a woman in, and their lust appeased, they lay contented in one another's arms. Charley smoked. He felt dull and flat. He did not think of anything in particular. At last he went back to bed and fell asleep.

ix

CHARLEY WAS AWAKENED by the maid bringing in the morning coffee. For a moment he forgot the events of the previous night.

"Oh, I was sleeping so soundly," he said, rubbing his eyes.

"I'm sorry, but it's half-past ten and I have an engagement at eleven-thirty."

"It doesn't matter. It's my last day in Paris and it would be silly to waste it in sleep."

The maid had brought the two breakfasts on one tray and Lydia told her to give it to Charley. She put on a dressing-gown and sat down at the end of his bed, leaning against the foot. She poured out a cup of coffee, cut a roll in two and buttered it for him.

"I've been watching you sleep," she said. "It's nice; you sleep like an animal or a child, so deep, so quiet, it rests one just to look at you."

Then he remembered.

"I'm afraid you didn't have a very good night."

"Oh, yes, I did. I slept like a top. I was tired out, you know. That's one of the things I'm most grateful to you for, I've had such wonderful nights. I dream terribly. But since I've been here I haven't dreamt once; I've slept quite peacefully. And I who thought I should never sleep like that again."

He knew that she had been dreaming that night and he knew what her dreams were about. She had forgotten them. He forebore to look at her. It gave him a grim, horrible, and rather uncanny sensation to think that a vivid, lacerating life could go on when one was sunk in unconsciousness, a life so real that it could cause tears to stream down the face and twist the mouth in woe, and yet when the sleeper woke left no recollection behind. An uncomfortable thought crossed his mind. He could not quite make it explicit, but had he been able to, he would perhaps have asked himself:

"Who are we really? What do we know about ourselves? And that other life of ours, is that less real than this one?"

It was all very strange and complicated. It looked as though nothing were quite so simple as it seemed; it looked as though the people we thought we knew best carried secrets that they didn't even know themselves. Charley had a sudden inkling that human beings were infinitely mysterious. The fact was that you knew nothing about anybody.

"What's this engagement you've got?" he asked, more for the sake of saying something than because he wanted to know.

Lydia lit a cigarette before she answered.

"Marcel, the fat man who runs the place we were at last night, introduced me to two men there and I've made an appointment to meet them at the Palette this morning. We couldn't talk in all that crowd."

"Oh!"

He was too discreet to ask who they were.

"Marcel's in touch with Cayenne and St. Laurent. He often gets news. That's why I wanted to go there. They landed at St. Nazaire last week."

"Who? The two men? Are they escaped convicts?"

"No. They've served their sentence. They got their passage paid by the Salvation Army. They knew Robert." She hesitated a moment. "If you want to, you can come with me. They've got no money. They'd be grateful if you gave them a little."

"All right. Yes, I'd like to come."

"They seem very decent fellows. One of them doesn't look more than thirty now. Marcel told me he was a cook and he was sent out for killing another man in the kitchen of the restaurant where he worked. I don't know what the other had done. You'd better go and have your bath." She went over to the dressing-table and looked at herself in the glass. "Funny, I wonder why my eyelids are swollen. To look at me you'd think I'd been crying, and you know I haven't, don't you?"

"Perhaps it was that smoky atmosphere last night. By George! you could have cut it with a knife."

"I'll ring down for some ice. They'll be all right after we've been out in the air for five minutes."

The Palette was empty when they got there. Late breakfasters had had their coffee and gone, and it was too early for anyone to have come in for an apéritif before luncheon. They sat in a corner, near the window, so that they could look out into the street. They waited for several minutes.

"There they are," said Lydia.

Charley looked out and saw two men walking past. They glanced in, hesitated a moment and strolled on, then came back; Lydia gave them a smile, but they took no notice of her; they stood still, looking up and down the street, and then doubtfully at the café. It looked as though they couldn't make up their minds to enter. Their manner was timid and furtive. They said a few words to one another and the younger of the two gave a hasty anxious glance behind him. The other seemed on a sudden to force himself to a decision and walked towards the door. His friend followed quickly. Lydia gave them a wave and a smile when they came in. They still took no notice. They looked round stealthily, as though to assure themselves that they were safe, and then, the first with averted eyes, the other fixing the ground, came up. Lydia shook hands with them and introduced Charley. They evidently had expected her to be alone and his presence disconcerted them. They gave him a look of suspicion. Lydia explained that he was an Englishman, a friend who was spending a few days in Paris. Charley, a smile on his lips which he sought to make cordial, stretched out his hand; they took it, one after the other, and gave it a limp pressure. They seemed to have nothing to say. Lydia bade them sit down and asked them what they would have.

"A cup of coffee."

"You'll have something to eat?"

The elder one gave the other a faint smile.

"A cake, if there is one. The boy has a sweet tooth, and over there, from where we come, there wasn't much in that line."

The man who spoke was a little under the middle height. He might have been forty. The other was two or three inches taller and perhaps ten years younger. Both were very thin. They both wore collars and ties and thick suits, one of a gray-and-white check and the other dark green, but the suits were ill-cut and sat loosely on them. They did not look at ease in them. The elder one, sturdy though short, had a well-knit figure; his sallow, colourless face was much lined. He had an air of determination. The other's face was as sallow and colourless, but his skin, drawn tightly over the bones, was smooth and unlined; he looked very ill. There was another trait they shared; the eyes of both seemed preternaturally large, and when they turned them on you they did not appear to look at you, but beyond, with a demented stare, as though they were gazing at something that filled them with horror. It was very painful. At first they were shy, and since Charley was shy too, though he tried to show his friendliness by offering them cigarettes, while Lydia, seeming to find no need for words, contented herself with looking at them, they sat in silence. But she looked at them with such tender concern that the silence was not embarrassing. The waiter brought them coffee and a dish of cakes. The elder man toyed with one of them, but the other ate greedily, and as he ate he gave his friend now and then little touching looks of surprised delight.

"The first thing we did when we got out by ourselves in Paris was to go to a confectioner's, and the boy ate six chocolate éclairs one after the other. But he paid for it."

"Yes," said the other seriously. "When we got out into the street I was sick. You see, my stomach wasn't used to it. But it was worth it."

"Did you eat very badly over there?"

The elder man shrugged his shoulders.

"Beef three hundred and sixty-five days of the year. One doesn't notice it after a time. And then, if you behave yourself you get cheese and a little wine. And it's better to behave yourself. Of course it's worse when you've done your sentence and you're freed. When you're in prison you get board and lodging, but when you're free you have to shift for yourself."

"My friend doesn't know," said Lydia. "Explain to him. They don't have the same system in England."

"It's like this. You're sentenced to a term of imprisonment, eight, ten, fifteen, twenty years, and when you've done it you're a libéré. You have to stay in the colony the same number of years that you were sentenced to. It's hard to get work. The libérés have a bad name and people won't employ them. It's true that you can get a plot of land and cultivate it, but it's not everyone who can do that. After being in prison for years, taking orders from the warders and half the time doing nothing, you've lost your initiative; and then there's malaria and hook-worm; you've lost your energy. Most of them get work only when a ship comes in to harbour and they can earn a little by unloading the cargo. There's nothing much for the libéré but to sleep in the market, drink rafia when he gets the chance, and starve. I was lucky. You see, I'm an electrician by trade, and a good one; I know my job as well as any-one, so they needed me. I didn't do so badly."

"How long was your sentence?" asked Lydia.

"Only eight years."

"And what did you do?"

He slightly shrugged his shoulders and gave Lydia a deprecating smile.

"Folly of youth. One's young, one gets into bad com-pany, one drinks too much and then one day something happens and one has to pay for it all one's life. I was twenty-four when I went out and I'm forty now. I've spent my best years in that hell."

"He could have got away before," said the other, "but he wouldn't."

"You mean you could have escaped?" said Lydia.

Charley gave her a quick, searching glance but her face told him nothing.

"Escape? No, that's a mug's game. One can always escape, but there are few who get away. Where can you go? Into the bush? Fever, wild animals, starvation, and the natives who'll take you for the sake of the reward. A good many try it. You see, they get so fed up with the monotony, the food, the orders, the sight of all the rest of the prisoners, they think anything's bet-ter, but they can't stick it out; if they don't die of illness or starvation, they're captured or give themselves up; and then it's two years' solitary confinement, or more, and you have to be a hefty chap if that doesn't break you. It was easier in the old days when the Dutch were building their railway, you could get across the river and they'd put you to work on it, but now they've finished the railway and they don't want labour any more. They catch you and send you back. But even that had its risks. There was a customs official who used to promise to take you over the river for a certain sum, he had a regular tariff, you'd arrange to meet him at a place in the jungle at night, and when you kept the appointment he just shot you dead and emptied your pockets. They say he did away with more than thirty fellows before he was caught. Some of them get away by sea. Half a dozen club together and get a libéré to buy a rickety boat for them. It's a hard journey, without a compass or anything, and one never knows when a storm will spring up; it's more by luck than good management if they get anywhere. And where can they go? They won't have them in Venezuela any longer and if they land there they're just put in prison and sent back. If they land in Trinidad the authorities keep them for a week, stock them up with provisions, even give them a boat if theirs isn't seaworthy, and then send them off, out into the sea with no place to go to. No, it's silly to try to escape."

"But men do," said Lydia. "There was that doctor, what was his name? They say he's practising some-where in South America and doing well."

"Yes, if you've got money you can get away some-

times, not if you're on the islands, but if you're at
Cayenne or St. Laurent. You can get the skipper of a
Brazilian schooner to pick you up at sea, and if he's
honest he'll land you somewhere down the coast and
you're pretty safe. If he isn't, he takes your money and
chucks you overboard. But he'll want twelve thousand
francs now, and that means double because the libéré
who gets the money in for you takes half as his commission. And then you can't land in Brazil without a
penny in your pocket. You've got to have at least thirty
thousand francs, and who's got that?"

Lydia asked a question and once more Charley gave
her an inquiring look.

"But how can you be sure that the libéré will hand
over the money that's sent him?" she said.

"You can't. Sometimes he doesn't, but then he ends
with a knife in his back, and he knows very well the
authorities aren't going to bother very much if a
damned libéré is found dead one morning."

"Your friend said just now you could have got away
sooner, but didn't. What did he mean by that?"

The little man gave his shoulders a deprecating
shrug.

"I made myself useful. The commandant was a
decent chap and he knew I was a good worker and
honest. They soon found out they could leave me in a
house by myself when they wanted a job done and I
wouldn't touch a thing. He got me permission to go
back to France when I still had two more years to go
of my time as a libéré." He gave his friend a touching
smile. "But I didn't like to leave that young scamp.

I knew that without me to look after him he'd get into trouble."

"It's true," said the other. "I owe everything to him."

"He was only a kid when he came out. He had the next bed to mine. He put up a pretty good show in the daytime, but at night he'd cry for his mother. I felt sorry for him. I don't know how it happened, I got an affection for him; he was lost among all those men, poor little chap, and I had to look after him. Some of them were inclined to be nasty to him, one Algerian was always bothering, but I settled his hash and after that they left the boy in peace."

"How did you do that?"

The little man gave a grin so cheerful and roguish that it made him look on a sudden ten years younger.

"Well, you know, in that life a man can only make himself respected if he knows how to use his knife. I ripped him up the belly."

Charley gave a gasp. The man made the statement so naturally that one could hardly believe one had heard right.

"You see, one's shut up in the dormitory from nine till five and the warders don't come in. To tell you the truth, it would be as much as their lives were worth. If in the morning a man's found with a hole in his gizzard, the authorities ask no questions so as they won't be told no lies. So you see, I felt a kind of responsibility for the boy. I had to teach him everything. I've got a good brain and I soon discovered that out there if you want to make it easy for yourself the only thing is to do what you're told and give no trouble. It's not justice that reigns on the earth, it's force, and they've got the force, the authorities; one of these days perhaps we shall have it, we the working-men, and then we shall get a bit of our own back on the bourgeois, but till then we've got to obey. That's what I taught him, and I taught him my job too, and now he's almost as good an electrician as I am."

"The only thing now is to find work," said the other. "Work together."

"We've gone through so much together we can't be parted now. You see, he's all I've got. I've got no mother, no wife, no kids. I had, but my mother's dead, and I lost my wife and my kids when I had my trouble. Women are bitches. It's hard for a chap to live without any affection in his life."

"And I, who have I got? It's for life, us two."

There was something very affecting in the friendship that bound those two hapless men together. It gave Charley a sense of exaltation that somewhat embarrassed him; he would have liked to tell them that he thought it brave and beautiful, but he knew he could never bring himself to say anything so unusual. But Lydia had none of his shyness.

"I don't think there are many men who would have stayed in that hell for two long years when they could get away, for the sake of a friend."

The man chuckled.

"You see, over there time is just the opposite of money; there a little money is a great deal and a lot of time is nothing very much. While six sous is a sum that you hoard as if it was a fortune, two years is a period that's hardly worth talking about."

Lydia sighed deeply. It was plain of what she was thinking.

"Berger isn't there for so long, is he?"

"Fifteen years."

There was a silence. One could see that Lydia was making a great effort to control her emotion, but when she spoke there was a break in her voice.

"Did you see him?"

"Yes. I talked to him. We were in hospital together. I went in to have my appendix out, I didn't want to get back to France and have trouble with it here. He'd been working on the road they're making from St. Laurent to Cayenne and he got a bad go of malaria."

"I didn't know. I've had one letter from him, but he said nothing about it."

"Out there everyone has malaria sooner or later. It's not worth making a song and dance about. He's lucky to have got it so soon. The chief medical officer took a fancy to him, he's an educated man, Berger, and there aren't many of them. They were going to apply to get him transferred to the hospital service when he recovered. He'll be all right there."

"Marcel told me last night that he'd given you a message for me."

"Yes, he gave me an address." He took a bundle of papers out of his pocket and gave Lydia a scrap on which something was written. "If you can send any money, send it there. But remember that he'll only get half what you send."

Lydia took the bit of paper, looked at it, and put it in her bag.

"Anything else?"

"Yes. He said you weren't to worry. He said it wasn't so bad as it might be, and he was finding his feet and he'd make out all right. And that's true, you know. He's no fool. He won't make many mistakes. He's a chap who'll make the best of a bad job. You'll see, he'll be happy enough."

"How can he be happy?"

"It's funny what one can get used to. He's a bit of a wag, isn't he? He used to make us laugh at some of the things he said. He's a rare one for seeing the funny side of things, there's no mistake about that."

Lydia was very pale. She looked down in silence. The elder man turned to his friend.

"What was that funny thing I told you he'd said about that cove in the hospital who cut his blasted throat?"

"Oh, I remember. Now what was it? It's clean gone out of my mind, but I know it made me laugh my head off."

A long silence fell. There seemed nothing more to say. Lydia was pensive; and the two men sat limp on their chairs, their eyes vacant, like the mechanical dolls they sell on the Boulevard Montparnasse which gyrate, rocking, round and round and then on a sudden stop dead. Lydia sighed.

"I think that's about all," she said. "Thank you for coming. I hope you'll get the job you're looking for."

"The Salvation Army are doing what they can for us. I expect something will turn up."

Charley fished his note-case out of his pocket.

"I don't suppose you're very flush. I'd like to give you something to help you along till you find work."

"It would be useful," the man smiled pleasantly. "The Army doesn't do much but give one board and lodging."

Charley handed them five hundred francs.

"Give it to the kid to take care of. He's got the saving disposition of the peasant he is, he sweats blood when he has to spend money, and he can make five francs go farther than any old woman in the world."

They went out of the café, the four of them, and shook hands. During the hour they had spent together the two men had lost their shyness, but when they got out into the street it seized them again. They seemed to shrink as though they desired to make themselves as inconspicuous as possible, and looked furtively to right and left as if afraid that someone would pounce upon them. They walked off side by side, with bent heads, and after another quick glance backward slunk round the nearest corner.

"I suppose it's only prejudice on my part," said Charley, "but I'm bound to say that I didn't feel very much at my ease in that company."

Lydia made no reply. They walked along the boulevard in silence; they lunched in silence. Lydia was immersed in thought the nature of which he could guess and he felt that any attempt on his part at small talk would be unwelcome. Besides, he had thoughts of his

own to occupy him. The conversation they had had
with the two convicts, the questions Lydia asked, had
revived the suspicion which Simon had sown in his
mind and which, though he had tried to put it aside, had
since then lurked in his consciousness like the musty
smell of a long closed room which no opening of
windows can quite dispel. It worried him, not so much
because he minded being made a fool of, as because
he did not want to think that Lydia was a liar and a
hypocrite.

"I'm going along to see Simon," he said when they
had finished luncheon. "I came over largely to see him
and I've hardly had a glimpse of him. I ought at least
to go and say good-bye."

"Yes, I suppose you ought."

He also wanted to return to Simon the newspaper
cuttings and the article which he had lent him. He had
them in his pocket.

"If you want to spend the afternoon with your
Russian friends, I'll drive you there first if you like."

"No, I'll go back to the hotel."

"I don't suppose I shall be back till late. You know
what Simon is when he gets talking. Won't you be
bored by yourself?"

"I'm not used to so much consideration," she smiled.
"No, I shan't be bored. It's not often I have the chance
to be alone. To sit in a room by oneself and to know
that no one can come in—why, I can't imagine a greater
luxury."

They parted and Charley walked to Simon's. He
knew that at that hour he stood a good chance of finding

him in. Simon opened the door on his ring. He was in pyjamas and a dressing-gown.

"Hulloa! I thought you might breeze along. I didn't have to go out this morning, so I didn't dress!"

He hadn't shaved and he looked as though he hadn't washed either. His long straight hair was in disorder. By the bleak light that came through the north window his restless, angry eyes looked coal-black in his white thin face and there were dark shadows beneath them.

"Sit down," he continued. "I've got a good fire to-day and the studio's warm."

It was, but it was as forlorn, cheerless and unswept as before.

"Is the love affair still going strong?"

"I've just left Lydia."

"You're going back to London to-morrow, aren't you? Don't let her sting you too much. There's no reason why you should help to get her rotten husband out of jug."

Charley took the cuttings from his pocket.

"By your article I judged that you had a certain amount of sympathy for him."

"Sympathy, no. I found him interesting just because he was such an unmitigated, cold-blooded, unscrupulous cad. I admired his nerve. In other circumstances he might have been a useful instrument. In a revolution a man like that who'll stick at nothing, who has courage and no scruples, may be invaluable."

"I shouldn't have thought a very reliable instrument."

"Wasn't it Danton who said that in a revolution it's

the scum of society, the rogues and criminals, who rise to the surface? It's natural. They're needed for certain work and when they've served their purpose they can be disposed of."

"You seem to have it all cut and dried, old boy," said Charley, with a cheerful grin.

Simon impatiently shrugged his bony shoulders.

"I've studied the French Revolution and the Commune. The Russians did too and they learnt a lot from them, but we've got the advantage now that we can profit by the lessons we've learnt from subsequent events. They made a bad mess of things in Hungary, but they made a pretty good job of it in Russia and they didn't do so badly either in Italy or in Germany. If we've got any sense we ought to be able to emulate their success, but avoid their mistakes. Bela Kun's revolution failed because people were hungry. The rise of the proletariat has made it comparatively simple to make a revolution, but the proletariat must be fed. Organization is needed to see that means of transport are adequate and food supplies abundant. That incidentally is why power, which the proletariat thought to seize by making the revolution, must always elude their grasp and fall into the hands of a small body of intelligent leaders. The people are incapable of governing themselves. The proletariat are slaves and slaves need masters."

"You would hardly describe yourself any longer as a good democrat, I take it," said Charley with a twinkle in his blue eyes.

Simon impatiently dismissed the ironical remark.

"Democracy is moonshine. It's an unrealizable ideal which the propagandist dangles before the masses as you dangle a carrot before a donkey. Those great watchwords of the nineteenth century, liberty, equality, fraternity, are pure hokum. Liberty? The mass of men don't need liberty and don't know what to do with it when they've got it. Their duty and their pleasure is to serve; thus they attain the security which is their deepest want. It's been decided long ago that the only liberty worth anything is the liberty to do right, and right is decided by might. Right is an idea occasioned by public opinion and prescribed by law, but public opinion is created by those who have the power to enforce their point of view, and the only sanction of law is the might behind it. Fraternity? What do you mean by fraternity?"

Charley considered the question for a moment.

"Well, I don't know. I suppose it's a feeling that we're all members of one great family and we're here on earth for so short a time, it's better to make the best of one another."

"Anything else?"

"Well, only that life is a difficult job, and it probably makes it easier for everybody if we're kind and decent to one another. Men have plenty of faults, but there's a lot of good in them. The more you know people the nicer you find they are. That rather suggests that if you give them a chance they'll meet you half way."

"Tosh, my dear boy, tosh. You're a sentimental fool. In the first place it's not true that people improve as you know them better: they don't. That's why one should only have acquaintances and never make friends. An acquaintance shows you only the best of himself, he's considerate and polite, he conceals his defects behind a mask of social convention; but grow so intimate with him that he throws the mask aside, get to know him so well that he doesn't trouble any longer to pretend; then you'll discover a being of such meanness, of such a trivial nature, of such weakness, of such corruption, that you'd be aghast if you didn't realize that that was his nature and it was just as stupid to condemn him as to condemn the wolf because he ravens or the cobra because he strikes. For the essence of man is egoism. Egoism is at once his strength and his weakness. Oh, I've got to know men pretty well during the two years I've spent in the newspaper world. Vain, petty, unscrupulous, avaricious, double-faced and abject, they'll betray one another, not even for their own advantage, but from sheer malice. There's no trick they won't descend to in order to queer a rival's pitch; there's no humiliation they won't accept to obtain a title or an order; and not only politicians; lawyers, doctors, merchants, artists, men of letters. And their craving for publicity; they'll cringe and flatter a two-penny-halfpenny journalist to get a good press. Rich men will hesitate at no shabby dodge to make a few pounds that they have no use for. Honesty, political honesty, commercial honesty—the only thing that counts with them is what they can get away with; the only thing that restrains them is fear. For they're craven. And the protestations they make, the high-flown humbug that falls from their lips, the shameless lies they tell themselves. Oh, believe me, you can't do the work I've been doing since I left Cambridge and preserve many illusions about human nature. Men are vile. Cowards and hypocrites. I loathe them."

Charley looked down. He was a little shy about saying what he wanted to. It sounded rather silly.

"Haven't you any pity for them?"

"Pity? Pity is womanish. Pity is what the beggar entreats of you because he hasn't the guts, the industry and the brains to make a decent living. Pity is the flattery the failure craves so that he may preserve his self-esteem. Pity is the cheap blackmail that the prosperous pay to the down-and-out so that they may enjoy their own prosperity with a better conscience."

Simon drew his dressing-gown angrily round his thin body. Charley recognized it as an old one of his which he had been going to throw away when Simon asked if he could have it; he had laughed and said he would give him a new one, but Simon, saying it was quite good enough for him, had insisted on having it. Charley wondered uncomfortably if he resented the trifling gift. Simon went on:

"Equality? Equality is the greatest nonsense that's ever muddled the intelligence of the human race. As if men were equal or could be equal! They talk of equality of opportunity. Why should men have that when they can't take advantage of it? Men are born unequal; different in character, in vitality, in brain; and no equality of opportunity can offset that. The vast majority are densely stupid. Credulous, shallow, feckless, why should they be given equality of opportunity with those who have character, intelligence, industry and force? And it's that natural inequality of man that knocks the bottom out of democracy. What a stupid farce it is to govern a country by the counting of millions of empty heads! In the first place they don't know what's good for them and in the second, they haven't the capacity to get the good they want. What does democracy come down to? The persuasive power of slogans invented by wily, self-seeking politicians. A democracy is ruled by words, and the orator seldom has brains, and if he has, he hasn't time to use them, since all his energy has to be given to cajoling the fools on whose votes he depends. Democracy has had a hundred years' trial: theoretically it was always absurd, and now we know that practically it's a wash-out."

"Notwithstanding which you propose, if you can, to get into parliament. You're a very dishonest fellow, my poor Simon."

"In an old-fashioned country like England, which cherishes its established institutions, it would be impossible to gain sufficient power to carry out one's plans except from within those institutions. I don't suppose anyone could gain support in the country and gather round himself an adequate band of followers to effect a coup d'état unless he were a prominent member of one of the great parties in the House of Commons. And since an upheaval can only be effected by means of the people it would have to be the Labour party. Even when the conditions are ripe for revolution the possessing classes still retain enough of their privileges to make it worth their while to make the best of a bad job."

"What conditions have you in mind? Defeat in war and economic distress?"

"Exactly. Even then the possessing classes only suffer relatively. They put down their cars or close their country houses, thus adding to unemployment, but not greatly inconveniencing themselves. But the people starve. Then they will listen to you when you tell them they have nothing to lose but their chains, and when you dangle before them the bait of other people's property the greed, the envy, which they've had to repress because they had no means of gratifying them, are let loose. With liberty and equality as your watchwords you can lead them to the attack. The history of the last five-and-twenty years shows that they're bound to win. The possessing classes are enervated by their possessions, they're humanitarian and sentimental, they have neither the will nor the courage to defend themselves; their counsels are divided, and when their only chance is in immediate and ruthless action they waste their time in recrimination. But the mob, which is the instrument of the revolutionary leaders, is a thing not of reason but of instinct, it is amenable to hypnotic suggestion and you can rouse it to frenzy by catchwords; it is an entity, and so is indifferent to the death in its ranks of such as fall; it knows neither pity nor mercy. It rejoices in destruction because in destruction it becomes conscious of its own power.

"I suppose you wouldn't deny that that entails the killing of thousands of inoffensive people and the destruction of institutions that have taken hundreds of years to build up."

"There's bound to be destruction in a revolution and there's bound to be killing. Engels said years ago that the possessing classes must be expected to resist suppression by every means in their power. It's a fight to the death. Democracy has attached an absurd importance to human life. Morally man is worthless and it's no loss to suppress him. Biologically he's of no consequence; there's no more reason why it should shock you to kill a man than to swat a fly."

"I begin to see why you were interested in Robert Berger."

"I was interested in him because he killed, not for any sordid motive, not for money, nor jealousy, but to prove himself and affirm his power."

"Of course it remains to be proved that communism is practicable."

"Communism? Who talked of communism? Everyone knows now that communism is a wash-out. It was the dream of impractical idealists who knew nothing of the realities of life. Communism is the lure you offer to the working classes to rouse them to revolt just as the cry of liberty and equality is the slogan with which you fire them to dare. Throughout the history of the world there have always been exploiters and exploited. There always will be. And it's right that it should be so because the great mass of men are made by nature to be slaves; they are unfit to control themselves, and for their own good need masters."

"That's rather a startling assertion."

"It's not mine, old boy," Simon answered ironically. "It's Plato's, but the history of the world since he made it has amply demonstrated its truth. What has been the result of the revolutions we've seen in our own lifetime? The people haven't lost their masters, they've only changed them, and nowhere has authority been wielded with a more iron hand than under communism."

"Then the people are duped?"

"Of course. Why not? They're fools, and they deserve to be. What does it matter? Their gain is substantial. They're not asked to think for themselves any more; they're told what to do, and so long as they're obedient they have the security they've always hankered after. The dictators of our own day have made mistakes and we can learn by their errors. They've forgotten Machiavelli's dictum that you can enslave the people politically if you leave their private lives free. I should give the people the illusion of liberty by allowing them as much personal freedom as is compatible with the safety of the state. I would socialize industry as widely as the idiosyncrasy of the human animal permits and so give men the illusion of equality. And since they would all be brothers under one yoke they would even have the illusion of fraternity. Remember that a dictator can do all sorts of things for the benefit of the people that democracy is prevented from doing because it has to consider vested interests, jealousies and personal ambitions, and so he has an unparalleled opportunity to alleviate the lot of the masses. I went to a great communist meeting the other day and on banner after banner I read the words Peace, Work and Well-Being. Could any claims be more natural? And yet here man is after a hundred years of democracy still making them. A dictator can satisfy them by a stroke of the pen."

"But by your own admission the people only change their master; they're still exploited; what makes you think that they'll put up with it?"

"Because they'll damned well have to. Under present conditions a dictator with planes to drop bombs and armoured cars to fire machine guns can quell any revolt. The possessing classes could do the same, and no revolution would succeed, but the event has shown that they haven't the nerve; they kill a hundred men, a thousand even, but then they get scared, they want to compromise, they offer to make concessions, but it's too late then for concession or compromise and they're swept away. But the people will accept their master because they know that he is better and wiser than they are."

"Why should he be better and wiser?"

"Because he's stronger. Because he has the power, what he says is right *is* right and what he says is good *is* good."

"It's as simple as A B C but even less convincing," said Charley with some flippancy.

Simon gave him an angry scowl.

"You'd find it convincing enough if not only your bread and butter but your life depended on it."

"And who, pray, is to choose the master?"

"Nobody. He's the ineluctable product of circumstances."

"That's a bit of a mouthful, isn't it?"

"He rises to the top because he has the instinct to lead. He has the will to power. He has audacity and enthusiasm, ability, industry and energy. He fears nothing because to him danger is the salt of life."

"No one could say that you hadn't a good conceit of yourself, Simon," smiled Charley.

"Why do you say that?"

"Well, I suppose you imagine yourself to possess the qualities you've just enumerated."

"What makes you suppose it? I know myself as well as any man can know himself. I know my capacities, but I also know my limitations. A dictator must have a mystic appeal so that he excites his followers to a religious frenzy. He must have a magnetism which makes it a privilege for them to lay down their lives for him. In him they must feel that they more greatly live. I have nothing in me of that. I repel rather than attract. I could make people fear me, I could never make them love me. You remember what Lincoln said: 'You can fool some of the people all the time, and all the people some of the time, but you can't fool all the people all the time.' But that's just what a dictator must do; he must fool all the people all the time and there's only one way he can do that, he must also fool himself. None of the dictators has a lucid, logical brain; he has drive, force, magnetism, charm, but if you examine his words closely you'll see that his intelligence is mediocre; he can act because he acts on instinct, but when he begins to think he gets muddled. I have too good a brain and too little charm to be a dictator.

Besides, it's better that the dictator brought to power by the proletariat should be a member of it. The working classes will find it more easy to identify themselves with him and thus will give him more willingly their obedience and devotion. The technique of revolution has been perfected. Given the right conditions it's easy for a resolute body of men to seize power; the difficulty is to hold it. The Russian revolution in the clearest possible way, the Italian and the German revolutions in a lesser degree, have shown that there's only one means by which it can be done. Terror. The working man who becomes head of a state is exposed to temptations that only a very strong character can resist. He must be almost superhuman if his head isn't turned by adulation and if his resolution isn't enfeebled by unaccustomed luxury. The working man is naturally sentimental; he's kind-hearted and so accessible to pity; when he's got what he wants he sits back and lets things slide; he forgives his enemies and is surprised when they stick a knife in him as soon as his back is turned. He needs at his elbow someone who 'by his birth, education, training and character, is indifferent to the trappings of greatness and immune to the debilitating influence of success."

Simon for some time had been walking up and down the studio, but now he came to an abrupt halt before his friend. With his white unshaven face and dishevelled hair, in the dressing-gown huddled round his emaciated limbs, he presented a grotesque appearance. But in a past that is not so distant other young men as pale, as thin, as unkempt as he, in shabby suits or in a student's blouse, had walked about their sordid rooms and told of dreams seemingly as unrealizable; and yet time and opportunity had strangely made their dreams come true, and, fighting their way to power through blood, they held in their hands the life of millions.

"Have you ever heard of Dzerjinsky?"

Charley gave him a startled look. That was the name Lydia had mentioned.

"Yes, oddly enough I have."

"He was a gentleman. His family had been land-owners in Poland since the seventeenth century. He was a cultivated, well-read man. Lenin and the Old Guard made the revolution, but without Dzerjinsky it would have been crushed within a year. He saw that it could only be saved by terror. He applied for the post that gave him control of the police and organized the Cheka. He made it into an instrument of repression that acted with the precision of a perfect machine. He let neither love nor hate interfere with his duty. His industry was prodigious. He would work all night examining the suspects himself, and they say he acquired so keen an insight into the hearts of men that it was impossible for them to conceal their secrets from him. He invented the system of hostages which was one of the most effective systems the revolution ever discovered to preserve order. He signed hundreds, nay, thousands of death warrants with his own hand. He lived with spartan simplicity. His strength was that he wanted nothing for himself. His only aim was to serve the revolution. And he made himself the most powerful man in Russia. It was Lenin the people acclaimed and worshipped, but it was Dzerjinsky who ruled them."

"And is that the part you wish to play if ever revolution comes to England?"

"I should be well fitted for it."

Charley gave him his boyish, good-natured smile.

"It's just possible that I'd be doing the country a service if I strangled you here and now. I could, you know."

"I daresay. But you'd be afraid of the consequences."

"I don't think I should be found out. No one saw me come in. Only Lydia knows I was going to see you and she wouldn't give me away."

"I wasn't thinking of those consequences. I was thinking of your conscience. You're not tough-fibred enough for that, Charley, old boy. You're soft."

"I daresay you're right."

Charley did not speak for a while.

"You say Dzerjinsky wanted nothing for himself," he said then, "but you want power."

"Only as a means."

"What to do?"

Simon stared at him fixedly and there was a light in his eyes that seemed to Charley almost crazy.

"To fulfil myself. To satisfy my creative instinct. To exercise the capacities that nature has endowed me with."

Charley found nothing to say. He looked at his watch and got up.

"I must go now."

"I don't want to see you again, Charley."

"Well, you won't. I'm off to-morrow."

"I mean, ever."

Charley was taken aback. He looked into Simon's eyes. They were dark and grim.

"Oh? Why?"

"I'm through with you."

"For good?"

"For good and all."

"Don't you think that's rather a pity? I haven't been a bad friend to you, Simon."

Simon was silent for a space no longer than it takes for an over-ripe fruit to fall from the tree to the ground.

"You're the only friend I've ever had."

There was a break in his voice and his distress was so plain that Charley, moved, with both hands outstretched, stepped forward impulsively.

"Oh, Simon, why d'you make yourself so unhappy?"

A flame of rage leapt into Simon's tortured eyes and clenching his fist he hit Charley as hard as he could on the chin. The blow was so unexpected that he staggered and then, his feet slipping on the uncarpeted floor, fell headlong; he was on his feet in a flash and, furious with anger, sprang forward to give Simon the hiding he had often, when driven beyond endurance, given him before. Simon stood quite still, his hands behind his back, as though ready and willing to take the chastisement that was coming to him without an effort to defend himself, and on his face was an expression of so much suffering, of such consternation, that Charley's wrath

was melted. He stopped. His chin was hurting him, but
he gave a good-natured, chuckling laugh.

"You are an ass, Simon," he said. "You might have
hurt me."

"For God's sake, get out. Go back to that bloody
whore. I'm fed to the teeth with you. Go, go."

"All right, old man, I'm going. But I want to give
you a little presy that I brought you for your birthday
on the seventh."

He took out of his pocket one of those watches,
covered in leather, which you open by pulling out the
two sides, and which are wound by opening.

"There's a ring on it so you can hang it on your
key-chain."

He put it down on the table. Simon would not look
at it. Charley, his eyes twinkling with amusement, gave
him a glance. He waited for him to say something, but
he did not speak. Charley went to the door, opened it
and walked out.

It was night, but the Boulevard Montparnasse was
brightly lit. With the New Year imminent there was
a holiday feeling in the air. The street was crowded and
the cafés were chock-a-block. Everybody was taking
it easy. But Charley was depressed. He had a feeling
of mortification, as one might have if one had gone
to a party, expecting to enjoy oneself, and because one
had been stupid and tactless, had come away conscious that one had left behind a bad impression. It
was a comfort to get back to the sordid bedroom at
the hotel. Lydia was sitting by the log fire sewing, and
the air was thick with the many cigarettes she had

smoked. The scene had a pleasant domesticity. It reminded one of an interior of Vuillard's, with its intimate, cosy charm, but painted by Utrillo so that it had at the same time a touching squalor. Lydia greeted him with her quiet, friendly smile.

"How was your friend Simon?"

"Mad as a hatter."

Lighting his pipe, he sat down on the floor in front of the fire, with his back against the seat of her chair. Her nearness gave him a sense of comfort. He was glad that she did not speak. He was troubled by all the horrible things Simon had said to him. He could not get out of his head the picture of that thin creature, his pale face scrubby with a two days' beard, underfed and overworked, walking up and down in his old dressing-gown and with a cold-blooded, ruthless malignance delivering himself of his fantastic ideas. But breaking in upon this, as it were, was the recollection of the little boy with the big dark eyes who seemed to yearn for affection and yet repelled it, the little boy with whom he went to the circus during the Christmas holidays and who got so wildly excited at the unaccustomed treat, with whom he bicycled or went for long walks in the country, who was at times so gay and amusing, with whom it was jolly to talk and laugh and rag and play the fool. It seemed incredible that that little boy should have turned into that young man, and so heart-rending that he could have wept.

"I wonder what'll happen to Simon in the end?" he muttered.

Hardly knowing that he had spoken aloud, he almost

thought Lydia had read his thoughts when she answered:

"I don't know the English. If he were Russian I'd
say he'll either become a dangerous agitator or he'll
commit suicide."

Charley chuckled.

"Oh well, we English have a wonderful capacity for
making our wild oats into a nourishing diet. It's equally
on the cards that he'll end up as the editor of *The
Times.*"

He got up and seated himself in the armchair which
was the only fairly comfortable seat in the room. He
looked reflectively at Lydia busily plying her needle.
There was something he wanted to say to her, but the
thought of it made him nervous, and yet he was leaving
next day and this might well be his last opportunity.
The suspicion that Simon had sown in his candid heart
rankled. If she had been making a fool of him, he
would sooner know; then when they parted he could
shrug his shoulders and with a good conscience forget
her. He decided to settle the matter there and then, but
being shy of making her right out the offer he had in
mind, he approached it in a round-about way.

"Have I ever told you about my Great-Aunt
Martha?" he started lightly.

"No."

"She was my great-grandfather's eldest child. She
was a grim-featured spinster with more wrinkles on her
sallow face than I've ever seen on a human being. She
was very small and thin, with tight lips, and she never

looked anything but acidly disapproving. She used to terrify me when I was a kid. She had an enormous admiration for Queen Alexandra and to the end of her days wore her hair, only it was a wig, as the Queen wore hers. She always dressed in black, with very full long skirts and a pinched-in waist, and the collar of her bodice came up to her ears. She wore a heavy gold chain round her neck, with a large gold cross dangling from it, and gold bangles on her wrists. She was appallingly genteel. She continued to live in the grand house old Sibert Mason built for himself when he began to get on in the world and she never changed a thing. To go there was like stepping back into the eighteen-seventies. She died only a few years ago at a great age and left me five hundred pounds."

"That was nice."

"I should have rather liked to blue it, but my father persuaded me to save it. He said I should be damned thankful to have a little nest egg like that when I came to marry and wanted to furnish a flat. But I don't see any prospect of my marrying for years yet and I don't really want the money. Would you like me to give you two hundred of it?"

Lydia, going on with her work, had listened amiably, though without more than polite interest, to a story that could mean nothing very much to her, but now, jabbing her needle in the material she was sewing, she looked up.

"What on earth for?"

"I thought it might be useful to you."

"I don't understand. What have I done that you should wish to give me two hundred pounds?"

Charley hesitated. She was gazing at him with those blue, large, but rather flat eyes of hers, and there was in them an extreme attention as though she were trying to see into the depths of his soul. He turned his head away.

"You could do a good deal to help Robert."

A faint smile broke on her lips. She understood.

"Has your friend Simon been telling you that I was at the Sérail to earn enough money to enable Robert to escape?"

"Why should you think that?"

She gave a little scornful laugh.

"You're very naïve, my poor friend. It's what they all suppose. Do you think I would trouble to undeceive them and do you think they would understand if I told them the truth? I don't want your money; I have no use for it." Her voice grew tender. "It's sweet of you to offer it. You're a dear creature, but such a kid. Do you know that what you're suggesting is a crime which might easily land you in prison?"

"Oh well."

"You didn't believe what I told you the other day?"

"I'm beginning to think it's very hard to know what to believe in this world. After all, I was nothing to you, there was no reason for you to tell me the truth if you didn't want to. And those men this morning and the address they gave you to send money to. You can't be surprised if I put two and two together."

"I'm glad if I can send Robert money so that he can

buy himself cigarettes and a little food. But what I told you was true. I don't want him to escape. He sinned and he must suffer."

"I can't bear the thought of your going back to that horrible place. I know you a little now; it's awful to think of you of all people leading that life."

"But I told you; I must atone; I must do for him what he hasn't the strength to do for himself."

"But it's crazy. It's so morbid. It's senseless. I might understand, though even then I'd think it outrageously wrong-headed, if you believed in a cruel god who exacted vengeance and who was prepared to take your suffering, well, in part-payment for the wrong Robert had done, but you told me you don't believe in God."

"You can't argue with feeling. Of course it's unreasonable, but reason has nothing to do with it. I don't believe in the god of the Christians who gave his son in order to save mankind. That's a myth. But why should it have arisen if it didn't express some deep-seated intuition in men? I don't know what I believe, because it's instinctive, and how can you describe an instinct with words? I have an instinct that the power that rules us, human beings, animals and things, is a dark and cruel power and that everything has to be paid for, a power that demands an eye for an eye and a tooth for a tooth, and that though we may writhe and squirm we have to submit, for the power is ourselves."

Charley made a vague gesture of discouragement. He felt as if he were trying to talk with someone whose language he could not understand.

"How long are you going on at the Sérail?"

"I don't know. Until I have done my share. Until the time comes when I feel in my bones that Robert is liberated not from his prison, but from his sin. At one time I used to address envelopes. There are hundreds and hundreds of them and you think you'll never get them all done, you scribble and scribble interminably, and for a long time there seem to be as many to do as there ever were, and then suddenly, when you least expect it, you find you've done the last one. It's such a curious sensation."

"And then, will you go out to join Robert?"

"If he wants me."

"Of course he'll want you," said Charley.

She gave him a look of infinite sadness.

"I don't know."

"How can you doubt it? He loves you. After all, think what your love must mean to him."

"You heard what those men said to-day. He's gay, he's got a soft billet, he's making the best of things. He was bound to. That's what he's like. He loved me, yes, I know, but I know also that he's incapable of loving for very long. I couldn't have held him indefinitely even if nothing had happened. I knew that always. And when the time comes for me to go, what hope have I that anything will be left of the love he once bore me?"

"But how, if you think that, can you still do what you're doing?"

"It's stupid, isn't it? He's cruel and selfish, unscrupulous and wicked. I don't care. I don't respect him, I don't trust him, but I love him; I love him with my body, with my thoughts, with my feelings, with every-thing that's me." She changed her tone to one of light raillery. "And now that I've told you that, you must see that I'm a very disreputable woman who is quite unworthy of your interest or sympathy."

Charley considered for a moment.

"Well, I don't mind telling you that I'm rather out of my depth. But for all the hell he's enduring I'm not sure if I wouldn't rather be in his shoes than yours."

"Why?"

"Well, to tell you the truth, because I can't imagine anything more heart-rending than to love with all your soul someone that you know is worthless."

Lydia gave him a thoughtful, rather surprised look, but did not answer.

CHARLEY'S TRAIN left at midday. Somewhat to his surprise Lydia told him that she would like to come and see him off. They breakfasted late and packed their bags. Before going downstairs to pay his bill Charley counted his money. He had plenty left.

"Will you do me a favour?" he asked.

"What is it?"

"Will you let me give you something to keep in case of emergency?"

"I don't want your money," she smiled. "If you like you can give me a thousand francs for Evgenia. It'll be a godsend to her."

"All right."

They drove first to the Rue du Chateau d'Eau, where she lived, and there she left her bag with the concierge. Then they drove to the Gare du Nord. Lydia walked along the platform with him and he bought a number of English papers. He found his seat in the Pullman. Lydia, coming in with him, looked about her.

"D'you know, this is the first time I've ever been inside a first-class carriage in my life," she said.

It gave Charley quite a turn. He had a sudden realization of a life completely devoid not only of the luxuries of the rich, but even of the comforts of the well-to-do. It caused him a sharp pang of discomfort to think of the sordid existence that had always been, and always would be, hers.

"Oh well, in England I generally go third," he said apologetically, "but my father says that on the Continent one ought to travel like a gentleman."

"It makes a good impression on the natives."

Charley laughed and flushed.

"You have a peculiar gift for making me feel a fool."

They walked up and down the platform, trying as people do on such occasions to think of something to say, but able to think of nothing that seemed worth saying. Charley wondered if it passed through her mind that in all probability they would never see one another again in all their lives. It was odd to think that for five days they had been almost inseparable and in an hour it would be as though they had never met. But the train was about to start. He put out his hand to say good-bye to her. She crossed her arms over her breast in a way she had which had always seemed to him strangely moving; she had had her arms so crossed when she wept in her sleep; and raised her face to his. To his amazement he saw that she was crying. He put his arms round her and for the first time kissed her on the mouth. She disengaged herself and, turning away from him, quickly hurried down the platform. Charley got into his compartment. He was singularly troubled.

But a substantial luncheon, with half a bottle of indifferent Chablis, did something to restore his equanimity; and then he lit his pipe and began to read *The Times.* It soothed him. There was something solid in the feel of the substantial fabric on which it was printed that seemed to him grandly English. He looked at the picture papers. He was of a resilient temper. By the time they reached Calais he was in tearing spirits. Once on board he had a small Scotch and pacing the deck watched with satisfaction the waves that Britannia traditionally rules. It was grand to see the white cliffs of Dover. He gave a sigh of relief when he stepped on the stubborn English soil. He felt as though he had been away for ages. It was a treat to hear the voices of the English porters, and he laughed at the threatening uncouthness of the English customs officials who treated you as though you were a confirmed criminal. In another two hours he would be home again. That's what his father always said:

"There's only one thing I like better than getting out of England, and that's getting back to it."

Already the events of his stay in Paris seemed a trifle dim. It was like a nightmare which left you shaken when with a start you awoke from it, but as the day wore on faded in your recollection, so that after a while you remembered nothing but that you had had a bad dream. He wondered if anyone would come to meet him; it would be nice to see a friendly face on the platform. When he got out of the Pullman at Victoria almost the first person he saw was his mother. She threw her arms round his neck and kissed him as though he had been gone for months.

"I told your father that as he'd seen you off I was going to meet you. Patsy wanted to come too, but I wouldn't let her. I wanted to have you all to myself for a few minutes."

Oh, how good it was to be enveloped in that safe affection!

"You are an old fool, mummy. It's idiotic of you to risk catching your death of cold on a draughty platform on a bitter night like this."

They walked, arm in arm and happy, to the car. They drove to Portchester Close. Leslie Mason heard the front door open and came out into the hall, and then Patsy tore down the stairs and flung herself into Charley's arms.

"Come into my study and have a tiddly. The whiskey's there. You must be perished with the cold."

Charley fished out of his great-coat pocket the two bottles of scent he had brought for his mother and Patsy. Lydia had chosen them.

"I smuggled 'em," he said triumphantly.

"Now those two women will stink like a brothel," said Leslie Mason, beaming.

"I've brought you a tie from Charvet, daddy."

"Is it loud?"

"Very."

"Good."

They were all so pleased with one another that they burst out laughing. Leslie Mason poured out the whiskey and insisted that his wife should have some to prevent her from catching cold.

"Have you had any adventures, Charley?" asked Patsy.

"None."

"Liar."

"Well, you must tell us all about everything later," said Mrs. Mason. "Now you'd better go and have a nice hot bath and dress for dinner."

"It's all ready for you," said Patsy. "I've put in half a bottle of bath salts."

They treated him as though he had just come back from the North Pole after a journey of incredible hardship. It warmed the cockles of his heart.

"Is it good to be home again?" asked his mother, her eyes tender with love.

"Grand."

But when Leslie, partly dressed, went into his wife's room to have a chat with her while she did her face, she turned to him with a somewhat anxious look.

"He's looking awfully pale, Leslie," she said.

"A bit washed out. I noticed that myself."

"His face is so drawn. It struck me the moment he got out of the Pullman, but I couldn't see very well till we got here. And he's as white as a ghost."

"He'll be all right in a day or two. I expect he's been racketing about a bit. By the look of him I suspect he's helped quite a number of pretty ladies to provide for their respectable old age."

Mrs. Mason was sitting at her dressing-table, in a Chinese jacket trimmed with white fur, carefully doing her eye-brows, but now, the pencil in her hand, she suddenly turned round.

"What *do* you mean, Leslie? You don't mean to say you think he's been having a lot of horrid foreign women."

"Come off it, Venetia. What d'you suppose he went to Paris for?"

"To see the pictures and Simon, and well, go to the Français. He's only a boy."

"Don't be so silly, Venetia. He's twenty-three. You don't suppose he's a virgin, do you?"

"I do think men are disgusting."

Her voice broke, and Leslie, seeing she was really upset, put his hand kindly on her shoulder.

"Darling, you wouldn't like your only son to be a eunuch, would you now?"

Mrs. Mason didn't quite know whether she wanted to laugh or cry.

"I don't suppose I would really," she giggled.

It was with a sense of peculiar satisfaction that Charley, half an hour later, in his second-best dinner-jacket, seated himself with his father in a velvet coat, his mother in a tea-gown of mauve silk and Patsy maidenly in rose chiffon, at the Chippendale table. The Georgian silver, the shaded candles, the lace doyleys which Mrs. Mason had bought in Florence, the cut glass—it was all pretty, but above all it was familiar. The pictures on the walls, each with its own strip-lighting, were meritorious; and the two maids, in their neat brown uniforms, added a nice touch. You had a feeling of security, and the world outside was comfortably distant. The good, plain food was designed to satisfy a healthy appetite without being fattening. In the hearth an electric fire very satisfactorily imitated burning logs. Leslie Mason looked at the menu.

"I see we've killed the fatted calf for the prodigal son," he said, with an arch look at his wife.

"Did you have any good food in Paris, Charley?" asked Mrs. Mason.

"All right. I didn't go to any of the smart restaurants, you know. We used to have our meals at little places in the Quarter."

"Oh. Who's we?"

Charley hesitated an instant and flushed.

"I dined with Simon, you know."

This was a fact. His answer neatly concealed the truth without actually telling a lie. Mrs. Mason was aware that her husband was giving her a meaning look, but she paid no attention to it; she continued to gaze on her son with tenderly affectionate eyes, and he was much too ingenuous to suspect that they were groping deep into his soul to discover whatever secrets he might be hiding there.

"And did you see any pictures?" she asked kindly.

"I went to the Louvre. I was rather taken with the Chardins."

"Were you?" said Leslie Mason. "I can't say he's ever appealed to me very much. I always thought him on the dull side." His eyes twinkled with the jest that had occurred to him. "Between you and me and the gatepost I prefer Charvet to Chardin. At least he is modern."

"Your father's impossible," Mrs. Mason smiled indulgently. "Chardin was a very conscientious artist, one of the minor masters of the eighteenth century, but of course he wasn't Great."

In point of fact, however, they were much more anxious to tell him about their doings than to listen to his. The party at Cousin Wilfred's had been a riot, and they had come back so exhausted that they'd all gone to bed immediately after dinner on the night of their return. That showed you how they'd enjoyed themselves.

"Patsy had a proposal of marriage," said Leslie Mason.

"Thrilling, wasn't it?" cried Patsy. "Unfortunately the poor boy was only sixteen, so I told him that, bad woman as I was, I hadn't sunk so low as to snatch a baby from his cradle, and I gave him a chaste kiss on the brow and told him I would be a sister to him."

Patsy rattled on. Charley, smiling, listened to her, and Mrs. Mason took the opportunity to look at him closely. He was really very good-looking and his pallor suited him. It gave her an odd little feeling in her heart to think how much those women in Paris must have liked him; she supposed he'd gone to one of those horrible houses; what a success he must have had, so young and fresh and charming, after the fat, bald, beastly old men they were used to! She wondered what sort of girl he had been attracted by, she so hoped she was young and pretty, they said men were attracted by the same type as their mother belonged to. She was sure he'd be an enchanting lover; she couldn't help feeling proud of him; after all, he was her son and she'd carried him in her womb. The dear; and he looked so white and tired. Mrs. Mason had strange thoughts, thoughts that she wouldn't have had anybody know for anything in the world; she was sad, and a little envious, yes, envious of the girls he had slept with, but at the same time proud, oh, so proud, because he was strong and handsome and virile.

Leslie interrupted Patsy's nonsense and her own thoughts.

"Shall we tell him the great secret, Venetia?"

"Of course."

"But mind, Charley, keep it under your hat. Cousin Wilfred's worked it. There's an ex-Indian governor that the party want to find a safe seat for, so Wilfred's giving up his and in recognition he's to get a peerage. What d'you think of that?"

"It's grand."

"Of course he pretends it means nothing to him, but he's as pleased as Punch really. And you know, it's nice for all of us. I mean, having a peer in the family adds to one's prestige. Well, it gives one a sort of position. And when you think how we started . . ."

"That'll do, Leslie," said Mrs. Mason, with a glance at the servants. "We needn't go into that." And when they left the room immediately afterwards, she added: "Your father's got a mania for telling everyone about his origins. I really think the time has now arrived when we can let bygones be bygones. It's not so bad when we're with people of our own class, they think it's rather chic to have a grandfather who was a gardener and a grandmother who was a cook, but there's no need to tell the servants. It only makes them think you're no better than they are."

"I'm not ashamed of it. After all the greatest families in England started just as humbly as we did. And we've worked the oracle in less than a century."

Mrs. Mason and Patsy got up from the table and Charley was left with his father to drink a glass of port. Leslie Mason told him of the discussions they had had about the title Cousin Wilfred should assume. It wasn't so easy as you might think to find a name which didn't belong to somebody else, which had some kind of connection with you, and which sounded well.

"I suppose we'd better join the ladies," he said, when he had exhausted the subject. "I expect your mother will want a rubber before we go to bed."

But as they were at the door and about to go out, he put his hand on his son's shoulder.

"You look a bit washed out, old boy. I expect you've been going the pace a bit in Paris. Well, you're young and that's to be expected." He suddenly felt a trifle embarrassed. "Anyhow, that's no business of mine, and I think there are things a father and son needn't go into. But accidents will happen in the best regulated families, and well, what I want to say is, if you find you've got anything the matter with you, don't hesitate but go and see a doctor right away. Old Sinnery brought you into the world and so you needn't be shy of him. He's discretion itself and he'll put you right in no time; the bill will be paid and no questions asked. That's all I wanted to tell you; now let's go and join your poor mother."

Charley· had blushed scarlet when he understood what his father was talking about. He felt he ought to say something, but could think of nothing to say.

When they came into the drawing-room Patsy was playing a waltz of Chopin's and after she had finished his mother asked Charley to play something.

"I suppose you haven't played since you left?"

"One afternoon I played a little on the hotel piano, but it was a very poor one."

He sat down and played again that piece of Scriabin's that Lydia thought he played so badly, and as he began he had a sudden recollection of that stuffy, smoky cellar to which she had taken him, of those roughs he had made such friends with, and of the Russian woman, gaunt and gipsy-skinned, with her enormous eyes, who had sung those wild, barbaric songs with such a tragic abandon. Through the notes he struck he seemed to hear her raucous, harsh and yet deeply moving voice. Leslie Mason had a sensitive ear.

"You play that thing differently from the way you used," he said when Charley got up from the piano.

"I don't think so. Do I?"

"Yes, the feeling's quite different. You get a sort of tremor in it that's rather effective."

"I like the old way better, Charley. You made it sound rather morbid," said Mrs. Mason.

They sat down to bridge.

"This is like old times," said Leslie. "We've missed our family bridge since you've been away."

Leslie Mason had a theory that the way a man played bridge was an indication of his character, and since he looked upon himself as a dashing, open-handed, free-and-easy fellow, he consistently overcalled his hand and recklessly doubled. He looked upon a finesse as un-English. Mrs. Mason on the other hand played strictly according to the rules of Culbertson and laboriously counted up the pips before she ventured on a call. She never took a risk. Patsy was the only member of the family who by some freak of nature had a card sense. She was a bold, clever player and seemed to know by intuition how the cards were placed. She made no secret of her disdain for the respective methods of play of her parents. She was domineering at the card table. The game proceeded in just the same way as on how many evenings it had done. Leslie, after overcalling, was doubled by his daughter, redoubled, and with triumph went down fourteen hundred; Mrs. Mason, with her hand full of picture cards, refused to listen to her partner's insistent demand for a slam; Charley was careless.

"Why didn't you return me a diamond, you fool?" cried Patsy.

"Why should I return you a diamond?"

"Didn't you see me play a nine and then a six?"

"No, I didn't."

"Gosh, that I should be condemned to play all my life with people who don't know the ace of spades from a cow's tail."

"It only made the difference of a trick."

"A trick? A trick? A trick can make all the difference in the world."

None of them paid any attention to Patsy's indignation. They only laughed and she, giving them up as a bad job, laughed with them. Leslie carefully added up the scores and entered them in a book. They only played for a penny a hundred, but they pretended to play for a pound, because it looked better and was more thrilling. Sometimes Leslie would have marked up against him in the book sums like fifteen hundred pounds and would say with seeming seriousness that if things went on like that he'd have to put down the car and go to his office by bus.

The clock struck twelve and they bade one another good-night. Charley went to his warm and comfortable room and began to undress, but suddenly he felt very tired and sank into an armchair. He thought he would have one more pipe before he went to bed. The evening that had just gone by was like innumerable others that he had passed, and none had ever seemed to him more cosy and more intimate; it was all charmingly familiar, in every particular it was exactly as he would have wished it to be; nothing could be, as it were, more stable and substantial; and yet, he could not for the life of him tell why, he had all the time been fretted by an insinuating notion that it was nothing but make-believe. It was like a pleasant parlour-game that grown-ups played to amuse children. And that nightmare from which he thought he had happily awakened—at this hour Lydia, her eyelids stained and her nipples painted, in her blue Turkish trousers and her blue turban, would be dancing at the Sérail or, naked, lying mortified and cruelly exulting in her mortification, in the arms of a man she abhorred; at this hour Simon, his work at the office finished, would be walking about the emptying streets of the Left Bank, turning over in his morbid and tortured mind his monstrous schemes; at this hour Alexey and Evgenia, whom Charley had never seen but whom through Lydia he seemed to know so well that he was sure he would have recognized them if he met them in the street; Alexey, drunk, would be inveighing with maudlin tears against the depravity of his son, and Evgenia, sewing, sewing for dear life, would cry softly because life was so bitter; at this hour the two released convicts, with those staring eyes of theirs that seemed to be set in a gaze of horror at what they had seen, would be sitting, each with his glass of beer, in the smoky, dim cellar and there hidden amid the crowd feel themselves for a moment safe from the ever-present fear that someone watched them; and at this hour Robert Berger, over there, far away on the coast of South America, in the pink-and-white stripes of the prison garb, with the ugly straw hat on his shaven head, walking from the hospital on some errand, would cast his eyes across the wide expanse of sea and, weighing the chances of escape, think for a moment of Lydia with tolerant affection—and that nightmare from which he thought he had happily awakened had a fearful reality which rendered all else illusory. It was absurd, it was irrational, but that, all that, seemed to have a force, a dark significance, which made the life he shared with those three, his father, his mother, his sister, who were so near his heart, and the larger, decent yet humdrum life of the environment in which some blind chance had comfortably ensconced him, of no more moment than a shadow play. Patsy had asked him if he had had adventures in Paris and he had truthfully answered no. It was a fact that he had done nothing; his father thought he had had a devil of a time and was afraid he had contracted a venereal disease, and he hadn't even had a woman; only one thing had happened to him, it was rather curious when you came to think of it, and he didn't just then quite know what to do about it: the bottom had fallen out of his world.

THE END

THE WORKS OF
W. SOMERSET MAUGHAM

An Arno Press Collection

NOVELS

Ashenden: Or, The British Agent. 1941
The Bishop's Apron. 1906
Cakes and Ale. 1935
Catalina: A Romance. 1948
Christmas Holiday. 1939
The Explorer. With Four Illustrations by F. Graham Cootes. 1909
The Hero. 1901
The Hour Before the Dawn. 1942
Liza of Lambeth. 1936
The Magician: Together with a Fragment of Autobiography. 1957
The Making of a Saint: A Romance of Mediaeval Italy. 1966
The Moon and Sixpence. 1919
Mrs. Craddock. 1903
The Narrow Corner. 1932
Of Human Bondage. 1915
The Painted Veil. 1925
The Razor's Edge. 1943
Then and Now. 1946
Theatre. 1937
Up at the Villa. 1941

ESSAYS

The Art of Fiction: An Introduction to Ten Novels and Their
    Authors. 1955
Books and You. 1940
Points of View: Five Essays. 1959
Selected Prefaces and Introductions. 1963
Strictly Personal. 1941
The Summing Up. 1938
The Vagrant Mood: Six Essays. 1953
A Writer's Notebook. 1949

TRAVEL

Andalusia: The Land of the Blessed Virgin. 1935
Don Fernando: Or Variations on Some Spanish Themes. 1935
France at War. 1940
The Gentleman in the Parlour: A Record of a Journey from
    Rangoon to Haiphong. 1930
On a Chinese Screen. 1942

PLAYS

East of Suez: A Play in Seven Scenes. 1922
For Services Rendered: A Play in Three Acts. 1933
The Letter: A Play in Three Acts. 1925
The Sacred Flame: A Play in Three Acts. 1928
Sheppey: A Play in Three Acts. 1933
Six Comedies. 1939

SHORT STORIES

Ah King. 1933
Casuarina Tree. 1926
Cosmopolitans. 1938
Creatures of Circumstance. 1947
First Person Singular. 1931
The Mixture as Before. 1940
The Trembling of a Leaf. 1934
Seventeen Lost Stories. Compiled and with an Introduction by
    Craig V. Showalter. 1969

LIBRARY
FLORISSANT VALLEY COMMUNITY COLLEGE
ST. LOUIS, MO.

INVENTORY 1983